THE QUEEN AND THE HALF-BLOOD

THE UNFORGIVEN: BOOK ONE

JAYNE CASTEL

WINTER MIST PRESS

Published by Winter Mist Press

ISBN: 978-1-991280-30-5 (paperback)

Edited by Tim Burton
Cover design by Winter Mist Press
Fantasy map design by Winter Mist Press

Visit Jayne's website: **www.jaynecastel.com**

His army is the only thing that can save her people … but his loyalty comes at a price. When a determined young queen makes a pact with a ruthless outcast, she finds herself at the mercy of a man with nothing to lose—and everything to gain.

Scottish folklore meets The Rings of Power and A Game of Thrones. THE QUEEN AND THE HALF-BLOOD is an epic Fantasy Romance, set in a dark and lush world inspired by Celtic myth, with a marriage of convenience, delicious spice, and a morally-grey hero who will break your heart.

One fateful night, when Lara is lured into the woods by corpse candles, a stranger saves her from a grisly death.

It's her first meeting with the Half-blood … but it won't be her last.

She's a High Queen without allies. The enemy rules half her realm, and the other half is on the verge of rebellion. She needs help, or Albia will fall to the fae.

But at her darkest hour, an unlikely ally emerges—the stranger who saved her life. And he leads an army of wulvers.

Half-fae, half-human, Alar was cast out of society and has lived too long in the shadows. Now he's ready to step into the light once more. He'll fight for her, if she allows him to co-rule.

Her kingdom is dying, and Lara will do anything to save it … even shackle herself to a dangerous stranger.

From best-selling author Jayne Castel comes a Romantic Fantasy duology set in the same world as The Enforcer's Bride, where druids, mortals, and Fae collide with Celtic myth.

For the ones who didn't know they were warriors until the battle began.

CONTENT WARNINGS

THE QUEEN AND THE HALF-BLOOD is a fantasy romance set in a brutal Pict-inspired world. It's intended for mature (18+) readers and contains the following triggers:

Violence
Graphic sex
Discrimination/racism
Coarse language

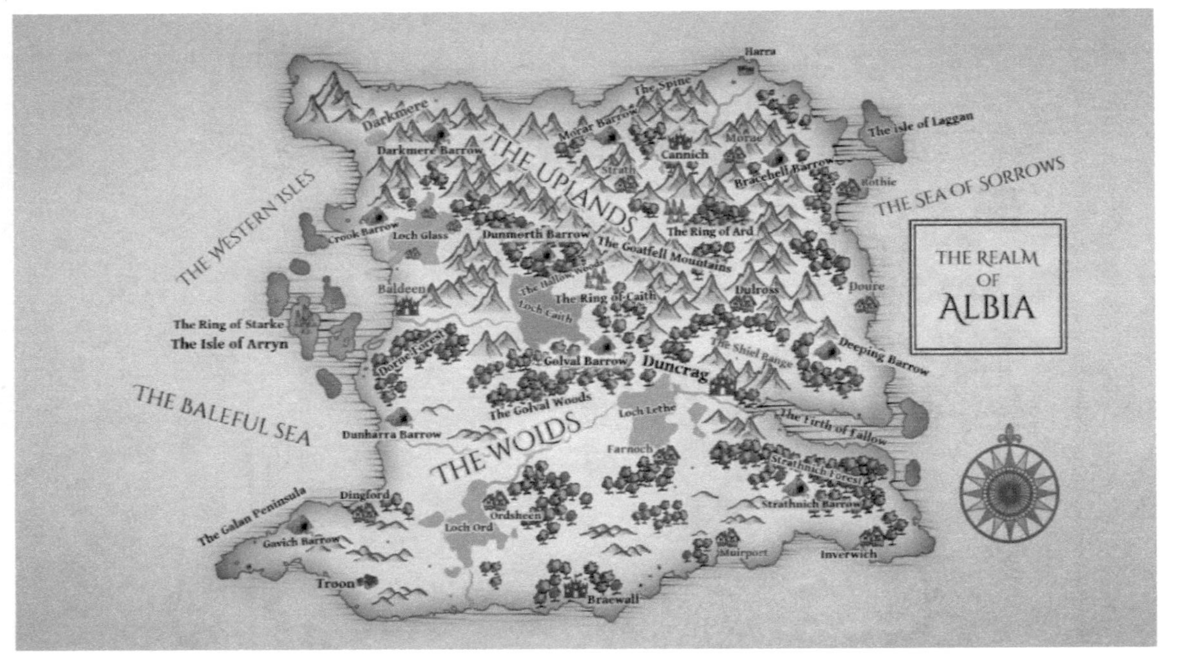

THE REALM OF ALBIA
THE SEA OF SORROWS
THE WESTERN ISLES
THE BALEFUL SEA
THE UPLANDS
THE WOLDS
Harra
The Spine
Darkmere
Morar Barrow
Morae
The Isle of Laggan
Darkmere Barrow
Cannich
Strath
Bracehell Barrow
Rothie
Crook Barrow
Loch Glass
Dunmerth Barrow
The Ring of Ard
The Goatfell Mountains
Dulross
Douire
The Hallow Woods
The Ring of Caith
Baldeen
Loch Caith
The Ring of Starke
The Isle of Arryn
Dorne Forest
Golval Barrow
Duncrag
The Shiel Range
Deeping Barrow
The Golval Woods
Loch Lethe
The Firth of Fallow
Dunharra Barrow
Farnoch
Strathnich Forest
Dingford
Strathnich Barrow
The Galan Peninsula
Ordsheen
Loch Ord
Gavich Barrow
Muirport
Inverwich
Troon
Braewall

MAP

Visit my website to view a larger version of the Realm of Albia map.

It is a brave flame that holds fast when darkness falls.
—**Shee proverb**

1: PROMISES

A PROMISE MEANT nothing, if you didn't keep it.

Lara had made herself two, and she intended to honor them.

Wincing, she pushed wet hair off her face and shifted uncomfortably in the saddle. Her arse was sore, and her leathers chafed. Rain had drifted down in a soft, thick veil all day, soaking through her layers of clothing. Cold, tired, and grumpy, she longed to sink up to her neck in a hot bath with a cup of sweet plum wine in hand. Unfortunately, such luxuries wouldn't be forthcoming.

Ahead, a horn's mournful wail shuddered through the damp gloaming, announcing that the day's long march had ended.

Lara heaved a sigh, drew up her horse, and glanced around. They'd stopped in a shallow glen bordered by woodland. The sky pressed close. Mist wreathed like smoke between the nearby press of pines. It had been wet and grey ever since they'd departed from Duncrag days earlier. She, like everyone else who traveled with her, was sick of the weather.

But she wouldn't let it douse the fire in her belly.

No, she'd make the Shee taste iron.

That was the first of the promises she'd made herself.

Swinging down from the saddle, she gritted her teeth as her booted feet hit the ground too hard. On the first day out, one of her Guard had tried to help her off her horse, but she'd brushed his assistance aside. She wasn't an invalid. Even so, she hadn't yet mastered an elegant dismount.

"How far are we from Doure, Captain?" she called out, trying to ignore her stinging feet.

Ahead, a big man with shaggy red hair turned in the saddle. Cool blue eyes settled on her. "We shall reach it before noon tomorrow, My Queen."

Acknowledging Roth's answer with a nod, she then glanced over at where Bree was also dismounting, although with a lot more grace than her queen. Lara's warder was now surveying their surroundings, hazel eyes slightly narrowed.

"All is well?" Lara asked.

Bree nodded. "As far as I can see … although this close to Doure, Shee scouts will be watching us. They'll have spied our approach a day or two ago."

Her stomach tensed. "I'm sure they did."

The moment she'd been building up to for so long had finally arrived. Doure had fallen to the Shee eight turns of the moon earlier. But the enemy would go no farther. The reckoning her people cried out for was beginning.

Her pulse quickened then. So much depended on this campaign's success. When her father had lost the North, and his life, he'd left his daughter with a massive task. Lara's reign hadn't been easy so far, for there were many who believed a young, untested woman shouldn't wear the crown. This campaign wasn't just about victory—it was about proving herself. She couldn't return to Duncrag defeated.

"Bree!"

A tall, broad-shouldered figure clad in black strode toward them: Cailean mac Brochan. A striking man with close-cropped black hair and startling woad-blue eyes, his brawny arms covered with druidic tattoos, Lara's chief-enforcer could be intimidating. A massive dog with a shaggy dark-green coat and glowing amber eyes padded behind him. Skaal.

Once—years ago now—Lara had been infatuated with Cailean. He'd never returned her interest, and just as well too, for her father would have forbidden a union between his chief-enforcer and his daughter. Those days of girlish infatuation were far behind her though.

It felt like someone else's life.

"What is it?" Bree stepped forward to meet him. In her Shee form, she'd been tall, towering above most Marav women, yet these days, she had to crane her neck to meet her husband's eye. It was foolish to underestimate her though, for even in a 'weaker' body, Bree Fellshadow was a force of nature.

"I'm going out to patrol the approach to Doure," he rumbled. "I need you with me."

His announcement didn't surprise Lara. This close to the enemy, Bree would provide valuable insight. She'd likely notice things others would miss.

However, Bree frowned. "I shouldn't leave the High Queen's side."

"Aye, you can," Lara cut in before Cailean could respond. She motioned then to where Roth had also dismounted. "Captain mac Tav will accompany me while I see to my horse, and escort me back to my pavilion afterward."

Bree looked unconvinced. "Are you sure?"

"I am." Lara glanced back at Cailean. "Report back to me later."

The chief-enforcer nodded.

With a sigh, Bree handed her reins to one of the High Queen's escort. "We won't be long."

Lara waved her away. "Go."

They went—the warrior druid and the warder walking side by side—with Skaal silently following in their wake.

Watching them, Lara smiled. Cailean and Bree were a formidable team. She liked knowing they were at her side, that she could depend on them.

Turning, Lara caught Roth's eye. "Come, Captain … let's see to our mounts."

"One of your warriors can take care of that, My Queen," he replied.

"I think not." She liked to unsaddle and rub down her own horse. Bracken was a sturdy bay mare who'd carried her well these past few days. Tending to the horse at the end of each day relaxed Lara and gave her a little time with her own thoughts.

The captain huffed a sigh. He knew better than to argue. Turning, they led their horses toward the enclosure that was being erected on the southern edge of the camp. A dark wall of pines reared up just a few yards distant, shadowy and brooding in the grey dusk. The rain had finally ceased, yet the air was thick and heavy with the fragrance of conifers.

Tying Bracken up to the railing, Lara then set about unsaddling the mare.

Roth did the same with his heavy-set bay stallion. Working back-to-back, they had to be careful not to knock elbows or stand on each other's feet. Meanwhile, two lads appeared bearing nets stuffed full of hay—carted with the baggage train at the back of the army.

Bracken started to snatch mouthfuls of hay, and Lara smiled. "You've been waiting all day for this, haven't you?"

Behind her, the captain snorted. "It's the nosebag of oats she'll be after."

"Aye … and she's earned it."

Twisting a large handful of hay into a knot, Lara used it to rub Bracken down in long, firm strokes. The mare gave a gentle huff. She enjoyed this ritual as much as her rider did. One of the lads returned with hog bristle brushes then. Taking one, she started to groom her horse.

She worked silently, while around her the rise and fall of gruff voices drifted through the camp, punctuated by the thud of iron tent pegs being driven into damp soil. The swiftness with which the warriors put up the tents, built enclosures for the horses, and lit cookfires always took her by surprise. They'd only recently stopped for the day, and already, a small village surrounded her. The scent of woodsmoke permeated the air.

But as Lara groomed Bracken, nervousness twisted under her ribcage. After days of travel, she was about to conduct her first siege. So much depended on her success. Albia's future hung in the balance. If she didn't push the Shee back, the Raven Queen would one day rule both Sheehallion and Albia. Lara and those who protected her would be put to the sword.

"Are your warriors ready for tomorrow, Captain?" she asked finally as she knelt to brush the feathers on Bracken's heavy feet.

"Aye, My Queen."

"How is morale?"

"Good. They are eager to fight for you … as am I."

Something in his voice made her stiffen. Straightening up, she glanced over her shoulder. To her surprise, Roth had turned—and was right behind her. The captain stood well over six feet. She turned too and had to step back to meet his eye properly. When she did, she marked the intensity of his gaze.

Warmth rolled over her. He shouldn't stare at her like that. It occurred to her then that they were alone here, hemmed in by their horses. It was the only time she and Roth had ever been on their own together.

Embarrassed, she cleared her throat. "Captain—"

"I would ride through the stones into Sheehallion, if you asked it," he said, his voice low and intimate now.

"Then you would die," she replied crisply, irritation flaring. What was this nonsense?

"Maybe," he said, the edges of his lips lifting in his usual arrogance. "But for you, I'd do it." His gaze roamed over her face. "I know you refuse to take a husband, Lara … but a lover isn't forbidden to you."

Her breathing caught. *Lara?* Bree was the only one she permitted to speak to her so informally. Shades, she should have seen this coming, for she'd noted the way Captain mac Tav looked at her sometimes. She could take him to her furs—the man was certainly attractive enough—but she wouldn't.

Seemingly oblivious to the indignance that rose within her, Roth moved closer, bridging the gap between them once more.

Lara stood her ground, even as heat ignited in the pit of her stomach.

He'd crossed a line.

"I would be your lover," he murmured. "I would give you long … hot … nights to remember."

The fire in her belly started to pulse. "Is that so?"

"Aye." He reached out then, a hand brushing a damp strand of hair off her cheek. "It would be such a shame to allow your loveliness to go to waste."

A heartbeat passed. "I won't be taking a lover," she said coldly.

His gaze shadowed, and he pulled his hand back. "Why?"

"That's my business, not yours."

Jaw clenching, she shoved the brush she'd been using at him before ducking around his broad body and heading toward the edge of the enclosure. She'd had enough of this conversation.

"Wait, My Queen." Alarm edged his voice now, his arrogance faltering. "You can't go off on your own. I must escort you."

Lara halted and swiveled, pinning him with a glare. "I don't require your company, Captain." She bit the words out. "Finish seeing to our horses. I can find my own way back to my tent."

And she could. It was safe enough now that they'd almost finished making camp. The enforcers would have dropped most of the ward-stones, and the faint strains of singing, as the bards wove a protection sain, reached her now.

Meanwhile, stubbornness hardened Roth's features. His lips then parted. He was about to argue with her. "Enough,

Captain," she cut him off. "I will give you grace this time … but don't speak to me like that ever again."

Roth's mouth closed, his strong jaw flexing. He understood his mistake now.

Turning on her heel, she stalked out of the enclosure. Wisely, he didn't follow.

And as she walked, Lara seethed.

How dare he?

When she'd taken the throne, she'd made it clear she was 'handfasted' to Albia. She wouldn't marry again. She'd meant it too. And no, she didn't need to deny herself lovers, but she would.

That was the second thing she'd promised herself.

No man would ever dominate her again. She was High Queen now. *She* made the rules.

Her captain wasn't the first man to show interest in her since she'd taken the throne—the overking of Braewall had proposed marriage and been swiftly rejected—but he was the first bold enough to offer to *service* her.

Heat rose to her cheeks, embarrassment prickling over her. Things would be strained between them after this. It was the last thing she needed on the eve of battle.

As she strode, mist swirled in, drifting sinuously through the camp.

Lara was about to turn right then and make her way into the press of conical hide tents when something to her left caught her attention.

A beguiling flame flickered within the pines.

Her step faltered, and she drew to a halt. Suddenly, her anger at Roth, and her humiliation, faded.

The flame transfixed her.

She loved fire—the way it chased away cold and darkness, and how red and gold danced in its depths. It had always been her friend. She'd secretly played with fire over the years—on the rare occasions when she was alone—yet a warning whispered to her now. This was no friendly lantern flame.

Never follow the lights.

She'd been cautioned countless times as a child. Her mother had repeated it to her regularly, as had her nursemaid. Corpse candles were lethal. You couldn't let one ensnare you, or you'd be lured into a treacherous bog or a marsh and meet a watery end. If you were out in the wilderness and happened to spy a flickering light in the darkness, you should immediately avert your gaze.

But she didn't. *She couldn't.*

Her surroundings disappeared. Suddenly, there was just her and the beckoning light.

Look away!

It was too late. The warning died to a whisper then as the desire to get closer to the light overwhelmed her.

Drawing up the hood of her cloak, she moved—not right, toward the heart of the camp, where her pavilion waited—but left, toward the woods.

2: NEVER FOLLOW THE LIGHTS

LARA APPROACHED THE perimeter, her soft-soled boots squelching over the wet ground. Her hooded cloak obscured her identity. The mist wreathed thick now, turning the encampment into a shadowy grey world, where the figures of warriors and druids moving around her appeared distant, wraiths lost in smoke. Even their voices seemed far away.

The surrounding fog wrapped her in its cool embrace. It was the beginning of autumn, and the air had a bite to it. And all the while, the glowing flame up ahead promised warmth and comfort. She had to reach it.

For the first time since ascending the throne, taking back her lands from the Shee ceased to matter. Everything, including the gnawing worry that she'd fail to take back the North, merely melted away. All she cared about was that single beckoning flame. It drew her to it as if by an invisible cord.

Her breathing grew shallow, and she quickened her step. *I'm coming.*

She passed behind two tall, broad shapes then: enforcers were dropping the final ward stones.

Neither warrior druid saw her.

Ahead, the light amongst the trees grew brighter, joined by more flickering flames. They were so beautiful that Lara's throat tightened.

She increased her pace. She had to get closer. She had to let the flames dance in her hand as she'd managed once with a candle flame. These days, four attendants slept in her alcove, and the rest of the time, Bree shadowed her. There had been no time, or opportunity, to make fire dance on her palm.

She was dimly aware that the camp was now behind her. She was alone, but it didn't bother her. If anything, it was a relief. Let someone else worry about what the next day might bring. All she wanted was to reach the lights.

Finally, she was gaining on them. And so, she broke into a run, navigating tree roots as she went. The trees drew back then, and she stepped into a glade. The lights surrounded her, illuminating the murky twilight like fireflies.

Lara breathed an oath. Up close, they were even bonnier— and some of the flames fluttered and cavorted like fairies. They were mischievous, playful. Laughter bubbled up as she halted amidst them, and she suddenly felt like a carefree lass again, the young woman she'd once been before the war. "Good eve, my lovelies," she whispered, holding out her hand, palm upward. "Would you care to dance?"

The fires bobbed and dipped in the misty air, and then one of them—one that resembled a woman with long robes and flowing hair—leaped onto her palm, spinning around so that golden sparks rained over Lara's hand.

She didn't flinch, for the sparks didn't burn her. Instead, she raised her other hand and was about to whisper to the flames once more when a noise broke through her reverie—a grating sound like iron dragging over stone.

The golden fairy that had been spinning on her right palm leaped high into the air at the sound, and all the flames scattered to the edge of the glade. Blinking, Lara glanced around her. She felt drowsy, as if she'd just emerged from a pleasant dream, and her mind still wished to cling to it.

What am I doing here? Alarm washed over her. *Why am I alone?*

A rustling noise made her turn, drawing the dagger at her hip. She always carried a weapon these days.

She spied something she had completely missed earlier then: a crumbling stacked-stone wall. She ran her gaze over it, ice settling in her gut. The glow of the flickering lights, most of which now hovered on the fringes of the clearing, illuminated a ruin. Partially swallowed by creeping ivy and growths of nettles, it was possibly a watchtower from many years earlier.

Her breathing grew shallow. *Shit.*

Her pulse then started to pound in her ears. What was she doing out here? How had she let that dancing flame ensnare her?

Tightening her fingers on the grip of her dagger, she backed away. "Captain!" she called out, hoping Roth had ignored her command and followed her, after all.

Only silence answered her.

Instead, something was moving inside the ruin. A moment later, stocky figures clambered over the wall, their heavy boots thudding onto the mossy ground.

Lara whispered an oath, raising the iron blade. Bree had taught her how to wield a dagger, and they still had regular lessons. Nonetheless, she'd never been in a proper fight before.

She *had* encountered powries though—during her father's ill-fated campaign, when the military camp she'd been sheltering within had been attacked. Shee warriors had stormed it, bringing with them a vicious host of the imps.

There were five of them now. They grasped pikestaffs in their left hand and drew daggers with their right. Bright silver gleamed in the light of the corpse candles, and Lara's belly swooped.

Sheehallion steel.

It wasn't like any metal forged in the mortal realm—not an alloy of iron and carbon—but made from elements only mined in Sheehallion. All faerie creatures, including the Shee, abhorred iron. However, ever since the Raven Queen had taken the North, she'd equipped some of her allies with Sheehallion steel. Armed with such blades, powries could stray from the ruins they inhabited, and could venture out in daylight. But they'd done neither tonight. Instead, they'd somehow used the corpse candles to lure her into a trap.

"Captain," she shouted, her voice shrill now.

She continued to back away, keeping her blade raised. Her mind racing, she glanced around the clearing. Shades. She was up to her neck now. Maybe she could fight off one powrie, but not five. The imps' fiery red eyes burned as they continued to advance on her.

One of them grinned then, revealing long, prominent, rabbit-like teeth. Stringy grey hair flowed over his broad shoulders, framing a leathery face. And atop his head sat a dark-red cap—a grisly accessory that obtained its color from being soaked in the blood of his victims.

The powrie's long, thin, claw-tipped fingers flexed around the hilt of his pikestaff, and then he rushed her.

Whoops cut through the clearing as his companions did the same.

Lara dropped into a fighting stance and slashed her dagger at him. However, the next thing she knew, she was on her back, and the powrie was driving his blade toward her face.

Iron met steel as she blocked him, the sound ringing through the woods. The powrie laughed before raising his pikestaff.

A scream ripped from her throat.

The Gods save her.

And then, the powrie who was about to stab her through the chest let out an unearthly howl. An instant later, a ball of flame erupted in Lara's face. Crying out once more, she raised her free arm to protect her eyes, and when she lowered it, the powrie had gone, taking the pikestaff with him. Only its steel dagger fell onto the mossy ground next to her.

Blinking, she scrabbled to her feet. She didn't know what had just happened to her assailant, but she needed to be ready for the others. Blood roaring in her ears, she scooped up the fallen dagger—for two blades were of more use than one—and crouched, readying herself.

But the remaining powries weren't focused on her.

Instead, they were fighting someone else.

A tall, lean figure, cloaked in black, danced in their midst. The stranger wielded two long fighting daggers.

And as Lara looked on, frozen in place—her fingers clenched tight around the grips of her own knives—the newcomer drove a blade into one of the powries. With a shriek, the imp burst into flames, but its companions didn't draw back. Instead, teeth bared, the other three rushed at their attacker.

Skillfully avoiding being stuck by a pike, and moving with fluid grace, the cloaked one slashed their way through the powries, dispatching the last of them with a vicious downward cut using both blades.

A final ball of fire erupted in the glade. Meanwhile, the corpse candles still hovered on the tree line, as if curious to see what would happen next, their pale glow illuminating the clearing.

Heart pounding, Lara straightened up, watching as the stranger turned to her. They then advanced, walking in long, smooth strides until they were around four feet distant. Stopping, they sheathed the fighting daggers at their back in one smooth movement.

A hand pushed back their hood.

Lara stilled.

A man stood before her—whether he was Marav or Shee, she couldn't tell at first. A thick mane of long, tangled dark hair framed a pale face with high cheekbones and sharp features that made him look eerily fae. And yet, he didn't have cat-like eyes, with elongated pupils, like one of the Shee. His eyes were slate-grey and slightly slanted, with round pupils just like hers.

Lara had never seen a man of his like. It was difficult to place his age. He could be just a couple of years older than her—or a decade. She marked the long, thin silver scar that slashed down one side of his face then. It started just above the left eyebrow to level with his mouth. A second scar encircled his throat.

"You should be careful," he said, his voice low with a gravelly edge. "Didn't anyone tell you never to follow the lights?"

Lara swallowed, heat flushing through her. Indeed, she felt foolish. "It enchanted me," she replied, still breathless. "I don't know how—"

"Lara!" A man's voice rang through the trees, echoing in the mist. "Where are you?"

"Captain!" she shouted back, her heart kicking hard against her ribs. "I'm here!"

Meanwhile, her savior slowly backed away, even as his gaze never left her face.

"Wait!" she gasped.

He paused, inclining his head.

"I should thank you."

His dark-grey eyes glinted. "You're welcome ... *Your Highness.*"

Heat crept up her neck now. So, he knew who she was. "What is your name?"

Her savior paused an instant before replying. "Alar mac Struana."

He pulled up the hood of his cloak then and, before she could ask him anything else, melted like a shade into the swirling mist.

Lara stared after him, heart still pounding, her breathing still labored.

Thanks to this stranger, she'd just dodged The Reaper's scythe.

A moment later, the sound of twigs cracking underfoot made her spin on her heel and raise her daggers once more.

Roth erupted from the tree line, face taut, and broadsword at the ready, with three black-clad enforcers behind him.

Relief barreled through Lara, making her knees wobble. Never had she been so relieved to see anyone.

3: AT FAULT

"IT WAS A TRAP." Lara's declaration fell heavily in the damp, smoky air within the tent. "Those powries were waiting for me."

A few yards away, Cailean growled a curse. He and Bree had just returned from scouting and come straight to the meeting pavilion. Skaal was with them, sitting at the chief-enforcer's side as if she too were a member of Lara's council. "Mor's fucking servants."

Silence fell, drawing out until Lara broke it. "I came close to being impaled on a powrie's pikestaff," she admitted huskily. In truth, in the aftermath, she felt a little sickly and shaky, although she was careful not to let anyone see. She was also still berating herself for giving in so easily to the lure of the corpse candles. "But luckily, someone got there first."

"And who is this 'Alar mac Struana'?" Roth muttered. The captain wore a thunderous expression. Since her brush with the powries, he hadn't met her gaze squarely—and didn't even now.

Blank looks followed. No one gathered around the table, Lara included, had ever heard of him. The name 'Struana' was unusual, for it was female. It was tradition in Albia to take your father's name, not your mother's.

Cailean snorted. "What interests me is what he was doing out there in the midst of the woods."

"A hunter, perhaps," Lara replied. The chief-enforcer's gaze narrowed. Lara wasn't surprised. It was his job to be suspicious. "When the captain called out to me, he melted into the shadows as if he were one of the Shee."

Cailean's frown deepened. "Are you sure he wasn't?"

"He had Marav eyes."

"Aye, but he could have been glamored."

"If he were Shee, why would he have saved my life?"

The chief-enforcer didn't answer. She had him there. Besides Bree and her brother, Gil, who now worked as Lara's archivist back at Duncrag, no Shee would save the High Queen of Albia's neck.

Another silence followed. As it drew out, Lara reached out and traced a finger across the large unfurled map of Albia upon the table. Her fingertip traveled east over the lower Uplands to where Doure sat upon the coast. Trying not to let the penetrating gazes of her council unnerve her, Lara focused on Doure and its surroundings. Over the past moons, they'd discussed the best way to take the fort at length. Like most

Albian forts, it sat upon high ground and was protected by lofty stacked-stone walls.

Impatience fluttered up then. *We need to get back to the task at hand.*

Nonetheless, her council wasn't ready to discuss the siege yet.

"How could a single corpse candle lure you out of this camp?" Annis mac Gord, her chief-counsellor asked. The woman's round face, framed by hazel-colored braids, was strained, with a deep crease between her eyebrows.

"It all happened so quickly," Lara muttered, defensiveness rising. "One moment, I was walking back to my tent … the next, the light ensnared me." And it had. The flame had consumed her, and for a short while, all that mattered was reaching it. When she'd let it dance upon her palm in the clearing, joy had erupted like a cloudburst inside her.

But she wouldn't admit that part.

Gods, she didn't want anyone to think she was a 'fire-wielder'. Sweat beaded upon her skin then. She wasn't, anyway. She couldn't be. That ability had been lost centuries ago, after all those who could wield fire were tracked down and killed. The bloodlines had been lost. No, her ability to call to fire, to play with it, wasn't dangerous, forbidden magic. It was innocent. Innocuous.

"I take responsibility for this," Roth said gruffly then, drawing everyone's gaze. A nerve flickered in his cheek. "I should have escorted you to your pavilion."

"And why didn't you?" Bree demanded. "You were supposed to shadow the High Queen while I went out on patrol. I entrusted *you* with her safety."

The captain's broad shoulders went rigid at this, while the other members of Lara's council shared veiled glances. Indeed, it looked to them as if Roth had been grossly incompetent.

But Lara couldn't let him shoulder the blame. "Captain mac Tav isn't at fault here," she said softly. "*I* insisted on walking back to my tent alone."

Bree's eyes snapped wide. "Why?"

Lara favored her with a sheepish smile. "I just wanted some time alone, I suppose … and thought I'd be safe within the perimeter of the camp." She didn't look Roth's way as she spoke.

The chief-sacrificer, Gregor mac Hume, muttered something under his breath. He was a big, rawboned man with a shaven head and high cheekbones, who wore blood-red robes. And he wasn't one to bandy words. "That was foolish, My Queen."

"It was," she murmured, even as warmth spread across her chest. Gregor had never missed an opportunity to patronize her since she'd replaced her father on the throne—and now, she'd played straight into his hands. Clearing her throat, she met his eye. "But it won't happen again, I assure you."

Gregor gave her a look that made the heat burning between her breasts creep up her neck.

Curse it. She was the High Queen, but sometimes both Annis and Gregor made her feel like a goose-witted lass who should be weaving by the fireside, not leading warriors into battle.

Swallowing, she dragged her attention to Cailean.

The chief-enforcer wore a scowl. He wouldn't criticize her like the others, although his unspoken censure was almost worse. "Cailean … did you note anything of concern on your patrol?"

He shook his head. "With Skaal guiding us, we managed to draw close to Doure. They have sentries around twenty furlongs out from the fort … but no farther."

"That doesn't mean they aren't watching us," Bree replied, her voice unusually brittle. Her gaze was shadowed as she met Lara's eye. "However, they should leave us in peace tonight."

Lara nodded, even as an ache rose under her breastbone. Her friend's disappointment in her was a blade to the chest. She'd let her anger at Roth's presumption cloud good sense.

"Shall I gather my bards for another protection sain on the western perimeter, My Queen?" A sharp-featured young woman with red-gold hair, robed in green, asked then. "Just in case more powries are lurking in the woods."

"Aye, thank you, Ren." Lara placed her hands firmly upon the table before her. She was relieved to see the tremor she'd marked following the attack had gone. Even so, the stares around the table were getting to her. "Shall we go over our plans for tomorrow now?"

Her gaze lingered on her hands for a moment then. On each one, she bore rings that had once belonged to her parents. Upon her left hand, she wore her mother's delicate silver ring with a rose-colored garnet. A chunky amber stone upon an iron band—her father's signet ring—sat upon her right ring finger. It was the *Ord-ree Seal*. But for the first time in many generations, it sat on the hand of the High Queen, not a High King.

Her father hadn't carried the ring into battle. Sometimes, Lara wondered if things might have gone differently for him if he had. Instead, wary of damaging the precious ring, he'd handed it to his wife on that fateful morning.

The *Ord-ree Seal* was the color of flame, gold with flecks of red at its heart. Its gleaming surface flickered in firelight sometimes. It symbolized the indomitable spirit of the Marav. Her people weren't blessed with lifespans that reached thousands of years like the Shee, but they ruled this land, nonetheless. Or they had, before her father's inglorious defeat in The Uplands.

"As discussed, Doure will be a challenge," Cailean replied after a lengthy pause. "I just hope your warriors understand this siege won't be a short one. It could last days … or even a moon's turn."

Nerves fluttered under Lara's ribcage. Like many Albian forts, Doure perched upon a high crag. It could only be taken from the west. She'd also discovered that there was a deep, spike-filled ditch defending the landward side. They'd put up ladders, but if anyone fell, they'd be gored.

"The warriors all know," Roth assured him. "And they're ready."

"The omens have been conflicting since we left Duncrag," Annis spoke up then. "I do not trust them."

Lara glanced over at her chief-counsellor, alarmed. "Such as?"

"Odd numbers of geese flying overhead, the sight of a lamb in the fields at the wrong time of year … and a blight upon all the apple trees we've passed." Annis's lips pursed. "We should proceed with caution."

Lara fought to keep her worry from showing.

Like most Marav, she wasn't one to discount omens. All the same, her father's ill-fated campaign—which he'd believed was Gods-favored—had taught her the folly of putting too much store in such signs.

She'd heed the warning, yet she couldn't let Annis's words get to her.

"What do the bones tell you, Ruari?" She shifted focus to the lanky, solemn-faced man clad in blue who stood next to the chief-bard.

"Little, My Queen," he replied.

"No troubling dreams?"

The chief-seer shook his head. He then glanced nervously over at Annis. "None."

Lara sank down into the furs and rubbed at her temples. A headache thumped behind her eyes. A few feet away, her handmaid, Mirren, warmed some milk in a pan over the nearby brazier, while her other attendants—Florie, Ani, and Lilith—readied clothing and food for the morning, for they'd be making a swift and early departure.

As she worked, Mirren kept darting Lara concerned looks. "Should I get Eldra to mix you a tonic?"

Lara shook her head. "I'm fine."

Her maid gave a soft snort. "You were attacked by powries this evening, My Queen … no one would think less of you for being shaken."

Lara grimaced. "I'm not so sure about that," she replied. "By now, everyone will be gossiping about the foolish woman who recklessly left her escort behind before allowing a corpse candle to lure her away."

Ani and Lilith—two red-haired sisters who'd only recently joined the High Queen's personal staff—stilled in their work, their gazes flicking up. Meanwhile, Florie's already doe-like eyes grew huge upon her thin face. Although Lara spoke informally with Mirren and Bree at times, she rarely did when anyone else was present.

Tonight though, in the aftermath of the attack, and with her temples pounding, her defenses had lowered.

Mirren shook her head, causing her curly brown hair, which often had a life of its own, to bounce. "No, they won't … instead, they'll be thanking The Mother that you're alive." Pouring the milk from a pot into an earthen cup, she then carried it across to the furs.

Lara sighed, wrapping her fingers around the cup. "All the same, I'll be more careful in future."

Mirren's sea-blue eyes shadowed. "Good," she said softly. "Albia needs you … *we* need you."

Lara smiled. Mirren had been with her since before her marriage to Dunchadh of Braewall. Their friendship was a gentle one, and their differing ranks meant there was a reserve between them that didn't exist between Lara and Bree. But it was something she could count on.

"Thank you, Mirren," she murmured. "I will remember that."

4: BY A THREAD

A STORM OF yew arrows flew from the walls, peppering the Marav front ranks.

The High Queen's army was prepared. Led by Roth on one flank and Cailean on the other, they raised their sturdy oak and iron shields, forming a tight vee-shaped shieldwall as they advanced.

Lara watched from astride her feather-footed mare, upon the crest of a hill west of the fort. They'd reached Doure mid-morning to find it shrouded in sea fret. And, of course, the enemy had marked their approach and was ready for them.

Sucking in a deep breath of the damp, smoky air, she scanned the walls. She could see the outlines of Shee up there, dark silhouettes against the grey. Silver glinted in the dull light. Sheehallion steel.

Lara's fingers tightened around the reins.

She had to take this fort back. Over the past turn of the year, the Raven Queen had stretched out her hand, pulling the villages and smaller forts in the southern reaches of The Uplands within her grasp. If something wasn't done, they'd cross into The Wolds.

Lara cut Bree a look then. Her warder was mounted upon a stocky dun gelding, watching their army edge its way toward the defile.

"I didn't realize just *how* high Doure's perch is," Lara admitted then, raising her voice to be heard above the thump of marching feet, the rattle of iron, and the whistle of flying arrows. Indeed, with the fog curling around it, obscuring the Sea of Sorrows farther east, the fort—with its lofty stone walls— appeared a crow's nest. Seemingly impenetrable.

"Aye," Bree replied. "The Marav have always excelled at building well-defended forts."

A roar went up then. Their army had reached the defile and was now putting up long ladders. And all the while, arrows rained down upon them. Flaming projectiles followed, lighting up the gloomy morning.

Lara's breathing grew shallow. How many of those arrowheads were coated in Nightbane? Thanks to Bree, they now knew the name of the poison and how to counteract it. The problem was though that Nightbane worked swiftly. They had to remove the arrow and administer the mashed root of mugwort as soon as possible, or an excruciating death would follow.

"They need to get those ladders up faster," Bree muttered. "They're leaving themselves too exposed."

Lara's heart kicked. Gaze narrowing, she watched as, one by one, the tall wooden ladders inched up the stacked-stone walls. She couldn't see how they could work any quicker. Warriors were now scaling them—men and women clad in leather with iron helms jammed upon their heads to protect them from above.

But fast and nimble as their warriors were, the Shee were swifter.

Many of the archers shifted focus now, aiming directly below. And even from this distance, Lara spied the cauldrons the Shee had dragged to the edge of the walls. As she looked on, they emptied one of them—a stream of hot oil followed.

Screams knifed through the cool, damp air.

Bodies fell, writhing into the spike-filled ditches beneath the walls.

Nausea washed over Lara. How had her father stomached this? Talorc mac Brude had made many mistakes during his reign and created a mess that she wasn't even close to untangling, but he'd loved the chaos of battle. She'd never seen him afraid, not even on that fateful day he'd led his army to Cannich and met his doom. The High King had possessed nerves of iron, but he'd been callous too. His people, even his kin, were tools for him to use.

Lara's mare shifted under her then, tossing her head. She leaned forward, stroking Bracken's neck. "Hold fast," she murmured.

Bitter smoke caught in Lara's throat, and she coughed. Eyes streaming, she watched as flaming arrows hailed down on Marav warriors from the walls. Even from here, she could see her army was struggling, staggering with exhaustion as they pressed on.

They'd held fast—but they were close to breaking now.

It was the afternoon of the third day since they'd begun their siege of Doure—and in that time, they hadn't managed to breach the walls as she'd hoped. They'd gotten close, but each time, the Shee foiled them. Their longbows had quite a reach, and they seemed to have an inexhaustible supply of boiling oil, rocks, and flaming projectiles within.

"Yield, you bastards," she muttered.

"You'd be surprised just how tenacious they can be," Bree replied, her voice hoarse from the drifting smoke.

Lara breathed a curse. They wouldn't have any warriors left at this rate.

Bodies—most of them Marav—filled the deep ditch at the foot of the defile. They'd broken like waves against the walls of the fort, yet were no closer to getting inside, and the Shee had destroyed their battering ram by raining down hot oil upon the siege weapon and setting fire to it. She'd brought six hundred warriors north—fierce men and women carrying spears, axes, and swords—and had already lost too many.

The mist had burned off this afternoon, revealing a pale sky where buzzards now circled. A salty breeze feathered in from the sea, pushing the stench of offal and burned flesh over the hill where Lara waited.

"Fall back!" A male voice, rough with fury and exhaustion, cut through the chaos below, drifting up to the hill to the west.

Lara's breathing hitched.

Captain mac Tav had just ordered a retreat.

Dizziness swept over her. *No!*

Roth was indomitable, but The Reaper was standing over them now. She too could feel his cold breath.

Tears stung her eyelids—although not from the smoke now. Instead, frustration pummeled her like heavy fists, impotent rage thumping through her. "Withdraw!" she shouted.

A few yards away, one of her escort heeded his queen. Grim-faced, he unslung the battle horn from over his shoulder, lifted it to his lips, heaved in a deep breath, and blew.

The deep bellow shook the smoky air and echoed into the defile, reaching the warriors and druids who fought there. Moments passed, and then, slowly, the army started to retreat.

A fur cloak slung about her shoulders, for the wind held a bite this evening, Lara moved through the crowd of bloodied warriors. Bree stalked at her side, hand upon the pommel of her longsword. The High Queen's shadow.

Their encampment, fifty furlongs west of Doure, was in chaos this evening. As the last of the long twilight drained from the sky, those who'd survived the day's siege limped across the perimeter, where enforcers were laying ward stones.

Lara's gaze roamed the blistered, grime-smeared faces of the warriors and druids gathered around cookfires. She noted their bound wounds, as well as the gathering despair in many of their gazes.

They were holding on by a thread.

Gods, so was she.

Their despair worried her. If they lost hope, this was over. She couldn't let them give up. Fire had to keep burning in their bellies.

"We shall rally," she assured them, wishing her voice were stronger. "Doure *will* be ours."

Some of those she passed nodded, murmuring, "We shall rally," and someone managed, "Aye, we shall drive those Shee bastards out!" But their response was scattered, weak.

A brick settled in Lara's gut as she walked on, making her way to the healing tent.

Ducking inside the large rectangular pavilion crammed with pallets and the injured, she found the healer and her assistants—all garbed in distinctive mauve robes—hard at work. One glance at their pinched expressions and Lara knew they were struggling. There weren't enough healers for the number of injured.

"Eldra!" Lara called out to her as she shrugged off her fur cloak and handed it to Bree. "I'll assist."

The royal healer—a statuesque woman with silver-blonde hair—glanced up from where she was sewing a gaping leg wound. Eldra's grey-blue eyes then narrowed; however, she didn't argue with her queen.

Moving to a trestle table, Lara deftly washed her hands in soap and water. She wasn't a warrior. She couldn't join Roth and Cailean as they led assault after assault on the walls, but she could assist in other ways. Before taking the throne, she'd spent many mornings in Eldra's healing chamber underneath Duncrag broch, helping the healer prepare poultices, ointments, and salves. She'd discovered a natural talent for healing, an instinct for what was needed and when. It had been a while since she'd rolled up her sleeves and worked alongside Eldra, although she'd forgotten nothing.

Drying off her hands, she headed toward a woman who lay groaning upon a pallet a few feet away. The warrior had taken an arrow to the flank. The shaft still pierced her. The woman's eyes were glazed in pain, and she was clinging to consciousness.

Leaning forward, Lara inspected the wound. They needed to remove that arrow, although in doing so, the warrior risked bleeding out. At least there was no tell-tale yellow cast to her skin, nor was the wound starting to bubble. The arrow hadn't been poisoned by Nightbane.

Straightening up, she glanced over at where Bree looked on, Lara's heavy fur cloak in her arms. "Put that down," she ordered brusquely. She wasn't usually sharp with Bree—and her friend's eyes narrowed at her tone—but the cracks were now starting to show. "I need your help here."

Lara's back ached, and her eyes stung from fatigue, when she finally left the healing pavilion. It was getting late, and a full moon sailed high above the encampment. Shoulders sagging, yet once again grateful for her thick cloak, which warded off the chill, she made her way to the heart of the slumbering camp.

Assisting the injured hadn't been easy. Her gorge had risen numerous times as she cleaned and dressed wounds, some of them grievous, and tried to give solace to the dying. Nonetheless, she'd done all she could. Her body cried out for rest, but it wouldn't receive any—not yet. Instead, she and Bree crossed to the meeting tent, pushed aside the flap, and ducked inside.

Her council—five druids and the captain of her army—was waiting for her. As was Skaal.

Apart from the fae hound, who'd remained at camp while they lay siege to the walls, they all looked as drained as she felt.

Grime, ash, and blood still streaked the chief-enforcer's face, as they did her captain's. Fortunately, both men appeared uninjured. The chief-sacrificer and chief-bard's cloaks were singed, and the former bore a cut upon his temple.

"Apologies for the delay," Lara greeted them huskily. "I was needed in the healing pavilion."

She halted before the table, her gaze sliding over the faces of each member of her war council. Her gut tightened. She didn't like their stern expressions and shadowed gazes. "Don't look so grim," she muttered. "We aren't defeated yet."

"No," Roth replied curtly. His gaze was wary. Ever since he'd overstepped, things had been strained between them. "Not yet."

A heavy silence followed these words. Eventually, Lara broke it. "So, where do we go from here?"

"We'll need a breather before hitting the walls again," her captain answered.

Her pulse quickened. "How long do you need?"

"Three days ... at least."

"Then you will have them."

Actually, the thought of waiting so long galled her. Nonetheless, she wasn't a warrior. She had little experience with battle and needed to take instructions from those who'd been fighting on the front line.

"We'll use that time to build more battering rams and ladders," Cailean added. "We've run out."

Lara's palms started to sweat. They could replace those things, but they couldn't bring all those who'd already fallen back from the dead.

"We must also ensure the Gods favor us," Gregor announced. The chief-sacrificer's expression was stone-hewn, his thick arms folded across his chest. "My sacrificers will bleed twice the number of pigeons as usual over the coming nights."

"What if the Shee use this wait to their advantage?" The chief-seer spoke up then. Ruari's long face was pale and taut this evening. "They might attack our camp."

"Let them," Cailean growled. "If they emerge from behind their stone walls, it'll be a fairer fight."

Next to Lara, Bree shifted uneasily and cut her husband a veiled look. "They won't attack," she murmured. "They know they have the advantage and will wait us out."

Another, troubled, silence followed these words.

Queasiness rolled over Lara as she rubbed her aching back; today had taken its toll on her. She imagined then, limping back to Duncrag with her army in tatters and Doure still in Shee hands—and the disappointment, and scorn, on her people's faces when they learned of her failure.

How would she live down the shame? Worse still, how would she stop Mor's army when it eventually did march south?

"My Queen!" A leather-clad figure ducked through the tent flap. "You have a visitor."

Lara's heart bucked. "Have the Shee sent an emissary?"

The warrior shook his head, discomfort flickering across his features. "A man approached our northern perimeter, from the woods … we were about to see him off."

"Why didn't you then?" Cailean growled.

The warrior's face flushed, and he cut the chief-enforcer an apologetic look. "We would have … but he insists he can help us take back Doure."

5: NAME YOUR PRICE

LARA WAS WAITING in her own tent, with Bree standing next to her and her attendants gathered a few feet away, when they brought the visitor in.

The chief-enforcer and the captain escorted him. Cailean led the way into the pavilion while Roth brought up the rear. And between them was the man who'd saved Lara's life three evenings earlier.

Lara stiffened at the sight of him, and Alar mac Struana's lips curved. "Didn't think you'd ever see me again?" The power in that voice, the low rasp of it, made her suppress an involuntary shiver.

"Do you know him?" Cailean asked, scowling.

"Aye," she murmured. "This is the man who rescued me from the powries." Meanwhile, it was hard not to stare at her visitor. In the misty clearing, illuminated only by pale corpse candles, Alar had been a shadowy figure. Now, she could see him properly.

He was dressed entirely in black, from the hooded cloak to his hunting boots.

In the glow of the nearby brazier and the lanterns that hung from the roof, the sharpness of his cheekbones was even more evident, as was the disfiguring scar that slashed down his left cheek. His skin was unusually pale—in stark contrast to his hair, long and jet-black, which hung over his shoulders. His woolen cloak was open, revealing a leather breastplate. Two flames, one curving upward, the other reaching down, had been embossed upon it.

Her gaze narrowed. *The Endless Flame.* Wasn't that a wulver sigil? The half-man, half-wolf creatures that inhabited the dark woods of Albia worshipped the Hearthkeeper—but Alar was no wulver.

Under the breastplate, he wore a long-sleeved tunic made of thick wool. Tooled leather bracers covered his forearms, and fitted leather breeches encased his long legs. The blades she'd seen him sheath upon his back were missing. He'd either come to her unarmed, or his escort had taken his weapons.

Even so, despite that he was at a disadvantage here, he dressed as if he was *someone* and walked boldly into her tent as if he were one of Lara's overkings.

And if she were honest, she found him a little intimidating.

"Talk then," Roth ordered.

Alar inclined his head. "What I have to say is for the High Queen's ears only."

Cailean made a warning noise in the back of his throat. "You don't walk in here and make demands."

"That's right," Roth agreed, his hand straying to the pommel of his sword.

Alar merely shrugged, a slight smile still playing upon his lips.

Lara's heart started to beat faster. His arrogance was galling. Fatigue pressed down on her shoulders, and impatience shortened her temper. Nonetheless, right now, she was desperate enough to hear him out.

"Cailean … Roth … wait outside," she said after a pause.

Both men stiffened at the command, but she gestured to her warder. "Bree will watch over me."

"For *your* ears only, Your Highness," Alar reminded her.

Lara frowned, anger spiking through her. Of course, she was grateful to this man for saving her, but ever since he'd stepped into her tent, he'd had the upper hand. She didn't like it. "My bodyguard and one of my attendants will stay," she told him coldly. "Or *you* can go."

Their gazes fused before, eventually, he nodded.

Both her chief-enforcer and her captain reluctantly moved back. "We'll be just outside the entrance, My Queen," Roth said brusquely, meeting Lara's gaze squarely for the first time in days. "Call if you need us."

"I will."

The two men departed, and Lara glanced over at where her attendants stood at the back of the pavilion. "Florie, Ani, and Lilith … leave us," she said, even as her pulse continued to race. "Mirren, pour some wine."

As her attendants did as bid, she settled herself on a wooden stool by the brazier and gestured to the unoccupied one opposite. Her feet felt as if they had millstones chained to them, and her back now ached viciously after working in the healing tent. She wasn't going to conduct this meeting standing, but she didn't want him looming over her either. "Please sit."

Moving with the same fluid grace she'd seen when he'd come to her aid, Alar settled onto the stool.

Mirren brought over two cups of bramble wine before retreating once more. Bree, however, moved closer so she stood at her queen's shoulder. A silent warning.

"So …" Lara took a sip of wine, feigning a calmness she didn't feel. "How exactly can you help me?"

He mirrored her action, drinking from his cup. "I lead an army of wulvers … and should you wish it, they're at your disposal."

She stilled. Whatever she'd thought he might say, this wasn't it. So, that was why he bore the wulver sigil?

"You're the *Half-blood?*"

Surprised that Mirren would speak up so boldly, Lara cut her handmaid a sharp look. She was staring at their visitor as if he'd just turned into the botach before her eyes.

For a heartbeat, irritation flickered across Alar's face before he covered it up with another sly smile. "Aye, that's what some call me."

Uneasiness curled up inside Lara.

The Half-blood?

She'd heard of him too. He was supposed to be an exile, of Marav mother and Shee father, who'd taken up with the wulvers. She should have guessed it from his looks. She'd heard the whispers but had dismissed them as fanciful. The Half-blood, who was said to dwell somewhere in the mid-Uplands, wasn't a threat to her, and wulvers weren't causing her any problems either. She had far too many other things to worry about.

There hadn't been any stories about him being a military commander though.

"An *army* of wulvers," she said finally, even as her mind raced. "How many exactly?"

"Close to a thousand at hand."

Her heart kicked hard. By The Warrior's Blade, his army was bigger than *hers*. Her breathing quickened then, the despair that had been nipping at her heels all evening drawing back. Such a force could turn the tide against the Shee. With his help, she could take back Rothie, and Strath too. She'd be near Cannich then and—

Don't get ahead of yourself.

This man had saved her life, but she didn't know him at all. He was bold and cunning. She needed to handle him carefully. "And they'd fight for me … after all the years of persecution they suffered at my father's hands?" she asked warily.

Alar's grey eyes fixed upon her. "You aren't your father."

Once again, the gravelly timbre to his voice made a strange, unsettling sensation shiver through her.

She swallowed. No, she didn't hold many of her father's views. He'd persecuted wulvers, as he had many of the faerie creatures who lived in Albia. "And what do you want in return?"

Alar gave a low laugh before raising his cup to her in a vaguely mocking toast. He then lifted the cup to his lips and drained it. "You understand how the world works then?"

Yet again, the sensation that he was the one in control of this meeting, not her, washed over Lara. Was her predicament a game to him?

"Aye," she replied, her tone cooling. "What's your price?"

Alar leaned forward, resting his elbows on his thighs. He then captured her gaze boldly with his. "Your hand in marriage."

Lara stared back at him.

Your hand in marriage.

She couldn't help it—she screwed her face up. It took all her effort not to call out to Cailean and Roth and order them to drag this dung-eater from her sight. "You ask too much."

"Do I?"

"Aye." Her voice was icy now, yet he seemed oblivious.

"So, victory isn't important to you?"

"Oh, it is."

"I'm a valuable ally."

"I have no wish for another husband." And even if she did, this sly man who lived amongst wulvers would be at the bottom of her list. His proposal was an insult.

He inclined his head. "King Dunchadh of Braewall was a disappointment then?"

A brittle silence fell in the pavilion. Meanwhile, Bree and Mirren's gazes drilled into Lara. They were waiting for her to respond—and she would.

Rising to her feet, she handed her half-finished cup of wine to Mirren before smoothing her palms on the skirt of the ankle-length tunic she wore. The garment was slit at the sides to allow her to stride out properly and to ride a horse without impediment. However, after a long day, the pine-green wool was stained with rain, mud, and blood from the healing tent.

She didn't feel particularly regal at present, for she was sure the rest of her clothing, and her face, were as dirty as her skirts, but she cut Alar an imperious glare, all the same. He'd never know just how much he rattled her. "Why do you want to marry me?"

"I want a better life for my brothers and sisters. Wulvers have always been gentle creatures. In the past, they'd often guide the lost and leave fish for the poor. But your people turned on them." His eyes glinted then. "And I'm ambitious … I want to co-rule Albia with you."

His last words hung heavily in the air.

Heat started to pulse in her belly. "What, no flattery?" Her marriage proposals so far had been tedious, but this one was a slap across the face. Unlike Niall of Braewall—her new southern overking—he hadn't droned on about her beauty, about how he wished to protect her.

She almost wished he had.

He arched an eyebrow. "Would you like me to sweeten my words?"

"It wouldn't matter if you did," she shot back, her anger surfacing. "The answer is still no."

That wiped the smile off his face. "Nearly a thousand wulvers at your command … an army that would take back, not just Doure, but *all* of The Uplands," he replied, his tone cooling. "You'd throw that aside?"

"That's right." Gods, how she wanted that army. However, his price was too high.

"Then you're a fool."

Bree made a hissing noise between her teeth. Her warder stepped forward then, the scrape of a blade drawing filling the tent. "Watch yourself."

Alar ignored her. Instead, his slate-colored eyes bored into Lara, holding her fast. "You won't take Doure without help. You know it as well as I."

Lara's hands curled into fists at her sides. Sourness flooded her mouth as despair rose like a specter once more. Viciously, she shoved it down. "My warriors will see you out of the encampment." She paused then before calling out, "Cailean.

Roth." Immediately, two tall, broad-shouldered figures shoved aside the tent flap and pushed inside. Lara nodded to them, even as her pulse thundered in her ears. "We're finished here. Take him away."

The Half-blood stood up and held out his empty cup to Mirren. The maid approached him warily, as if she expected him to leap for her throat. Once Alar had handed over his cup, the chief-enforcer stepped forward, his hand fastening around his upper arm.

Lara thought he might try and shake off Cailean's grip, but he didn't. Instead, he allowed the warrior druid to steer him toward the exit. However, just before he reached it, he glanced over his shoulder, his gaze spearing hers once more. A challenge glinted in his eyes. "My offer still stands," he said softly. "I will be waiting in the woods north of here. Send word, if you change your mind."

6: A BLADE OFFERED HILT-FIRST

ALAR WALKED THROUGH the High Queen's encampment, his pace unhurried. He was aware of his escort—the bullish chief-enforcer and the glowering captain of the army—stalking at his heel, but he ignored them.

Something wet and cold pushed against his neck then. Stumbling under the force of the nudge, he turned to find a huge dog with a shaggy dark-green coat and massive jaws looming at his shoulder. The beast—at least four times larger than the biggest wolf he'd ever seen—had massive jaws that could crush a man's skull like a walnut, yet its amber-hued gaze was adoring.

"Hello there," he murmured, wary. He was used to wolves and dogs responding well to him, but it was wise to be careful around a fae hound. He'd never stood so close to one before.

The dog gave a low whine and nudged him once more.

"Skaal!" The chief-enforcer's tone was sharp. "Back!"

Reluctantly, the fae hound obeyed, and Alar turned, resuming his journey through the camp.

Warriors watched as he passed, curious gazes tracking him. They were trying to decide who he was. Later, they'd discover that 'The Half-blood' had walked amongst them, but for the moment, they were mystified.

"Walk faster," the chief-enforcer growled, "Or I'll wedge my boot up your arse."

Alar glanced over his shoulder, meeting mac Brochan's hard blue gaze. He'd heard of this big, tattooed man and the fae hound that followed him—few in Albia hadn't. He'd once hunted and killed Shee for the High King and now served Talorc mac Brude's daughter. "Am I making you nervous?"

"No, you're pissing me off."

"It's not my fault your dog likes me."

"Shut your mouth, Half-blood," the captain added tersely. "You've said enough for tonight."

Alar smirked. "Eavesdropping, were you?"

Of course, these two pricks had been standing right outside the tent while he'd been speaking to the High Queen. They'd listened to every word.

"He insulted our High Queen," mac Tav muttered. "Maybe we should rough him up a bit."

Mac Brochan cracked his knuckles. "Don't tempt me."

Alar's smile didn't slip, although his instincts sharpened at the threat in the chief-enforcer's voice. Shifting his attention ahead once more, he slowed his stride further, hands flexing at his sides. "You'd attack an unarmed man?"

Mac Brochan shoved Alar between the shoulder blades. "Keep moving."

They reached the edge of the camp, where mist wreathed around the warded perimeter. Druidic magic hung heavily in the air here, and the pungent scent of ash and pine filled Alar's nostrils. As he walked through the wards, his skin prickled, the tattoo on his chest warming as it responded to earth magic.

Ignoring the sensation, he turned then to face his escort. The chief-enforcer held out his twin fighting daggers, which he sheathed, one over each shoulder, with deft, practiced movements.

"Slither away now." The captain raked a gaze over Alar. "And don't bother returning."

Alar took a step backward, his attention shifting to mac Brochan. "I won't need to," he replied softly. "Because you'll come looking for *me*."

The chief-enforcer's features pinched at this, while the captain spat on the ground between them.

Unbothered, Alar turned away. Years, he'd prepared for this moment—and now his time had come. Finally, justice was about to be served. For him. And for the wulvers. He then walked off, covering the ground in long, easy strides. All the while though, he was aware of stares digging into his back. The skin between his shoulder blades itched in response.

Moments later, he entered the woods that fringed the northern edge of the High Queen's camped army, his boots sinking into peaty soil. He wove his way through the trees, his keen eyesight picking out the dark outlines of twisted oaks, birches, and pines frosted in the light of the waxing crescent moon. It was a still night, eerily so, and he caught movement out of the corner of his eye as he walked. These woods weren't slumbering tonight. Ever since the Shee had occupied the North, the faerie creatures that roamed Albia had been more active.

He spied deep claw marks scored upon the trunk of one of the birches then and stopped to examine them. Reaching out, he rubbed a finger over where sap oozed onto the silvery bark. A shiver tickled his spine, and he glanced around. Moonlight filtered through the branches overhead, yet the shadows were deep. Anything could be lurking there. Watching. Waiting.

He moved on then, his right hand lifting to the hilt of the blade jutting at his shoulder. And as he walked, he kept a sharp eye upon his surroundings. Presently, he came to a small glade where a burn trickled over mossy rocks.

Lyall and Dolph were waiting for him there. His brothers. Two large wulvers—shaggy wolf heads on rangy men's bodies—their eyes glowed gold in the light of the torches they held. Lyall was the bigger of the two, with a thick black and grey ruff above his shoulders. Dolph, his mate, was smaller and lithe, with a coat the hue of weathered oak.

"Well?" Lyall rumbled.

"The seed has been sown."

"The queen didn't swoon at your proposal then?" Dolph crossed arms corded with ropey muscle across his chest, where heavy knife belts had been strapped. Unlike most of the faerie creatures that inhabited Albia, wulvers could tolerate iron. Over the long age since they'd been cast out of Sheehallion, whatever faerie magic they'd once possessed had been lost. These days, wulvers had more in common with the Marav than the Shee—a fact Lara's father had wished to ignore.

Alar halted before them. "No … although you knew she likely wouldn't. She's proud." He paused then. "She thinks herself too good for me."

Lyall snorted. "She's no better than any of us."

"That's right, brother," Alar replied before shrugging. "However, her imperious manner is merely a shield … in reality she's isolated … and desperate."

Lyall's feral gaze glinted. "But not yet desperate enough to agree to marry you?"

"She will be."

Dolph muttered something under his breath.

"It's all part of the game," Alar assured him. He paused then, glancing back over his shoulder. His instincts stirred once more. Something *was* watching him. "It's her move now."

"Let her sweat," Lyall agreed with a nod, his mouth curving into a smile that revealed sharp canine teeth. "Wait until despair creeps in. She can't win this battle without us."

"This is our moment," Dolph added. "Finally, we'll step into the light."

"Aye … and not before time," Alar replied before slowly reaching over his shoulders and drawing both his daggers.

The wulvers tensed and unsheathed blades of their own. "What is it?" Dolph murmured.

"I was tracked through the woods."

"The Marav?" Lyall's voice hardened.

"No." Alar turned then, his gaze sweeping the edges of the glade. "Something else. I noticed claw marks on one of the trees … there could be a clag-doo nearby."

Lyall cursed.

Clag-doos were rare, yet deadly. The lean, cat-like hunters were territorial and marked their domain with deep scratches that never healed. It had been years since Alar had last seen a 'Black-claw', although he wasn't in a hurry to do so again.

He caught sight of movement then, sinuous dark shapes wreathing between the trees. Low, thin voices followed, moaning, hissing, and snarling.

Alar stiffened. "The Slew?" There was something worse than a clag-doo in these woods.

"Can't be," Lyall answered, his golden eyes snapping wide. "The nearest burial site is half a night's walk away."

More shapes appeared, slithering around the edges of the clearing, as if they were wary of moving out of the shadows. The Slew were the spirits of men and women who'd committed terrible deeds during their lives and so were forbidden from entering the Otherworld. Their crimes were so awful that they couldn't enter the Underworld either—a cold, hostile place, where winter storms raged—and so they lurked in the Threshold or Albia's dark corners waiting to feed on the souls of the living.

Dolph breathed a curse. "It's still two moons until Gateway."

"That may be so," Alar replied, his skin prickling as he watched the shadows creep through the trees. Indeed, the only night of the year when the Slew ventured forth was the eve autumn slid into winter—the night when the veil between the living and the dead was at its thinnest. On that night, they took to the skies and went hunting. "But they're hungry *now*, it seems."

"They have been for a while," Dolph answered as he too tracked the Slew. All three of them hadn't moved since spotting the wraiths. The Unforgiven fed on the weak and fearful—and as such, the wulvers and their half-blood companion stared them down, even as their bodies tensed, readying themselves to run. "I think the Shee have something to do with it."

Alar harrumphed. "It's possible."

His pulse quickened then. The balance between the living and the dead, and fae and mortal, was delicate at best. The last High King had hated that the fae could cross between realms while his people couldn't. Talorc mac Brude was a butcher who loathed the Shee and all faerie kind, including wulvers and half-breeds like Alar. But now that mac Brude was dead, and the Raven Queen sat on the throne in Cannich and ruled The Uplands, Albia was changing.

Maybe the Slew knew it and grew bold as they prepared themselves for a new age.

Alar was readying himself too.

Even so, the restless dead made him uneasy. He wasn't foolish enough to let fear creep in, or they'd sniff it like hounds on the scent, but it was wise not to linger here any longer.

"Come on." He moved toward the trees on the northern side of the glade, where the Slew hadn't yet reached. "Let's get back to the others."

"Are you sure?"

Lara stared down at where the yellowed pieces of bone, with symbols inscribed upon them, lay scattered over the sheepskin. She swallowed hard then, for it felt as if a plum had lodged in her throat.

After dismissing the Half-blood, she'd come straight to the seer's tent looking for answers. But she hadn't liked what he'd just told her. Maybe he'd misread the bones.

Ruari knelt before her, his brow creased in concern. "The Cauldron, The Wolf, and The Endless Flame," he murmured, pointing to where the three bones had fallen side by side. "The Wolf represents Albia's ruling family … your family … The Endless Flame is the wulver mark … and The Cauldron symbolizes unity. It looks as if you *will* agree to marry the Half-blood."

Queasiness rolled over her. Upon entering the tent, she'd told the chief-seer about her meeting with Alar. "No," she ground out, even as she started to sweat. "I won't do it." The Hag spare her, she couldn't make an alliance with that man, even for his army.

Ruari cast her a sidelong look, his pale-blue gaze veiling. "The bones have more to say." His hand gestured to where two knucklebones overlapped. "The Square Knot lies atop The Shield Knot."

Her already racing pulse leaped. "What does that mean?"

"It's not a combination that often falls together … for it urges both trust and courage." He paused then, his expression suddenly wistful. "It reminds me of something my grandfather used to say. *'Trust is a blade offered hilt-first—dangerous to give, deadly to refuse'.*"

Lara sat back on her heels, frowning. They were words spoken by someone who had no idea what it was like to be a woman in a man's world. "No," she murmured. "Trust is just betrayal waiting for the right moment."

Guards escorted Lara back to her pavilion. It was strange to walk around the camp without Bree at her side. However, since it was late, she'd bid her warder to retire. On the way, they passed a smoldering fire pit where warriors gathered, warming their hands. "Good eve," she greeted them, injecting a heartiness into her tone she didn't feel.

The men nodded back. Some of them murmured responses, although she marked the sullenness on their faces, the wariness in their eyes. Her pulse quickened. It was bad enough that her overkings and the chieftains scattered throughout The Wolds doubted she could take back the North—but if her warriors lost faith, it was over.

Spine stiff, she walked on, head held high. Around her, the night was windless and silent, with a watchful quality, like an indrawn breath. The eerie stillness put her already strained nerves on edge.

Were the Half-blood and his wulvers watching from the woods to the north?

Her breathing grew shallow then. Alar commanded a formidable army, and if he chose to attack this camp, they'd be in trouble.

"Have you ever fought a wulver?" she asked one of the men flanking her.

"No, My Queen," he replied. "They're craven bastards. Wulvers don't fight … they cower."

"And yet the Half-blood says he has amassed an army of them … and that they'll fight for me."

The warrior pulled a face, giving her his answer.

They reached the royal pavilion then, and Lara left her escort outside while she pushed aside the flap. Yawning, she ducked inside.

The brazier had burned down low now, just a couple of faintly glowing coals holding back the darkness. The gentle sound of breathing greeted Lara. All four of her attendants were fast asleep, curled up like kittens on sheepskins. Skirting around

Mirren's sleeping form, and careful not to wake her, Lara moved to her furs and heeled off her boots. She sighed then. Shades, she was weary. Her feet were heavy, and it felt as if she were dragging rocks behind her.

Turning to the brazier, she raised a clenched hand and let her fingers unfurl. The coals brightened and then burst into flame.

Her lips curved then, as the familiar sensation of greeting an old friend washed over her, easing a little of her fatigue. A moment later, her smile faded. Of course, she'd felt the same way when she'd let the corpse candle dance on her palm. She wouldn't dare play with fire with an audience, but the brazier had almost gone out. The women who served her were all slumbering deeply, and she wished to have some light to see by.

Shrugging off her fur cloak, she hung it up on a stand. She then moved to a low table in the corner of the tent, kneeling before it. Four rosewood figurines sat there, their polished, carven surfaces gleaming in the light of the brazier. She blinked a few times as her gaze slid over them, her eyes gritty and blurred. The Mother. The Maiden. The Warrior. The Hag. Four of the five Gods of Albia. The fifth, The Reaper, was never represented in art—to do so was to invite ill fortune.

Lara's chest tightened as she silently whispered a prayer to each God, a ritual that usually steadied her. Kennan had carved these figurines. He'd whittled them over many evenings, especially for her. An image of his handsome face, his teasing smile flashed before her then. Gods, how she missed him. Her brother had died a few turns of the moon before her father— ambushed by the Shee.

Her jaw tightened then, a familiar anger quickening in her belly. Her father had killed him, as surely as if he'd plunged a blade into his son's chest himself. His lust for power, for revenge, had turned him blind to all else. *The bastard sacrificed us all.*

Kennan would have made a good High King. He'd spent his life preparing for it, whereas the role had been thrust upon her. However, she'd worked tirelessly to catch up. Ever since taking the throne, she'd studied history and battle tactics. She'd worked closely with her overkings, even though both men patronized her, and rebuilt her army. She'd given rousing speeches to the people of Duncrag, promising them that she'd reclaim the lands that had been taken, that she'd drive the Shee out of Albia.

But she'd yet to deliver. Of course, for all her determination, she was inexperienced in the art of war.

What advice would you give me now, Kennan? Sometimes she liked to think her brother's shade was near, watching over her. She asked him things she wouldn't ask others. *Did I make a mistake laying siege to Doure?*

Reaching out, she picked up the figurine of The Warrior. The feel of the smooth rosewood in her grip made the tension under her breastbone ease a little. Moments passed, and her eyes flickered closed.

No, this was the right path. The *only* path.

The Gods were with her, and The Warrior would guide them in the coming days.

Her people required action. She'd waited long enough, gaining strength, but now was the time to strike. She squeezed the figurine tightly. She'd known this wouldn't be easy. She was ready for a fight.

Lara opened her eyes and replaced The Warrior next to the others on the low table. Rising to her feet, she padded across to her furs, sliding into their soft embrace. She then heaved a heavy sigh. This was a day she desperately wanted to forget.

Shifting her attention to the flickering brazier, she surveyed the prone figures lying nearby to reassure herself that everyone was still sleeping. Then, she extended her hand, stretching out her fingers. The flames flickered and danced, and something inside her unraveled as she gazed at their beauty.

With another sigh, she sharply drew her fingers back, snapping them into a clenched fist.

The flames in the brazier flared bright once more and died, plunging the tent into darkness.

7: FIND THE HALF-BLOOD

Ten days later …

WATCHING THE REMAINS of her army retreat in the grey gloaming, Lara's stomach dropped. It was as if she'd just jumped feet first into a bottomless well. The acrid odor of burnt tar mixed with the stench of offal drifted over her. It was the smell of defeat. She could see it in the warriors' rounded shoulders, their haggard faces.

They had nothing left to give.

A group of red-robed men and women limped into view then, climbing up from the smoking defile. Gregor and his enforcers had done their best to keep the Gods close over the past days, braving fire, arrows, spears, and stones to do so. But even they were beaten. The last of the pigeons and hares they'd brought from Duncrag had been sacrificed.

The sight of the chief-sacrificer shocked Lara. She'd never seen him look so downcast. The big man staggered as he made his way up the slope.

Throat constricting, her attention flicked to the walls of Doure. They were smoke-blackened now, yet stood as strong as ever. As did the gates. Over the past days, four battering rams had been built and then destroyed.

Her breathing came shallow and fast—it was hard to draw in enough air.

But underneath her despair, fury pulsed in her gut. Curse the fucking Shee for eternity. This couldn't be the end. She wouldn't accept it. She couldn't let the Shee take Albia, fort by fort, until they ruled everywhere.

A glimmer caught her eye then. The ring on her right hand—the *Ord-ree Seal* that had once belonged to her father—had just flashed at her.

Stilling, she stared down at the chunky amber stone set on a thick iron band.

I must have been imagining things.

She was about to lift her chin once more when fire flickered in the heart of the amber.

Cold washed over her, dousing the heat of her anger. What was this?

"Come, Lara." Bree's voice intruded. "We must follow the others."

"Aye." Heart hammering, she yanked her attention from the ring and reined Bracken around before urging her into a canter.

But as she rode away from Doure, trying not to think about the flame she'd seen dance in the amber, the skin between her shoulder blades burned. She imagined the Shee standing on the walls, jeering at her.

They were stronger and quicker than her people and certainly knew how to defend a fort. Their greatest weakness was iron—even the proximity weakened them, and the merest touch burned like fire upon their skin—yet her warriors couldn't scale the walls to use it on them. They also feared earth magic, which her enforcers wielded, although the warrior druids couldn't get close enough to use it effectively.

Humiliation bit at her like cold steel then, and she forgot all about the ring.

Maybe this was the real reason her father had loathed the Shee so. The tales went that his first wife had been stolen away by the Shee, never to be seen again, and it had left him bitter. But Lara realized that it went deeper than that. Her father feared the fae race that dwelled in Sheehallion. They lived for thousands of years, whereas if one of the Marav was blessed with a century, it was considered a miracle. The Shee were swift and, although lean in build, tall and incredibly strong. Not only that, but they could glamor themselves, share thoughts with animals, and blend in with the shadows when they wished to.

In short, they were superior to the Marav in most ways. Talorc mac Brude had known this and had feared that they'd one day decide to take Albia for their own. And now, the thing he'd dreaded most was about to happen.

It was a bitter irony then that he'd been the one to start this.

Back at the encampment, the mood was grim, and the healing tent was fuller than ever.

Lara had ridden straight there, not allowing herself to catch anyone's eye. She couldn't bear to see the disappointment, the judgment, in their gazes. Dismounting, she'd handed the reins over to one of her guards before ducking into the pavilion. Bree followed her inside. Every evening after battle, the High Queen continued to help tend to the injured.

The iron tang of blood assaulted her nostrils as she walked down the narrow aisle between tightly-packed pallets. The groans and whimpers of the injured and dying drove into her like blades.

This is my doing.

Indeed, these brave warriors had marched here and laid siege to Doure for her.

So many had fallen. A fresh funeral pyre had burned every night, illuminating the darkness like a beacon. Another would burn tonight too.

Moving through the tent, she spoke to some of the dying. There was little to be done for these men and women, other than to give them some water with a tincture of hemlock mixed in, just enough to sedate them and dull the pain.

"We have failed you, lass," a warrior rasped as she took his hand.

Lara squeezed gently. His fingers were strong yet clammy. The man had taken a spear, thrown from the ramparts, to the belly. She'd administered a strong dose of hemlock for him earlier. "What is your name?" she asked gently.

"Aonghus," he rasped.

"Well, Aonghus, you fought like a wolf … and I will never forget it." She paused, her grip on his hand tightening further. Her heart was in her throat now. "Ever."

Her chest clenched then. Curse it. She couldn't let this man's death—and those of so many others—be all for nothing. Aonghus thought he'd failed her, but it was the opposite. She'd failed *them*. She'd promised her people she'd take back Doure, yet she couldn't.

Hope isn't lost ... all you must do is make a deal.

Biliousness rose in her chest.

She'd done her best not to think about the Half-blood's offer. None of the members of her council had brought it up since. They'd dismissed his proposal out of hand, yet she hadn't. Every evening when they met to discuss how the siege was going and plan the way forward, it was as if Alar were standing in the shadows behind them, smirking, biding his time.

He'd known this moment would come.

Murmuring a soothing word to Aonghus, she released his hand and straightened up. Her attention shifted to where Bree stood in the aisle between the rows of pallets. Her friend's face was strained, her eyes shadowed.

"Call my council," Lara said, even as dread closed her throat. "I must speak with them now."

"Marrying that man would be a mistake, My Queen." Annis leaned forward and placed her hands on the table between them. "One *all* of us would come to regret."

"Would we?" Lara replied, wishing her voice didn't sound so rough. "If we want to take Doure ... or indeed win the war against the Shee, we need allies."

"You can't trust wulvers." Gregor's scowl was so deep it risked cleaving his forehead in two.

"*Or* the Half-blood," Cailean growled.

"It's a risk," she admitted, even as dizziness assailed her. "But it's either that or we retreat."

"Then we retreat," the chief-counsellor shot back. Lara had never seen Annis look so fierce. "We return to Duncrag and rebuild our strength. We take the North on *our* terms … no one else's."

Lara's pulse started to thud in her ears. She'd gathered her council and told them that she wished to accept the Half-blood's proposal; however, they weren't responding well. Over the past three years, she'd nearly always heeded their advice—but this time, she resisted it. They were all giving up the fight too easily, but she didn't have that luxury.

They didn't carry the responsibilities she did. She'd promised her people the Shee wouldn't take The Wolds, but if she retreated, there was a real possibility they would. And soon. Defeating her could give the Shee the confidence they needed to push south again.

"Annis is right," Roth spoke up then, breaking the brittle silence. "We don't need the Half-blood and his flea-bitten wulvers." He paused then. "Besides, you swore never to take another husband, remember?"

There was no mistaking the accusation in his voice.

Lara's chin kicked up. She then cut the captain a glare. "Do you think I want this?" He stared back at her stonily, his pale-blue eyes glinting. "Trust me, Roth … I'd rather swallow nails."

They had no idea just how much she abhorred the idea. Her chest constricted then with an emotion that felt very much like grief. She was about to lose something very precious: her autonomy. Aye, she depended heavily on her council at times—but she was her own woman.

If she accepted the Half-blood's offer, that would end.

Silence followed her outburst.

"I will not return to Duncrag defeated," she said finally, her gaze sweeping the taut faces of those gathered around the table.

"If you don't want me to forge an alliance with the Half-blood, give me a better solution ... one that will win us Doure."

No one answered.

Ren and Ruari, the newest members of her council, exchanged worried looks. They hadn't spoken up after her announcement, yet their frowns made their displeasure clear. Meanwhile, across the table, Cailean's blue eyes narrowed. His jaw set in that bullish expression she'd come to know well over the years. To his right, Bree's face was pinched, while to his left, Gregor looked mutinous. Annis pursed her lips unhappily and folded her arms across her ample bosom.

"So, no one here has one?" Lara threw down the challenge.

Roth muttered a curse under his breath.

"I didn't think so." She turned to her captain, pinning him with a hard stare. "Find the Half-blood."

"Please reconsider, Lara." Bree stepped close, her brow deeply furrowed.

"I know you want victory," Cailean rumbled, his gaze shadowed. "But this is going too far."

Muttering an oath under her breath, Lara turned to face her friends. They were inside the royal pavilion now. Unsurprisingly, they'd followed her in here after the meeting. They wanted to speak to her alone. Skaal had padded into the tent behind them and was now seated in front of the brazier, scratching. Unlike Cailean and Bree, the fae hound seemed unconcerned about Lara's decision.

"I can't let the Shee get a foothold," she replied, trying to ignore her pitching belly. "We have to take Doure back."

"And you *will*," Cailean countered. "Just not like this."

"The Half-blood is an outcast … you know nothing about him, or his true motives," Bree added.

"Maybe not, but since I'm going into this with my eyes open, he's not likely to take me by surprise." Lara's temper simmered now. "He has a large army … one that can turn the tide for us. The Raven Queen uses faerie creatures as her weapons. Why can't we use the might of the wulvers?"

Neither of them had a reply for this, although Cailean's jaw bunched, and Bree shook her head in exasperation.

"So, you're determined to go through with this?" the chief-enforcer asked finally.

Lara nodded.

"Even knowing that your council disagrees?"

"Aye." Her pulse quickened. This was the first time she and Cailean had ever truly locked horns. He was her friend, and she valued his opinion, but in this instance, he was wrong. "There are some things a queen must decide for herself."

His lips thinned, and he favored her with a curt nod. Then, without another word, he turned and pushed his way out of the tent. Skaal gave a low whine and rose fluidly to her feet. Her golden eyes flicked to Lara then, holding her fast for an instant, before she followed the chief-enforcer.

Bree remained though. Observing Lara with a look she'd come to know well, she folded her arms across her chest. "I've never seen you like this," she murmured finally. "Reckless. Desperate."

"And you'd be too, in my place," Lara snapped, even as her chest grew tight. "I can't turn my back on Doure. I won't."

"But marrying *him?*"

"It's the only way, Bree."

Her friend's eyes shadowed. "No," she said softly, "it isn't."

"Enough." Lara stepped back then, gesturing to the flap where Cailean had just exited. "You can leave too … I will meet Alar alone."

Bree's chin lifted. "What?"

"The nature of our arrangement is … personal … and I wish for some privacy."

"Do yourself a favor and negotiate hard." Bree's voice was forceful now. "If you're going to get into the furs with this man, make sure it's worth your while."

Lara flinched. There was no need to be crude. Giving Bree her back, she moved to one of the two stools before the glowing brazier. "Don't worry … I will."

"Do you want anything, My Queen?" Mirren asked then. Florie and the twins had already left the pavilion, yet her handmaid lingered. Worry filled Mirren's blue eyes; she looked as unhappy as Bree and Cailean about this.

"Just leave a jug of wine and two cups on the table." Lara sank down on the stool. The warmth of the brazier was welcome. It was a cold, damp evening. That morning, she'd noticed many of the trees in the woodland now wore cloaks of red and gold. Winter was marching toward them.

Mirren did as bid. Lara watched her, marking the tension in her movements, the way her full lips now turned down at the corners.

"For the love of the Gods," Lara muttered. "I'm not going to my execution."

"I know … but this solution just seems" —Mirren broke off there searching for the word— "Extreme."

"It is," Bree replied. She hadn't yet left the pavilion. Instead, she lingered near the doorway. "You're wrong, Lara. Failing to take back Doure this time doesn't mean Mor will win. Why won't you return to Duncrag and rally yourself?"

Lara heaved in a shaky breath before glancing her way. "Rally? With what resources exactly?" Her pulse fluttered then. "We no longer can recruit warriors from The Uplands … and if I take many more warriors from The Wolds, I risk an uprising." It was true, her overkings—King Artair of Baldeen and King Niall of Braewall, who were both as new to their roles as she was—had started to push back of late. Artair, especially, had grown difficult. The Southerners, who'd lived for centuries in relative prosperity and safety, didn't appreciate sending their sons and daughters off to war, and when they heard of what had transpired before the walls of Doure, they'd be looking for someone to blame.

Bree scowled, heat flaring in her eyes. "You have an answer for everything, don't you?"

Lara glared back at her. "Aye."

Mirren cleared her throat, shattering the tense silence that followed. "Come on, Bree," she whispered. "Let's go."

And they did, although not without backward glances. Guilt tugged at Lara as she watched them leave. Mirren and Bree had become her family over the past years. They'd been through much together. They meant well, but they were just making this all the harder.

As soon as she was alone, she rose from the stool, went to the table, and poured herself a large cup of wine. She then slugged it back.

Eyes watering and throat burning, she set the cup down and crossed to the makeshift shrine in the shadowy corner of her tent. There, she knelt before reaching out and picking up the figurine of The Mother. She then bent her head, closed her eyes, and whispered a prayer. The Goddess was the bringer of change, and if there was ever a time she needed her strength, it was now.

75

8: A PROMISE MADE IN BLOOD

ALAR DUCKED INTO the tent and let the flap fall behind him. Casting a gaze around the warm interior, illuminated by a brazier and hanging lamps where pots of oil burned, he was surprised to find the High Queen alone.

Lara was sitting by the brazier, small pale hands folded demurely upon her lap. Her posture was straight, almost unnaturally so.

She was bracing herself for this meeting.

For his part, Alar hadn't expected her to wait ten days before calling for him. As the time had slid by, and his wulvers grew restless, he'd secretly begun to worry that Albia's High Queen would prefer to suffer a humiliating defeat rather than shackle herself to a half-blood outcast—even one who'd promised her an army. Of course, he'd kept his concerns to himself. He'd assured his brothers and sisters that Queen Lara would eventually capitulate, and this evening, finally, she had.

Justice was so close, he could smell it.

"Your Highness."

"Alar." She rose from her seat, her lips pursing as if something unpleasant had just slithered into her tent. "Wine?"

He nodded, pretending not to notice her unwelcoming expression. "Thank you."

He moved over to the brazier but didn't sit down. Instead, he watched Lara cross to the low table and pour them both cups. It seemed odd to see her perform such a menial task, especially since the last time they'd met, her handmaid had served them both.

But this evening, she'd sent her attendants—even her bodyguard—away.

While the High Queen's attention was elsewhere, he took the opportunity to take a good look at her.

She was comely—which certainly would make this task easier—with a heart-shaped face and fine features. A fetching high-necked and fur-trimmed emerald tunic encased her supple body. Bronze, silver, and gold arm rings decorated her bare arms, and amber combs held back thick auburn hair from her face, while the rest of her mane tumbled down the long sweep of her back.

Lara turned back to him then, terminating his scrutiny, and carried the wine across to the brazier.

He took the cup she offered him. "So, you have failed to take back Doure?"

A nerve flickered in her cheek. "Evidently."

"None of the battering rams you've constructed were sturdy enough to breach the gates," he replied. "We have one that is."

Her pine-green eyes, fringed with thick dark-auburn lashes, widened. He noted then, for the first time, the light scattering of freckles that dusted the bridge of her nose and cheeks. "Aye?"

He nodded. "It's not just built of oak … but of *iron*. We call it the *Fire Wyrm* … and the gates of Doure won't withstand its might."

"You've *named* your battering ram?"

He favored her with a slow smile, one that made a delightful blush stain her smooth cheeks. "Of course."

Clearing her throat, Lara settled herself onto a stool, and Alar followed her lead. They now sat facing each other with a little over four feet between them. He held his tongue, instead taking a sip of the sweet plum wine. He'd let the High Queen take the lead now, let her think she was the one in control of this discussion.

Of course, she wasn't. Tonight, he had the upper hand.

Silence settled in the pavilion, broken only by the pop of embers in the brazier and the muffled rumble of the surrounding camp. Earlier, as he'd followed the chief-enforcer and his monstrous fae hound through the tents, he'd noted the despondency among the Marav had worsened. He'd heard the rasp of fear in the voices of those gathered at firesides, had marked their hollowed gazes and taut faces.

Aye, they were desperate. The timing was perfect.

"You know why I've called you here?"

He nodded.

"If I can't take Doure, it will send a message to Mor that I'm weak … and that Duncrag is ripe for the seizing." Her throat worked then. "This is the beginning of the end ... unless ..." Her voice trailed off as if she couldn't bear to continue.

"You agree to marry me."

The High Queen winced before lifting the cup to her lips and taking a gulp of wine, a slight tremor in her hand. She wouldn't look at him now. "There must be another way."

He swallowed a smile. She wanted to play, did she? "Go on."

She shifted on her stool, still avoiding his eye. "Surely, there is something else you want ... besides this? Coin ... lands? Name your price."

Alar didn't answer right away. Instead, he took a sip of wine and pretended to consider her words. He almost felt sorry for her. Albia's young High Queen carried much responsibility upon her shoulders. However, he wouldn't let the vulnerability she was doing her best to hide sway him. "No," he said finally. "Only becoming your husband will do. In return for my army, you must agree to be handfasted to me ... to allow me to co-rule." He had to spell it out to her. He wanted no ambiguity in this.

Her chin jerked up, her eyes glinting as anger surfaced. "You want to be High King of Albia, is that it?"

He shrugged. "The title of prince consort will do ... what matters more is that you share power with me." His heart kicked then. That wasn't part of the plan. He'd promised his brothers and sisters that he'd negotiate hard, that he'd push for as much as he could.

He'd just made quite a concession, but the High Queen didn't look grateful. Instead, her pretty mouth twisted. "You're all the same."

He inclined his head. "Who are?"

"*Men,*" she clarified, biting out the word. "There's nothing you wouldn't do for control."

Alar huffed a laugh. She had *no* idea what he was prepared to do to achieve his ends.

"And what will you *do* once you're prince consort?" Her eyebrows lowered as she glared at him. "Attempt to overthrow me?"

He snorted, both entertained and irritated by her spirited response. "I give you my word that I won't."

"No offense, but you've given me no reason to trust you."

Alar leaned forward, ensnaring her gaze with his. "No offense, but you have no choice *but* to trust me." He paused then. "I'm your bridge to victory, Lara. Without my army, you'll never make it."

Another silence fell in the pavilion, the brazier crackling gently between them. The High Queen's expression was pinched now. She was looking at him as if a warty puddock had just hopped into her tent and proposed marriage.

Perhaps she would have preferred a toad to a half-blood outcast.

"I have no interest in taking Duncrag for my own," he said finally. "You are its rightful ruler."

She snorted. "You expect me to take you at your word?"

His gaze never wavered. "Aye, I'm not doing this for you … but for the wulvers. When we're done, with their leader as prince consort and with victory over the Shee, they will have earned the respect they deserve in Albia."

Her gaze narrowed once more. "And why does that matter to you so much?"

He leaned forward. "Long have my brothers and sisters been ill-treated by your people, shunned from settlements, and pushed into the fringes of Albia. They deserve better."

That was an understatement. They deserved to stand on their own—to rule land as the Marav did. He kept these sentiments to himself though.

"But you aren't one of them. Why take up their cause?"

He sat back. "They gave me shelter … and kindness and respect … when no one else would."

Her fingers tightened around her cup. "How long have you lived with them?"

"Decades."

Surprise rippled over her delicate features. "Really? You can't be any older than thirty winters."

A smile tugged at his lips. "You'd think that, aye … but I'm a half-blood remember. This is my seventy-second summer."

Her face paled, panic flaring in her eyes. "Do you expect me to bind myself to a man who's literally immortal?" she rasped. "A man who'd rule for many centuries after my death?"

"I don't have the lifespan of a Shee," he assured her. "My blood is too diluted for that … all the same, half-bloods can often live up to three hundred years."

She drew in a deep, shuddering breath and cut her gaze away. Alar watched her struggle.

"How did I not know this?" she asked finally.

"Likely because it never mattered to you before now." He paused then before adding. "However, *I* won't live three hundred years." Once again, the strange urge to reassure her rose.

"And why not?"

"An aughisky stole a century from me."

Lara jolted. "What?"

"Nearly thirty years ago, I journeyed to one of the crannogs on Loch Glass in the North. Tired after days of travel, I was resting, thinking how I could do with a sturdy pony to carry me, when I spied a fine garron grazing a few yards away … a grey pony with feathered feet, and a flowing mane and tail." He pulled a face as he recalled the incident. It wasn't one he spoke about often. "Of course, I shouldn't have acted on impulse. The moment I swung up onto its back, my hand stuck fast to its neck, and I realized my mistake."

Lara shook her head, clearly thinking him a fool. The vicious water spirits lived in the sea and lochs. There were few tales of anyone surviving an encounter with one. Once you touched an aughisky, you couldn't get free. After that, it dragged you deep into the water and feasted on you.

"I had to think fast … for an instant later, we were lurching toward the water's edge," he continued. "Before we reached the loch, I called out … and offered up a hundred years of my life, if it released me."

"And it agreed?" She was incredulous, and he didn't blame her.

"Aye … aughiskies hunger for the lives of others. But few people know that if you give up *years* of your life willingly, it might spare you. Such a *gift* will satisfy its appetite for a time. Luckily, my grandmother once mentioned this to me."

The High Queen frowned. "That's still a costly price when you're Marav. Our lives are too brief as it is."

"Aye … although a shortened life is better than a grisly death. I learned years later from the crannog-dwellers there that the Loch Glass ausghisky had been known to take several lives a year … it must for its survival. Lying in wait on the shore for someone ignorant or stupid enough" —he grimaced once more— "to touch it, is long, boring work. That's why it took my offer, dumped me onto the loch shore, and plunged into the water … and didn't take any more lives for a while after that."

Lara arched an eyebrow. "So, you'll live *two* lives of a Marav now, rather than three?"

He shrugged, eager to move the conversation on. "Aye."

"I suppose when you have so many years to play with … what's a century?"

He barked a laugh. "So young and fair … and yet so bitter," he teased.

She scowled. "So, are there others … like you?"

Ashes, the woman wouldn't let this go.

"Aye … although we're rare. In all my years, I've only ever crossed paths with two … and briefly. Like me, they were both outcasts."

Silence fell once more, and Alar observed her pale, tense face. Her eyes were shadowed, and a muscle feathered in her jaw. She looked young. Out of her depth. Lost.

"I'm not planning to usurp you, Lara," he said after a lengthy pause. "And if we have children, I am happy for one of them to take the throne upon your death."

"And you'd swear this … sign a document before our handfasting?"

His gaze held hers, even as his pulse quickened. "If that's what you wish … aye."

Lara stared back at him for a few moments before lifting her cup and draining its contents in a long draft. Alar watched her, uneasiness feathering through him.

When she lowered the cup, her lips were stained red. "Very well," she said hoarsely. "I shall wed you."

Alar's heart kicked hard, although he kept his expression veiled. "You do me an honor."

Tension rippled through her body, and for a moment, he thought she might withdraw her agreement. Instead, she cleared her throat. "I shall call in my chief-enforcer … so he can witness this."

He shook his head. "I'm sorry, but I'll need something more binding than that."

Enough feeling sorry for her. Lara would try to wriggle out of this the moment his back was turned. He had to make their pact ironclad.

She stilled. "Excuse me?"

"I require you to make a blood oath."

Her breathing hitched. Her lips then compressed. "Is that necessary?"

"Aye."

And it was. This was one thing he wouldn't yield on.

"Do you think I'll go back on my word?"

"You're in a corner right now and will do anything to get out of it." Her pine-green eyes darkened to jade, and her full lips thinned, yet he continued, "The blood oath requires but a small nick in the flesh … it won't take long."

Her fingers clenched so tightly around her empty cup that her knuckles turned white.

Alar stilled. Had he gone too far? It wouldn't help him if she shouted to her chief-enforcer and had him hauled from the camp. His breathing grew shallow as he waited for her to weigh up his words.

The blood oath was something you only resorted to when desperate. The people of Albia believed that if you broke a promise made in blood, The Five would damn you.

Lara squeezed her eyes shut then, as if praying to the Gods for strength, and Alar drank her in. She *was* young, around five and twenty summers at most. At first glance, she appeared soft, pliable, yet he sensed a steeliness to her. She'd bend, but she wouldn't easily break. The High Queen was no fool.

The realization both pleased and unsettled him.

He had no wish for a mewling, whining wife, although he could see Lara mac Talorc wouldn't be easily manipulated. He, on the other hand, had to be wary of being played.

"Very well," she ground out finally. "Get it over with."

"I'll need a knife … as you can see, I don't carry one at present."

Jaw set, she put aside her cup and drew a thin-bladed dagger from the leather scabbard at her belt. Alar recognized it. The knife was the same one she'd defended herself with against the powries days earlier. Now, as then, she drew the weapon with confidence—someone had clearly shown her how to use it—before holding it out to him, grip first. Her throat worked as she did so.

It was a vulnerable gesture, one that surprised him.

Putting down his wine, Alar took the dagger. He then rose to his feet and stepped toward her. "Stand up." She obeyed, even though the groove between her eyebrows had deepened. She'd gone the color of milk. "Hold out your left hand."

A tremor went through her, and for a moment, he thought she might change her mind. But then, she thrust out her hand. Her gaze glinted as she dared him to hurt her.

Gently, he took hold of her wrist and turned it over, exposing the translucent skin underneath. It was the finest skin he'd ever seen, and Alar hesitated a moment. He was loath to mar it, but this was necessary.

He drew the sharp blade swiftly across her wrist, hearing the hiss of her breath follow. Then, he turned his right hand over and cut himself. A sting of pain followed, and a sensation of warmth followed as blood welled. Usually, he wore leather bracers upon his forearms, but he'd removed them before coming here this evening, in anticipation of making the blood oath.

Aye, he'd planned this.

He then placed his wrist against hers, curling his fingers around her slender forearm. The flesh beneath his was soft, the bones delicate. "Grip my wrist tightly," he commanded, and a moment later, her fingers formed a bracelet around his arm, her hold surprisingly strong. It struck him then that this act was very similar to the handfasting that would soon bond them as husband and wife. Indeed, the words of the blood oath were similar to handfasting ones.

"You have my word that my hand and my army are yours," he murmured as heat pulsed upon his wrist, where their skin met. "We have made a promise in blood … and blood remembers … or may The Five damn my soul."

"You have my word that my hand and my throne are yours," she whispered back, her gaze riveted upon their joined hands. "We have made a promise in blood … and blood remembers," she whispered back. "Or may The Five damn my soul."

9: WITH THE DAWN

LARA LOWERED HERSELF back onto the stool and tried to ignore the dull throb in her wrist. Alar was right: he hadn't hurt her overly. All the same, some things stung more than a cut to the skin.

She'd just agreed to bind herself to a man of questionable morals. She'd accused him of lusting after power, yet was she any different?

Bile surged up, stinging the back of her throat. *What have I done?*

Too late, she wished she'd taken the advice of her council— and her friends—and accepted defeat. Now, whether she wanted it or not, she shared a bond with the Half-blood.

She was glad Mirren and Bree hadn't been present to see her perform the blood oath, to witness just how low she'd stoop to get what she wanted.

She'd have to watch Alar. He'd assured her he didn't covet Duncrag, but she didn't believe him. She'd put measures in place once she returned home to ensure he and his wulvers couldn't stage a rebellion.

Viewing the man whom she'd just made a pact with—as he retrieved his wine, yet didn't drink any of it—she decided to focus on practicalities. Perhaps if she did, this sickening sensation would retreat. Maybe then she wouldn't feel as if she'd just put her head in a noose.

"Is your army ... and your *Fire Wyrm* ... ready to attack with the dawn?" she asked briskly.

Alar nodded. "We have been waiting for your command."

"Good." She rose to her feet, wishing her belly would stop churning. "We must now meet with my chief-enforcer and the captain of my army ... to discuss tactics for tomorrow morning."

Lara's skin prickled as she watched the wulvers advance.

These creatures were reclusive by nature, and so she'd never actually seen one. They stalked rather than walked, moving with rounded shoulders and a loping gait. Rangy in build, they dressed lightly. The males were clad in leather trews and heavy boots, with knife belts strapped across their naked chests, while the females bound their breasts with leather. Pelts of different hues—from smoke or ash grey, to tawny brown, peat, and black—covered their shoulders, necks, and heads.

Lara noted their powerful canine jaws and their feral golden eyes, which fixed ahead at where the first glimmers of light warmed the eastern sky, gilding Doure's walls and turning the Sea of Sorrows molten bronze. Like most of her people, she'd believed wulvers were a craven lot—but they didn't look like cowards this morning.

And the snarls and barks they made chilled her blood. Pride gleamed in their eyes.

As promised, they'd been ready to attack with the dawn.

Alar strode by then, flanked by two male wulvers—one of which was huge, his grey and black hackles raised. The Half-blood was clad in leather breeches, a breastplate, and arm bracers. His long black hair had been braided at the sides and pulled back from his face, and he was armed as she'd seen him on their first meeting, with two fighting daggers strapped to his back.

He nodded to her as he passed, and she mirrored the gesture, acknowledging him too.

They didn't speak though. Enough words had passed between them for the moment.

She'd regretted every one of them.

But now, as Alar and his wulvers strode toward Doure, her regret slid into something else. Hope. Maybe this would work out. Maybe she hadn't made a huge mistake.

Lara watched him go until the swelling ranks swallowed him. Her wrist started to tingle then, and she turned her hand over and drew back her sleeve. The cut he'd given her the night before had scabbed over, yet it had prickled intermittently ever since. She'd deliberately not told anyone about the blood oath and had covered up the cut. She wasn't sure how her council would react to what she'd done—on top of her obstinance the day before—and so she decided to keep it secret.

In the aftermath, all her advisors had been aloof with her, even Bree and Cailean, but once Doure was taken, they'd realize that she'd done the right thing. Sometimes sacrifices had to be made.

Pulling her sleeve back down, she raised her chin, her gaze travelling to where the *Fire Wyrm* emerged. She murmured an oath under her breath as she tracked the path of the battering ram.

It made those they'd constructed look feeble indeed. The weapon was pulled in on wheels, by lines of heaving wulvers. It was long, around twelve feet, and swung on heavy chains. And as Alar had described, it had been forged of iron. Pitch burned within, flames erupting from the wyrm's open jaws and slitted eyes. The weapon rolled on, while the wulvers—wearing heavy iron helmets and plate armor—hauling it chanted in a rough tongue that Lara didn't understand. The iron began to glow. Before her eyes, the *Fire Wyrm* illuminated the dawn.

Her heart started to pound.

Beside her, Bree breathed a curse. "I've never seen the like." They were the first words her friend had spoken since they'd left the camp.

"Let's hope that the Shee have seen it too … and are now shitting themselves," Lara replied huskily.

Bree snorted, making it clear that the enemy wasn't so easily cowed.

Shifting in the saddle, Lara peered into the carpet of leather and mail-clad bodies moving toward the gates. Somewhere in there was her husband-to-be. Alar had advanced with the front ranks, along with Cailean and Roth.

And then, the great horde surged forward, a vast wave that rolled down the defile. Iron glinted dully as sunlight caught the edges of shields and blades. The shouts of men and women, and the chants of druids, mingled with the growls and snarls of wulvers, shook the sky.

But they didn't waste time trying to scale the walls this morning. Instead, they fell in behind the *Fire Wyrm* and headed toward the gates.

Arrows slammed into the battering ram as it rumbled up the other side of the defile, flying from the ramparts. Rows of figures clad in gleaming silver wielded longbows. They aimed at the *Fire Wyrm* first, but when their quarrels merely ricocheted off the glowing iron, they focused their attention upon the rows of wulvers that drew the weapon ever closer to their destination.

Just a few yards remained now.

But these wulvers had come prepared. Their heavy helmets and plated shoulder guards protected them. Heads bowed, they plowed on, and although some of them fell under the onslaught, the *Fire Wyrm* kept up its slow, inexorable progress.

Lara held her breath now, her heart kicking against her breastbone.

Just a few feet more.

With a lurch, the battering ram halted.

Fiery debris now rained down on it, as the Shee tried to set fire to the wooden scaffold that held up the *Fire Wyrm*. However, the wulvers had covered the scaffold with a canopy of wet animal hides. Steam rose as fireballs hit, but the battering ram under it swung back on chains, pulled by the wulvers.

Lara's ears started to ring, and she let out a sharp exhale. *Breathe, you idiot!* She'd look like a fool indeed if she fainted and toppled off her horse into the mud.

Boom!

Solid iron hit the gates.

Of course, although the Shee hated iron, they couldn't escape it in Doure. The gates themselves were made of iron and oak. They were sturdy, yet they'd already taken a hammering over the past days.

Boom!

"Come on," Lara growled as sweat now slid down her back between her shoulder blades. "Break, you bastards!"

Boom!

The scream and creak of both metal and wood sundering ripped through the smoky air, and a great roar went up.

But the *Fire Wyrm* wasn't yet done. It swung on its heavy chains once more, and this time—even from this distance—Lara saw the gates give way.

A whoop tore from her throat, and Bracken danced under her. And then, the army outside the walls surged forward into the breach, pushing into the fort.

The roar from the Marav and the wulvers broke over her in waves, and the air vibrated from the force of it. Presently, the rows of Shee archers on the walls disappeared, rushing down to the lower levels to fight.

Lara cut Bree a glance then. Her warder was staring at the fort. Cailean was in there, no doubt fighting in the thick of things. The tension in Bree's body, the way her hand gripped the pommel of her sword, betrayed her hunger to be at his side. "What now?" Lara gasped, excitement pitching in her gut.

Bree tore her gaze from the fort and met her eye squarely for the first time that morning. "Now the *real* battle begins."

Lara rode into the smoking fort, flanked by her Guard. The army had cleared a path for her, dragging debris and corpses out of the way so that the High Queen could enter.

Heart pounding, she urged her mare across the large open ground at the base of the fort, an area lined by storehouses and stables. *Victory.* Her breathing grew shallow, her skin prickling with elation.

Alar had done what he'd promised.

Riding on, she found herself peering into shadowed wynds, steps, and the doorways of turf-roofed roundhouses and cottages. They'd won—the surviving Shee had surrendered—although it paid to be cautious. They could never be underestimated. Her warriors had scoured Doure and had assured her that the enemy was either dead or captured. But she was on edge, all the same. Bree traveled alongside her, one hand still resting on the pommel of her sword.

As she made her way up the narrow road that snaked up to the top of the promontory, the people of Doure—the Marav who'd continued to live here under Shee rule—ventured out to see their queen. Thin, haggard faces turned up to the pale sun.

She wondered how greatly they'd suffered under their Shee overlords. She'd expected to see relief in their eyes at being liberated, yet many of them just looked stunned. And those who didn't wore sullen expressions.

Lara's lips thinned, her jubilation fading. Were they angry the wulvers were here? The arrangement didn't suit her either, but it couldn't be helped.

Nodding to her people—and trying to overlook their accusing stares—she urged her horse on. Anger sparked then, its heat rolling over her. *Ungrateful turds. You'll thank me one day.*

Still scanning her surroundings, for she half-expected a Shee clad in steel armor to leap out from behind a wall or emerge from one of the narrow vennels—walkways that provided shortcuts for those on foot to reach the summit of the fort—Lara crested the top of the crag. Here, the beehive-shaped broch, a smaller version of her own in Duncrag, rose against the sky. The tightly-packed dwellings drew back, and she rode across a wide dirt square before the gates of the broch. Her banner, a white wolf's head against a field of black, fluttered from the wooden palisade that surrounded the broch. Dark splotches stained the ground up here—blood—although the bodies had been dragged aside. The Marav and wulver dead now lined the northern wall, while a pile of Shee corpses rose on the southern side of the square. Steel scale armor glinted in the sunlight.

Queasiness rolled over Lara, and she swallowed hard.

So many dead—on both sides.

What did you expect? This is only the beginning. If she wished to take back The Uplands, she'd have to do this again, many times over, before she drove the Shee back. She'd have to get used to death.

Tearing her gaze from the corpses, she straightened her spine and focused on the gates ahead.

And when she rode through them, she found the three men who'd led her to victory standing on the steps to the broch: Cailean, Roth, and Alar. A large fae hound, her green coat ruffling in the wind, stood with them. Skaal's coat was singed in places and clumped with gore. Fortunately, she appeared unhurt.

The chief-enforcer, captain, and the Half-blood were also blood-splattered, and they bore what looked like superficial cuts on their arms and faces, yet their gazes gleamed. Cailean and Roth weren't happy with her decision, but hopefully, today's win would ease things a little between them.

Maybe they'd understand why she'd done this.

"Well fought," she greeted them, pride flushing through her.

Cailean nodded brusquely, and Roth flashed her a tight smile, while Alar inclined his head.

"Where is the Shee commander?" she asked, trying not to let their muted responses bother her.

"Dead inside the broch," Cailean replied. "He's on the dais. I think you'll recognize him."

Lara tensed. Would she? Sliding her feet from the stirrups, she prepared to dismount. Behind her, she heard the thud of boots hitting the ground then, as one of her Guard swung down from the saddle to help his queen. Irritation flared under her ribs. "It's all right." She waved the man away. "I told you I can manage."

"Allow *me* then."

Lara's attention snapped right to see Alar descending the steps toward her.

10: SPOILS OF WAR

WATCHING ALAR DRAW near, Lara tensed.

What are you up to?

She was aware that everyone present was observing their interaction.

Warmth flushed over her chest and crept up her neck. Humiliation. All her life, she'd had little privacy. It was part of being born into Albia's ruling family, and for the most part, she'd accepted it. Her life wasn't her own. She belonged to her subjects.

But now, she didn't want to be the center of attention. This arrangement was demeaning enough without Alar putting on a show for them all.

Lara silently bristled as he approached. Two could play this game. She'd made him a promise, but they weren't yet handfasted. Things could change before then, and she certainly wasn't in any hurry to set the date. The Half-blood might come to regret looking so smug.

Stopping before her, he held out a hand. "My Queen." A challenge glinted in those iron-grey eyes.

"Alar," she replied coolly before taking his hand.

Like the eve before, she noted the warmth and strength in those lean fingers. Moving nearer, he helped her down from her mount before placing a solicitous hand upon her back to guide her up the steps to the broch.

The gesture was innocuous enough, yet Lara stiffened at the contact. Despite the layers of clothing she wore, she felt the heat of his palm against her spine. It was a possessive gesture. Once again, the Half-blood knew he had an audience and was playing up to it.

The urge to tell him to stand back surged up then, but she choked it down. She'd dismissed her council's advice to make a pact with this man; there was little point in making a scene now. As High Queen, she had to give the outward appearance of dignity, even if she was seething inside.

So, she mounted the steps. The open doorway yawned before her, torchlight flickering beyond. She was vaguely aware of Bree moving to her left side, while Alar remained on her right. Glancing her warder's way, she marked the rigid set of Bree's jaw. She wondered then, how it must feel to see so many Shee dead. She might have even recognized some of them.

Lara's chest tightened. She was sorry her friend had to witness this, but it couldn't be helped. Bree had chosen her side.

Stepping inside the broch's entrance hall, she came to an abrupt halt.

It was clear the Shee had been living here. Her people's brochs were windowless structures of stacked-stone, but the new residents of this one had counteracted the darkness with banks of candles lining the walls and lanterns that hung from the rafters. Unlike her broch, there were no rushes on the floor; instead, the sandstone pavers beneath their feet had been scrubbed and polished until they shone.

Lara sniffed. The air was fresh and scented with rose, despite the fatty odor of burning tallow.

"I never thought a Marav broch would smell like Caisteal Gealaich," Bree murmured.

Lara marked the sharp look Alar cut Bree then—of course, he didn't know about her origins.

Skirting around the body of a female Shee warrior who lay face-down near where the doors to the main hall were open, they passed within.

And just like the entrance hall, this much larger space glowed with light. The lanterns that swung from the high ceiling shone like corpse candles, and pine logs smoldered in the hearths on the far side of the space. Everything was brighter, cleaner, and less cluttered than Lara's own broch—but that wasn't what drew her attention now.

There were more dead in here, mostly Shee with a few wulvers and Marav warriors among them, their blood pooling on the pavers.

The metallic stench of death made her gorge rise. Breathing shallowly now, she picked her way across the floor, her gaze traveling over the faces of the fallen. Cailean had told her she'd recognize the Shee commander, but she hadn't so far.

However, when she caught a flash of white-blond hair upon the dais at the far end of the hall, her step slowed. And when she heard Bree's sharp intake of breath next to her, her suspicion was confirmed.

She stopped before the high seat. The male sprawled on his back upon it was tall and lean, like many of his race, with chiseled features, yet his handsome face was contorted in a terrible grimace. A fine longsword, its steel blade gleaming in the light of the bank of candles behind him, lay next to his limp fingers. A dark puddle of blood had pooled under him. His throat gaped.

Lara's lips thinned as she surveyed the injury. Fitting, considering how her mother had died.

"Do you know him?"

She glanced over at where Alar was watching her intently.

"Aye," she murmured. "Our paths have crossed before … unfortunately."

"Frostshard fought like a cornered wolf."

Lara looked over her shoulder to meet Cailean's eye. "Did you kill him?"

"Aye."

She shifted her attention back to Gavyn Frostshard. It seemed Mor had forgiven him for failing to abduct Lara and her mother. She'd put him in charge of one of her outposts, but he'd failed his queen again—for the last time.

"How many captives are there?" she demanded, shaking herself free of memories of her mother on that fateful day—her blind panic and all-consuming terror. Frostshard's companion had slit her throat.

"Around thirty, My Queen," Roth spoke up from behind her. "Shall we put them to the sword?"

Lara stilled as she considered the question. Her father would have answered 'aye' without any hesitation. But she wasn't quite as bloodthirsty. Perhaps those Shee who hadn't fallen during the siege and the battle that followed would wish for death, but she wouldn't be giving it to them—not yet anyway. "No," she replied, turning to her captain. "They'll return south with us … as spoils of war."

Lara sank down into the hot water with a deep sigh.

By the Gods, she'd never take a hot bath for granted again.

Steam enveloped her as she closed her eyes and leaned her head back on the rolled rim of the iron tub. Four husky male slaves had lugged the iron tub up to the alcove she had temporarily made her own before a procession of servants hauling buckets of hot water followed. She'd deliberately not taken the commander's quarters—she had no wish to crawl into the same sleeping nook that Gavyn Frostshard had used, even if Mirren had dragged the old furs out and replaced them with fresh ones.

Eyes still closed, she listened to the muffled sounds of her attendants moving about the alcove. The peace in here, after the chaos and filth of battle, was a balm on her soul. "Go down and fetch some drying sheets, Florie." As usual, Mirren was ordering the others about. "Ani and Lilith … bring up more pails of hot water, while I see about finding some drinkable wine for our queen." The handmaid approached the tub then. "Will you be all right on your own for a short while?"

Lara cracked open an eye. "Of course … I've got guards outside my quarters."

Mirren headed toward the heavy hanging that divided the alcove from the landing beyond. "I won't be long."

Moments later, all four lasses departed, leaving Lara alone.

Alone. She didn't close her eyes again. Instead, she reveled in the strangeness of it. A queen's time was never her own. To have some solitude was an even greater luxury than a bath. Picking up a cake of fine lavender soap, she lathered a soft cloth and began to wash. The gentle splashes filled the alcove, as did the pungent, woodsy scent—so different from the sweetness of rose.

Her wrist started to sting then, and she examined the fresh scab. It was healing well enough, although she'd taken care to hide it from Mirren when she helped ready her for the bath.

Turning her wrist over, she tried to banish the wound—and the blood oath—from her mind. She didn't want to think about her impending handfasting. She wished to enjoy some peace.

She sighed then, letting the tension of the past days ebb from her.

She'd done it. Taking back Doure had required a sacrifice on her part—one she didn't wish to dwell on—but her council, and her people, would come to realize she'd made the right choice.

Mor would think twice before pushing south now.

Lara's eyes fluttered shut once more. This space, high up in the broch, was an oasis of calm. Outside, her army of Marav and wulvers were repairing the gates and ensuring the fort was secure, while the servants she'd brought from Duncrag were making themselves at home in the kitchens and preparing a feast for the evening.

She and Alar would break bread together for the first time.

The reminder punctured her bath-time bliss like a thorn, and her eyes snapped open.

Curse it, the prick kept intruding. She wasn't allowed any respite, it seemed.

She wasn't looking forward to having everyone's eyes upon her while she sat with her betrothed upon the high seat. Nonetheless, it was necessary after the bargain she'd struck.

"Enough," she muttered. "Don't let him ruin your bath."

Soaping up her hair, she massaged her scalp before ducking under the water to rinse it. Then, wringing the water out of her hair, she pinned it to the crown of her head and leaned back against the rim once more. Drowsiness settled over her. *That's better.*

"Shades, it's chaotic out there."

Mirren shoved aside the hanging and entered the alcove. She carried a tray with a ewer and a pewter goblet, her cheeks flushed from the climb from the lower levels of the broch.

Bree followed at her heels. "That's right … you can't walk two paces without running into a wulver."

Florie entered then, a large basket of linen in her arms. "Aye," the lass muttered. "They're everywhere!"

Setting the tray down near where Lara still reclined up to the neck in the tub, Mirren shuddered, a hand lifting to the small dull-grey protection amulet that hung around her neck. The Hag's staff.

"Iron won't protect you from wulvers," Bree replied with a glint in her eye. "Nor will salt … they aren't like the other faerie creatures."

Mirren swallowed. "What works against them then?"

"The same things that work against any Marav." Bree paused then, casting Lara a sidelong glance. "Although, we shouldn't be talking about such things. They're our *allies* now, remember?"

Spearing a piece of dried fruit with his eating knife, Alar watched the High Queen pick at her meal. "Enjoying the Shee fare?"

Her chin kicked up, those penetrating pine-green eyes settling on him. Of course, they both knew that wasn't what he was really asking. What he really wanted to know was whether she was regretting their 'arrangement' yet.

Of course, she was. He'd given her what she wanted—but now, she'd be hoping there would be a way out of this.

There wasn't.

The night before, after they'd sworn the blood oath, he'd left her tent with a sour taste in his mouth. He'd gotten what he wanted, but in doing so, he'd also made Lara promises—ones he hadn't yet shared with his brothers and sisters.

"It's different from what I'm used to," she replied stiffly. "But tasty enough."

An array of dishes lined the long table upon the high seat. They bore a selection of cheeses, fruits, custards, poached fish, and light, crispy bread. Two slaves bearing dull-grey iron collars stood discreetly at the back of the high seat, jugs of wine in hand.

There were four people seated at this table, but only one of them was eating with relish: Bree, the High Queen's warder. When they'd taken a seat at the table earlier, Bree had scowled at Alar—as had the chief-enforcer who joined her—but now the food had her full attention. Her gaze was eager as she helped herself to one of the pale custards garnished with violet petals, a dish no one else had dared to sample.

Taking a mouthful, she sighed with pleasure. Silence fell at the table, and when Bree realized everyone else was looking her way, she frowned. "What?"

"You actually enjoy that?" Cailean mac Brochan asked, incredulously.

Bree snorted, looking at him askance. The pair sat so close that their elbows brushed. "Aye … it's delicious."

Alar took a bite of the dried fruit he'd speared. It was both tart and sweet, a desiccated plum. Not unpleasant, although having lived amongst the wulvers for so long, he was used to smoked or fried trout and thick eel stews. This food wouldn't satisfy him for long.

The chief-enforcer clearly agreed, for a groove had etched between his dark brows as he glanced down at the selection of fruit and cheese on his platter. Alar noted the lines of fatigue upon the chief-enforcer's face. Wielding earth magic had drained him, and the other enforcers too. They needed to take part in the blood-letting. However, the next full moon was still over twenty days away. "No wonder the Shee are all so lean," he muttered. "Where's the meat?"

Mac Brochan then offered a sliver of cheese to his fae hound, who sat behind him, but the beast merely sniffed at it dismissively.

"They don't typically eat much of it," Bree replied.

Mac Brochan pulled a face. "Even slaves eat more heartily than this."

Bree snorted and dug an elbow into his leather-covered ribs. "It won't do you any harm."

The chief-enforcer made a growling sound in the back of his throat, his attention shifting to the woman next to him. His expression was still disgruntled, although his gaze was not.

Alar watched their interaction with interest. It appeared that these two were a couple.

"I hear the broch's kitchen and stores were fully stocked when we arrived," he said, focusing on Lara once more. Once again, he deliberately spoke of trivialities. It helped him gauge the High Queen's mood.

"They were." Lara took a bite of soft goat's cheese. "Fresh food shouldn't go to waste." She then picked up a heavy goblet and sipped her wine. Her expression was veiled now; he could almost taste her wariness.

Swallowing a smile, Alar continued eating. This was his victory meal, and although the food was admittedly a little strange, he'd savor every mouthful. His brothers and sisters had done him proud today. For the first time ever, wulvers had left the sheltering woods and fought alongside the Marav. They'd shown everyone what they were capable of. From this day forth, neither the Marav nor the Shee would underestimate them.

This wasn't just about reclaiming territory for the Marav queen. It was about the wulvers finally getting the respect they deserved.

The attack had gone better than he'd anticipated. The *Fire Wyrm* had destroyed the gates spectacularly, and the Shee garrison within had been smaller than expected. They'd fought viciously, but it hadn't been enough to save them.

Around him, conversation rose and fell in the cavernous hall. After clearing away the bodies and scrubbing away the blood, servants and slaves had packed the space with long trestle tables. As he ate, Alar surveyed the rows of tables below the high seat:

Marav filled one side, while wulvers dominated the other. They didn't mix. Instead, the warriors and druids viewed his brothers and sisters with distaste. It was hard to ignore the whispers, the sneers. The glowers.

Chewing slowly, his gaze narrowed. Their lack of gratitude pissed him off. Marav and wulvers were equal here. They'd fought shoulder to shoulder with these people today, but it wasn't enough. The Marav still held onto their prejudices.

Well then, let me hold onto mine.

He swallowed his mouthful, even as his gut clenched. The slate wouldn't be easily wiped clean. He wasn't about to forget the wrongs of the past. The Marav seated below the high seat didn't realize this was just the beginning—the wulvers were rising, and they wouldn't be dismissed any longer.

"Your wulvers fought well today," Lara said, her tone veiled.

"They did," he agreed, pushing aside bitter, vengeful thoughts and lifting his goblet to his lips. It was a light and dry apple wine that fizzed slightly on his tongue. He'd never tasted anything like it. "But then, we've been waiting a long while for this moment."

Her features tightened. "I'm still surprised you convinced the wulvers to help us."

He smiled. "Maybe they'd prefer Albia was ruled by Marav … not Shee."

Her frown deepened. "They would?"

"Wulvers have more in common with your people than you'd think. A half-blood lives a few centuries … but wulvers have lifespans of similar lengths to the Marav. Unlike many of the faerie folk, they can venture out in bright sunlight and aren't tied to waterways, mounds, or ruins." He paused then. "Did you know the Raven Queen sent emissaries to request their alliance three years ago?"

Her jaw tightened, making it clear she didn't. "What did she promise them?"

Alar speared another piece of dried fruit with his eating knife. "What she promised the other faerie creatures who now fight for her: five years of loyalty for a return to Sheehallion."

Her gaze narrowed. "They weren't tempted?"

He shook his head. "The dark forests of Albia are their home." Irritation speared him then. Typical Marav arrogance. They thought they were the only ones who truly belonged to this land.

"And *you* weren't tempted either?"

Alar snorted, even as his grip on the eating knife tightened. "Do you think a half-blood is any more welcome in Sheehallion than here?"

A faint blush rose to her cheeks. She then glanced away and picked up an apple. "Probably not."

A brittle silence fell. Alar let it lie. He wasn't going to give her anything else. A sheltered, privileged woman such as Lara wouldn't understand what life for wulvers was like—or for him.

Meanwhile, the High Queen neatly peeled her apple before cutting it up into dainty slivers.

Alar cleared his throat. "There are a few things we must discuss, Lara."

She stiffened before casting him a sharp look. "Can't it wait?"

"I'm afraid not." Enjoying the panic that flared in her eyes, he drained the dregs of wine in his goblet and waved away the slave who tried to pour him some more. No, she wasn't going to put this off. "The supper table isn't the place for such a discussion though." Indeed, he was aware of the warder and chief-enforcer both watching him with naked suspicion in their eyes. He didn't want these two listening in on their conversation. "Come … let's take a walk together outside."

11: AT A CROSSROADS

LARA DREW HER fur-lined cloak close as she followed Alar up onto the walls. The light was fading, color slowly leaching from the world. The sky was a dark-blue velvet curtain, and the first of the stars twinkled to life against it. Braziers burned upon the ramparts, both illuminating the pitted stone and throwing deep shadows.

Cold, damp air feathered against Lara's cheeks. She was glad for her cloak, although Alar hadn't bothered to put one on to go outside. Clad in a black leather vest that left his arms bare, fitted leather trousers, and long boots—with his fighting knives still strapped to his back—he was a disquieting sight. His unbound hair flowed like ink over his shoulders, while his pale skin contrasted with its darkness, and in the gloaming, his eyes looked as black as pitch. There was a feral edge to him. He might not be a wulver, but he carried himself like one.

Her pulse quickened then, her palms growing damp. They were alone up here. He'd insisted on it.

Bree hadn't been pleased, and Cailean's glare could have melted iron, but Alar hadn't backed down. He'd pointed out that they were within Doure's sturdy walls, and Marav guards stood watch nearby should Lara need them.

It had looked as if her friends weren't going to let the matter lie either. However, Lara had de-escalated the situation by assuring them she'd be safe in Alar's company. She'd then bid a slave to fetch her mantle.

She now wished she'd refused him. She didn't want to discuss her upcoming handfasting or the other details of their agreement. The longer she could put it off, the better. Nonetheless, she couldn't risk falling out with the Half-blood either.

Not when his wulvers outnumbered her warriors inside this fort.

The atmosphere inside the hall during supper had been tense. The wulvers and Marav had sat apart, and she hadn't missed the looks the latter had given the former. There was no gratitude or camaraderie in their gazes, just resentment and suspicion.

Reaching the top of the steps, she surveyed the darkening world beyond. North of the walls, the remnants of a pyre smoldered—the Shee dead had been piled up there and torched.

A shiver traced down her spine then. Bree had told her that the Shee never burned their dead; they buried them instead. This disposal of the bodies was an insult to them. The Marav who'd fallen would burn the following eve though, as was their way, with bards singing their final lament.

She and Alar walked along the wall, stopping halfway. Sentries, some Marav, others wulver, lined the defenses, but none were now within earshot.

"I suggest you leave a strong garrison in Doure," he said without preamble. "This fort isn't an easy one to take, but the Shee succeeded once … and they'll no doubt try again."

Lara clenched her jaw. They'd only just taken it, and already he was telling her how to defend Doure.

"Captain mac Tav will make the necessary arrangements," she replied, not bothering to disguise the irritation in her voice.

"Why don't we leave two hundred wulvers here to help protect the fort?"

A brittle silence followed. She didn't want any of his army remaining here. Nonetheless, his suggestion wasn't a foolish one. Leaving a large Marav garrison here would cut her dwindling army in half.

Curse him, she *did* need his help.

After a heavy pause, she cleared her throat. "I'll consider it."

He flashed her a smug half-smile that made her want to slap him before glancing over at where a waxing crescent moon rose over the edges of the mountains to the north. "I wish for us to be handfasted, one turn of the moon from today … if that's agreeable to you?"

Lara cut him a surprised look. She'd expected him to want them to be wed as soon as possible. "Why the delay?" she asked lightly. She was hesitant to pry, for she didn't want to hurry their union along. All the same, she wondered why he wished to wait. What was he up to?

Maybe in the meantime, she could find a way out of fulfilling her side of the agreement.

His gaze gleamed in the glow of the nearby brazier. "I must return to my brothers and sisters … and let them know what we have agreed. I will then rally more warriors and bring my host south."

Lara frowned. "I was hoping we might use this victory to our advantage and push on, up the east coast," she said firmly. "We could take Rothie next before cutting west to Cannich."

He raised an eyebrow. "Ambitious, aren't we?"

Heat washed over Lara. Was he mocking her? Her plan was an embryonic one that she'd mulled over in the bath earlier. She hadn't said anything to her council yet. Instead, she wanted to talk to him first. "It makes sense," she said stiffly.

"You're rushing," he answered, holding her eye. "And taking Cannich from the east is the hardest route. Best to strike out from Dulross instead."

"Why?"

"Dulross is still yours, so you won't waste resources winning it back. 'The Brooch of Albia' sits at a strategic point in the southern Uplands."

Lara's jaw tightened. He was right about that. Dulross was important. It was said that whoever held Dulross, held the realm. The Raven Queen would want the fort, but she wouldn't get it.

"But that's not the only reason why your plan is flawed," Alar went on. "The road from Rothie to Cannich takes you right by Bracehell Barrow. It's too risky to march an army through there. The Shee will swarm us before we get as far as Morae." He paused then. "Our alliance isn't just about reclaiming The Uplands, Lara … it's about Marav and wulvers living as equals. You'll need time to return to Duncrag and prepare your people.

Soon, my brothers and sisters will reside at the capital … and its residents must be ready."

Lara's stomach clenched. Once again, he was telling her what to do. Curse him though, was he right? Was she in too much of a hurry? He did have a point; she had to warn the residents of Duncrag before an army of wulvers turned up. Her breathing grew shallow at the thought. Who was she fooling? It didn't matter how much time she had. Her people were never going to like this.

It galled her to wait though, especially when her gut told her they should keep going. But she wasn't a military strategist. Alar had more experience in these matters, and she'd be a fool to disregard his advice.

"So be it," she finally managed. "I shall await your arrival." Feeling sick, she turned from him, her fingers curving around the rough stone wall. It bore scorch marks and grooves, scars from the recent battle.

To her consternation, Alar moved closer. His proximity made her freeze. He smelled of leather, mixed with the woodsy, earthy scent of oak, with the undertone of something fresh like mint. It wasn't unpleasant, yet she wanted him to step back, to give her space. Pulse racing, she shifted forward, pressing herself against the sturdy bulk of the wall. It steadied her.

"Have your overkings been putting pressure on you?" he asked finally.

"Of course … and they're right to. They know what will happen if the enemy crosses into The Wolds."

"The Shee will never take the South, Lara," he replied, steel creeping into his voice then. "I promise you that."

Surprised by the vehemence of his answer, she drew in a steadying breath, her gaze traveling over the dark pinewood that covered the hills to the north. She was about to ask how he could make such assurances when something in the sky above the forest caught her eye. "Shades … what's that?"

The scuff of boots on stone followed as Alar stepped up to the wall next to her, so close that their elbows accidentally brushed.

Ignoring him, she craned her neck forward and narrowed her gaze. The last glimmers of daylight were fading now, yet there was no mistaking the dark shapes that twisted and dove like monstrous swallows above the tree line.

Alar whispered an oath under his breath. "It's the Slew."

Alarm shivered through her. "But it's not yet time."

"No … they've grown … active … of late."

Lara's pulse sped up. Over the past years, the Slew had become more vicious at Gateway—even forcing their way into dwellings to steal the souls of the sick, weak, or frightened. But seeing them on the wing outside of Gateway made her belly churn.

This is the last thing we need.

"There's a burial ground in the middle of that pine forest, and they've been straying from it," Alar added. "But this … is not something I've yet seen."

As they watched, the dark shapes rose and fell. From this distance, it resembled a great swarm, and Lara held her breath, readying herself to flee from the walls should they head in her direction. But they didn't. Instead, they arched high once more before diving beneath the canopy of dark conifers again.

Lara's heart pounded as she continued to stare at the pinewood and the sky over it, searching for more black, writhing shapes. But The Unforgiven didn't reappear. Only then did she exhale, her lightheadedness returning.

"We should probably get off the walls," Alar murmured.

"Aye," Lara agreed. "Let's go."

They stepped away from the edge, turned, and made their way back toward the steps leading down to the inner ward.

"Before we go inside … there's something I'd like you to see," Alar said then.

Lara cut him a sidelong glance. "Not more malevolent spirits on the wing? Or maybe, there's a family of powries living inside the walls I don't yet know about?"

Alar surprised her by grinning then, revealing a dimple in his left cheek. His smile was disarming, and she stumbled. His hand shot out, his fingers curving around her upper arm to steady her.

Extracting herself gently from his grip, she halted on the walkway and turned to face him squarely. "I don't like surprises … best you tell me what you've got planned."

His mouth twitched once more. "You'll like this one … I swear."

Lara stepped through the rose-covered archway and stopped short. "The Mother's tits," she whispered, momentarily forgetting her manners. "What is this?"

"The Shee love their gardens, it seems," Alar replied, his voice unnervingly close. "So, they have grown one here."

She took a smart step forward to put some more distance between them. All the while, she gazed at the beauty around her. White trailing roses covered all the surrounding walls, their sweet perfume heavy in the air. The usual stone pavers had been replaced with gleaming white stone, and a fountain made of the same material tinkled at the heart of the courtyard. Stone cressets dotted the space, where fires glowed.

"I had the fires lit earlier … for you."

Lara cut Alar a sharp look over her shoulder, to find him watching her. His words set her already tight nerves further on edge. Their upcoming marriage was an arrangement. He didn't need to impress her—in fact, she wished he wouldn't.

"Apparently, this area was once the guard barracks," he added. "Although you'd never know to look at it."

Lara turned away from him and walked into the heart of the courtyard. Her gaze rested on the fountain once more—the smooth stone had been carved into the form of a bird. The Great Raven. The Shee didn't worship The Five. Water gushed from its beak and fell into a basin that drained away beneath the fort. She guessed a well had once sat here, but since Doure already had one well in the inner ward, the Shee had turned this one into a decorative feature.

How decadent. Her people wouldn't put that much energy into something that served no practical purpose. She couldn't help but marvel at the fountain's beauty though, and wondered how they'd managed to create it.

Eventually, she turned her attention away from the fountain and surveyed the rose-covered walls around her. "Bree told me that the Shee love roses," she murmured to herself. "White ones especially." She shook her head incredulously then. "But how did they grow them so fast?"

"The Shee have their own magic … different from the earth magic of druids." To her consternation, Alar was standing right behind her again. "Haven't you heard the tales of how they can whisper to animals and plants?"

Lara's skin prickled. Aye, she had. But stories were one thing; seeing it with her own eyes was another.

"Can I ask how Bree knows so much about the Shee?" Alar's tone was casual, although she detected sharpness just beneath.

"I was wondering when you'd ask me that," she admitted, turning to face him. "The tale hasn't spread as far and wide as I'd thought, after all."

He inclined his head, inviting her to continue.

"Bree was once one of the Shee … an assassin sent by Mor to Duncrag as a spy."

Alar stilled at this admission, and a frisson of satisfaction rippled through Lara. It was a relief to see *him* on the back foot for once. The bastard always looked so sure of himself. He had answers for everything.

"And?" he prompted.

"And … she posed as the Maid of Albia Cailean ordered himself."

"The chief-enforcer *ordered* himself a bride?"

"Aye … my father insisted he take a wife … but the Shee intercepted her on the way to Duncrag."

Alar frowned. "How did he not see through her glamor?"

"She didn't glamor herself … she passed through The Ring of Caith into our realm … and in doing so became Marav."

He jerked as if she'd just jabbed him with a pin. "What?"

Lara favored him with a rueful smile. "Aye … it appears the Shee can pass through our stone circles … and change form when they do so. Only at certain times of year though." She paused then, marking the calculating glint that suddenly sparked in his eyes. "And no, Marav can't do the same apparently … although you could take your chances, if you wish." Certainly, that would be one way of ridding herself of him, although being a half-blood, he might survive the trip.

He snorted as if guessing her thoughts. "So, why is she still alive?"

Lara sighed. "It's a long tale … but let's just say that Bree and Cailean fell in love, and she chose him over her queen." She halted then, another wry smile tugging at her lips. "And she also proved her loyalty to me … which is why she's now my warder. And you might as well know that her brother lives at Duncrag too. He's taken Marav form as well and is now my archivist."

Alar considered her words, one long-fingered hand lifting to rub the lean line of his jaw as he observed her. Her admission had rendered him speechless.

"Are you conflicted when it comes to the Shee?" she asked then.

His gaze narrowed. "In what sense?"

"Their blood flows through your veins. Do you ever wonder if you're on the right side?"

He snorted. "I'm the result of one reckless encounter between a Shee warrior and a Marav lass. My father tumbled my mother in a forest glade and then disappeared. I have no loyalty to the Shee." His voice was low, yet she picked up the edge to it. This wasn't a subject he was comfortable discussing.

Silence fell between them, broken only by the soft tinkle of the fountain. The sky above was dark now, ropes of stars twinkling overhead.

Tiredness swept over Lara then, and she raised a hand to her lips, hiding a yawn. She couldn't wait to crawl into her furs. Today had exhausted her—as had her conversations with the Half-blood.

"Come," Alar murmured. "Let's go inside."

Lara nodded, moving away from the fountain. She headed toward the archway, not waiting for him to fall into step next to her. They'd spent enough time together today.

However, she'd only gone a few steps across the smooth pavers when a lithe figure burst out from the shadows. Steel flashed in the firelight then, as a blade flew at her throat.

12: FROM THE SHADOWS

THE BLADE NEVER bit. Instead, something heavy crashed into her back, knocking her flat.

Winded, Lara gasped as she tried to suck in a breath. Meanwhile, the clang of blades rang out behind her. Scrabbling along the ground, she reached for the dagger at her side. Then, managing to draw air into her lungs now, she rolled onto her back, blade raised.

Alar was fighting her assailant.

In the light of the flickering cressets, a young Shee female wielding a longsword dueled with vicious determination. Long hair, the color of a raven's wing, streamed behind her as she struck at Alar repeatedly. Black leather encased her tall, lean form, and she moved with the fluidity that Lara had seen in Bree when she'd been Shee.

No Marav could move like that.

However, Alar matched her. He'd drawn both his long fighting daggers and circled the Shee, pushing her away from where Lara still lay.

The sound of running feet—boots slamming against stone— intruded then.

Heaving in a lungful of air, Lara rolled to her feet and backed away from the dueling pair.

"Lara." Bree was at her side, weapon drawn. Her gaze tracked Alar and the Shee warrior. "Where the fuck did she come from?"

"From the shadows," Lara replied breathlessly, watching as Alar drove the warrior back farther. The fountain was now behind her. "She must have hidden herself amongst the roses." Indeed, the banks of carpet roses were thick in places. Nonetheless, it would have been a thorny hiding place.

Steel clattered against stone as Alar bested his opponent. An instant later, the Shee warrior was sprawled on her stomach, writhing as he held her down, a knee pressed into the small of her back.

Two Marav guards were at his side then, helping him subdue her.

The Shee's vicious curses rang against stone, shattering the peace of this rose-scented courtyard. They were binding her wrists behind her, and she wasn't taking kindly to it.

Sheathing her dagger, Lara shivered. "She almost had me."

Beside her, Bree was silent. She tore her gaze from the struggling captive then and looked at her warder. "I thought you had retired for the evening."

Bree's lips thinned. "No."

Murmuring an oath, Lara pushed strands of hair off her face. Her attention shifted then to where Alar had risen to his feet. He stared down at his snarling captive before bending to retrieve his fighting daggers. He didn't sheath them though. His tall, lean form tensed then, his fingers flexing around the grips of his weapons.

Meanwhile, the Marav warriors hauled the dark-haired Shee female to her feet.

"What do you want us to do with her, My Queen?" one of them grunted.

Lara hesitated, observing her would-be assassin. "Who sent you?" she asked after a pause, relieved that her voice was steady.

The Shee's face contorted, and she spat on the ground.

Heat flared under Lara's ribs. However, before she could answer, Alar stepped forward, the flat of his iron blade pressing down upon the female's bare bicep.

This hiss of iron on flesh followed, and the Shee choked out a curse, struggling in her captors' holds.

"Answer the High Queen," Alar commanded. "Or this blade will kiss your throat." He then lifted the fighting dagger from her skin.

Panting, the Shee glared at him. "The commander bade me to wait," she gasped.

Lara's lips thinned. Even dead, Gavyn Frostshard was dangerous. "You were waiting for *me*?"

The female sneered. "I was hoping for the chief-enforcer, but you're a much better prize."

"What is your name?" Bree demanded.

"Fuck off, Marav bitch."

Alar brought the flat of his blade down once more, and the female shrieked, writhing under the contact. "Answer."

His ruthlessness was shocking, and Lara averted her gaze. She reminded herself then that this Shee had tried to kill her. She didn't deserve mercy.

"Fern Sablebane!"

Alar jerked the dagger away, as if scalded. He then took a rapid step back from the captive. In the flickering light of the surrounding torches and braziers, his face had gone pale and taut.

Focusing on the Shee once more, she studied the proud, haughty lines of her face. Even in pain, she was defiant. An angry red welt of blisters had come up on her smooth upper arm. "I have some more questions for you, Fern," she said finally. "And I suggest you answer them."

"Mor divides her time between Sheehallion and Cannich." Seated at the long table upon the high seat, her fingers wrapped around a cup of warm broth, Lara surveyed her council. "She leaves her trusted commanders to control her conquered territory. She's in Cannich at present ... but will leave at Gateway." She paused then, giving a soft snort. "Our winters are too bitter for the Raven Queen."

"Did your prisoner tell you anything of Mor's plans?" Cailean's expression was hard this morning, his big body tense.

Lara could guess the reason.

There were eight—rather than the usual seven—members of her council this morning, for Alar had joined them. Her chief-enforcer wasn't the only one who didn't want the Half-blood present. Roth wore a deep scowl, and Gregor's mouth was pursed as if he'd just taken a sip of horse piss rather than broth from his cup.

Despite that Doure was now theirs, none of her council looked that happy this morning.

Alar ignored their displeasure. One elbow resting on the table, he trailed his fingertips lazily upon the tabletop, tracing the whorls in the oak. His expression was shuttered.

"It took more iron to convince her," Lara answered, even as her mouth soured. The char of burning flesh had lingered in her nostrils for a while after the questioning. Alar had seemed reluctant to touch the prisoner with his blade again, so a guard had done it. Torture had been Talorc mac Brude's favorite pastime, but it wasn't his daughter's. All the same, she'd allowed it. "And even then, she gave us little. We did learn though that Mor intends to make Albia hers within the turn of the next year." Her pulse started to race then. "And that she'll burn every druid. Earth magic will be outlawed ... as fire magic is."

Cailean sneered at these words. However, a few yards away, Ren swallowed audibly. The chief-bard's eyes were large upon her sharp-featured face. Lara was inclined to share Ren's concern. She'd known Mor wouldn't be content with The Uplands. This was proof.

Suddenly, she wished she hadn't agreed to Alar's plans to wait before striking north. What if Mor attacked first?

"What have you done with the prisoner?" Annis asked, speaking up for the first time.

"She's still alive ... just nursing some nasty burns," Bree replied.

"Aye … she's with the other captives now," Lara added. "And will return to Duncrag with us." She glanced over at Alar then, to find him watching her.

"Are you going to tell them what we witnessed from the walls last night?" he asked, gaze sharp now. "Or shall I?"

Heat flushed over Lara. "I'll do it," she muttered before shifting her gaze to the others. A pause followed before she spoke once more. "We saw the Slew."

A breathless hush fell.

"Outside the fort?" Gregor asked, leaning forward.

"In the sky … above the woods to the north," Alar replied.

The chief-sacrificer snapped upright, his eyes narrowing, while next to him, the chief-seer's long face pinched. Cailean growled a curse.

"We've all seen how the Slew have changed over the past years." The broth and oatcakes that Lara had just consumed churned in her belly. "They're more vicious at Gateway than they've ever been."

"Aye … but what if they start hunting more than one night a year?" Alar answered.

13: STORM CLOUDS

LOCALS GATHERED ALONG the roadside to see their High Queen off. However, there were no smiles, no cheering and waving at her departure. Just stony silence.

Riding astride Bracken, Lara's chest tightened as she marked their angry faces. Initially, the people of Doure were shocked at the sight of the wulvers pouring into their fort. Now, they were angry. Alar's army had helped take back Doure, but that didn't mean the people were grateful, or that they wanted them to remain here.

And today, they'd learned that a garrison of three hundred would remain at the fort: half wulver, half Marav.

Lara's council didn't like it either. They'd pushed back, Cailean and Roth in particular. Her chief-enforcer and captain had met privately with her to discuss it, but she'd reminded them that Mor had already succeeded in taking Doure once, and she'd likely try to take the fort again. Only a powerful garrison would prevent it. Reluctantly, they'd accepted her choice. All the same, arguing with them had left her drained and worried.

She didn't like locking horns with her advisors, especially Cailean. He wasn't pleased with her these days.

No one, except Alar, was, it seemed.

She glanced at him then, stalking by her left side while Bree rode at her right. Clad in black and armed with his blades, he unnerved her.

And, of course, his presence just made the locals *more* resentful.

Impatience twisted her belly then. Her stay in Doure had been a brief one, yet she wished she were already back in Duncrag, making plans. Instead, a journey of around eight days awaited her. Gods, she needed to get this cursed handfasting out of the way so she could march north. Since Alar was leaving many wulvers behind in Doure, he'd need to gather more warriors. However, she wouldn't tolerate any further delays.

To make matters worse, her council was also divided about her decision to return to Duncrag. None of them had wanted her to make a deal with the Half-blood. But now that she had an army of wulvers behind her and had retaken Doure, Roth and Gregor urged her to exploit her advantage—to travel down to Dulross immediately and then strike north from there. But Annis, Ruari, and Ren insisted she should wait. The chief-counsellor said that the omens weren't good, while the chief-seer warned that the bones were conflicting at present.

Meanwhile, Cailean and Bree both advised her to be wary, no matter what path she chose.

And at each meeting, Alar observed them silently—only offering his opinion when asked.

"Traitor!" Her chin jerked up, her gaze scanning the crowd to see who'd just shouted out, but it was impossible to tell.

"Don't let them get to you, Lara," Alar said softly. "Change is always difficult at first … but they'll get used to the new way of things soon enough."

Tension rippled through her. "Will they?"

"Aye, just give them time."

Unconvinced, she shifted her gaze ahead, focusing on Bracken's furry ears.

They left the fort and rode down the steep defile before climbing to the hill west.

A cool salt-laced breeze feathered across Lara's cheeks as she turned to look back at Doure.

High upon the walls, she spied the outlines of figures—the dull-grey iron helmets of Marav warriors and the beastly profiles of wulvers—against the pale sky.

She twisted back then to see that Alar now stood a few yards away with two of his captains—the wulvers she'd seen him with during the siege, introduced afterward as Lyall and Dolph.

The rest of his army, those who wouldn't remain in Doure, waited on the edge of the tree line to the north. The breeze stirred the thick fur that covered their faces and necks. The rising sun, and pride, reflected in their yellow eyes.

"Everything is in place," Alar said, drawing her attention once more. "Our captains will co-rule the fort … they will ensure no Shee will set foot in it again."

There was a hardness in his voice that made Lara scrutinize him. In the bright morning light, his skin was so pale it was almost translucent, and the scars upon his cheek and neck gleamed like quicksilver. She wondered where he'd gotten them. There was so much she didn't know about this man.

And yet, she'd made a pact with him.

"I can return to Duncrag with peace of mind then?"

He nodded. "Of course."

"You'd better be right, Half-blood," Cailean muttered. "Or we've just created more problems than we've solved."

Stiffening, Lara cast a glance over her shoulder at her scowling chief-enforcer. A few yards away, Roth waited, astride his stallion, his strong jaw bunched. Meanwhile, the rest of her council gathered farther back—none of them were smiling.

Her skin prickled then. The tension in the air was unbearable. Everyone was watching her, judging her.

"Right … it's time to go." She was suddenly desperate to take her leave of this man and his silently watching wulvers. Their stares held a challenge.

He smiled. "You and I shall meet again at Duncrag within the turn of the moon."

There was a promise in the way he'd said those last words. He might as well have said: *You will soon be mine.*

Dread lodged like a brick in her gut. She didn't want to think about what that entailed. She didn't want to think about being bedded by him. Her brief marriage to Dunchadh had made her swear never to suffer a man's touch again—and now, here she was about to go through the same ordeal.

Making a deal with the Half-blood had seemed like a wise choice when she'd been staring defeat in the face, but with each passing day, regret gathered like storm clouds within her.

Nonetheless, she had to keep focused on why she was doing this and just what was at stake. Someone had to make the hard choices.

"I shall bid you safe travels then," she replied stiffly, gathering her reins. "And shall await you in Duncrag in due course." She paused for a moment. "As soon as the handfasting is done, we must make plans to march north."

He inclined his head. "We can leave just after Gateway … if that suits you?"

"It does."

"Until our next meeting," he answered, with a smile, taking a step back. His black cloak billowed behind him as he turned and strode away, Lyall and Dolph flanking him.

Lara watched him go.

The High Queen's army moved with frustrating slowness, snaking through the thickly wooded hills of the borderlands. They brought their captives with them. The Shee walked ahead of Lara and her escort, with their wrists bound at their backs.

They didn't wear iron shackles or collars, for the metal would burn their skin and eventually kill them. Even so, Cailean and Roth didn't trust their captives—least of all Fern Sablebane— not to make trouble. As such, enforcers flanked them, as did blue-robed bards. The low hum of voices drifted through the air that was thick with the scent of pine, ash, and damp, peaty earth. The bards sang a dirge as they walked, weaving earth magic about their captives.

Many of the Shee's faces were set, their shoulders rounded under the weight of the druidic magic that flowed around them. They hated it almost as much as they did iron.

And as the morning drew out, and they inched their way southwest, Lara's gaze often flicked to her would-be assassin. There was something about the Shee female that needled her. Even with her wrists bound, Sablebane was defiant. Unlike most of the other captives, she wasn't cowed. She held her chin at an arrogant tilt, her black hair tumbling down her straight back. Even being burned by iron hadn't broken her.

Lara hated to admit it, but the female unsettled her. She was a reminder of what dangerous adversaries the Shee were.

"Do *all* Shee females have backbones of tempered steel?" she asked Bree eventually.

Her warder laughed, and her response made the knots in Lara's belly loosen just a little. Things had been strained between her and Bree over the past days, but she was relieved to see her thaw a little. "Aye … most do."

Lara studied Bree's face, remembering just how intimidating she'd been in her Shee form. "It might sound foolish … but I thought you were unique."

Her friend shrugged. "Aye, well … your captives are all warriors too … and they've had *centuries* to hone their skills."

Lara's palms grew damp at these words. The Shee couldn't be underestimated. How she wished they were heading to Dulross right now. But she couldn't. Not without the Half-blood's army. Without them—even with druids—they'd never take back the North.

"We can't rely on the wulvers, My Queen."

Lara swallowed a sigh. She'd been dreading this meeting and had known her advisors wouldn't hold back. Alar's presence at every council in Doure had checked them. However, the first words out of Annis's mouth were a direct challenge.

After a long day's travel through glorious autumn sunshine—where the light was deep gold and every detail was etched in sharp relief—they'd just made camp. Lara was weary and hungry, but she had to face her council first.

"No, we can't," Cailean agreed roughly, even as he gently stroked the thick fur on Skaal's back. The fae hound had pressed her large hairy body up against his as he stood before the meeting table. "Once we get back to Duncrag, we should increase security."

"Aye … the Fort Guard will need to be ready for them," Roth said, folding his muscular arms across his chest. "I shall recruit more warriors from The Wolds … although that might prove a challenge these days."

Lara nodded briskly, even as misgiving clutched at her. She'd deliberately avoided issuing a draft, but they were getting to the stage where one might be necessary. "See it all done then." Surprise rippled over Cailean and Roth's faces, as if they'd expected her to argue, and irritation spiked through her. "Don't you think I understand the risks that come with allowing an army of wulvers to reside within Duncrag's walls?"

Both men frowned, making it clear they had indeed doubted her.

Sucking in a deep breath, Lara resisted the urge to rub her temples. Another headache loomed.

"I suggest sending word to the Isle of Arryn," Ren added, a trifle timidly, for she wasn't one to speak up at meetings. "We require more enforcers and bards for the fight ahead."

"I shall," Lara assured her. She didn't hold out much hope though. The Arch-druid had warned just a year earlier that they weren't getting enough initiates these days. There weren't as many druids being trained as before.

A brittle silence followed before Annis spoke once more. "All of this is sage counsel, My Queen … but I was referring to something else when I said we shouldn't 'rely' on the wulvers." Her gaze was sharp as it met Lara's. "If you find more allies, then you won't be so dependent on the Half-blood and his army."

The chief-counsellor was right, of course. Depending wholly on the wulvers would give her husband too much power. She couldn't let him think he was indispensable. And she had to be ready, if he tried to overthrow her.

"Go on," Lara murmured.

"For centuries, the rulers of Albia have relied on the might of The Uplands to fill the ranks of their armies," the chief-counsellor replied. "The hill-tribe warriors are fierce fighters. You need them on your side."

Lara stilled. Aye, she did.

"The Circines serve the Raven Queen now, not the High Queen of Albia," Gregor reminded Annis sourly.

Lara's pulse quickened. "Aye, but don't you wonder what she promised them?"

Gregor frowned.

"Didn't the Raven Queen assure the faerie creatures they could re-enter Sheehallion after five years of service?" Ruari asked.

"Aye, but that's no good to the Circines," Gregor replied. "Since our kind can't pass through the barrows or the stone circles."

"And nor would we want to," Ren murmured.

"We must learn what Mor has promised them … so we can offer something better." Annis drew herself up then, her gaze sweeping over the circle of men and women gathered in the meeting pavilion. "I have an idea."

Lara observed her warily. "Aye?"

"Let me choose two of my most able counsellors. They shall travel to The Uplands and track down the Circines chieftain. They will then assure him that the High Queen of Albia will better any terms the Raven Queen has offered."

Lara considered this plan for a few moments. It had merit. Unlike her father, who'd ill-treated the hill-tribes and ended up earning the resentment of their chieftains, she'd gain their respect. Their love.

"That could work," she murmured. "Although they can't go on their own."

"You'll need some enforcers," Cailean said gruffly.

"And an escort of warriors," Roth added.

Lara drew in a deep breath. She was pleased they were all working together again—instead of arguing—although her chief-enforcer and captain's grave expressions were yet another reminder of their dwindling resources.

Encouraged, Annis folded her arms across her chest. "The Shee took The Uplands because they understood the power of alliances, My Queen. We need to do the same … and I'm not talking about wulvers."

"It'll also weaken the Shee's hold on the North before we get there," Gregor flashed Annis a grudging smile. "Well, done."

Annis's lips curved in response. The chief-sacrificer wasn't one to hand out praise.

Moments passed, and Lara surveyed the faces of those gathered around her. They were watching her keenly, waiting for her answer.

"Very well," she said after a pause. "A peace envoy shall leave for The Goatfells with the dawn."

14: A GREATER GOOD

"THIS IS AN insult."

Leaning back in her carven throne, Lara swallowed a sigh. "Come, Artair … let's not be overly dramatic."

The overking of Baldeen's face turned the color of liver, his ring-encrusted hand tightening around the stem of his goblet. A few feet away, King Niall of Braewall had stilled, his dark-blue eyes fixed upon Lara as if she'd just turned into one of the Slew.

"You have doomed us!" Artair was determined not to be silenced.

Lara met the overking's eye, her own temper quickening now. These two pricks wouldn't have dared to challenge her father's decisions. "No, I did this to save my people."

Artair let out a harsh laugh. "What? You think sharing the furs with that half-breed outlaw … and allowing wulvers to dwell amongst us, will turn the tide?"

Her heart started to thump against her ribs. "It already has … Doure is ours, and we couldn't have taken it without his help."

"Alar mac Struana has a price on his head in Baldeen," Artair shot back. "Did you know that?"

Lara stilled. No, she hadn't, although she wouldn't embarrass herself by admitting such, or asking what he was wanted for.

The three of them sat at a table upon the high seat at the end of her hall. Bree, Cailean, and Skaal stood behind Lara, silent and watchful. Annis was also present. She looked on from the far end of the high seat, hands folded in front of her. The chief-counsellor's gaze was narrowed, her white robes glowing in the light of the two large hearths that burned against the northern wall. Pungent peat smoke drifted up through the air vents. It was mid-afternoon, and both of her overkings had just arrived.

Upon Lara's return to Duncrag, she'd let the fort elders and the headmen who kept order in the various levels of the fort know what had transpired. She'd also sent word immediately to both Baldeen and Braewall, informing her overkings as well.

The elders and headmen weren't happy about her choice, and so she hadn't expected a warm response from her overkings either. Their presence here wasn't a surprise. What had taken her aback though, was that they'd turned up *together*. A united front. Did they hope that by ganging up on her, they'd have their way?

It was too late for that. The wheels of war were already moving. Ever since her return, Cailean and Roth had been busy preparing for their campaign to The Uplands. Gateway was just over a moon's turn away now, and as soon as it passed, they'd march north.

"The deal has been struck," she said, breaking the heavy silence. "I agreed to wed Alar … and in a few days, he shall bring his wulvers south." Her belly churned as she said these words. She'd accepted what needed to happen, but it didn't mean she wasn't dreading his arrival, or their handfasting. Where was Alar now? Had he managed to rally more wulvers, as promised? "Duncrag shall welcome them. I will then become his wife."

"You said you'd never take a husband." Niall found his tongue then. Ruddy spots of color had appeared upon his high cheekbones. "*I am married to Albia*, you said … remember?"

Aye, she remembered. It was what she'd told Niall when he'd lowered himself onto one knee before her two years earlier and proposed. Tall and rakishly handsome, with thick oak-colored hair combed back and fastened at his nape, he was around her own age. The young overking of Braewall was full of himself. He'd been sure Lara would agree to wed him and was insulted when she turned him down.

Lara didn't like his tone. Gripping her carven armrests, she leaned forward, spearing him with her gaze. "I *am* wedded to Albia," she replied coldly, "even more than before. That's why I have sacrificed my own wishes, my own *happiness*, for the greater good. Do you think I wanted to make such an alliance?"

Annis shifted her weight from one foot to the other, her lips pursing slightly. A warning to keep her temper in check.

A nerve ticked in Niall's cheek, while Artair's face was still dangerously red. The King of Braewall had always been strong and well-built, yet a surfeit of rich food since he'd been crowned was taking its toll. The past couple of winters had been harsh, and The Wolds had teetered on the edge of famine, but Artair mac Neathan clearly hadn't been going without.

The silence drew out, the air sharp with tension.

Lara heaved in a deep breath. It was time to try and rescue this situation. They needed to talk about something else while they composed themselves. "How are things at Braewall, Niall?" she asked. When he didn't answer, she pressed on. "Is there any word on your brother?"

A muscle flexed in the overking's strong jaw. "None."

She inclined her head. Just after Mid-winter Fire, news had reached Duncrag that the overking's younger brother had disappeared under suspicious circumstances. There were rumors that Niall had something to do with it. Braewall's new overking was ambitious—perhaps he worried his brother had designs on his throne. There was no evidence though, just whispers.

It wasn't the best choice of subject, especially since she was supposed to be smoothing Niall's ruffled feathers. She should have left things there, yet she couldn't help but dig deeper. "Do you suspect foul play?"

"Possibly," Niall replied coolly. "He went out for an evening's drinking at an ale-hall ... but hasn't been seen since."

"I'm sorry to hear that."

He pulled a face, making it clear he didn't care.

Lara shifted her attention to Artair. "And what of Baldeen? I hear it was a much better harvest this year."

"You won't change the subject so easily," Artair ground out, his peat-brown eyes glittering. "Not after what you've done."

Lara frowned. The bastard was like a dog with a bone.

"You have made a grave mistake," Artair went on. "The people of Albia won't follow a High Queen who makes pacts with wulvers."

"The folk of Duncrag know of my alliance." Lara's pulse now beat in her ears. "But I see no riots in the streets ... do you?"

Best she didn't admit that there had been unrest ever since her return home. At first, there had been grief, as news of their losses filtered through the fort. A sorrowful lament had lifted high into the damp air on the eve of her arrival. She'd stood on the walls listening to those mourning their dead.

She was responsible.

But then, once the grief had settled, and Duncrag's residents learned of the bargain their High Queen had struck, they'd turned angry. The elders had led protests before the gates to the broch, their insults and accusations drifting over the ramparts. Fortunately, the Fort Guard had handled the situation, although the rumblings of discontent continued in the days following.

Artair lurched to his feet, the wooden stool he'd been seated upon clattering to the ground behind him.

Beside Cailean, Skaal gave a low growl. The sound rumbled dangerously in her throat.

"Careful, mac Neathan." The chief-enforcer's warning swiftly followed. "Consider your next words to our High Queen carefully."

The overking's broad chest rose and fell quickly now, expanding and contracting like forge bellows. Watching the fury smoldering in his eyes, Lara knew that only a healthy fear of her chief-enforcer stopped him from unleashing it. Even so, she didn't want her alliance with the wulvers to ruin her relationship with her overkings. She needed to build a bridge—and quickly.

"I would have consulted you, Artair," she said, deliberately gentling her voice. "But there was no time ... surely, you understand that?"

A nerve flickered in his cheek.

"We can't waste time arguing, not when our freedom hangs in the balance. You know the Shee have allies. I'm trying to find a way forward … but to do that, I need you at my side. We must remain united. The Wolds have already given so much … but I must ask more of you. We're recruiting more warriors for my army … and I need Braewall and Baldeen's cooperation."

Her attention shifted to Niall then, who'd been silent as the exchange heated up. The younger man shifted uncomfortably upon his stool, a deep frown creasing his brow—but she seized his gaze with hers and held fast. "Can I rely on you both?"

Standing on the walls, Lara watched the overkings of Braewall and Baldeen depart. Their banners—the leaping black stag of Braewall and the iron shield of Baldeen—bristled above the procession of helmed warriors clad in leather armor who led the way down The Thoroughfare, the main road that descended from the broch at the fort's summit.

It was a raw afternoon, and Lara's breath steamed in front of her. A frost would settle tonight, heralding the return of the bitter season.

Jaw firming, she pulled her fur-lined mantle closer. Her gaze then swept over the wooded hills that surrounded the fort, alighting on a grassy one to the north. Even from this distance, she spied red-robed figures. There would be a full moon tonight; the sacrificers were readying themselves for the blood-letting. It was a much-needed one too. Cailean and the other enforcers who'd accompanied her to Doure had to replenish their earth magic.

They needed to be at full strength for the campaign to come.

"Do you trust the overkings, Annis?" she asked finally.

Next to her, the chief-counsellor murmured something under her breath before adding. "No … I can't say I do."

"I don't either." Her gaze returned to where Artair and Niall rode side by side, lingering upon them for a few moments. Huffing a sigh, she then turned to the white-robed woman standing beside her on the walls. Bree and Cailean had also come up here with them, yet they waited a few yards away. "Should I have stopped them from leaving?"

Annis raised a brow. "To what end?"

"I could have arrested them … on suspicion of treason … thrown them both into the dungeon and found replacements." Frustration churned in her chest. Maybe she should have done just that.

Annis favored her with a speculative look. "Aye … you could have … but you have no proof."

Lara's belly tightened. "That wouldn't have stopped my father. The slightest whiff of dissent and he'd have brought the mallet down."

"You're right … but do you wish to be like him?"

Lara swallowed. No, she didn't. Few here knew of the bitterness she held toward her sire, for she'd never told anyone about how badly he'd let her down. Nonetheless, that was the closest Annis had ever come to making an outright criticism of the former High King—a man she'd served for twenty years.

Her chest tightened as she watched the receding banners. She needed Braewall and Baldeen's resources and hated feeling so reliant on her overkings. She'd bid them both to send weapons and warriors to Duncrag before Gateway—but what if they didn't?

No, she wasn't like her father, but she didn't want to be perceived as weak either. "Shouldn't I?" she countered, deliberately challenging her chief-counsellor.

The older woman sighed, brushing a thin brown braid off her cheek. "Talorc was a strong ruler … and feared … but if Albia is in pieces, it is because of him."

15: TRUST, ONCE BROKEN

MIRREN WAS UNUSUALLY quiet while she readied Lara for supper—her movements jerky as she took out the High Queen's braids and brushed her hair.

"Ouch." Lara winced as the hog bristle brush caught. "What's up with you this evening?"

"Nothing," Mirren replied quickly. "Sorry, My Queen!"

Lara swiveled on the stool where she perched before the hearth in her alcove, her attention settling on her handmaid.

Mirren wasn't herself. Her face was pinched, and her blue eyes were slightly red.

Lara frowned. "Have you been crying?"

Mirren waved her concern away, a little of her usual spirit returning. "No."

Lara fixed her with a level look. "You'd tell me if you were in any bother, wouldn't you?" She didn't want Mirren to keep her worries to herself. Guilt stabbed at her then. She'd been so caught up in her own problems of late, she hadn't given anyone else much thought.

Mirren gave a wan smile in response.

"I'm sorry if I haven't been myself recently," Lara said with a grimace. "I hope I haven't been overly demanding with you?"

"Of course not."

"Well then." Lara folded her arms across her chest. "What is it?"

Her handmaid swallowed. Clearing her throat, she lowered her gaze to the hairbrush she still gripped. She then began turning it over and over in her hands. "Tonight is the blood-letting."

Lara nodded. "Aye ... and what of it?"

"Torran has asked me to partner with him."

The words were whispered, as if she were revealing a terrible thing, and Lara stilled. Torran mac Rab was Cailean's second-in-command. While they'd been on campaign, he'd held the fort in Lara's stead. She trusted his loyalty as much as she did Cailean's. Nonetheless, Mirren now trembled at the thought of taking part in the blood-letting with him.

Rising from her stool near the sleeping alcove, Lara took a step closer to Mirren and laid a hand on her shoulder. "Hey ... it's all right."

But she knew it wasn't.

Over three years earlier, two enforcers had cornered Mirren outside the broch and brutally raped her. Overnight, she'd gone from a light-hearted lass who saw the best in others, to a cynical one who feared men—warrior druids especially. She'd also insisted that Bree teach her how to fight and wield knives. She'd even asked one of the Guard to tutor her in knife throwing—a skill that had come in handy when Lara and her mother had been attacked in the North, for Mirren had thrown the blade that brought down the queen's killer.

"Are you afraid of him?" Lara asked softly.

Mirren grimaced. "I'm not sure. I find it hard to see the good in any enforcer these days."

"Even Cailean?"

"Aye … even him."

A pause followed, while Lara considered how to respond. Once, she would have been at a loss for how to speak of such things, having had little worldly experience. But now, after her marriage to Dunchadh of Braewall, she knew what it was to fear a man—what it was to hate one. Nevertheless, she'd tread carefully here. "You know that I partnered with Cailean at the blood-letting … twice?"

Mirren's blue eyes widened. "You did?"

"Aye … it was before you came to live in the broch." Lara flashed Mirren a sheepish smile. "Just between you and me, I was smitten with him at the time … so when he asked me to partner with him, I fell over myself to accept."

Mirren's eyebrows rose, her lips curving. "What was it like … to bond with someone in that way?"

"Exciting … intimate. You share more than blood … it's as if your life forces entwine for a short while. Afterward, you feel … close."

"You weren't jealous when he ordered himself a bride then?"

Lara sighed. "No, I always knew my father would arrange a match for me … for the good of Albia."

"I can't believe you weren't bitter about that." Mirren was watching her closely, as if trying to catch her out.

"I wasn't," she replied honestly. Bitterness had come later. "I was told of my duty from an early age … and accepted it." She halted then, studying Mirren's pale face. "Torran is a decent man … but you don't have to partner with him, if you don't want to. You have freewill, Mirren."

The lass stiffened then, and Lara wondered if she'd overstepped. Despite their differences in rank, they were friends—but they both had held back certain things. Mirren had never learned about what had happened on Lara's wedding night or the morning after.

Lara wouldn't confide in her now either. Some things were best left unspoken.

Her handmaid lowered her gaze. "I wanted Torran once." A blush rose to her cheeks then. "I watched him like an adoring puppy … and dreamed that one day he'd actually notice that I breathed. It's ironic that he finally has … although I don't understand why he'd choose me."

Lara watched her for a few moments before giving a soft snort. "Well, I'd say it proves he has good taste."

During supper, Lara picked at her venison stew and dumplings, letting conversation swirl around her. It had been an exhausting day, and concern about her overkings gnawed at her. Not only that, but the days were passing with frightening swiftness. They were doing their best to prepare themselves for their upcoming campaign, but it didn't feel like enough.

After her meeting with Artair and Niall, she worried she wouldn't have enough spears, blades, arrowheads, and fighters ready in time. Their losses in Doure had to be replaced. Just another reason why they needed the Circines to partner with them. The less reliant they were on the wulvers, the better.

And soon, the Half-blood would arrive.

Despite that she was impatient to strike north, she wasn't ready to see him again. And she definitely wasn't ready for their handfasting. He'd share her alcove, her furs. He'd do what Dunchadh had—

No! She swiftly cut herself off. She couldn't let herself think about such things, or she'd claw Alar's face off if he tried to touch her.

Pushing aside her stew, she picked up her goblet of wine and took a large gulp.

Her gaze then traveled along the table, and she surveyed those who'd joined her on the high seat. Bree's brother, Gil, was deep in discussion with Cailean and Torran. The chief-enforcer looked exhausted. His chiseled features were drawn, and he had dark smudges under his eyes. He'd worked tirelessly since his return to Duncrag, but that wasn't the reason for his fatigue. He needed tonight's blood-letting. In contrast. Gil's lean face was animated.

It pleased Lara to see her archivist happier here these days. When he'd first come to live at Duncrag, he'd been traumatized—ripped from his old form and reluctantly living amongst the Marav. Unlike his sister, Gil hadn't chosen Albia as his home. Instead, the Raven Queen had cast him out when she'd discovered his sister had left Sheehallion.

Her attention shifted then to Torran.

Tall, lanky, and covered in woad tattoos, with close-cropped dark-blond hair and grey eyes, the enforcer was undoubtedly attractive. She could see why Mirren had been drawn to him.

Worry tightened her belly as she took another sip of wine. Maybe it *was* best Mirren kept her distance from the warrior druid. Torran had always seemed decent; however, the earth magic that flowed through enforcers' veins made them aggressive, unpredictable.

She was pondering this when Cailean and Torran excused themselves from the table.

It was time for the blood-letting.

Flanked by two of the Fort Guard, Lara climbed the steps to the walls. Usually, Bree would accompany her, but this evening, she was with Cailean.

Inhaling the frosty air, Lara pulled her fur cloak tighter about her to ward off the chill. Above, the sky was a glittering carpet of stars. There was no veil between the world and the Gods tonight. Perfect weather for the ritual that would take place on the hill northwest of the fort.

As she stepped up to the ramparts, the glow of torches below caught her eye.

There they were walking in pairs down The Thoroughfare—enforcers and the women they'd chosen to partner them. Only women partnered with the warrior druids for the blood-letting, for they were closer to earth magic and provided a better channel during the ritual. Cailean led them, Bree at his side. As always, they made a striking couple. Cailean was brawny and raven-haired, and although Bree had taken Marav form, she still walked with the posture and smooth stride of one of the Shee.

Of course, not all the enforcers were men. Thalia strode among them. Tall and proud, her long dark hair plaited in thin braids, the female enforcer walked alongside the woman who'd partner her for the ceremony.

And toward the end of the procession, Lara caught sight of a small woman with curly dark hair, walking next to a tall, blond, tattooed enforcer.

Mirren and Torran.

Lara was sitting by the fire in her alcove when Mirren returned.

Florie and the twins were downstairs, helping clean up after supper, and so she'd enjoyed a rare moment of solitude. She nursed a cup of warm wine. Earlier, she'd even risked whispering to the flame burning on the low table beside the hearth—and had made it dance for her. Playing with fire helped relax her. It was a welcome distraction from her worries.

However, the flame now flickered sedately once more as the curtain swished open and Mirren hurried inside.

Her blue eyes were bright, her cheeks flushed. She'd never looked prettier.

"Sorry for keeping you waiting," she greeted Lara breathlessly. "As soon as the ritual was done, I—"

"Don't worry about that." Lara waved her apology away. "You went in the end then?"

"Aye." The blush upon Mirren's cheeks deepened. "You were right … it's quite an experience."

"And Torran … he was respectful?"

Mirren nodded, hurrying past her to start preparations so her queen could retire to the furs. Swiveling on her chair, Lara noted how flighty she was, how she deliberately avoided her eye as she poured water into an earthen bowl and fetched a drying sheet.

"So, you're more comfortable around him now?" Lara pressed.

Mirren cast her a sidelong glance. "I suppose so," she answered, wary now. There was a skittishness in her gaze that warned Lara she should leave this be, but she couldn't. Part of her wanted to know if it was possible to heal a deep distrust of men.

"And if he shows interest in other ways ... will you encourage him?"

Her handmaid's face stiffened. She turned away then, busying herself in folding some washing that Florie had brought up from the laundry earlier. "Probably not," she said huskily, the excitement she'd entered the alcove with fading like a doused candle. "He's an enforcer, after all ... and I won't let one of them near me ... ever again."

Lara watched the rigid line of her handmaid's back as she worked, her movements jerky. She was upset now. "Apologies, Mirren," she said softly. "I shouldn't have asked you that."

"It's fine." Mirren still didn't look her way.

No, clearly, it wasn't.

"I guess I hoped that if you could let the past go, so could I," Lara whispered.

Mirren stilled then before glancing over her shoulder. Their gazes met and held, and as the moments slid by, her handmaid's blue eyes widened, understanding dawning.

"Aye," Lara added. "I know what it's like to dread a man's touch."

16: UNWORTHY

HALTING AT THE top of the last hill before Duncrag, Alar swept his gaze over the vast fort that he'd soon co-rule.

A slow smile curved his lips.

"Gloating?"

He glanced over his shoulder at where Dolph had stepped close. The Sweeper buffeted them, ruffling the plush fawn-colored fur that covered Dolph's head and neck, and making Alar's thick cloak billow and snap around him. The wind had followed them all the way south for days now, and today, it pushed fat clouds across a leached-out blue sky above.

"Aye," he admitted. "Aren't you?"

"Of course. This is the next step … and we're ready for it. Ready to take our rightful place."

"So, you have taken the High Queen at her word?" Lyall moved up next to Dolph. The huge wulver loomed over them both. "We'd better not be walking into a trap."

"I can make no such promises."

Neither wulver replied to this, although both their amber gazes glinted.

"Lara mac Talorc isn't her father," he went on. "But she hasn't proved herself to us … or me."

Turning, he surveyed the long column of wulvers, all of them on foot, that stretched up the highway. Wulvers didn't travel on horseback, and so the journey had taken several days. Of course, Duncrag scouts had already marked their passage south.

Lara would be waiting for him.

And as he'd promised, his arrival was one turn of the moon after Doure. Gateway was half a turn away, and autumn was sliding toward winter.

"Come." He swiveled on his heel once more and started off down the final slope. Ahead, lay the sparkling waters of the River Lethe, spanned by a wooden bridge. "Let's prepare ourselves for a warm Duncrag welcome."

The wulvers entered the fort to the clang of iron.

The noise didn't surprise Alar. In every Marav settlement in The Wolds, smiths were hard at work forging weapons to combat the Shee—they had been for years now.

It didn't surprise him either that their arrival drew crowds.

Men, women, and bairns gathered around the large dirt meeting ground inside the gates and lined The Thoroughfare, all gawking rudely at Alar and his companions. Of course, many of them had never seen wulvers before.

Today changed all that.

It wasn't Alar's first trip to Duncrag in his seventy-two summers. He'd visited a few times, mainly to pick up weapons or supplies. He'd always enjoyed the vibrancy of Albia's capital, even if the acrid tang of iron in the air mixed with the ripe odor of too many bodies living in close quarters, and the stench from the open sewers on the lower levels, called for a strong stomach.

Fortunately, as they climbed The Thoroughfare through the various levels, with densely-packed roundhouses and sod-roofed cottages lining the way, the smell improved.

However, the mood amongst the inhabitants didn't.

He caught their muttering, the growled curses. Some even spat on the ground as the wulvers approached, although the timid amongst them clutched iron protection amulets and murmured prayers to the Gods.

Alar couldn't help but smirk at their superstition. *Fools.*

He noted then, on the fringes of the swelling crowd, many leather-clad warriors, domed iron helmets jammed upon their heads and spears in their hands. The High Queen had sent out her Fort Guard to ensure Alar and his army could enter unmolested.

Or to prevent fighting from breaking out.

Up they climbed, until finally, they crested the tip of the promontory.

Duncrag was immense, many times larger than Doure, and from the top, Alar had a wide view of pinewoods and hills to the south and west, the edge of an estuary to the east, and the craggy outline of the Shiel Range to the north.

But his attention didn't linger on the views for long. Instead, he focused on the high walls surrounding the massive beehive-shaped broch.

Anticipation tightened his stomach.

Lara would be waiting for him.

He had to be wary of his bride-to-be. She'd made that blood oath in an act of desperation, but a moon had turned since then. No doubt, she was looking for an excuse to break their agreement.

He wouldn't let her.

Alar strode through the open gates and into the wide courtyard before the broch. He spied Lara then, standing in front of the vast oaken doors leading inside. His step slowed as he raked his gaze over her, from the crown of her head to her sandalled feet. Her thick auburn waves had been tamed into twin coils, amber pendants hung from her ears, and a gleaming bronze torque encircled her throat, while bronze, silver, and gold rings decorated her bare arms. She wore a gold-trimmed, jade-green sleeveless tunic that reached the ankle, and a thick wolf's pelt hung from her shoulders.

Her warder and the chief-enforcer flanked her, while more black-clad enforcers stood below them on the steps. Mac Brochan's fae hound was present too—and its golden eyes fastened on Alar. Despite that the beast had displayed a surprising affection for him in Doure, the hound's stare was a little unsettling.

Lara held herself proudly. However, her heart-shaped face was pale, strained.

Discomfort flickered through Alar then, catching him unawares.

What was this?

When they'd met outside Doure, she'd been dressed in hard-wearing, practical tunics, for she was on campaign, with little jewelry or finery. But now she was back in Duncrag and dressed like a High Queen once more, he suddenly felt unworthy of her. Scarred and covered in dirt and sweat from days on the road, he looked like the outcast he was.

Irritation sliced through him then.

Unworthy?

He'd spent most of his life clawing out of that fucking pit. He wasn't going back there. Ever.

His bride-to-be might look as untouchable as The Maiden, but he'd earned a place at her side. He'd worked up to this moment for so long, the fact that it was finally coming true made the situation feel surreal, as if it were happening to someone else.

But it was his moment, and he'd grasp it with both hands.

Halting at the bottom of the steps, Alar nodded. "We meet again."

"I trust you had a safe journey south?" Lara's voice was low, only a slight huskiness betraying her nerves.

"Aye … some bother with a clutch of trows a few days ago, but we saw them off." Actually, both trows and powries had been plentiful during the journey, harassing them nightly. He decided not to burden the queen with this though. They could talk about such things when they were alone.

Lara cleared her throat. "A feast has been prepared for this evening in honor of your arrival."

Alar inclined his head in thanks. "Are you happy for our handfasting to take place tomorrow?"

"So soon?"

"Why wait?"

Bree and Cailean both scowled at his glib tone, yet Alar ignored them. Instead, his attention remained upon the High Queen.

Her throat worked. "As you wish … tomorrow it is."

"Good." He motioned to where Lyall and Dolph stood behind him, followed by the ranks of wulvers who now filled the yard. "I trust accommodation has been organized for my host?"

Lara nodded stiffly. "The Fort Guard will escort them down to the two levels beneath us, where they will be lodged. Six wulvers will share each roundhouse." She didn't add that she'd had to move out many residents from that level and provide accommodation for them elsewhere in the fort—yet another thing her people had complained about. "There is space there for them to train."

"Is the meal to your liking?"

"Aye. It's delicious."

Despite that her appetite was poor this evening, Lara cut herself a sliver of cheese from the round upon the table before them and placed it upon her trencher. And all the while, she was aware of Alar's gaze.

The Mother's tits, did he have to watch her so closely?

He wasn't a wulver, yet there was something vulpine about his gaze. A cunning that set her nerves on edge. It made her want to do anything to break the tension, including asking simpering questions. What did she care if Alar liked his meal or not? With any luck, he'd choke on it so she wouldn't have to go through with this handfasting.

That wouldn't solve her problems though. She wouldn't have to wed him, but she'd be without his army. And since the envoy they'd sent into The Goatfells hadn't yet returned, she had to be careful.

"I plan to push north as soon as Gateway is over," she said after a pause. "Are your wulvers ready?"

He inclined his head. "Of course. Is your army?"

Her spine stiffened at the challenge in his voice, and she raised her chin. "It will be."

Around them, warriors and wulvers crammed the hall of Duncrag broch. Extra trestle tables had been carried in to accommodate the huge numbers. The slaves serving the feasters had to squeeze their way in between the tightly-packed rows. Rumbles and growls echoed up, mingling with the pall of blue-black peat smoke that hung beneath the heavy rafters.

Nonetheless, it didn't escape her notice that the wulvers sat on one side of her hall, and her warriors on the other. Just like in Doure—it was as if they were oil and water, never meant to mix. And when she looked closely, she noted that it wasn't just her warriors who weren't making an effort. Back in Doure, the wulvers had been elated by their victory, yet still humble. But this evening, many held themselves with a new arrogance. They stared down the men and women seated on the other side of the hall.

Nervousness tightened her belly. Over a thousand wulvers now resided in this fort. What if they ran amok?

Next to her, Alar helped himself to more braised boar and onion stew. His gaze then shifted down the table to where Gil sat to Bree's left. Eight of them sat upon the dais this evening:

Lara, Alar, Bree, Cailean, Torran, Gil—as well as the Half-blood's captains, Lyall and Dolph.

Alar studied Lara's archivist with interest. Feeling the weight of his stare, Gil raised his chin, his hazel eyes narrowing under the scrutiny. "Our queen has told you who I am then?"

Alar nodded.

Gil smirked. "It doesn't matter how long you scrutinize me … you won't see any of who I was before."

Beside him, Bree snorted before flashing her brother a warning look.

"I had no idea," Alar murmured. "That the stone circles had such power."

"Aye, well, I wouldn't try it for yourself," Gil replied, helping himself to some bread studded with walnuts. "With Marav blood in your veins … you'd be dead before you got three paces inside."

Despite herself, Lara swallowed a smile. She'd missed Gil while she'd been on campaign. Like his sister, he didn't attempt to flatter or ingratiate himself. His bluntness was refreshing. She'd also missed paying visits to his archive and learning about the things he'd uncovered for her.

"So, how does it feel to travel through the stones?" Alar asked then.

"Painful," Gil replied. "It's like pushing through water at first … and then the air starts to crush you."

"Not an easy trip, then?"

Gil huffed a laugh. "Not when your eyeballs feel like they're about to explode."

As the two men continued their discussion, Lara's attention shifted to the others at her table.

Torran was attempting to converse with Lyall, the bigger of the two wulver captains. The blond enforcer's brow was furrowed as he listened to Lyall's growled words. She was too far away to catch their conversation though.

The sight of Cailean's second-in-command made her think of Mirren.

Her handmaid had been subdued ever since the blood-letting. She hadn't spoken of Torran again, and Lara had wisely left the subject alone. These days, Mirren let Florie, Ani, and Lilith chatter away in the mornings and evenings while she went about her chores with a distracted air. Bree had also marked Mirren's subdued mood, and tried to draw her out of it, with little success.

Something subtle had shifted between the High Queen and her handmaid ever since the eve of the blood-letting too. Lara had revealed more than she'd intended—Mirren knew that she too feared a man's touch. They had something in common, yet it hadn't brought them closer. Instead, it had driven a wedge between them. It was as if they shared a guilty secret, and the realization vexed Lara.

Neither of them had done anything wrong.

She was sorry Mirren was wary of her now, for her circle of friends was a tight one. She couldn't afford to lose any, and ever since striking a deal with Alar, things hadn't been the same between her, Bree, and Cailean. She caught both of them watching her sometimes, their gazes shadowed as if they worried what she'd do next.

Lara was still picking at her meal when Alar leaned close. "Will you take a walk with me on the walls after supper?"

Chin kicking up, she met his gaze. Her pulse quickened then. It was a good idea for them to talk privately before their handfasting, as they had things to discuss—nonetheless, she'd have preferred to retire early and enjoy her last night of freedom.

Pushing aside her reaction, she favored him with a tight smile. "Really … you want to risk it … after last time we took a stroll together?"

"I take it there aren't any lurking Shee at Duncrag?"

She snorted. "You don't have to worry about that … not here."

"The Shee female who attacked you … what became of her?"

Lara gave him a probing look. His tone was light, yet she hadn't forgotten his strange reaction when they'd interrogated the Shee warrior. "Fern Sablebane is still my captive."

He raised a dark eyebrow. "Locked away in the dungeon, eh?"

"No." She shook her head. "We've put all the Shee captives to work … filling cesspits in the lower levels."

"And you don't worry they'll try to escape?"

"We have them barricaded in a roundhouse with an iron door at night," she assured him, "and guarded by druids while they work. That should be enough."

"I'm happy to put some of my wulvers on guard duty as well." He flashed her an easy smile she didn't trust in the slightest. "If it helps?"

"That won't be necessary. We have the situation well in hand." She twisted then, beckoning to a white-clad figure who had been waiting in the shadows behind them—one of the counsellors, a young woman with curly flaxen hair. "Ruatha, do you have the document?"

"Aye, My Queen." The counsellor stepped forward and withdrew a scroll from the basket she carried, handing it to Lara.

She then reached back into the basket and produced a bottle of ink and a freshly sharpened quill.

Lara turned back to find Alar watching her. His smile had faded. "What's this?"

"You promised to sign an agreement, remember?" Around them, the table went silent. "If we have any children, you assured me you shall step aside and allow our firstborn to rule after my death."

His gaze hardened. "That's right."

He wouldn't like her bringing this up with an audience, yet she'd done so deliberately. She needed witnesses when he signed. She wanted him to know that she wasn't a lamb to be meekly led to slaughter.

"And if we don't have any children?" he asked after a pause.

"Then my council will name an heir." She held the rolled parchment aloft. "It's all written here."

A muscle flexed in his jaw. He didn't like that either. "You've thought this through, Lara," he said finally, a warning creeping into his voice now.

"I have." Unfurling the parchment, she placed it in front of him. Her pulse quickened as she did so. For the first time, she felt truly in control of their interactions. She then unstoppered the pot of ink and placed the quill next to it. "Go ahead … take a look. Then, we can both sign at the bottom. Of course, you aren't just agreeing personally … but on behalf of the wulvers."

Moments passed before Alar's jaw tightened. "I can't read."

Lara stiffened. She should have realized. The man had lived wild for most of his life. Only the druids and Albia's high-born learned their letters and numbers. She'd humiliated him.

"Very well," she answered, picking up the document. "I shall read the agreement out to you … and you shall sign it with a cross."

17: YOU NEED NEVER BE ALONE

THE SWEEPER BUFFETED them when they stepped up onto the walls. Drawing her cloak tightly about her, Lara led the way past guttering braziers to the terrace that looked southwest. Bree and two of the Fort Guard followed at a discreet distance. "You get the best views from here," she said as she drew to a halt.

Deliberately not looking Alar's way, she looked down at where the home fires of Duncrag burned, illuminating the fort. The waxing moon was rising: a pale-silver half-circle in a jet sky.

The atmosphere had been strained between them since the signing of the agreement. Alar's mood had turned sullen, and she'd been dreading going up on the walls with him.

A brittle silence settled, and eventually, Lara cleared her throat. "Have you been to Duncrag before?"

"Aye, many times." His voice was aloof.

"My father always said there's no fort as beautiful as Duncrag … especially at night."

"I've always preferred Dulross, actually."

Relieved that he was at least engaging with her, Lara nodded. She could see why he liked Dulross. The 'Brooch of Albia' had a picturesque setting, surrounded by rolling meadows to the south, and dark pinewood to the north. It sat under the majestic shadow of The Goatfell Mountains. Dulross was a little smaller than Duncrag yet had a grace that the capital lacked.

She reflected then that Alar must have traveled far and wide over his seven decades, yet she'd seen little of Albia—aside from Doure and Dulross, she'd visited Braewall a few times and Cannich twice. Nowhere else. Before taking the throne, she'd led a sheltered life, and after her father's death, she'd been catapulted into a world she wasn't prepared for.

Another hush fell. Alar made no move to break it. He'd been the one to suggest coming up here, but he was still brooding now.

Eventually, she huffed a frustrated sigh. If he wasn't going to make an effort, she'd dispense with pleasantries. "I hear you are a wanted man in Baldeen."

He snorted. "Who told you that?"

"King Artair."

"I've had no dealings with him."

Lara studied his profile. The nearby brazier gilded the sharp lines of his features. "Well, he certainly knows who you are."

His gaze flicked to her. "He didn't take the news of our impending handfasting well then?"

"No."

"And the King of Braewall?"

"He isn't happy either." She pulled a face then, glancing away. "Unfortunately, Niall offered for me a couple of years ago. His pride was bruised … but he accepted my decision to remain unwed in the end. As such, he's taken our impending handfasting as a slight."

"Ah, so I have a rival?" She shifted her attention back to Alar, to find him watching her. His coldness had gone, although she preferred it to the smug expression he now wore.

Eyeballing him, she folded her arms across her chest. "So, are you going to tell me *why* there's a price on your head?"

"Is it important?"

Lara frowned. His slippery responses were starting to vex her. "Aye."

He reached up, his fingers rubbing the lean line of his jaw—something he did when thinking.

Her wariness grew to misgiving. By the Gods, whom was she binding herself to? She hadn't even been born for most of his time alive. He cloaked himself in layers of secrecy, and she wondered if she'd ever find her way through them to discover the real man beneath it all.

"I killed the king's brother."

Lara stiffened. "King Beorn's brother?" Beorn was the previous overking of Baldeen, who'd fallen alongside her father outside Cannich.

"No, Col mac Darach was overking then. As I said, it was a while ago … I must have been your age at the time."

"And why did you kill him?"

His iron-grey eyes hardened. "Revenge."

"For what?"

"A few years earlier, King Col charged his younger brother Evin with keeping peace in the villages of Dorne Forest," Alar answered, his attention shifting west, in the direction of Baldeen and its territories. "Like your father, Evin had no love for the Shee or anything faerie. He discovered that a Half-blood lad lived among the locals and turned them against me." He paused then, his profile almost harsh. "I was around ten at the time … and my mother had just died. They chased me from our bothy and hunted me like a dog through the woods. Evin caught me though and strung me up on a tall pine before leaving me to slowly choke to death."

Lara's breathing grew shallow. "But you lived."

He cut her a veiled look before one hand lifted to the scar upon his throat. "I did … but that's another story." He paused then, absently stroking the raised silver line. "Fifteen years passed, but I never forgot Evin mac Darach. And when I was ready, I hunted him as he'd once done me and hanged him from a tall pine."

His words were uttered matter-of-factly. Nevertheless, Lara suppressed a shiver. She deliberately looked away, focusing on the glowing half-moon.

"Does my tale appease you?" Alar asked, a challenge in his voice now.

She nodded, even as her gut tightened. Moments passed before she finally spoke. "There has been another development since I saw you last."

"Aye?"

She turned to face him, her arms still folded protectively across her chest. "I've sent an envoy of counsellors to seek out the chieftain of the Circines."

He stiffened. "Why didn't you tell me this earlier?"

"I wanted some privacy."

"That didn't stop you from waving that agreement in my face in full view of your hall."

Heat flushed over Lara. Aye, she'd vexed him. "That was necessary," she answered crisply. "Besides, you already agreed to sign it."

His gaze narrowed. "And why have you sent an envoy into The Goatfells?"

"My father made the hill tribes of The Uplands his enemies … but I will change things," she replied, relieved they weren't going to argue about the document he'd just signed. "Anything Mor has offered the Circines, I will better. They should have met with them by now. When we march north to take back Strath, the Circines will hopefully rally at our side."

Silence followed her words. Eventually, he broke it. "You should have discussed this with me in Doure."

Irritation spiked through her. She didn't answer to him. "My chief-counsellor didn't bring up the idea until we'd left."

His brows drew together, his mood darkening once more. "If you'd told me what you were planning, I'd have warned you that Beathan mac Glen, the chieftain of the Circines, hates you and everything you stand for. Your father captured, tortured, and killed his brother … that's why he allied himself with the Shee."

"But I'm not my father," she replied, her belly clenching. "My envoy will make that clear."

"Well, I hope you sent your best to speak on your behalf … and that you've offered them something that'll make Beathan see you in a different light."

Lara scowled. "Of course. In return for their loyalty, they will live without my interference. No longer will we draft hill-tribe warriors into our armies. The Goatfell Mountains will be their domain … there will be no taxes, no laws, but their own."

Alar barked a humorless laugh. "And you think that'll be enough?"

Heat rolled over her. "Aye."

His gaze flicked to where her right hand clenched around her left bicep, his brow furrowing. Stiffening, Lara glanced down. He was staring at her father's ring, the *Ord-ree Seal*. She was about to ask him why, when his attention snapped up to her face once more.

"When did you send your emissaries north?"

"Just over half a moon's turn ago." Worry clutched at her belly then. Time was marching on.

"Aye, well, they should have sent word by now." His dark brows drew together over the bridge of his nose. "You do realize they're likely all dead?"

Her heart kicked against her ribs, although she covered up her response with a scowl. "You don't know that." She stepped abruptly back from him. "This conversation is over, Alar. When we discuss this again, it will be with my council present."

Lara climbed the stairs to her quarters, quietly simmering.

Her exchange with the Half-blood upon the walls had left a sour taste in her mouth. His revelations about his past had been unnerving, and his reaction to her sending an envoy to the Circines angered her.

He had no right to question her decisions.

Not yet … but he will soon.

Dread clutched at her as she pushed aside the curtain to her alcove and strode inside. This evening hadn't gone well from start to finish. The two of them were locked in a duel. Her trick at supper had angered him, but his behavior afterwards had riled *her.* Gods, was there any way out of this marriage?

Her attendants were all in here already, preparing the alcove and sleeping nook for their queen's arrival. Mirren was putting another brick of peat on the fire, Florie was tidying the furs, and the twins were fussing over the pretty tunic Lara would wear for her handfasting the following day.

Lara halted, her throat constricting as she surveyed them.

This was the last night the four women would reside in this alcove with her. From tomorrow, only she and her husband would sleep in here. Her attendants would share a small alcove on the floor below.

Dizziness swept over her then.

She'd be alone … with *him.*

"Would you like a cup of wine, My Queen?" Mirren asked, straightening up from her task.

"Aye," Lara said huskily, "but pour a cup for yourself, Florie, Ani, and Lilith, as well."

Mirren stilled. "My Queen?"

"Go on." Lara moved over to one of the high-backed chairs flanking the hearth and sat down heavily. "Things will be different from tomorrow … I'd like to remember what it was like to spend the evening with you all."

Mirren still looked surprised by the command, but heeded it, nonetheless.

A short while later, they'd pulled up stools and sat near their queen, sipping at their wines.

The red-haired twins, Ani and Lilith, both perched nervously, thin fingers clasped around their cups, while Florie wore a stunned expression. It wasn't customary for servants to eat or drink with the ruling class—but Lara had no patience for such things tonight.

None of her family were alive to chide her for it.

She attempted to draw the twins into conversation, yet they were too shy to answer with any more than one-word responses, and Florie was too awed to engage. Only Mirren managed—as always.

Eventually, Lara gave up trying to chat with them—it seemed the gulf between their ranks couldn't be breached, after all—and let them get on with their evening chores. The twins rushed off, relieved, to fetch her hot water and drying clothes, while Florie took the dirtied cups and empty ewer down to the kitchen. She'd bring back a fresh jug of sweet plum wine.

Lara intended to have a few swigs of it before her handfasting ceremony. Anything to get her through it.

Seated alone with Mirren, Lara sifted through her jewelry box, trying to decide on what earrings, torque, and arm rings to wear to the ceremony. It was difficult to concentrate on her task, for such details seemed trivial. She then picked up a golden torque engraved with ferns, a lovely neck decoration that had belonged to her mother. Holding it up to the light, she remembered how beautiful the queen consort had looked wearing it.

She hadn't worn the torque since her mother's death. Maybe now was the time.

"The golden arm rings would go well with that … and they'd both look good with the woad-blue of your tunic," Mirren suggested.

"Gold it is," Lara replied listlessly, passing the maid the box. "Go ahead and pick out some earrings for me then."

Mirren's brow furrowed. "You don't want to choose them?"

Lara sighed. "I don't care what I wear tomorrow … it's not going to make the day any easier." She looked away then, seeking solace in the warmth of the flickering hearth. "Or the *night*."

Her handmaid didn't answer. However, a moment later, a small hand rested on her forearm. "Are you afraid?"

"A little," she admitted, even as her pulse leaped into a canter. *Liar.* She was *terrified* of Alar touching her.

"Dunchadh … was he—"

"A foul brute … aye, he was." She started to sweat then. She wasn't sure she could discuss her late husband without losing her composure.

As if sensing this, Mirren didn't press further. But as silence swelled between them, the need to confide in someone started to throb under her breastbone. Sometimes, she felt so alone. It was exhausting, keeping everything to herself.

"I knew that Dunchadh had buried three wives … just not how he treated them," she said, wishing her voice didn't sound so brittle. "But on our wedding night … I learned."

Another pause followed before Mirren gently squeezed Lara's arm. It was a kind gesture, although one that made tears burn behind her eyelids. The Mother give her strength, she didn't want to start weeping.

"No matter what happens tomorrow, or in the days to come, I am here," she said, her voice low and firm. "Whenever you need an ear, I will listen." She paused then, her lips curving.

"And remember that Bree and Cailean are here for you too. You need never be alone with your worries."

Lara swallowed, trying to loosen her tight throat. "What if I've ruined our friendship? They opposed my decision to make this pact with the Half-blood. Maybe they think I should suffer for it."

Mirren shook her head. "You don't give them enough credit. They will always stand by you … as will I."

18: THE THREADS OF TRUST

LARA APPROACHED THE riverbank barefoot and clad in flowing blue. Her auburn hair was unbound and tumbling over her shoulders, gold shimmered upon her earlobes and arms, and a torque glinted at her throat. She looked untamed, as if a wood nymph had just strolled from the trees rather than the Queen of Albia.

Alar tracked her progress along the mossy bank, toward the flat stone where he waited for her. Like his bride-to-be, he didn't wear boots or shoes. The Marav always handfasted barefoot, for they believed it brought them closer to the Gods.

Alar wouldn't have cared either way. When he'd visited Lara's tent outside Doure, he'd seen her tiny shrine to The Five in the corner. It meant nothing to him. These gods had forsaken him a long time ago, and in turn, he'd turned to the Hearthkeeper.

The Lethe flowed by, whispering around clumps of rushes. A large crowd had gathered here. Every druid in Duncrag, resplendent in their different colored robes, as well as the highest ranking of the fort's inhabitants: elders and headmen. A pack of wulvers, Lyall and Dolph among them, looked on from the fringes of the crowd. They were here to witness this, to ensure their leader did marry the Marav High Queen.

But Alar paid none of the crowd any mind.

Lara held his attention.

He shouldn't stare at her like this. It was a habit he'd gotten into in Doure, one that he found hard to break. The truth was, he'd seen few things as lovely as the High Queen of Albia. Lara was young and fresh, untainted by bitterness. She was also determined to do whatever it took to serve this realm, even if it meant shackling herself to a twisted creature such as him.

And he *was* twisted.

If she knew how much, she'd never have made an alliance with him.

He didn't deserve such a woman. He shouldn't have put her in such a position. He should have offered her his army of wulvers out of loyalty to the realm, but he hadn't.

Instead, he'd greedily take her as his own.

She was the key he'd spent decades searching for.

The chief-counsellor, a heavy-set woman clad in flowing white with a thick mane of brown braids and a stern face, stepped up to the stone, waiting as Lara closed the remaining gap.

His bride-to-be wore a composed expression, one she'd likely learned to put in place from an early age. A king's daughter knew how to behave when the eyes of all were upon her. Nonetheless, he guessed she wasn't so calm on the inside.

They'd locked horns the night before. When she'd produced that document for him to sign at the supper table, fury had knifed through him. He'd been the one to suggest it, but she could have warned him before waving it in his face, before revealing to everyone that he couldn't read.

His illiteracy had bothered him little over the years—none of the wulvers knew their letters or numbers either—but seated in the hall of Duncrag, next to the haughty young woman who'd soon become his wife, it had suddenly mattered.

It pissed him off that it did.

They'd clashed on the walls too, especially after she told him about the peace envoy she'd sent north. When her anger spiked, he could have sworn the amber ring on her right hand flickered, as if a flame had ignited in its depths.

How strange.

He couldn't dwell on that at present—not with his bride-to-be just a few yards away.

The High Queen's druids and warriors were staring at him now. These people had never accepted him, but soon, they'd have a Half-blood prince consort.

Lara stepped up before him and halted.

The chief-counsellor cleared her throat. "Ready, My Queen?" There was a sharpness in the woman's voice. Annis mac Gord was looking for a sign that the High Queen wished to call this whole thing off.

But she wouldn't.

She couldn't.

The blood oath would hold her to her promise.

Lara nodded, a nerve flickering in her cheek.

"Very well … face each other, and clasp hands."

Alar and Lara swiveled so they were before each other, and then Alar took the initiative, reaching out and taking her hand. It was ice-cold, and as his thumb brushed over the soft skin of the underside of her wrist, he felt the flutter of her pulse.

The chief-counsellor began to wrap a length of pine-green ribbon around their clasped hands. "Alar mac Struana, Commander of the wulvers, I join you with Lara mac Talorc, High Queen of Albia." She paused then, her gaze flicking between them. "May The Mother light your paths. May The Warrior protect you. May The Maiden grant you a bounteous family. May The Hag bless you both with long, healthy lives … and may The Reaper stay far from your door."

Alar's pulse quickened. He'd made his pact with Lara without giving any thought to the ceremony that would bind them. It was nothing but a means to an end. He'd planned to get through it as quickly as possible. But the words that the druid spoke, in her low, solemn voice, made him uneasy.

He was making a mockery of this ceremony, of the promises he'd made, and for an instant, he was sorry.

"Alar, repeat these vows after me," the chief-counsellor instructed. "I, Alar mac Struana, Commander of the wulvers, pledge to protect you, Lara mac Talorc, High Queen of Albia, with my body and my life."

Alar did as bidden, speaking the words slowly and deliberately, as if they meant something to him. And when it was Lara's turn, she held his gaze, her voice husky yet steady. "I,

Lara, mac Talorc, High Queen of Albia, pledge to honor you, Alar mac Struana, Commander of the wulvers … with my body and my life."

They stared at each other then, as if seeing each other properly for the first time. The moment drew out until the druid's voice intruded. "You are now wed." She unwrapped the length of ribbon from around their hands before retreating a few steps. "You may kiss your bride."

Lara's face blanched at this, and something deep inside him clenched.

Did she dread his touch so much?

Sidestepping his reaction, he moved close to his bride, cupped her face with his hands, and lowered his mouth to hers.

Lara didn't glance her husband's way as they rode, side by side, up The Thoroughfare. A crowd had gathered by the roadside, curious gazes tracking the newlyweds. There was no cheering or fanfare though.

No one threw rose petals or called out well-wishes. Many brows were furrowed.

Although their reaction didn't bode well, Lara was relieved that no one was making a fuss. She was also thankful the ceremony was over, for she'd been dreading the kiss. Fortunately, he'd kept it brief and chaste. Perfunctory.

That was good. Once today was done with, they could focus on what really mattered: taking back The Uplands.

The wedding party reached the top of the fort, riding into the yard before the broch and dismounting from their horses. Alar swung down from his horse first and helped her down from hers. His behavior was expected, a gesture she'd already seen from him in Doure. Nonetheless, his hand on her back made her mouth go dry and her pulse race.

It was a reminder of what was to come.

Within the broch, the hall had been decorated for their arrival, with boughs of fragrant pine and trailing streamers of ivy. Banks of candles flickered against the walls.

"It smells like a forest in here," Alar noted as they crossed the floor, covered in fresh rushes and dried lavender and rosemary.

"Aye … it's customary for a royal handfasting."

"It's … pleasant."

She cast him a sidelong look, surprised. She never knew what to make of this man.

They took their places at the long table upon the high seat, waiting while everyone else filed into the hall. Cailean and Bree flanked them—Cailean seated next to Alar and Bree next to Lara. Her warder's proximity reassured Lara a little. Bree's quiet strength never failed to calm her.

Gil took his place upon the high seat next to his sister, while Roth sat down next to Cailean. Below them, warriors, wulvers, druids, and high-ranking servants took their places upon long benches at the trestle tables while slaves entered the space carrying trays of roast boar and venison. And like the eve before, Marav and Wulvers sat separately.

Lara spied Mirren then. Her handmaid had just taken her place at the table nearest the high seat.

A moment later, Torran sat down next to her.

"It's time for a dance. It's expected."

"As you wish." Alar rose to his feet and offered Lara his arm. They'd barely spoken through the feasting, for the din of conversation in the hall made it difficult to talk without shouting. However, once the feasting was done and the tables pushed back, the noise lowered. Two musicians sitting in the corner of the hall then struck up a tune on a bone whistle and a lyre.

Lara didn't want to step out onto the floor with Alar, to have all eyes upon her as she moved around the hall in her husband's arms. But it was tradition, just like feeding each other honey cake, as they'd done earlier.

The intimacy of breaking off a piece of cake and sliding it between Alar's parted lips had made her cheeks burn. She'd shared the same ritual with Dunchadh years earlier and found it embarrassing then too. But now, she had to get through the dancing.

Just play the role you were taught. Smile, dance, and act the part.

The musicians were playing a slow, lilting melody, and she and Alar began a traditional Marav dance—one where the partners moved around each other in slow steps while holding eye contact. They danced to one song, and then another, finally returning to the high seat when the musicians struck up a livelier tune.

On the way back to her seat, Lara caught sight of Mirren and Torran again.

The enforcer appeared to be urging her to dance with him. Yet, the lass, her face flushed, shook her head. Torran stepped closer, murmuring something, and Mirren answered him sharply. She then spun on her heel and pushed through the crowd.

Lara watched the lass go, her chest constricting.

No, the threads of trust weren't so easily spun. She knew that as well as her handmaid did.

Sitting down upon the high seat, she took the goblet of wine Alar passed her.

"Your eyes are shadowed," he observed. "Am I such a bad dancer?"

His comment roused her, and she blinked. "No," she murmured. "My mind is occupied by thoughts of our campaign," she lied. "I find it difficult to focus on much else these days."

"We'll be marching north soon enough," he replied with a half-smile. "You should enjoy the peace and comfort … while you can."

Easy for him to say. Impossible for her though. An awkward pause followed before she cleared her throat. "You dance well … who taught you?"

His features tightened slightly. "My mother."

"Struana?"

"Aye."

"You took your mother's name … rather than your father's. That's unusual."

He gave a soft snort. "It was necessary … since my father was Shee."

Of course. "Do you know his name?"

He shook his head, glancing away. He didn't want to talk about his father; that much was clear—and understandable.

19: WHAT ARE YOU WAITING FOR?

"IT'S GETTING LATE. Shall we retire?"

Panic surged up Lara's throat. She'd been dreading this moment all day—and finally, it had arrived. Her mind scrambled as she desperately tried to think of an excuse, one that would delay her performing her wifely duties.

But her mind went blank.

There was no getting out of this.

Swallowing the hard lump that had just lodged like gristle in her throat, she managed a tight nod.

A moment later, Alar smoothly rose to his feet and held out his hand. Dizziness washed over her as she took it—fearing her own was clammy—and stood up.

The dancing had ended, and everyone now sat at the long tables once more, lingering over wine, mead, and ale. Meanwhile, the musicians played a gentle, beguiling melody. The music was likely meant to be seductive, but instead, it only served to remind her of the humiliation that lay ahead.

You're doing this for Albia, she reminded herself doggedly. *Keep that in mind when he ruts you.*

Her pulse went wild then. That didn't help.

As they stepped down from the high seat, Lara's gaze flicked to where Bree and Cailean were sitting together now at the far end of the table. Skaal sprawled by the fire behind them, her large paws holding down an ox bone she gnawed upon. The chief-enforcer had slung his arm around his wife's shoulders, and Bree was leaning into him. They looked so right together, and Lara's heart squeezed.

Once, she'd dreamed of finding an epic love like they had, but that wasn't to be her destiny.

Cailean scowled at the prince consort, while Bree ignored Alar completely, focusing instead on Lara.

Her friend knew enough of Lara's history to understand what tonight was costing her.

Lara attempted a shaky smile yet failed.

Leaving the hall, the newly handfasted couple climbed the narrow, winding steps of the broch to the topmost level, where the High Queen's extensive quarters lay.

When they entered her alcove, Alar surveyed his surroundings with interest. "Nice," he murmured. "Although less adorned than I expected."

Surprised by his reaction, Lara looked at her alcove with fresh eyes. Sheepskins covered the floors, and colorful hangings and tapestries hung from the stacked-stone walls. This space had once belonged to her parents, but after she'd moved in, she made it her own. It felt wrong to live with her mother and father's belongings around her, as if their shades lingered.

The large alcove had a sleeping nook in one corner and two additional alcoves leading off it. One was a space where she or her husband could bathe in a large iron tub, and the other was a study or private meeting space.

It was her sanctuary, the place she could retreat to for a short while to escape the weight of attention that usually rested upon her shoulders.

But it wouldn't be hers alone any longer.

"I prefer simplicity," she replied, wishing her heart wasn't slamming against her ribs like a trow with a pick, digging itself a fresh knowe.

His gaze settled upon her. "Nervous?"

"A little." Gods, her voice sounded like a sheep's bleat.

"Shall I pour us some wine?"

"No, I'll do it." She moved over to where Florie had brought up a clay jug of her favorite plum wine. She then poured them both large cups. They'd both drunk sparingly over the evening. Earlier, she'd told herself that it was best to stay sharp—but now, she wanted something, anything, to help calm her.

Panic lay just beneath the surface, like a lurking aughisky— waiting.

Handing Alar his wine, she then raised her cup to her lips and took a long draft.

He then drank from his before blinking. "Mother, this is strong enough to fell a troll."

Lara took another gulp. *Not strong enough.*

He gestured to the two high-backed wooden chairs that flanked the flickering hearth. "Do you want to sit?"

Grateful to be able to flee to a chair rather than the shadowy sleeping nook to their right, Lara hurried over to the fire and seated herself.

Sinking down into the chair opposite, Alar eyed her. "It's all right," he said, his lips curving. "I'm not going to maul you."

Her blood started to roar in her ears, and she took yet another large swallow of wine. "You aren't?"

His expression sobered then. A groove etched between his dark brows as he continued to study her.

Lara made a choking sound. "For the love of the Gods, do you have to stare so? You're like a wolf sizing up its next meal."

He snorted. "Sorry. After years amongst the wulvers, I've adopted many of their ways."

"Aye, well … can you look elsewhere?"

"Maybe I don't want to. You are lovely to look upon."

Her fingers clenched at her cup. By the Gods, it was starting.

He leaned forward, his elbows resting on his thighs. "I will do my best to make tonight easy for you."

The wild urge to laugh ripped through her. *Easy?*

Downing the last of her wine, she set the cup down on the hearth with a thump. She then stood up and moved back from the fireplace. Heat flowed through her now, giving her the courage she needed.

The sooner they consummated their union, the sooner they could focus on their campaign to take Strath.

"Right then." She tugged at the laces on the side of her fitted, ankle-length tunic. "Let's get started."

What are you doing? Ignoring the screaming in her head, she loosened the last of the laces and wriggled out of the tunic. Then, clad only in a thin sleeveless shift that reached mid-thigh, she began tearing off the golden arm rings she'd donned for today's celebrations, tossing them carelessly onto the sheepskins at her feet. Afterward, she tore off the restrictive torque from around her throat.

Breathing hard, she looked Alar's way once more.

He hadn't moved from before the fire.

"Come on," she challenged him. "What are you waiting for?"

A moment passed before he rose smoothly to his feet. He then cocked an eyebrow, a challenge glinting in his eyes.

Her heart kicked violently, dizziness sweeping over her. This was false courage. Indeed, her heart quailed as he unlaced his vest and shrugged it off. He was now clad in nothing but tight leather breeches.

The first thing she noticed was the wolf's head tattoo inked over the left side of his chest. It had been done by a master, in exquisite detail. The wolf's jaws were open, revealing sharp teeth, although it was the beast's eyes that held her fast.

For a moment, they appeared to glow red in the firelight.

Lara blinked. *No, surely not.*

She was loath to admit it, but he had a beautiful body, graceful yet strong. However, when her gaze traveled down the smooth, sculpted muscle of his lean torso, to where his breeches sat low on his hips, it settled upon a bulge at his crotch.

Those trousers left little to the imagination.

He then took a step toward her, and Lara's bravery fled. Panic slammed into her breastbone like a mallet. And then, suddenly, all the strength went out of her legs. Gasping for breath, she fell to her knees, onto the sheepskins.

"Lara?" A moment later, Alar was there, kneeling too, in front of her. There was no mockery in his eyes now, no teasing smile. "What is it?"

"Nothing," she choked out.

"You—"

"I'm all right."

"No, you aren't." He placed a steadying hand on her shoulder. "Breathe."

"I am," she snarled.

"Slowly." He ignored her venom. "Draw air in deeply through your nose … into your belly, not your chest." He paused for a moment, waiting until she complied. "Hold it for a few moments … and let it out slowly."

Choking down the urge to snap at him again, Lara obeyed. At first, it was hard; it felt as if a boulder sat on her chest. But then, her ribcage gradually loosened.

Breathing slowly and deeply, she lowered her gaze, focusing on where their knees nearly touched on the sheepskins. Her cheeks then started to burn. The Reaper take her, she'd just humiliated herself.

"Am I that terrifying?" he asked gently.

She swallowed hard. "It's not you."

A pause followed. "Dunchadh?"

She squeezed her eyes shut. Just the memory of her first husband's brutal hands and rending prick made her break out into a cold sweat—even three years on.

Silence followed before Alar gently took hold of her chin. He then raised her face so she met his gaze. "I heard the rumors about him."

She licked suddenly dry lips. "Rumors?"

His grey eyes glinted. "Aye … that he liked it rough."

Lara jolted before jerking free of his touch. She then lowered her gaze once more. "So, you know?"

"Aye … and I shall tell you this. It wasn't your fault."

Her chest tightened once more, her breathing coming in shallow gasps now. She hadn't expected him to ever say something like that; it confused her. Was there actually some decency in him?

"Look at me, Lara."

With an effort, she obeyed.

His gaze was deadly serious now. "We don't have to do this."

Her chest heaved. He was giving her a way out, and she longed to take it, but there was no escaping her obligation. "We must lie together," she managed. "Or the Gods will curse us."

He gave a soft snort.

"They will!"

"I didn't realize you were so devout."

She swallowed hard. How she wished she weren't, but her mother had brought her up to respect The Five in all things, and to fear their wrath. She and Alar were handfasted, and the Gods were waiting for them to consummate their union. The Mother and The Maiden would withhold their blessings if it didn't happen. She might never take back the North then. "I'd rather not lie with you … but it must be done."

She clamped her lips shut then. Curse her, she wasn't supposed to admit that.

Alar grimaced. "I prefer my women willing." She didn't answer, and he eyed her. "I repeat … we don't have to lie together." Something flickered across his face then, and she wondered if he regretted being so 'understanding' about this. If they didn't lie together, they weren't really husband and wife. He knew that as well as she.

"Aye, we do."

"But you don't—"

"Just get on with it, Alar!"

Long moments passed before he raked a hand through his hair and murmured a curse under his breath. "Are you *sure?*" he asked, eyeing her with exasperation.

She nodded, not trusting herself to speak.

"You're not going to start shrieking the moment I touch you?"

"No."

"I won't hurt you … but you must tell me if you want me to stop."

She managed another, jerky, nod. "I will."

Another silence fell, drawing out for a long while.

Lara was beginning to wonder if he'd heed her—and tried to fight the relief that washed over her at the thought he might not—when he reached out, stroking the hair that hung in her face with his fingertips.

She remained frozen, as still as a standing stone, even as her heart bucked wildly. No, she wouldn't shriek, but it took all her will not to shrink away from his touch. He promised he wouldn't hurt her, but what if he was lying?

Courage.

His fingers traced down her cheek before following the line of her jaw. He moved then—shifting behind her now and sweeping the curtain of her hair aside—so he could explore her neck and shoulder.

His caress was light, and Lara shivered. His calmness soothed her. Maybe this wasn't going to be an ordeal, after all. However, when his lips brushed her neck, she jolted.

"You have beautiful skin," he murmured, as his breath feathered across her neck. "Like milk."

She swallowed, suddenly faint. And when he dragged his lips down to her right shoulder and gently nipped her skin with his teeth, she started to tremble.

"Do you want me to stop?" he asked as his hands skimmed down her arms.

Lara closed her eyes. "No," she managed. "Go on."

"Relax, lass." The teasing note had returned to his voice. "And let me teach you a thing or two."

Heat flushed through her. The arrogance of the man.

She murmured a curse under her breath, and he laughed, his breath feathering against her shoulder. And then his hands slid to her torso. The thin linen of her undertunic provided a flimsy barrier, and the heat of his palms scorched her skin. He moved up, over the arch of her ribcage, before he cupped her breasts with both hands.

And then, as he stroked her nipples with his thumbs, his lips traveled back up her neck. A moment later, his tongue explored the shell of her ear.

Lara's breathing caught. She didn't want to like what he was doing, yet her body suddenly felt as if it were melting. Her nipples became hard and sensitive as he continued to stroke them, her breasts heavy. All the while, she was aware of the heat of his body like a furnace against her back.

A long, shuddering sigh escaped her.

"That's it … ease into it," Alar whispered as he pushed her hair to the other side and lavished attention on her neck and other shoulder. "You'll enjoy this. I promise."

Lara swallowed, not trusting herself to speak. He was taking his time, allowing her to get used to him. He'd sworn he'd treat her gently, and he was. Even so, her pulse still fluttered like a trapped moth.

Eventually, Alar moved so that he faced her once more. Her eyes flickered open, her gaze meeting his.

His lips curved, although his eyes were hooded now.

His expression made her breathing grow shallow. An odd sensation, almost like excitement, quickened in her lower belly.

What was this?

He then gestured for her to change position so that her legs were no longer folded underneath her. And when she stretched her legs out on the sheepskin, he started to caress her ankles and calves. Slowly, he pushed up the hem of the tunic as he worked his way up her legs.

Lara watched his progress. He took his time, exploring her skin with exquisite slowness. And as he did, she started to feel overly warm and flustered.

What was wrong with her? She didn't feel like herself at all.

Eventually, he gently parted her legs and pushed the tunic up farther so that it bunched around her hips—and when he did, panic twisted under her ribs. Her body went rigid as she leaned back on her hands, her fingers digging into the sheepskin.

The Mother forgive her, she wasn't ready for what would come next—for rough fingers, probing, invading, hurting.

20: ONLY YOU AND ME

"EASY, LARA." ALAR stroked his fingers up the inside of one of her thighs. His fingers brushed the nest of soft auburn hair between her legs then, and she squeaked. He glanced up at her, his iron gaze glinting, before he stroked her again in the same place. This time, she bit down on her lower lip.

She couldn't believe she'd made such a noise.

And then, his finger slid down, into the cleft between her spread thighs.

She gasped, a tremor rippling through her.

In response, Alar murmured something she didn't catch under his breath. A moment later, he parted her with his other hand, exposing her fully to his hot gaze.

Lara's eyes flickered shut, humiliation washing over her. What an idiot she was. Why had she insisted they do this?

He started to caress her with the pad of a finger then, stroking, rubbing, and circling. Gently.

Sensation clutched at her lower belly, and her eyes snapped open to find Alar looking up at her, watching her reaction. "How's that then?"

She stared back at him before swallowing hard. Words failed her.

In return, he favored her with a wicked smile. He lifted his other hand then, and, while continuing to stroke her, slid a long finger into her. "And this?"

Lara shuddered, and she bit down hard on her lower lip. *Gods!*

He moved his finger in and out of her before inserting another. A moment later, he curled his fingers up, touching a place deep inside her that made her choke back a gasp. She became aware then of just how aroused she was. Legs splayed wide, she stared down at where his hands slowly worked her. Wet sounds filled the alcove. This shouldn't feel so delicious, but it did. Her thighs started to tremble, tension coiling low in her belly.

Her gasp filled the alcove as she climbed to the brink. She couldn't help it; she was pushing her hips against him now, encouraging him deeper, while his finger circled the swollen pearl of flesh above her hungry quim.

"Aye," he murmured, a rasp to his voice. "That's it … let go."

A moment later, she did. Her head fell back, her body shuddering as pleasure crested like a wave and then pulsed through her loins.

Trembling, she collapsed onto the sheepskin, panting. She looked up at Alar then, but he wasn't looking at her. Instead, he was watching the fire, his gaze wide.

"What is it?" Lara gasped, breathless from her climax.

"The fire in the hearth just flared bright," he replied. "As did the burning cressets."

She froze. *Shit.* Had the flames surrounding her responded to her loss of control? No, that couldn't be right. "It's windy outdoors," she answered, still breathless. "There must have been a draft."

He inclined his head, considering her explanation for a moment before accepting it. And then, as she lay there, spread out before him, her body flushed and damp with sweat, he rose smoothly to his feet.

A moment later, he started unlacing his breeches.

Lara couldn't help it; her gaze slid down his lean torso to where the bold outline of his erection pressed against snug leather. Earlier, she'd panicked at the sight of his leather-clad groin, but she didn't now. Instead, curiosity wreathed up.

She couldn't believe she wanted to see him, but she did.

Alar pushed down his breeches and kicked them aside. His shaft had sprung up against his belly—long, thick, and slightly tapered. Its end leaked. Alar sank to his knees before her and took himself in hand, sliding his fist up and down its swollen length.

Lara started to sweat.

What a sight.

"Are you ready?" His voice was throaty, his gaze ravenous now. "Or shall I tease you for a bit longer?"

Sweat beaded across her chest at the sensual promise in his words. There was a traitorous part of her that wanted to rise to the challenge and ask him to do just that. However, she reminded herself that they needed to get this over with.

"I'm ready," she replied huskily. "If you are?"

The smile he gave her then made her pulse go wild. "Oh, aye," he murmured. "You have no idea, lass."

The Mother preserve me.

He shifted between her spread thighs once more and positioned the slick head of his rod at her entrance. But as he did so, fear flickered up again. It had hurt when Dunchadh took her. Hot, tearing agony that went on and on. Would there be pain now too?

Holding her gaze, a teasing smile still tugging at his lips, Alar eased himself into her. She'd tensed, and was tight, but he didn't rush her. Instead, he slowly rolled his hips, gently pressing against her.

And eventually, she opened for him.

Once again, his calmness quieted her fear, as did his ability to bring humor into this intimate moment.

However, the feel of his solid heat sliding deep, stretching her, made a whimper claw up her throat.

When he was all the way in, he let her adjust to him. Moments slid by, and then he undulated his hips. Pleasure rippled through her lower belly. Wetness flooded her loins, and she started to tremble.

Alar stared down at her, sweat glistening on his forehead and cheeks. He wasn't smiling now. Instead, his lean face was taut, his skin pulled tight across his high cheekbones. He almost looked as if he were in pain.

"Are you all right?" she asked breathlessly.

"Aye." His grey eyes gleamed as they held her fast. "Words fail me."

Lara couldn't help it; she gave a soft snort. "Well, that'll be a first."

His lips twitched. "Sometimes, talk isn't what's needed." And then he began to ride her in slow, deep strokes, holding her thighs apart as he did so.

Lara swallowed a groan. She'd only recently peaked, but with each thrust, something started to build inside her once more. Her eyes fluttered shut. The way he filled her, stretched her. She wanted more of him. And like earlier, she pushed up against him then, encouraging him.

Grunting, Alar pushed one of her legs up, holding it fast under the knee, so that he could penetrate deeper.

She bit down on her lower lip, her thighs trembling as tension coiled again. Moments later, wild pleasure twisted in her womb. She gave a strangled cry.

He rolled his hips and plunged into her again. "That's good, is it?"

"Gods!" she gasped.

His lips curved into a wicked, sensual smile. "The Five aren't here tonight, Lara," he murmured. "Only you and me."

The gravelly edge to his voice made her stomach muscles clench. His words were blasphemy, yet they sounded like a promise.

He took her in deep, measured strokes that stoked the fire in her belly.

Lara stared up at him, transfixed. She had no idea sex could feel like this. After Dunchadh, she'd looked upon a man's prick as an instrument of domination and torture. Tonight, she discovered that not all lovers were like her first husband. Some actually wanted to give their woman pleasure.

And as Alar took her, his own self-control frayed.

Panting, she continued to watch his face, fascinated. His expression was raw, almost feral. Sweat now gleamed upon his torso, his lean frame quivering as he climbed toward his own climax. "Fuck!" he choked out.

His reaction unleashed her, and she bucked against him, slapping a hand over her mouth to smother a cry.

Alar thrust deep one last time while his body arched back.

The cords of his neck tightened, and a nerve flickered in his cheek. He squeezed his eyes shut, his body trembling as he spilled inside her.

"I meant to be gentler than that."

Lara pushed herself off his sweat-damp chest, her gaze settling on Alar's face. He lay on his back on the sheepskins. Following their coupling, they'd collapsed there—and to her surprise, he'd pulled her close. There they'd lain, the rasp of their breathing joining the crackle of the hearth. "You *were* gentle," she assured him.

Alar pulled a face. "At the start maybe ... but then I got carried away."

Her belly fluttered. Aye, he had. And curse her, she'd enjoyed seeing his mask slip.

"Thank you," she said, averting her gaze then. "I was dreading that more than you know."

He huffed. "I won't take that personally."

"Please don't."

Her hand slid across his smooth chest, tracing the lines of the wolf's head tattoo. Once again, those eyes seemed to stare directly at her. Unnerved, she slid her fingertips up, across his collarbone, to the silvered scar upon his throat. She shouldn't be touching him so boldly, but in the aftermath of their coupling, she couldn't help herself. The memory of his tale about being strung up on that pine and left to die made something deep in her chest tighten.

Her fingers continued their leisurely progress, up, to the second scar. This one slashed down from his forehead to almost parallel with his mouth. "Will you tell me how you got this?" she asked softly.

He didn't answer, and her gaze lifted to meet his.

He pulled a face, and she braced herself for his refusal.

However, a moment later, he surprised her by answering. "When I was a bairn, my mother and I lived amongst others … in a village near Dorne Forest. We shared a bothy with my grandparents. My grandfather was a woodcutter … a big man with a soft heart." Something flickered in the depths of his iron eyes then. "He suspected that his grandson wasn't *right*. My mother refused to speak about my father … but my grandparents had an idea of what had happened. They never shunned us though."

He paused then, his jaw tightening. "As I grew from an infant to a child, the villagers grew suspicious. They whispered that I was strange and sly … that the woodcutter's wild daughter had fucked someone she shouldn't have."

Lara winced. His expression had hardened now. Suddenly, she wished she hadn't asked about the scar.

"One day, my grandfather took me to the village market," he went on. "I was no older than four … and excited by all the sights and sounds. But then, one of the villagers … the ironsmith … came at me with a blade, shouting that a half-blood couldn't be allowed to live. He slashed my face … but when he tried to stab me through the chest, my grandfather stopped the blade. It severed a large vein in his neck … and he bled out then and there."

Lara stiffened, her skin prickling at the brutality of his tale.

"The local chieftain had the ironsmith hanged for what he did … but things were never the same between our family and the villagers after that." Reaching up, Alar traced that silvered scar with his thumb. "And there you have it."

Lara swallowed, her throat suddenly tight. "I'm sorry," she whispered.

Irritation flickered over his face. "Why? It wasn't your doing."

"No, but I shouldn't have asked."

His lips quirked then. "You're curious about the man you married," he replied, his voice softening. "It's understandable."

21: A FORMIDABLE ALLY

STIRRING AWAKE, LARA found herself face down, sprawled amongst the furs in her sleeping nook. For a moment, she lay there, enjoying the sensation of languid wellbeing, before memories from the night before crept in.

She squeezed her eyes tightly shut then, heat rolling over her as she recalled every lewd thing Alar had done to her. How would she be able to look his way without turning the color of a plum?

Eventually, she opened her eyes and rolled onto her side.

The cressets had all gone out, yet the glow of the embers in the hearth cast a soft, ruddy light over the alcove. She was naked in the sleeping nook—as was the man who lay beside her. Like her, Alar slept on his belly, and Lara found herself studying him.

Mirren had told her once that folk who slept on their stomachs did so to seek comfort. It was a defensive position, revealing someone who didn't trust easily.

The irony wasn't lost on her. They had something in common, after all, it seemed.

Images crept back in then, of their coupling. Gods, the pleasure he'd given her. Brutally, she shoved the torrid memories aside. *The handfasting night is done with now*, she reminded herself firmly. *It's time to get to work.*

The furs had slipped off Alar in the night, and her gaze traveled along the length of his body. His buttocks were tight and muscular, his limbs long and finely muscled. And the long hair that spilled over his shoulders and down his back was the color of a raven's wing.

When he was awake, Alar had a coiled tension to him, but asleep, he looked different.

Younger.

He twitched then, waking up.

Hastily, Lara pulled one of the furs over herself to cover her nakedness. It was pointless really, since he'd already seen everything, but it made her feel more comfortable. More in control of things.

With a groan, he rolled over onto his back and gave a long, cat-like stretch. "Shades," he murmured. "I slept like a hibernating trow."

Lara's mouth curved. "Fortunately, you don't snore like one." When she was a bairn, her mother had told her that the rolling boom of thunder during a summer storm was the sound of trows snoring. The creatures hid away in their knowes during the warmer months, for sun on their skin would turn them to stone. However, ever since the Shee had taken the North, things had changed. News reached Duncrag regularly that trows ventured out in sunlight, and powries strayed far from their ruins. The reminder made Lara's mood sober.

With this man's help, she'd put things right.

"I'll be holding a council meeting this afternoon," she said then. "And you'll join us."

His lips quirked. "Of course."

"There's still so much to organize before we head north," she went on, ignoring the teasing edge to his voice. "We've had the ironsmiths working double shifts ever since we got back … and Captain mac Tav has managed to recruit more warriors from The Wolds. They're young … and green … but, hopefully, they should be ready in time."

"And what is the mood amongst your council these days?"

Lara frowned, wariness rising. "They are behind me."

"Really? Last time I joined one of your meetings, the atmosphere was … frosty."

"Aye, well … they were upset … concerned I'd made the wrong choice."

"They've forgiven you?"

"Aye."

That was a wee lie—for although she was getting along better with her advisors these days, they still weren't happy about the alliance she made. But once she drove the Shee from The Uplands, they would be.

"And what of the people of Duncrag? We didn't get a warm welcome upon our arrival."

Lara pursed her lips. "They've never had such close contact with wulvers before. Give them time."

"Perhaps we need to hurry things along."

Her gaze narrowed. "How exactly?"

He smiled. "Don't look so suspicious. I'm only suggesting we take a walk through the fort this morning. I'll take my captains with me … you bring your council. Seeing Marav and wulvers walking together, united, might help them thaw."

Lara stepped out into the overcast morning and pulled her fur cloak tightly about her. She and Alar had just breakfasted on oatcakes, butter, and honey together. Later, they'd meet with her council in the hall, as promised.

But now, she was, reluctantly, taking his advice.

He was right. They couldn't hide in her broch. The High Queen and the prince consort had to be visible. They had to encourage the residents of Duncrag to accept change. The wulvers were here to stay.

Her breathing grew shallow then.

Why did she feel as if she'd crossed a river and then burned the bridge down behind her?

Alar stepped up to her side, clad in black leather and armed with his blades, as usual. She eyed him, considering whether the events of the night before had changed her opinion of the Half-blood.

They had.

It wasn't just the sex—although the fact that he'd treated her gently and let it be her choice had surprised her—but that they'd both lowered their guard around each other. She'd revealed a vulnerability he could have exploited, while he'd told her a little about his past, a tale he didn't usually share by all accounts.

She still didn't trust him, and whenever their conversation shifted to war or politics, they often clashed. But the fact remained that Alar was a strong ally.

His gaze glinted as it met hers. "Ready?"

She nodded. "Let's face them."

They crossed the yard to the gates, following Cailean and Torran—and Skaal. Bree and Roth flanked the royal couple, while Lyall and Dolph strode behind them. The rest of the High Queen's council brought up the rear.

As soon as they left the broch's perimeter behind and stepped out onto The Thoroughfare, they drew a crowd.

That was a good thing, even if the atmosphere was strained. Bairns clung to their mothers' skirts as they eyed the wulvers, while the men and women of Duncrag watched their High Queen with resentment simmering in their eyes.

Lara pretended not to notice. Instead, she spoke brightly to them, stopping at intervals on the way down the hill to introduce her husband and his captains, and to assure them that the wulvers would help them win back the North.

It was hard work.

Many of those she approached were too distracted by the sight of the wulvers, Lyall especially—for he was a hulking figure—to concentrate on her words. Usually, it was Cailean's fae hound who drew the eye. But today, no one paid Skaal much attention.

"Where will the wulvers live once The Uplands are reclaimed?" One man asked, his tone belligerent. He was one of the ironsmiths, who'd ventured out of his forge wearing a soot-covered apron. "Will they remain here?"

"Aye," Lara replied with more conviction than she felt. In truth, she and Alar hadn't discussed what would happen afterward—she could only deal with one obstacle at a time—but this smith wanted a clear answer. "And you will welcome them."

"And what will they eat?"

"The same food as you. There's plenty for us all." Indeed, the fields around Duncrag were fertile, and it had been a good harvest this year. No one in this fort would go hungry.

"We are good at fishing," Lyall said then, his gravelly voice carrying across the crowd. "And we are happy to share our catches with you all."

The man scowled at this, eying the wulver captain as if he'd just offered him a turd.

"Wulvers aren't savages," Alar said smoothly, speaking up for the first time. "They're peaceloving by nature. They'd have lived alongside you years ago, if you hadn't shunned their kindness and driven them out."

Dolph growled something under his breath then, while a rumble went through the surrounding crowd.

"Gone are the days when the Marav had nothing to do with faerie creatures," her husband continued. "The world has changed … and we must adapt … or the Raven Queen will march upon Duncrag and take it for her own." He paused then. "Would you rather wulvers shared this fort with you … or that the Shee became your masters?"

Muttering began then, and they moved on.

Leaving the top terrace of Duncrag behind, they walked through the two levels of the wulver encampment. Here, Alar called for more of his brothers and sisters to join them. Lara's gut tightened when they did.

This 'stroll' wasn't going well, and the lower levels of Duncrag were rougher than the top ones. She hoped Alar knew what he was doing. At the same time, she wanted the wulvers with her. The unfiltered hostility toward their new allies was starting to leave a bitter taste in her mouth. This had always been a Marav problem: the belief that they were superior to the other races who inhabited Albia.

But their prejudice couldn't continue.

Farther down, they walked past the middens, where their Shee prisoners pushed barrows of rotting food, excrement, and offal over to deep pits before emptying them.

Lara wrinkled her nose. She usually only ever passed the middens on horseback and would urge Bracken into a brisk trot to escape the stench. But today she was on foot, and there was no escaping the putrid odors that enveloped her.

And as they walked by, she marked the way Alar watched the Shee.

"They fascinate you, don't they?"

His head jerked her way. "Not really."

She huffed. "You must want to ask them about your father."

An emotion she couldn't quite place rippled across his face. "Why would I?"

"Because everyone wants to know where they came from." She paused then. "I'm surprised your mother didn't tell you about him."

"Well, she didn't."

His answer was blunt, his tone a warning, and she heeded it. She'd touched a raw nerve.

They left the middens behind and descended lower still. The roundhouses flanking The Thoroughfare crowded closer together here, and half-naked bairns chased each other amongst the crowds. The air was only slightly less foul than the cesspits.

"Betrayer!" A woman shouted then from the front of the crowd. She was one of the fort elders, her white hair pulled back into braids, her dark eyes as sharp as flints of granite. "You will drag us all into darkness!"

Lara halted, her skin prickling at the woman's venom.

The gathering crowd lining the road rumbled with anger now, like an approaching storm. She couldn't walk on. She had to address this.

"My father already did that," she replied, her voice cutting through the muttering that swelled around them. "He angered the Shee and brought the Raven Queen's wrath down on us. And now they've allied themselves with trows and powries, and Gods-know who else." She paused, her pulse thumping against her ribs. "If we don't make strong allies ourselves, we'll never take back The Uplands. Worse still, The Wolds could be overrun."

Some of the faces around them screwed up. A man a few yards away even spat on the ground.

"Craven bitch," someone shouted from the back.

"Traitor!"

"Your High Queen didn't *want* to marry me," Alar cut in. To Lara's surprise, he'd stepped close to her, his stance protective as his gaze swept over the press of people. "But she did it anyway, to save *your* ungrateful lives. She's selfless and brave. Is this how you thank her?"

He broke off then as a brittle hush settled over the crowd. Meanwhile, Lara's chest tightened. She should be vexed that he'd stepped in to defend her, yet she wasn't. Instead, a knot deep within her chest loosened. No man had ever spoken up for her like this.

"Don't think the Shee aren't coming for you all," Alar went on, an edge to his voice now. "Don't stand here so smug and self-righteous. Duncrag isn't untouchable. Mor is merely sharpening her blade … and soon she'll march on The Wolds. When she gets here—*if* she gets here—there will be no mercy."

22: HARBORING SECRETS

ALAR STRODE OUT of the broch into the grey afternoon. The temperature had dropped. His breath steamed in the chill air, and the cold prickled his bare arms. Ignoring it, he made his way across the yard toward the gate.

On the way, he passed the chief-enforcer and his second-in-command. Cailean and Torran had been talking, but they halted their conversation as he walked by, their hard gazes tracking him.

Alar ignored the enforcers.

Let them stare.

"Off for another stroll?" the chief-enforcer called out as Alar reached the stone arch that led out of the enclosure and onto The Thoroughfare beyond.

"Aye."

"Without an escort this time?"

"I don't need one."

And he didn't. Alar carried his fighting daggers strapped to his back. Anyone foolish enough to take him on would regret it soon enough.

Neither man replied to this, and he walked on.

However, Skaal, who'd been sniffing at something by a nearby wall, spied Alar. The fae hound's ears pricked, and she trotted toward him.

"Skaal!" Cailean barked. "Stay!"

Surprisingly, the fae hound checked her stride before halting. Then, casting the chief-enforcer a reproachful look, she sat down.

Her longing stare followed Alar as he departed.

Outside the walls of the broch, he breathed a little easier.

After decades of living wild, amongst the dark forests of The Uplands, he wasn't used to being confined. Like all the brochs of Albia, Duncrag was a stifling, windowless tomb. The afternoon was dull and damp, but it was preferable to the heavy air within, acrid with peat smoke. There were numerous vents throughout the broch to let out the smoke, but there weren't nearly enough.

But that wasn't the only reason he'd slipped away this afternoon.

He needed some respite—from *her*.

The events of the past day had unsettled him. He had to find some detachment. Some distance.

He'd told himself he'd be careful with Lara, wary of what he told her, what he revealed about his past. But, already, he'd said too much. His lovely young wife had a way of prying things out of him. Before he knew it, he'd told her about how he'd gotten the scar on his face. He never told *anyone* that story.

Her vulnerability had done something to him. Her last husband had damaged her. And she tried to hide it, but she was lonely. She longed to let someone in—even the likes of him. Alar had been ready to do his duty and fuck her—and enjoy it too—but he hadn't been prepared for how it had made him feel.

He'd lost control. That couldn't happen again. Now that their union had been consummated, he wouldn't touch her again for a while.

And there was that strange incident with the fire. When she'd climaxed the first time, he'd been sure the flames in the hearth and in the cressets burning on the walls had flared bright. It reminded him of the fire he'd seen spark in her ring.

Curious.

There was definitely more to Lara mac Talorc than met the eye.

Jaw set, Alar headed off down The Thoroughfare. Along the way, he passed local women, wearing simple sleeveless tunics with woolen shawls to ward off the chill, who carried wicker baskets under their arms as they shopped.

Heads turned as he walked by. He caught the blend of fascination and distrust in the women's gazes—not that different from the way his wife looked at him.

After last night though, he'd sensed a change in Lara. There had been a camaraderie between them as they rode side by side through the fort that morning. She'd defended the wulvers' presence here, and he'd stepped in when she needed support.

She was still wary, but she was opening to him—like a timid flower opening to the early spring sun. She wanted to trust someone, even him.

She should be more careful … and so should I.

Alar continued walking, aware of the gazes that tracked him.

He'd given a few speeches during their walk through the fort that morning. The residents of Duncrag still didn't know what to make of the Half-blood. Nonetheless, they hadn't expected to see him out alone later in the day.

They all minded him though.

Deep in thought, Alar kept moving. He descended from the top level, through to where his brothers and sisters were housed. The aroma of smoking fish greeted him, a welcoming and familiar smell. Spying their leader, the wulvers called out to him. He waved back but didn't slow his stride.

Restlessness churned through him, as did the urge to break into a run. He wanted to get out of this stinking fort, to race over the fresh green hills outside Duncrag—sprint until exhaustion beat him down. Until thoughts of Lara no longer unsettled him.

Instead, he kept walking. And before he knew it, his feet had carried him down to the middens. Halting on the edge of them, he screwed up his face at the foul smells drifting across from the pits.

The skin on his back started to prickle then. Glancing over his shoulder, he spied two black-clad enforcers following him at a discreet distance. He'd been so lost in his brooding that he hadn't noticed them earlier. Cailean obviously thought he needed watching.

Irritated, Alar cut his gaze away, his attention traveling to where the Shee captives shoved piles of foul matter into barrows before wheeling them over to the pits.

And then, acting on instinct, he started walking toward them.

The stench grew eyewatering as he approached, and he took care to breathe through his mouth. His step slowed then. What was he doing?

A handful of enforcers oversaw the captives, their hands resting casually on the hilts of the swords at their hips. Blue-clad bards stood behind them, their voices merging into a low dirge that made the hair on the back of Alar's arms tingle.

Unlike for the Shee—who worked with pinched faces, their shoulders rounded—the earth magic surrounding them didn't press down on him like a smothering blanket. All the same, the odor of pine and ash that now blended with the reek of the cesspits put him on edge. He'd lived apart from the Marav and their druids for decades; it would take time to grow accustomed to their ways again.

Halting a few yards back, Alar did his best to ignore both the stench and the earth magic, his gaze traveling to where a Shee female with long braided black hair shoveled muck into a barrow.

Like the others, she wore a leather collar around her throat— rather than an iron one like slaves wore—with a rope attached. The ropes tied to each captive snaked along the ground and were secured to a heavy iron stake that had been driven into the ground.

The enforcers weren't taking any chances with these prisoners.

Standing in the shadow of a large conical-roofed storehouse, he folded his arms across his chest, observing the female.

She was tall, as most Shee females were—nearly his height—and as slender as a blade, although having fought her, he knew she was much stronger than she looked. She'd moved with a fluidity the Marav lacked, her thin steel longsword a blur in the darkness.

As skilled as Alar was, it had been an effort to best her.

Feeling his gaze upon her, Fern Sablebane straightened up, her grey eyes, with their slitted pupils, narrowing when she saw him. Her proud features tightened, and her mouth puckered as if she'd just tasted something foul.

One of the enforcers barked at her, warning her to keep working, but she ignored him. Instead, her baleful gaze drilled into Alar. She likely hadn't forgiven him for branding her with his iron blade back in Doure.

Moving out of the shadow of the storehouse, he approached her.

"Watch yourself," an enforcer warned gruffly. "I wouldn't get too close … these goat-eyed fuckers move like greased eels."

Alar nodded, taking the man's point. He halted a few yards distant from Fern, his right hand rising to the grip of one of his daggers. A warning.

A nerve flickered on her smooth cheek. "Come to gloat, have you?"

"Not at all."

Around them, the noise of the others working—the scrape and squelch, and the creaking of wooden barrows—mingled with the rumble of a busy fort. They stood apart from the other prisoners and the watching druids. If they kept their voices low, they wouldn't be overheard.

Fern studied him for a few moments before uncertainty flared in her eyes.

Alar knew why. "I look like *him*, don't I?"

She jolted. "What?"

"It was dark when we fought … maybe you didn't get a proper look at my face. But when I learned your name, I knew."

Her fingers tightened around the shovel she gripped. She looked like she wanted to swing it in his face. "You speak in riddles," she growled.

Alar held her gaze, tension coiling between them.

Is this wise? He checked himself then. He shouldn't be here—but when he'd found himself at the middens, he'd been unable to stop himself. In truth, ever since he'd heard the name 'Sablebane', it had lodged in his head and given him no peace.

Turn around and leave.

Wise advice, but he didn't heed it.

"Look closely at my face again," he murmured. "Whom do I remind you of?"

Her slender throat worked, her slitted eyes narrowing as she stared back. And then, when her chest hitched, he knew she'd made the connection. "No," she whispered, her voice brittle now. "It *can't* be."

Alar's chest clenched. He'd spent a lifetime being treated as an aberration. He was used to it, but the horror in her eyes cut deep. Moments passed, and then he forced a smile. "It is."

"Cailean tells me you took a walk this afternoon."

Alar glanced up from where he'd been watching the flames dance in the hearth. He and Lara had retired to their alcove after supper and were relaxing together before bed. However, it hadn't taken his wife long to pounce. "Aye … I saw the two enforcers tailing me earlier," he replied, even as irritation speared him.

He'd known this conversation was coming, but wasn't in the mood for it.

"Why did you leave the broch without an escort?"

"I don't need one."

"Maybe not before you married me … but now you do." Seated opposite him, her slender fingers tightened around the cup of wine she held. "You can't just wander where you want anymore."

His irritation slid into annoyance.

He wouldn't have his movements restricted, even by her.

Sensing his rising temper, her brows arched. "What did you have to discuss with Fern Sablebane?"

He sighed, leaning back in his chair and crossing a booted ankle across his left knee. Here was the real reason she'd brought up this subject. "Aren't I allowed to have any secrets?"

"No," she replied. "Not any longer."

"It's personal."

"And I'm your wife."

"So, you harbor no secrets then?"

A flush rose upon her cheeks at his challenge. A moment later, she swallowed. The sudden vulnerability of her expression made him kick himself. *Stop being such a prick.*

"I lied this morning … when I told you I didn't know who my father was," he said finally. "His name is Wynn Sablebane. Fern is my sister."

Lara stilled. Her eyes grew large.

"You didn't notice my reaction in Doure when we learned her name?" he asked.

"Aye," she whispered. "You went as white as a shade." Silence fell then, drawing out before Lara cleared her throat. "So, Fern didn't know you're her half-brother?"

He shook his head, even as something deep in his chest twisted. "She wasn't overjoyed … if that's what you're getting at."

Lara studied him, and he wished she wouldn't. This conversation needed to end.

"How did you leave things?" she asked, her tone softening. Her sympathy made his gut clench. He didn't need her kindness.

"She knows I exist," he ground out. "Although, she wishes I didn't."

23: THE RIGHT PATH

"PREPARATIONS ARE TAKING longer than I thought." Roth's voice echoed through the lofty hall. "We won't be ready till well after Gateway."

"Your recruits should be improving by now, Captain." Seated next to Lara, Alar leaned back in his carven chair, his gaze veiled. "And since the ironsmiths work late every night, your armory must be bristling."

Roth shot the prince consort a glare before he shifted focus to Lara. "I suggest we delay this until the spring, My Queen," he said, his tone clipped. "After the snows have come and gone. There's less risk of the weather hindering us."

"The weather is more of a problem for the Shee than us," Alar responded. "It sounds to me, captain, as if you're making excuses."

Silence fell in the hall. It was mid-morning, two days after the handfasting. As usual, everyone had emptied out of this space so that the High Queen could hold her council in private. Only a couple of servants waited in the shadows by the doors leading to the entrance hall.

Lara exhaled sharply. Roth's attitude frustrated her. He'd promised they'd be prepared to march soon, but was now having second thoughts. She wondered then if he was being deliberately obstructive. Did he still resent her for spurning his advances? "We can't wait," she replied. "The Shee certainly won't."

Indeed, they all remembered Fern Sablebane's admission. The Shee would invade within the turn of a year. Lara had to make the first move.

Roth frowned. "But we—"

"Get the army ready, Captain," she cut him off. "I'm counting on you."

He stared back at her, his pale-blue eyes hardening. However, this time he held his tongue. Good. She didn't want excuses. Alar was right. Roth had enlisted many more warriors from the villages around Loch Lethe and Strathnich Forest than they'd expected. Earlier that morning, she'd watched from the walls as they trained in the yard below. Meanwhile, the fug of smoke from the forges hung over Duncrag these days.

No, their army wouldn't equal the number of wulvers—but it *had* to be enough.

"The peace envoy hasn't yet returned, My Queen," Annis spoke up then, her voice shattering the brittle silence. The chief-counsellor's round face was unusually strained this morning. "They should have sent word by now. Something is wrong."

Shifting in her seat, Lara could feel Alar's gaze on her, yet she deliberately avoided looking at him. He'd warned her she'd sent those druids and warriors to their deaths, but she wouldn't hear of it. She didn't want him to be right. "They have time, Annis," she said finally. "We need to trust in them."

"Without the support of the hill-tribes, taking The Uplands will be difficult," Cailean reminded her.

"Difficult … but far from impossible," Alar replied. "You have my army, remember?"

Cailean's jaw tightened. "What if it's not enough?"

"There's also the issue of the Slew," Gregor interjected gruffly. "You all seem to have forgotten that they've taken to straying from their burial grounds."

Lara's pulse fluttered in her throat. The chief-sacrificer was right. She'd been so occupied by political matters of late that she'd given little time to The Unforgiven.

"There haven't been any sightings of them in the past moon," Cailean answered.

Gregor scowled. "Aye, but Gateway's looming."

Lara began drumming the fingertips of her right hand on the table. The light of the cresset burning behind her glowed in the amber depths of the *Ord-ree seal.* "We aren't leaving until *after* Gateway, anyway," she reminded her council, tempering her irritation. They'd all agreed on this plan, but now they were having second thoughts. "The Unforgiven hopefully won't give us any problems."

Gregor didn't look convinced.

"I've been searching the archives for information about the Slew," Gil said then. "Nothing new has cropped up yet … but I can keep looking."

Lara glanced her archivist's way. Gil sat to Bree's left, his eyes watchful, as always. "Aye … do that," she answered with a nod. Perhaps their odd behavior could be explained. There was nothing to say it wasn't cyclical.

She then shifted her attention to her husband. "What do you think, Alar?"

He inclined his head. "About the Slew?"

"About everything we've talked about." She could feel Roth's glare boring into her; he was angry that she sought the prince consort's opinion rather than her captain's. She did, for her husband was a clever strategist.

Alar stroked his jaw as he considered her question. "Who knows what will happen with the Slew," he replied finally. "I wouldn't let them sway you. I agree with you, Lara. We should march before winter … not wait for the Shee to attack first." His gaze glinted as he met her eye. "My wulvers are primed … you need only say the word."

Warmth flared under Lara's ribs. Once again, she appreciated his support. Sometimes she felt like a lone reed in the wind. She itched to get her campaign underway. She had to show her people that her word meant something. She would take back what the Shee had stolen. She would protect them.

Alar understood what drove her. Why didn't everyone else?

"It's settled then," she said with a decisive nod, catching Roth's eye to ensure he heeded her. "We move after Gateway, as planned. We shall strike out from Dulross and march on Strath."

Tension rippled around the table, yet no one argued with her this time. Only the chief-sacrificer dared speak up. "If you are truly resolved to take this path, My Queen, I shall ensure my sacrificers begin a nightly vigil," Gregor muttered. "We're going to need the Gods on our side."

Gil was hunched over a stack of dusty parchments, with a manuscript brush made of feathers in hand, when Lara pushed aside the heavy curtain and entered the alcove.

Three years earlier, she'd put him in charge of looking after the jumble of scrolls in her father's possession that recorded the history of Albia. Barely six moons later, they'd discovered another cache of ancient parchments in a vault under the broch, near the healer's chamber, and Lara had moved him to larger quarters—one with four smaller alcoves off this one, where he could store the scrolls he was slowly working his way through.

Straightening up, the archivist pushed the wavy brown hair out of his eyes. "I didn't expect a visit from you at this hour, My Queen," he greeted her. His expression grew teasing then. "Tired of your husband already?"

Lara snorted. "My husband is training with his wulvers."

"After dark?"

"Aye … it's their way."

In truth, she found this habit odd, but she didn't question it. Alar wanted his wulvers to be fighting ready, and she appreciated his dedication. Even so, it meant that they spent little time together.

And to her surprise, she found herself missing his company. They hadn't been married long, yet she was more comfortable with him than she'd expected.

He hadn't touched her since the handfasting though, and she found that strange too. A part of her was relieved. He supported his wife while giving her the space she needed, and she was grateful. Nonetheless, there was a traitorous, soft part of her that felt rejected.

Rejected? Irritation spiked through her. *Listen to yourself.*

"Have you managed to find anything at all of note about the Slew?"

Gil raised an eyebrow at her abrupt change of subject, yet took the point. "A few mentions, here and there. However, so far, I've found only one scroll that goes into detail about them." He motioned to where a rolled parchment sat on the desk nearby.

"Can I take a look?"

He nodded, gesturing to the stool next to the desk.

Lara settled herself before it and carefully untied the leather thong around the scroll. Then, unfurling it, she began to read. It wasn't easy to follow, and she had to concentrate on the loopy script on the parchment and the archaic writing style. "This was written by my great-great-grandfather's steward," she murmured after reading the introduction.

"Aye ... it seems the man had a curiosity about spirits ... both malevolent and kind. There are many manuscripts here in his hand."

Lara nodded before she continued to read, letting Gil get back to work.

The document told of how the Slew were the spirits of those who'd committed terrible crimes in life. Shunned from both the

Underworld and the Otherworld, they either dwelled in the 'Threshold'—the liminal space between worlds—or they lingered around cairns, barrows, and graveyards, where the veil was at its thinnest. They were active at night and preyed upon the weak and fearful, and once a year, at Gateway, they took to the skies and hunted. Your best protection was to stay strong and healthy and not let fear into your heart. At Gateway, it was also wise to sprinkle salt at your door, wear an iron protection charm, and ensure a fire was burning furiously in the hearth.

Pausing, Lara glanced across at the lantern that burned nearby. None of this was new to her, but the last line made her reflect. It made sense that fire warded against the Slew. The heat and light chased away the shadows.

Thinking about fire now reminded her of her handfasting night—and how Alar had insisted the flames in the chamber had flared when she climaxed. His comment had unsettled her.

Huffing a frustrated sigh, she rolled the scroll back up and secured it with its thong. "It's all interesting enough … but nothing here answers our questions."

"I'll keep searching." Across the room, Gil pulled a face. "The archives at Caisteal Gealaich likely have many more … older … manuscripts." She marked the longing that flickered across his features then. "But I no longer have access to them."

Moments passed, and then she asked, "Have you ever read anything about *fire* magic?"

Gil frowned. "Not much … the Shee have never used elemental magic. Indeed, most of them fear it."

"You know that fire magic was outlawed here … a long while ago?"

He nodded. "Why do you ask?"

"Reading about the Slew gave me an idea," she replied, thinking on her feet. "If we were able to harness the power of fire somehow, we might be able to protect ourselves against them."

"Maybe … but no one in Albia has that ability any longer." His frown deepened. "And I thought it was dangerous, anyway?"

"I know little about it, apart from the old tales," she replied with a shrug, even as her pulse quickened. "But there might be something in the archives about fire magic. Maybe in those ancient scrolls you dug out of that vault."

"Do you want me to have a look?"

She nodded, relieved that he wasn't suspicious. Her focus these days was on her upcoming campaign, but her connection with fire was starting to bother her increasingly. Alar had noticed it too, which was worrying. She needed to learn more about it. Could her ability be harnessed and used for good? Excitement fluttered to life in her belly. Could it help them in the war against the Shee?

24: BENEATH THE MASK

SEATED BEFORE THE looking-glass—a rectangle of polished silver—while Mirren brushed out her hair, Lara assessed her reflection critically. A pale, heart-shaped face, with a scattering of freckles over the bridge of her nose, stared back at her. In the light of the lamp nearby, her eyes were dark green.

She was attractive enough. Pretty even. Just not to her husband's taste.

Catching herself, she frowned.

Stop this. This marriage was an arrangement. They were working together surprisingly well these days; sex would just complicate things. She should be relieved he left her alone. She should *welcome* it.

It was growing late, and the flames in the fire guttered. Outdoors, The Sweeper had gotten up and was now battering the fort. There was a sharp chill in the air tonight, and despite the thick stacked-stone walls of the broch, drafts still managed to push their way in.

Her gaze lifted then to where Mirren ran the hog bristle brush through her hair in long, deft strokes. Her eyes were unfocused, as if she were leagues distant.

Mirren hadn't mentioned Torran again since the night of Lara's handfasting. Neither had they discussed Alar. Her handmaid would listen if she talked, Lara was sure of it, yet something held her back. In truth, she wasn't sure how to articulate how she felt about her marriage, or the man she'd bound herself to.

Shades, she was confused.

The heavy curtain swished open, and a tall, lean figure clad in black ducked inside the alcove. And to her consternation, her belly fluttered. However, a moment later, she marked his furrowed brow and tense jaw.

"Good eve," Alar greeted them, his tone distracted.

Lara tracked her husband as he crossed to a narrow table, where a stack of wooden cups and a jug of ale sat. He then poured himself a drink before draining it in one long draft.

She frowned. Was he upset about something?

"All done." Mirren stepped quickly back from Lara now. "Do you need anything else?"

Lara shook her head. "No … thank you."

The handmaid put away the hairbrush and scented oil she'd used to help Lara ready herself for the furs and then nodded to both the High Queen and the prince consort. A moment later, she turned and hurried from the alcove.

"I make your maid nervous," Alar murmured. "Every time I enter a chamber, she leaves."

Lara sighed. "It's not you personally. She's not comfortable around men, that's all." She turned to him then, her gaze sliding over the sweat that gleamed off his naked arms. "Didn't the training go well?"

"Well enough. Why do you ask?"

"You seem … on edge."

He huffed a sigh. "It was a tougher session than usual, that's all. Lyall was in an aggressive mood tonight. He bested Dolph and three other opponents before I took my turn with him. He then tried to hammer me into the ground." Setting his cup down, he reached up and massaged his shoulder before wincing. "I should wash before we retire."

Lara's belly did another traitorous wee dip. "There's fresh water and soap in the bathing alcove."

He drained the rest of his cup and nodded. A moment later, he disappeared through the curtain into the adjoining chamber.

Telling herself not to be a goose, Lara shrugged off the woolen shawl around her shoulders and hung it from the back of a chair. Then, clad only in a thin sleeveless tunic that reached mid-thigh, she padded across the sheepskins to the sleeping nook and climbed inside.

She was lying on her back, cocooned by furs, when her husband emerged from the bathing alcove. Clad in nothing but a pair of leather breeches, he walked barefoot across the alcove and lowered the iron cover on some of the lamps on the way, dimming the light. His expression had smoothed over now, his gaze no longer troubled.

When he reached the edge of the sleeping nook, he started to unlace his breeches, and Lara hastily cut her gaze away.

She was still looking up at the stone ceiling when he climbed in next to her and covered himself with furs. "The Sweeper has a vicious bite tonight," he said as he settled himself. "You can tell Gateway is just a couple of days away."

Lara sighed. Months of dark and bitter cold awaited, yet she wouldn't spend them huddled around a fire. Instead, she had The Uplands to take back.

"I appreciate you standing by me during our council meetings," she said, even as heat rose to her cheeks. It embarrassed her to bring this up, yet she couldn't help herself. Her advisors—especially Annis, Roth, and Gregor—continued to challenge her. "Your advice has been … valuable."

Silence followed these words, and she inwardly cringed, wondering if she'd just made a fool of herself. She'd told herself she'd never trust a man again, and here she was extending a blade, hilt-first, to her husband.

"You're making the right choice, Lara," he replied eventually, and—curse her—her breathing grew shallow under his praise. "This isn't the time for indecision. A wavering flame is easy to extinguish."

She grimaced, knowing he couldn't see her face. "I suppose my father never campaigned in winter."

"No, it's not the 'traditional' choice … but we have the advantage over the Shee in the cold, and we'd be fools not to use it." He paused then. "Besides, wulvers are hardy."

Lara's mouth curved. She glanced his way, observing his shadowed profile. The sleeping nook was wide, and he lay around three feet from her. "What was it like living amongst them?"

He didn't answer immediately, and when he did, his voice held a slightly strained edge. "They are my people … they gave me a home when everyone else turned their back on me. They saved me."

He didn't look her way, although she turned on her side now, observing him with interest. "They did?"

"Aye … remember that story I told you about how Evin mac Darach strung me up by the throat from that pine … and left me to slowly choke?"

"Aye." She wouldn't forget it.

"Well, a wulver named Hrol found me. He'd been out fishing in a nearby burn, and he cut me down." Alar paused then. "I was half-dead by that stage, but he carried me back to the lair he shared with his mate, and they healed me."

"And you stayed with the wulvers after that?"

"I did. Hrol and Isa became my family for a long while. I spent summers fishing with them in the deep, cold lochs of the north and wintered in the Hallow Woods with their pack. Dolph is their son."

"Hrol and Isa are dead now then?"

"Aye … they joined the Hearthkeeper over twenty winters ago."

Lara considered this story, imagining what it would have been like for him to live amongst people who weren't his own but who treated him like family. It reflected well on the wulvers. He'd piqued her interest, and she wished to learn more. "Did the wulvers make you their leader voluntarily?"

He snorted. "I didn't force myself on them … they'd never have accepted me if I had. Instead, I earned their respect."

"And you rallied them?"

"I did."

Lara propped herself up onto an elbow, eyeing him. "Do you think they'd have ever united without you?"

"Probably not." His tone had cooled.

"And they want this war?"

He glanced her way, and his grey eyes glinted in the shadows. "They want to live in peace in The Uplands as they once did," he replied, his tone cutting. "If fighting for you will get them that, they will do whatever it takes." His expression turned hard. "And so will I."

Lara observed him, surprised by the vehemence of his answer. She'd clearly poked him in a tender spot. His loyalty toward his wulver kin, his drive to get justice for them, appeared to be a subject that made his temper flare. "The Uplands?" she said finally, choosing her words with care now. "They won't remain in Duncrag then?"

"Some might," he replied, looking away. "But the North is where many of their hearts lie."

She took this in with interest, more questions bubbling up. However, his curtness made her hesitate.

Silence fell between them before Alar's expression shuttered. "It's been a long day," he said, his tone softening a little. "We should both get some sleep."

Alar laced up his vest, his gaze flicking to where Lara crawled from the sleeping nook. A thin tunic covered her modesty, although the curves of her supple body were clearly visible through it. His gut tightened in response.

A few nights had passed since their handfasting, and during each one, he'd been painfully aware of the woman who slept within arm's reach in the furs.

The Hearthkeeper forgive him, he wasn't made of stone. After their conversation the eve before—after he'd told her yet more details about his past—he'd lain awake for a long while, fighting the urge to roll toward her, to sink deep into that soft body again.

Fortunately, he'd restrained himself. He had more important things to worry about right now. Fucking his wife needed to be low on his list of priorities. He knew that, but that hadn't stopped him from sleeping fitfully and waking earlier than usual. However, studying Lara's pale face, she appeared to have had a much rougher night.

He frowned. "Is something wrong?"

"I sometimes have prophetic dreams," she admitted huskily.

He stilled. This lass was full of surprises. "Really."

She swallowed before nodding. "I had one when Bree first arrived … seven crows sitting on a yew tree. This one was the same."

Alar's heart kicked as he finished lacing his vest.

Like most folk, he knew of ill omens. That one warned that someone near Lara guarded a dangerous secret. It had been accurate too—for Bree had once been a Shee spy.

Lara reached for a woolen shawl then and wrapped it around herself. It was cold inside their alcove, for the lump of peat in the hearth had burned down.

Alar moved to the fireplace and took a brick of peat from a basket before adding it to the glowing embers. Moments later, it started to smoke. However, he pretended to study it so that he didn't have to meet Lara's eye.

Many things about his wife unsettled him. The way she'd made the fire flare on their wedding night was one. And now he'd just learned she had seer's abilities. There was far more to this woman than met the eye—which made her dangerous. "Do you think there's another Shee spy under this roof?" he asked after a pause.

Lara winced. "I hope not … or Mor will already know that we plan to strike soon."

"You should discuss this dream with your chief-seer." Alar straightened up and turned back to her. "He will, no doubt, have ways of assessing your household."

She nodded. "Aye … you're right. I will see what Ruari has to say." She drew her shawl tighter around her then. "Either way, it's a warning … one I shouldn't ignore."

"No," he replied softly. "You shouldn't."

"My Queen," a male voice traveled into the alcove, slightly muffled by the heavy curtain that blocked the entrance. "A missive has come for you … from Braewall."

Alar stiffened. He recognized Captain mac Tav's voice. The captain had come upstairs to deliver the message himself. His gaze flicked to his wife. Lara wore a startled expression. Dressed in nothing but a thin tunic and shawl, she wasn't in a fit state to receive visitors. So, nodding to her, Alar crossed to the curtain and pushed through it.

As expected, Roth stood on the other side. The captain's jaw tensed at the sight of him, his eyes narrowing when Alar held out his hand for the scroll.

"This is addressed to the High Queen," Roth growled. "Not you."

"And I'll see she gets it."

The captain hesitated, dislike simmering. Ever since his arrival at Duncrag, Alar had often caught the captain watching him. Like the chief-enforcer, he was protective of their High

Queen. Almost *too* protective. Alar wondered if his feelings for Lara ran deeper than just loyalty.

"Give it to him, Roth," Lara called.

Lips compressing, Roth shoved the scroll into Alar's hand. He then turned, crossed the landing, and descended the narrow stairs. Alar watched him go before retreating inside the alcove.

Lara was waiting for him.

He handed the missive to her, and their hands accidentally brushed.

Warmth shivered up his arm. Dropping his hand to his side, he flexed his fingers and hoped she hadn't noticed.

Fortunately, Lara was focused on the scroll. She broke the wax seal, which bore the sigil of the leaping stag. Indeed, this had come from the overking himself. She read the letter, her gaze narrowing as the moments drew out.

Alar didn't interrupt her, although as he watched her eyes harden, it was clear the news wasn't good. "The *bastards*," she eventually rasped. "I was wondering why Braewall and Baldeen hadn't yet sent the warriors and weapons they promised. Now, I know why."

Alar raised his eyebrows. "What is it?"

Her gaze snapped to his. "This letter is from *both* my overkings ... signed by Artair and Niall. They've annexed themselves from me ... and declared themselves separate kingdoms."

Alar went still.

"The Gods damn them, this is *all* I need." She held the parchment up to the light once more. He marked the slight tremble in her hands as she began to read it out to him. "In light of our High Queen's decision to wed the Half-blood, a notorious outlaw, the territories of Braewall and Baldeen cannot continue to be associated with Duncrag. Henceforth, the new Kingdom of Braewall will extend along the entire southern coast, extending up to Farnoch. The new kingdom of Baldeen will encompass Dorne Forest and stretch as far south as Dunharra Barrow, and as far east as Golval Barrow. Any attempt to cross our boundaries without invitation or to issue orders of any kind will be seen as an act of war." She broke off then, her chest rising and falling sharply. "What answer do you have to that?"

Silence followed before he responded, "It's high treason."

Her mouth twisted. "Aye." Lara hurled the missive onto the table next to her. "They'd never have dared do this to my father."

Alar didn't answer. She was right, of course. Nonetheless, it was just her anger talking. They both knew she didn't want people to obey her out of fear, but respect.

But Alar wasn't so decent.

For a wild instant, he hungered to teach both those fuckers a lesson. The urge to take his wulvers to Braewall, batter down its gates, and bring King Niall's head back to Lara on a pike, crashed over him. He'd then make for Baldeen and give King Artair the same treatment. A heartbeat later though, he reined the impulse in. He'd do no such thing.

Instead, he stepped closer to his wife. "You will respond, of course?"

Her chin kicked up, and their gazes met. He'd deliberately challenged her, and he liked the way she stared back at him. He marked then how her pupils dilated. Their proximity affected her as much as it did him. Her shawl had fallen away, and her delicious body and high, firm breasts were clearly visible through the fine weave of her tunic. The garment only reached mid-thigh, revealing her slender, pale legs. Alar couldn't help but stare at her—despite that he too was reeling from these tidings—for she was regal, lovely. "This is a blow … as I was counting on their resources," she replied huskily. "But my reckoning with Braewall and Baldeen will have to wait until I've dealt with the Shee."

"You're right … The Uplands must be taken back."

"Aye." A muscle flexed in her jaw then, and she clenched her hands at her sides. Behind her, the flames in the hearth guttered, and Alar's breathing grew shallow. *There it is again.* However, Lara was too incensed to notice what she'd just done. "But rest assured, I *will* make them pay."

"Write back to your overkings this morning," he answered, his tone sharpening. "Inform them that you refuse to acknowledge their annexation." He moved closer still, inhaling the scent of lavender and sweet woman. "And then, once you've knocked the Raven Queen off her perch, turn your rage upon The Wolds." Lara's jaw flexed, and the fire in the hearth started to roar then, sparks flying. "Make those two wish they'd never crossed you."

25: THE BEAST AND THE BROKEN ARROW

"HOW ARE THINGS with Alar?"

Lara stiffened before glancing Bree's way. Her cheeks warmed. "Better than expected … considering everything that's happened of late."

The two women stood on the walls, watching as the light gradually faded. It was the eve of Gateway. Shortly, they'd have to retreat inside the broch, for it wouldn't be safe out here.

It wasn't just the Slew that emerged on this night. On Gateway, the veil between worlds grew thin. Many people swore they saw the ghosts of dead kin on this night, while others had to deal with the botach and other mischievous or malevolent spirits, who'd try to claw their way in through air vents or gaps around shutters and doorways. It was on this night that faerie creatures were also on the prowl, often helping themselves to the cakes and other sweet treats left out as offerings for the dead.

A groove formed between Bree's eyebrows. Clearly, that wasn't the right answer.

Her warder was so serious these days. Lara missed the banter they'd once shared and Bree's wry sense of humor. Their relationship had developed a formality she hated, although she didn't know how to bridge the distance between them.

It didn't help that Lara could focus on little but her upcoming campaign. They were just a day or two from departing now. Even her overkings' treachery couldn't distract her from it. "He's surprised me at times," she admitted then.

Bree cocked an eyebrow, inviting her to elaborate.

"He was gentle on our wedding night." She cut her gaze away, her cheeks burning now. "He's often busy training his wulvers, but when we do spend time together, he listens to me. You've seen how he backs me up in council meetings. He's clever, Bree. I'm learning much from him."

Her friend paused before answering, "Just be careful. You *deserve* to be treated well. Don't let gratitude override good sense."

Lara's heart started to race as she turned back to Bree once more. "Is that what you think I'm doing?"

Bree grimaced. "I know how exhausting it's been for you … to shoulder all this alone. Alar will be only too happy to help … to make himself useful. Remember who he is though. The man's slipperier than a bog wight."

Queasiness churned in Lara's belly. Bree's words were cynical, but was she right? Was she that starved of attention that she wasn't seeing things clearly? Was she letting the pull between her and Alar blind her?

"I will be wary," she assured her friend. "I understand our marriage is nothing but an arrangement. He's using me to give the wulvers the freedom they deserve … but I'm using him too."

Bree nodded slowly. Worry flickered in her eyes, and her lips parted, as if she wished to say something else. However, she didn't.

Lara glanced up at the sky, her brow furrowing. "We should get inside," she murmured. "It looks as if a storm is on its way."

A pause followed, and when Bree replied, there was an edge to her voice. "That's not bad weather."

Lara stiffened and looked closer. Bree was right. At first, she'd thought it was dark, swirling clouds that approached from the west. Yet there wasn't any wind this evening. And when she narrowed her eyes, she swore she could see winged shapes, long, trailing hair, and snaking limbs.

Her heart jolted, and she drew her fur cloak tightly about her.

"Right." Bree took her arm firmly. "Inside."

The two women descended the steps from the wall, where the guards had just lit a line of braziers. Usually, the sentries would stay outdoors and keep watch overnight, but once the braziers and torches were all burning, they too would take refuge inside.

Lara crossed the yard beneath the walls, noting the hurried step of the servants and slaves finishing their chores. No one wanted to linger out here any longer than they had to.

They were climbing the steps to the broch when a shriek ripped through the air.

Lara's step faltered. "So soon?"

"Aye." Bree linked her arm through Lara's and quickened her step. "It's not even sunset, and they're on their way."

The guards within nodded to the High Queen and her warder as they stepped into the entrance hall.

"The Slew are coming early," Bree informed them. "Make sure everyone's inside and then secure the doors."

The guards hastened to obey, and Lara and her warder made their way into the hall.

"My Queen." The chief-seer rushed up to Lara, green robes swishing. She halted, wondering if he had discovered the cuckoo in their nest yet. As Alar had suggested, she'd spoken to her seer, and he'd set about 'interviewing' the broch's residents. So far though, no one had raised his suspicions. "I've just cast the bones … and they have a warning."

Her belly flipped. *Great.*

She was just about to question Ruari when Alar entered the hall and strode toward her. Their gazes met as he approached, and Lara's racing pulse settled a little. His presence often steadied her—but recalling her conversation with Bree on the walls, her spine stiffened.

She needed to be warier.

"The broch is secure," he announced. "Although it'll be a wild night."

Cailean, who'd just entered the hall with Skaal and Roth, snorted. "Aye … the fuckers are circling the broch like crows as we speak."

"The beast and the broken arrow." Ruari raised his voice to be heard over the howling and shrieking of the Slew. Even through the thick walls of the broch, it was an unearthly sound, full of desperation and rage. The Unforgiven were tormented, ravenous. "Danger and vulnerability."

Seated upon the high seat, Lara's palms grew damp. She, the five druids, her captain, warder, archivist, and husband all sat around the table, while a handful of warriors looked on from the shadows. She'd gathered her council for an emergency meeting. As often, Skaal had settled before one of the hearths. However, she wasn't relaxed this evening. Instead, the fae hound sat up, her amber gaze watchful.

On the eve of Gateway, the bones had delivered a warning; one she shouldn't ignore. However, it was too late to do anything about it.

"Something is different this year." Annis was the first to speak. "The Slew have never been this *loud* before."

"Aye." Cailean's gaze lifted to the sturdy walls surrounding them. "It sounds as if they'll actually manage to claw their way inside this year."

No sooner had the chief-enforcer spoken than a loud 'boom' echoed through the broch, and its very walls shuddered.

"Shit," Bree growled. "What was that? Has the main door been breached?"

Shouting started then, coming from the direction of the entrance hall.

Everyone surged to their feet, the rasp of drawing weapons filling the smoky air. Likewise, the warriors who'd been standing watch stepped forward, readying themselves.

Skaal rose swiftly to her feet and moved to the front of the high seat. As she did so, the fae hound's hackles lifted on the back of her neck and shoulders.

Alar now gripped his fighting daggers. He moved close to Lara. She'd also drawn her blade.

The shouting morphed into screams, and then the doors to the hall itself flew open.

A group of terrified servants rushed inside.

Then came the sound—a low hum that vibrated across the floor and up through Lara's feet.

A heartbeat passed before darkness surged into the hall, bringing with it a mass of writhing figures. And as she watched, transfixed, the mass separated into individual forms, each wrong in a different way. Arms that bent too many times. Faces stretched like melted candle wax. Some beat the air with leathered wings, while tattered cloaks fluttered and snapped behind others.

The humming slid into ear-splitting screeches. The sound of insatiable hunger.

Even at this distance, she could see their fingers. They were too long, ending in curved claws that caught the firelight. Their mouths hung open, but not to speak. It was as if they were tasting the air—readying themselves to taste *them*.

They caught up with the slowest of the servants then, swooping down on two lads and plucking them off the ground. An instant later, the Slew carried them away, while more writhing shapes boiled into the hall.

Lara gasped a curse, watching helplessly as iron blades sliced through the empty air. The warriors might as well have been fighting smoke. One man's broadsword clove into something massive—wings that blotted out the torchlight—but the wraith didn't flinch. Claws found the warrior's throat. His boots scraped against stone as he was lifted, then gone.

Ren sang from the high seat, her voice cracking. The melody wavered, but pine and ash still swirled through the air. Some of the Slew recoiled, shrieking. Others kept coming.

Lara's knuckles clenched white around her dagger hilt. Between her and the advancing darkness stood Alar and Bree.

Silver light erupted from Cailean's tattoos as he channeled earth magic through his blade. The pungent smell made her eyes water. For a heartbeat, the wraiths hesitated. Then they surged forward again, and Lara's stomach dropped.

Skaal leaped into the fray, snarling. The Slew scattered as she attacked, but then reformed immediately afterward. The fae hound was snapping at shadows.

Gregor stepped into their path. His knife opened his palm in one swift cut. Blood dripped as he chanted, calling on The Five. His raspy voice was almost lost in the chaos.

Lara found herself whispering too—to the Gods, even to The Reaper. *Please. Spare us!*

Her protectors closed ranks around her. Annis clutched her iron sickle charm, but her hand shook. They all knew. They couldn't hold back the flood.

A terrified wail tore through the hall as the Slew took another servant. Cailean, Roth, and the warriors were drowning in black shapes, sweat streaming as they fought the tide.

Then one broke through—a huge wraith with seaweed hair and teeth like jagged, broken blades.

Lara's breathing caught. This Slew was different from the others. Bigger. More solid. It shoved Cailean and Roth aside as if they were bairns. Gil and Ruari stabbed at it uselessly.

Bree threw herself forward, but it smacked her across the face and sent her sprawling.

And then it lunged.

Lara stared into its dead eyes, and her world narrowed.

It's over.

But then Alar stepped between them, twin blades catching the firelight. "Stand down."

The wraith's maw stretched impossibly wide—rows of jagged teeth glistening.

"If you want her," Alar snarled back, "you'll have to take me first."

Lara's chest clenched. *Gods, no!*

Her dagger felt useless in her grip. Behind her, the hearths blazed against her back, and suddenly she couldn't breathe.

The fire.

Her pulse hammered. She'd hidden this her whole life. But Alar was about to die, and everyone else would follow. Those who were taken by The Unforgiven were doomed to join their ranks, lost forever in the Threshold or the places where the veil between the living and the dead was at its most fragile.

And then, as she hesitated, Alar rushed forward, straight into the embrace of the grasping Slew. He moved with a swiftness that caught her off guard.

His act propelled her into action.

Lara sheathed her dagger and flexed her hands.

Heat flooded her veins. The roar in her ears drowned out everything else—the screaming, the clash of steel, her own thundering heartbeat. The hearth flames behind her blazed so hot her skin felt as if it were blistering.

What if I can't control it? What if I burn us all?

Alar was losing. Shadows wrapped around him like hungry vines.

She flung her hands wide.

Fire erupted from the hearths, arcing over her head in twin streams. It slammed into the writhing mass of Slew. Their shrieks changed—from hunger to pain.

The power nearly buckled her knees. Fire coursed through her blood, her bones, threatening to tear her apart from the inside. She gritted her teeth and held on.

Cast them out.

Another wave of flame. Warriors threw themselves flat as the heat washed over them. Skaal yelped, bounding out of the way. The Slew writhed, fought back, but the fire was relentless.

Sweat poured down her spine. Her mind went blank except for one hysterical, burning, thought—*push them back, push them out*—and the flames obeyed, hammering the wraiths toward the doorway like the fist of an angry god.

Climbing off the floor, Cailean, Roth, and the warriors moved cautiously after them, keeping clear as the wall of flame forced the Slew back. Alar and Ruari joined them. Her long coat smoking from where the flames had singed her, Skaal prowled forward.

Moments later, the fire had shoved the Slew into the entrance hall beyond. And then, it went out.

The strength drained from Lara's legs, and she collapsed onto the floor. The heat dissolved, shivers wracking her body instead.

"Ren!" Cailean shouted as he moved through the door. "We need you!"

The chief-seer stumbled forward. Ashen-faced and shaking, she followed the others out into the entrance hall.

Moments later, the chief-bard's singing began, rising above the fading shrieks of the Slew. A repelling sain.

Boom. The great iron doors to the broch swung shut.

"Secure them!" Cailean's voice echoed through into the main hall.

Gregor, who was bleeding from a cut to his forehead, lurched to his feet from the foot of the high seat and staggered through the debris that now littered the floor toward the entrance hall. They needed the chief-sacrificer too, if they were to keep the Slew out.

From where she sat crumpled upon the raised dais, Lara gazed around her. It was a mess in here. The fire had scorched the interior of the hall. The heavy wooden beams crisscrossing above smoked. Black scorch marks covered the stacked-stone walls.

Annis sat a few yards away, cradling what appeared to be a broken arm. Her face was blistered from the heat that had roared through the hall. Meanwhile, Gil crawled over to his sister. Bree had just roused herself from where she'd hit the wall earlier. Her hazel eyes were unfocused, her face flushed.

"Lara." A gravelly voice drew her attention then.

Her gaze jerked to where Alar limped toward her. He'd returned from the entrance hall. His left leg was bleeding, and claw marks bloodied his right shoulder and arm. Unlike Annis, he'd managed to avoid being burned. Nonetheless, sweat slicked his face, neck, and bare arms.

His gaze raked over her. "Are you hurt?"

Lara swallowed as her mouth filled with saliva. "I don't know."

He knelt before her and, reaching out, took one of her hands, checking it as if looking for blisters and burns. "How," he said roughly, "did you manage *that?*"

"I'm not sure," she whispered.

Their gazes met and held for a long moment. "I suspected … that you had fire magic in your veins," he murmured. "But I never imagined—"

"Neither did I." Lara shuddered as chills rippled through her. Now that she'd severed the link with the fire, she was suddenly cold. "I've been able to … play … with flames for a while now … but I've never wielded it properly. Not like that."

"You never confided in anyone?"

She shook her head, even as her teeth chattered. "Fire magic is o… outlawed, Alar … G… Gods know what my father would have done had he known."

His sharp features tightened. They both knew what he would have done. Daughter or not, Lara wouldn't have been allowed to live. The Royal line of Albia had made the law clear over the centuries. Fire magic was forbidden—even to a High Queen. She could try and change the law now, but that wouldn't change people's prejudices. They'd fear her. Turn on her.

"I shouldn't have used it," Lara said, her throat hurting with each word. "But I … I couldn't let you … all … die."

Alar stared down at her. She'd expected to see censure flare in his eyes, or even fear, after what she'd done. But instead, all she saw was concern, and something oddly tender that made her throat tighten.

"Can you stand?" he asked after a pause.

"I'm not sure."

"Let's see then."

Gently, he took hold of her arm and helped her up. Lara's legs trembled like a newborn foal's. Chills wracked her body. She felt ill, as if she had a fever. Wielding fire did indeed have its price, it seemed, and she was paying it.

26: THE FIRE-WIELDER

"LET ME LOOK at your injuries."

Lara's voice was surprisingly strong as she rose to her feet. Alar wasn't fooled though. Wielding fire had left her shaky and feverish. After the Slew attack, he'd bid one of the trembling servants to fetch a blanket for the High Queen. The lad had done so swiftly. Meanwhile, Alar had led his wife over to one of the hearths, which now burned sedately. She needed to keep warm.

"They can wait," he replied, even as the burning in his leg, upper arm, and thigh started to throb. *Fuck*. That Slew's claws had been like meat hooks.

Ignoring him, Lara shrugged off the blanket and crossed to where the broch's healer was bathing the blisters that marred one side of the chief-counsellor's face. Annis was fortunate not to have been roasted by the flames.

With a nod to the healer—a tall woman clad in mauve robes with short blonde hair and pale, knowing eyes—Lara dug around in the basket, extracting a stoppered clay bottle. She then helped herself to a clean piece of linen and gestured for Alar to take a seat upon the stool she'd just vacated.

Reluctantly, he obeyed. As a rule, he didn't enjoy being fussed over.

Despite that the Slew still wailed outdoors—a sound that reminded him of keening now—the interior of the hall was eerily silent. Acrid smoke caught in the back of his throat from the smoking beams overhead, and he coughed. Three of the warriors who'd been injured by the Slew, and blistered by their High Queen's wrath, lay upon the rush-strewn floor. Bree's brother, Gil, tended to them. It appeared the archivist had other talents besides sorting through dusty scrolls.

The doors to the broch had finally been secured once more, and the chief-enforcer had returned to the hall. Grim-faced, Cailean sat with his wife. Bree, who usually looked so indomitable, leaned against him. Her face was pale, although an angry red lump had come up on her forehead.

"I thought the Slew were drawn only to the weak and the fearful," Ruari muttered. The chief-seer sat on a stool near the hearth, his green cloak wrapped tightly around him. His thin face was pale and pinched.

"Maybe … once," Cailean replied tersely. "But things have clearly changed."

Alar's lips thinned. They had. That massive Slew that had lunged at Lara hadn't been like any he'd ever seen. And it wasn't entirely wraithlike either. There had been solidity to its form. His blades had collided with flesh, and the claws and teeth that had raked at him were Clag-doo-sharp.

Meanwhile, Lara unstoppered a bottle of what smelled like vinegar and herbs and poured a little onto a cloth. Her hands trembled slightly. "The Warrior's balls," she muttered. "When everyone finds out I wield fire, I'm done for."

Without thinking, Alar reached out, his fingers closing around her wrist. Her pulse fluttered against his skin. "Then, they *won't* find out."

Her eyes widened. "I don't see how—"

"No one in here will say a word." He raised his voice then, ensuring everyone inside the hall heard him. "None of *us* will betray you."

The faces of those around them were strained, their gazes shadowed, yet nods followed.

Warmth kindled in Alar's gut. Aye, they'd all stay silent about what Lara had done.

Cailean heaved himself to his feet then. "I'll make sure Ren, Roth, and the others at the doors keep their mouths shut," he said gruffly.

His gaze met Alar's, and for the first time, there wasn't any animosity in the chief-enforcer's dark-blue eyes. A glimmer of respect replaced it.

"Thank you, Alar." Lara's husky voice drew his attention once more. "Although I'm not sure how long we can keep this secret."

"Long enough for you to learn more about your gift." He released her wrist, sitting back to give her access to his wounds.

She pulled a face. "Gift? It feels more like a curse."

"One that saved our hides," Bree spoke up then, her voice rough with pain. "I don't have a problem with it."

An uncomfortable pause followed these words. Tellingly, no one else around them chimed in. Alar's gaze swept over their faces, marking their tensed jaws and veiled gazes. Ruari, Gregor, and Annis, especially, stared at their High Queen, as if the Ben Neeya sat amongst them and was about to reveal whose clothes she was washing—a portent of which of them was to die.

But Lara wasn't The Washerwoman.

She was a fire-wielder. Of course, there was a reason she'd kept her ability hidden. She feared persecution. Tales of power-hungry fire-wielders, who'd incinerated whole villages when angered, had been passed down through the generations. Alar's own mother had told him such tales before reassuring her young son that such terrifying individuals no longer existed.

But they did, and he was bound to a woman who'd just revealed a weapon that could be powerful in the right hands, and devastating in the wrong ones.

Lara leaned forward and started gently cleaning the cut on his arm. Hot, stinging pain followed, and Alar clenched his jaw tight to stop a hiss from escaping.

However, he'd been lucky not to have fared worse.

"It's not too deep." Lara bent close to inspect the wound on his upper arm. "You won't need stitches. Nonetheless, we need to make sure it doesn't fester."

Alar grunted, setting his teeth once more as she poured her vinegar and herb tincture directly on the wound. She then did the same with the one to his thigh—the Slew's claws had ripped straight through the leather of his breeches and raked across the flesh.

"This needs woundwort," Lara announced then, her brow furrowing as she knelt next to him. "You have to be careful with puncture wounds."

"Let's hope its claws weren't poisoned," Alar replied.

Her frown deepened at this, and his breathing grew shallow.

He wasn't worried for himself. He'd long ago stopped worrying about his own mortality. Pain and death weren't things that scared him. However, he wasn't used to anyone showing such concern over his welfare. It was touching—and unsettling.

"I've got some freshly made-up woundwort here," Eldra called over, catching their conversation.

Lara nodded to the healer and moved away to retrieve some of the paste. She then spread it over the wound to his thigh, using the knife at her side to cut away the leather of his breeches surrounding it. Then, brow still furrowed, she carefully bound each wound with strips of linen.

Alar watched her work. "You have a healer's hands," he admitted finally.

Her chin kicked up, and the tension on her pale face eased just a little. Her eyes took on a wistful look then. "It would have been my choice … to become a healer," she admitted with a rueful half-smile. "If I hadn't been the High King's daughter."

"The Shee prisoners have escaped."

After everything she'd witnessed and experienced the night before, Lara shouldn't have been surprised by this news. Even so, she breathed a curse. This was just another blow.

Seated upon Bracken, at the start of The Thoroughfare, she'd just encountered a member of the Fort Guard who'd rushed up the hill to find her.

The devastation surrounding her made it clear that the Shee had used the chaos to make their move. It looked as if a hurricane had torn through Duncrag overnight. Turf roofs had been pulled off many of the roundhouses, store huts had been flattened, and oaken doors hung off their hinges. The wailing of those who'd had loved ones carried away by the Slew drifted through the frosty air.

"They *all* got out of the fort alive then?" Alar asked.

"We don't know," the warrior answered, his chest still rising and falling sharply from his sprint up The Thoroughfare. "Since most of us spent last night just staying alive." He pulled a face then. "But surely, the Slew would have picked some of them off?"

"Maybe," Alar replied, his tone veiled now.

Twisting in the saddle, Lara glanced over at where Bree sat astride a feather-footed cob behind her. Despite the angry red lump on her forehead, her eyes were sharp this morning. "I thought the Shee weren't bothered by The Unforgiven?" she asked.

Bree frowned. "They never used to be."

Lara shifted her attention back to Alar, studying him. Was he upset that Fern Sablebane had escaped? It was impossible to tell.

Silence fell then, and as it drew out, it became clear everyone was waiting for her to issue an order. And despite that she was weary and shaken after the night's events, she knew what had to be done.

Turning back to the waiting guard, she met his eye. "Gather a company of warriors and go after them," she ordered. "They may be injured … it'll slow them down."

The man gave a brusque nod, turned on his heel, and strode off to do her bidding.

Glancing back at her husband, Lara caught him watching her. "What?"

His lips lifted at the corners. "That was decisive."

She snorted, urging Bracken on. "The Shee move like light and shadow … but we have to at least try and retrieve them." She paused then. "However, they're the least of our problems right now. We need to see the rest of the fort."

They rode down The Thoroughfare, reaching the second level, where Alar's army of wulvers resided in squat, tightly-packed huts. A number of these dwellings no longer had roofs, and many of the doors had been bashed in. Alar spoke in a low guttural tongue with the wulvers who came out to see them.

Concluding his exchange, he turned to Lara, his eyes hard now. "We lost over thirty last night."

Lara drew in a slow breath. Another blow. Nonetheless, the wulvers had fared better than the Marav. Whole families had been taken in the level above. She didn't want to think about how many lives had been lost during the attack.

They left the wulvers to repair the roofs and doors of their huts and descended to the lower levels of the fort. An entourage of warriors followed, silent and watchful. There was little danger now, for the dawn had chased the Unforgiven away, but everyone was on edge.

This year's Gateway would never be forgotten.

She appreciated Alar's gesture earlier—assuring her they'd all keep her secret. All the same, dread now sat like an anvil in her belly.

Everyone had agreed, yet she'd seen the look on their faces.

Gods, did they think she was a danger to them now? She recalled the way the fire had rushed through her veins, filling her with a fleeting sensation of invincibility. For a few moments, she'd felt as if she could take on the world. She'd heard her father talk once of the 'fire madness' that consumed the fire-wielders of old. Unlike earth magic, which was far more stable, fire was corrupting and volatile. Those who used it too frequently risked losing their wits.

Cold washed over Lara then. Could that happen to her?

Reaching the bottom level, she drew up her horse and looked around the large dirt-packed meeting ground. A statue of The Maiden, untouched by the night's chaos, gleamed in the morning light. However, the houses that fringed the area, and the ale-hall's roof, had large holes gouged in their thick thatch. It looked as if the Slew had tried to claw their way in there. Three bairns hunched under the eaves of the ale-hall, whimpering. The sight of their strained, tear-streaked faces made Lara's throat tighten.

"Bring the bairns up to the broch," she instructed one of her warriors. "We can't leave them out here."

27: SECRETS INTO THE LIGHT

"THESE ARE ALL the scrolls I could find about fire magic."
Gil set down four dusty rolled parchments upon the long table.
He then eyed Lara before adding quietly, "I wondered what was
really behind that request."

And now you know.

"And have you had a chance to study them?" Lara asked,
trying to ignore the way her council members were watching her.

They were all keeping her secret, but they didn't look happy.

Both the chief-sacrificer and chief-seer wore scowls, while
the chief-counsellor and the chief-bard looked as if they'd just
swallowed sour milk. Lara was surprised that Annis had joined

her council this morning. One arm was in a sling, and a thick unguent covered her left cheek, where she'd been blistered by fire earlier.

Lara's belly cramped. Fire *she'd* wielded.

Cailean was the only druid who didn't appear disturbed. That didn't surprise her. There was little that flustered the chief-enforcer.

"Aye, I've read them," Gil answered, settling himself onto the bench seat.

"We all know about fire magic," Gregor muttered. The cut to the chief-sacrificer's forehead had scabbed, although it only made his scowl even more formidable. "It manifests when you leave childhood behind. It starts with the ability to control small flames … but with guidance develops into something far more powerful." His lips pursed then, his dark eyes hardening.

"I haven't had any *guidance* though," Lara pointed out, making sure her tone remained firm. Gregor could be a bully, but she wouldn't let him get to her. "And since the last fire-wielder was executed centuries ago, there's no one left to teach me." Her gut clenched as she admitted this. She knew it was forbidden. There wasn't any point in avoiding the subject.

"And yet, you still managed to channel the fire in the hearths and use it to expel the Slew," Alar said, his low voice rumbling through the hall. "Impressive."

"Do you recall *how* you wielded it?" Bree asked.

"Not really … it was instinctive."

"Does anyone wish to hear what I uncovered?" Impatience laced Gil's voice now. "Or would you all prefer to sit around theorizing?"

Gregor cut the archivist a glare, but Gil ignored him.

"Go on then," Lara replied, favoring Gil with a tight smile. It was a relief to have the focus shifted off her for the time being.

Picking up one of the scrolls, he then unfurled it. "According to this manuscript, the most stable fire magic is wielded in a calm state," he began, his gaze scanning the sheet. "The more emotional you are, the more dangerous it is."

Lara prickled, recalling the terror that had raged through her the night before. She certainly hadn't been calm then. It was a miracle she hadn't burned everyone inside the hall to cinders.

"The manuscript suggests that those who wield magic can also have 'seer' abilities," Gil continued, glancing Lara's way. "But you don't … do you?"

Her skin prickled. *Gods, not another secret to reveal.*

Across the table, the chief-seer frowned. Aye, Ruari knew, as did Alar.

"I sometimes have … prophetic dreams," she admitted after a pause.

The chief-counselor shifted awkwardly in her seat. "Why have you never said anything about this before?"

Lara pulled a face. "I was never destined to be a druid. I thought it wise to keep my … abilities … largely to myself."

Silence fell then, swelling until, eventually, Roth cleared his throat. All gazes flicked to the red-haired warrior seated next to Cailean. His attention was focused, not on Lara, but on Gil. "So, our High Queen isn't a danger to herself … or the rest of us?"

Lara's pulse quickened. She didn't like the glint in Roth's eyes. It was a far cry from the smoldering looks he'd once given her.

Gil's brow furrowed. "She hasn't been so far, Captain."

"No … but that was before she nearly burned the broch down."

Lara's heart started to pound. She wanted to speak up for herself, but she had no idea what to say. Her abilities were a mystery to her. She could well be a menace to everyone.

"Her act saved our lives," Alar said then. "You'd do well to remember that, Captain."

Tension shivered across the table as Roth and Alar locked gazes.

Lara's gaze flicked between the two men. The captain stared her husband down, his nostrils flaring.

Finally, the chief-seer shattered the heavy silence. "I had no idea that fire-wielders had seer abilities," Ruari murmured.

Gil shrugged. "Knowledge gets buried … lost with time … unless there are those who take care of it. In Sheehallion, there's an entire guild of archivists. Their purpose is to preserve and guard knowledge. Here, you let your past rot behind you." He held the brittle manuscript aloft. "It's all written down … although many of the scrolls I took from that hidden vault are ruined."

Lara frowned at this news. She didn't like the thought of so much history being lost. She too valued knowledge, which was why she'd made Gil her archivist.

Nonetheless, his words reminded her that the rulers of Albia had made many poor choices over the centuries. And as a result, they continued to make the same mistakes, for history had a way of repeating itself.

"Do the manuscripts say anything else about my *seer* abilities?" she asked, her throat suddenly dry.

"Aye." Gil's attention flicked to her. "This one specifies that a fire-wielder doesn't 'see' like a druid. You can't read the bones or walk amongst the spirit world like Ruari can … nor can you probe the emotions of others … but your dreams have the power to bring secrets into the light.”

Secrets into the light.

“Seven crows sitting on a yew tree,” she murmured. “It’s always the same.”

This made everyone at the table, except Ruari and Alar, sit up a little straighter, gazes narrowing and jaws tightening. They all knew what that dream signified.

Bree’s gaze narrowed. She wouldn’t have forgotten it from four years earlier either. All the same, it was strange. Lara didn’t understand why the same dream kept visiting her.

Silence settled in the hall once more. Lara let it lie while she reached for her goblet of wine and took a fortifying gulp. It was sloe, and strong. She welcomed its burn. “My ability could prove a useful weapon against the Shee,” she said finally. Maybe if she changed focus, her druids and captain would stop seeing her as a threat.

“Maybe,” Cailean rumbled. “If you learned to control it.”

“There’s no time,” Bree answered. “We’re about to go on campaign soon, remember?”

The chief-enforcer pulled a face, acknowledging that his wife had a point.

“I’ll have to learn ‘on the road’ then,” Lara replied briskly.

Gil picked up another of the scrolls and unfurled it. “There is little written down about the ‘training’ of fire-wielders,” he said, passing the parchment to Lara. “Although this manuscript speaks of the use of a cairn stone … a lump of smoky quartz that can help a fire-wielder quiet the mind and detach from emotions.”

She nodded, taking the document. “I shall source one.”

"Seers learn to control their breathing, pulse, and thoughts," Cailean pointed out. "Ruari could teach our queen some techniques."

All gazes cut to the chief-seer. The young man grimaced, earning a scowl from the chief-enforcer, before he bowed his head. "I could."

They heard the brawl before they even reached the ale-hall. A dull roar.

Cailean breathed a curse and increased his stride. Alar followed suit. Neither of them commented on the din, yet it sounded like the brawlers were mauling each other.

Skaal bounded alongside them, her powerful limbs covering the ground in easy strides. Her amber eyes glowed like two hot coals in the dim light.

A short while earlier, word had reached the broch that a fight had broken out between Marav and wulvers in an ale-hall on Duncrag's second level. Alar had been outdoors at the time. He'd just finished training, but instead of retiring had lingered up on the walls for a while. He'd been watching the home fires of Duncrag flicker in the darkness, deep in thought, when a lad sprinted into the yard below, bringing word with him.

Gasping for breath, the youth had told them that a fight had broken out. The second level's headman—who was in charge of overseeing order in that part of the fort—had tried to break it up but now lay insensible on the floor of the ale-hall.

When Cailean and his enforcers stormed from the yard, Alar had joined them.

The chief-enforcer's lips had thinned when Alar appeared at his side, but he hadn't tried to send him away. Alar wouldn't have gone, anyway. If wulvers were part of this brawl, they were his responsibility.

Heart pounding and chest heaving from his sprint down The Thoroughfare, he spied the thatched roof of the ale-hall up ahead. The building—windowless, rectangular, and low-slung—sat just inside the wall to the level above. It was after dark, and so braziers burned on either side of the ale-hall, sending deep shadows into the narrow wynds flanking the building.

And as they approached it, the wattle door crashed open and a wulver hurtled outside. He sprawled upon the hard-packed dirt, rolling onto his back just in time as a rawboned man with a florid face charged out of the building and leaped on him.

Cailean and two of his enforcers were on them an instant later, pulling the two struggling, snarling figures apart.

"Mother humpers!" the man yelled, flailing in their grip. "Get your fucking hands off me!"

"Enough." Cailean's command was low, yet powerful.

The man froze, his head jerking sideways. His expression went slack when he realized who held him, his vitriol dying on his tongue. His throat worked as his attention settled upon Skaal. The fae hound had halted next to Alar, her stare pinning him to the ground.

Meanwhile, the wulver picked himself up. Blood trickled down his naked chest from what looked like a knife cut below his collarbone.

Heat rolled over Alar. "Who started this?"

The wulver met Alar's eye, his yellow eyes glinting. "They did," he barked. "Some of us came in earlier … for a tankard of ale after training. We'd just started drinking when a group of them set upon us."

"They don't belong here." The man wiped blood from a split lip when the enforcers let him go. "The *mongrels* have taken our houses ... and now they want to *drink* with us? Next, they'll want to fuck our women." He spat out a gob of blood and spit on the ground. "It's too much."

"You don't decide what's too much and what isn't," Cailean replied. He then cut the other enforcers a sharp look. "Thalia and Conn ... stay here and make sure these two behave themselves, while we deal with the rest."

The female enforcer with long dark hair braided in thin plaits and a bald male enforcer with massive shoulders both nodded.

Cailean shifted his attention to the fae hound. "Wait, Skaal." The chief-enforcer turned then and headed for the door.

Alar followed.

A wall of noise hit them as they entered. Grunts and curses, interspersed with shouting and snarling. Before them heaved a sea of men and wulvers. Fists flew, and the lanterns hanging from the beams overhead caught the gleam of flashing blades. The wet sound of iron cleaving into flesh followed.

Alar's gut clenched in anger. It was frenzied. There were already a few bodies on the ground, but no one seemed to notice. Instead, they were just crushed underfoot as the brawl continued.

Meanwhile, the proprietor—a short, squat man who'd sent his son up to the broch to raise the alarm earlier—stood, pressed up against one wall.

Relief bloomed across his strained face when he spied the chief-enforcer.

"Right," Cailean said as he flexed his hands at his sides. His tattoos started to glow dull silver in the dimly lit hall. He then glanced across at Alar, meeting his eye squarely for the first time since they'd left the yard before the broch. "Let's shut this down."

"There's been an *incident*, My Queen."

Lara glanced up from where she'd been studying the scrolls Gil had found, to see Florie in the doorway. It was getting late, and her attendants were supposed to be finishing their chores for the evening. However, the lass's face was flushed from her sprint up the stairs. "What's happened?"

"A clash between wulvers and fort residents … on the second level of the fort."

Murmuring an oath, Lara rose to her feet. "Is it still going on?"

"No … they managed to break the brawl up … but those responsible have been brought up to the broch." Florie swallowed nervously. "The prince consort has called for you."

Lara didn't need to be told twice. Slinging a cloak around her shoulders, she left her alcove. Out in the stairwell, she picked up her long skirts with one hand and descended the spiral staircase so quickly that she caused the cressets burning upon the stacked-stone walls to gutter.

And when she reached the entrance hall, she found Bree waiting for her.

"Do you know who started it?" she asked her warder as they pushed through the heavy doors.

"A group of drunken Marav, by all accounts," Bree muttered. "They took issue with wulvers drinking with them … and things turned very nasty."

Lara's jaw tightened. It was only a night after Gateway. She'd have thought the residents of Duncrag had better things to do than pick fights with each other. She'd also hoped that things between Marav and wulver had been improving. They'd had several days now to get used to each other, and the Slew attack should have united them.

Instead, it had made her people lash out.

Her temper flared then. She could understand that everyone was on edge after Gateway, but how could folk be so small-minded and foolish? The Shee were breathing down their necks, the Slew had just terrorized them—and the Marav couldn't see past old prejudices? The wulvers were here to help. They were beings worthy of as much respect as Marav. She wouldn't tolerate this.

Lara and Bree descended the steps from the broch and stepped out into the torchlit yard before it. The night was foggy, and mist wreathed around the ramparts. After the unearthly screeching of the Slew the night before, it seemed unnaturally quiet.

A bloodied crowd of men and wulvers was held captive by enforcers and warriors in the center of the yard. Cailean, Torran, and Alar stood before them. The chief-enforcer wore a deep scowl, as did his second. However, Alar's face was stone-hewn. Skaal was there too, standing close to the men, especially. One or two of the Marav cast the glowering fae hound nervous glances.

Uneasiness fluttered in Lara's belly as she halted before them. She hadn't seen her husband truly vexed before.

"Fucking wolf scum!" One of the Marav—a huge man with a jutting jaw—shouted then. "You brought the Slew down upon us!"

"Aye, that's right," one of the wulvers—young and lanky with a bleeding gash down one arm—snarled back, deliberately goading. "Pity they missed you … maybe they avoid the ones who are as thick as pig shit!"

With a roar, the big man twisted out of a warrior's grip and hurled himself at the wulver. An instant later, they were rolling on the ground.

And as Lara looked on, shocked by the hostility that crackled in the air now, the Marav, who had big scarred hands, started throttling his opponent.

Alar strode into the fray.

His booted foot struck out, catching the man in the ribs. Hard.

The man cursed, releasing his grip on the wulver's throat. A heartbeat later, warriors gripped both individuals and hauled them apart.

Lara stepped up to Alar's side. "These men think the wulvers brought the Slew here?"

"It's just an excuse," Alar said roughly, his gaze never leaving the big man who'd started the fight. She could feel the anger vibrating off her husband. "Earlier, they were whining about the smell of smoking fish. They wanted to lash out … and they have."

The man flexed his scarred hands at his sides and spat a gob of blood on the ground. "We don't want their kind living amongst us," he growled. "Send the craven, *unnatural* fuckers back to the woods, where they belong."

Lara drew in a deep breath, even as anger started to pulse in her stomach. Ignorance. It was written all over his face. He and his friends didn't care that Albia was teetering on a knife-edge, and that this alliance could save them. What mattered more was clinging to their prejudice. It gave them rules to live by and the illusion of control in a world where there was none.

But she wouldn't stand for it. She wouldn't continue her father's legacy.

She caught a glimmer out of the corner of her eye and realized her ring was responding to her kindling fury. Swiftly, she clasped her hands before her, covering the *Ord-ree seal* with her fingers lest it betray her.

Her gaze met the man's then. "The wulvers will give us back the North," she said coldly. "You should show them some gratitude."

He raked his gaze over her. He took his time, making sure everyone present marked his disrespect. His thick lips then twisted. "And you certainly have," he murmured. "I bet you thank the Half-blood every night in the furs when he humps you."

Heat washed over Lara. His insult wasn't original, yet it cut deep, all the same. Was that how her people saw her? The Half-blood's whore?

However, she never had a chance to answer him, for the rasp of iron against leather cut through the misty yard. An instant later, Alar lunged forward and drove a dagger into his throat.

The man choked, sinking to his knees. Shock flared in his eyes.

Yanking the blade free, Alar stepped back, watching while blood pumped from his thick neck. Clutching at the wound, his gaze frightened now, the man slumped on his side, twitching as he died.

A hush fell then, stretching out as Alar met Lara's eye. Her heart kicked hard against her ribs when his lips quirked. "Some people don't know when to stop talking."

28: DANGEROUS WATERS

PACING INSIDE HER alcove, Lara listened to the shrieks outside the walls. Panic thumped against her breastbone. "Gods … what are they doing back here?"

Two nights after Gateway, the Slew had returned. Fortunately, the guards on the walls had spied dark clouds boiling in from the west shortly before dusk. They'd managed to get everyone inside in time. Of course, some of Duncrag's residents were still without a home, or were still repairing their roundhouses—and so they'd sought refuge inside the broch. The building was now crammed with fort residents. They'd put down furs to sleep on in any available space, while warriors and druids kept vigil over the entrance. They'd boarded up the doors this time, and the bards had begun a protection sain the moment everyone was safely indoors. Outside, braziers burned bright upon the walls—many more than usual—to chase away the shadows.

"Clearly, Gateway wasn't enough. They're back for more souls."

Lara turned, her gaze spearing Alar. Her husband sat by the roaring hearth—all the fires in the broch had been stoked high tonight—a cup of wine in hand. In contrast to her, he appeared irritatingly at ease. Only the crease between his eyebrows hinted that the return of The Unforgiven bothered him.

Lara put her hands on her hips. "How can we march north with the Slew hunting us?"

Reaching up, he rubbed his jaw. "That's a problem, I grant you."

"Any solutions?"

His gaze met hers. "Luckily, we'll have a fire-wielder with us."

Lara pursed her lips. "A fire-wielder who doesn't know what she's doing." She swallowed then. "And I'm supposed to be hiding my abilities, remember? Not flaunting them."

"There are ways to keep the camp secure *and* keep your secret." Alar unfolded his long body from the chair and rose to his feet. He then gestured to where a jug of wine sat next to a stack of wooden cups on the nearby table. "I'm getting another … do you want one?"

She hesitated a moment before giving a stiff nod. She needed to calm down. The broch was secure tonight. Even so, she couldn't stop thinking about the havoc those vicious spirits were possibly wreaking in the fort. Would they rip apart the dwellings they'd already damaged as they hunted? Would they manage to claw their way into the buildings where Duncrag's residents sheltered?

Tonight would be endless as she waited to see the damage.

Alar crossed to the table, filled a cup with wine for her, and refilled his own. Their fingers brushed as he handed Lara her drink.

Her breathing hitched.

Her reaction to him unnerved her.

She was both attracted to and repelled by the man she'd married. He was clever and could be surprisingly protective and supportive of her. She liked his irreverent sense of humor, his aura of calm. And often when he looked at her, the intensity of his gaze left her lightheaded and unsettled. Whenever he walked into a space, her gaze tracked him, and sometimes she caught herself daydreaming about their handfasting night and wishing he'd touch her like that again.

But there was a viciousness to Alar as well.

Like when he'd killed that man. The lout had insulted her—and she'd been about to have him punished for it—but Alar hadn't shown a shred of remorse after taking his life. Instead, his manner had been aloof ever since.

Even more unsettling was the fact that there was a part of her that didn't shy away from his darkness.

Moving away from her husband, Lara sat down in her chair opposite him. The howling outdoors rose to a spine-tingling crescendo then, and the flames in the hearth guttered.

Lara's pulse leaped, and without thinking, she extended a hand toward the fire, clenching her fist and then snapping her fingers straight. The flames roared up toward the smoke vent, and the shrieking subsided.

"How did you learn to do that movement with your hand?" Alar asked, eyeing her as he sat down once more.

She lowered her gaze to the hand in question, frowning. "I don't know … it's instinctive. If I clench my fist and focus on the flames, it forms a … connection of sorts. And then, when I straighten my fingers, it seems to do my bidding."

"Do you have a cairn stone yet?"

She nodded, patting the pouch at her waist, where she kept a lump of smoky quartz. "Mirren found me one … her mother collects such things." She took a sip of wine then. "Ruari's been showing me some 'mind-clearing' techniques … but I'm not having much success."

He snorted. "Give yourself some time."

"That's the problem. I don't have any. We're supposed to be leaving any day now, remember?"

His gaze met hers. "And we shall," he said firmly. "And we'll ensure you have the privacy you need to practice every night on the road north. Ruari will help you … and so will I."

Silence fell in the alcove as their stare drew out.

Lara was the first to look away. "You're a man of contradictions, Alar."

"How so?"

"When we first struck our deal, I suspected you'd try to seize power once you got settled at Duncrag … that what you really wanted was my crown. That you were lying to me." She paused then, forcing herself to meet his eye. "But you've stood at my side … encouraged me."

Discomfort flickered across his proud features.

Warmth stole over her then, embarrassment rising. She should stop talking now, yet she couldn't seem to prevent herself. "I put on a brave front, but I used to feel a bit like a sheltered princess playing at being High Queen. I feared failure … and the judgment of others. But you treat me like there's nothing I can't achieve."

A pause followed, and Lara's chest tightened. She couldn't believe she'd blurted all of that out. His silence made her wish she could haul every word back. Curse her, she'd just handed him a weapon to use against her.

"You give me too much credit," he said finally, his voice gruff. "I'm not the only one who believes in you."

"No," she replied softly. "But you make me feel less alone."

Alar observed his wife over the rim of his cup.

They were straying into dangerous waters here. His proud young wife, who'd once been so cold, was warming to him. Her pine-green eyes were soft this evening, luminous.

She needed to hide her emotions better.

And he needed to be more careful.

Taking a sip of wine, Alar considered his next words. Things weren't going to plan at present. The warriors Lara had sent after the Shee had come back empty-handed. The Slew were a problem. His half-sister's escape had been a blow too. Fern would return to Sheehallion and tell their father about him. What would Wynn Sablebane do when he discovered that he had a half-breed son who was now wedded to the High Queen of Albia?

Alar's pulse quickened. Did he really care?

Meanwhile, Lara watched him expectantly. He wouldn't continue this conversation though; it was time to change the subject. "I wonder why the Slew have become so unruly," he murmured.

A nerve flickered in her cheek, disappointment flaring in her eyes. "Once we've dealt with the Shee, I intend to find out." She swallowed, even as her chin lifted. "Then, we'll put things back the way they were."

Heat ignited in the pit of Alar's gut. He welcomed it. Here was his chance to distance himself a little from his wife. "Maybe, there's no going back." He swirled the dregs of his wine in his cup. "Have you considered that when your father fell, it marked the beginning of the end?"

She stiffened in her chair, her fingers tightening around her cup. "I refuse to believe that."

He shrugged. "Look around you. Albia is fractured. The faerie creatures and spirits no longer hide in the shadows. You can defeat the Shee and beat your overkings into submission, but the old order … your *father's* world … is dying."

Her chest rose sharply, anger flaring in her eyes. Jaw tight, she got swiftly to her feet and slammed her cup down on the ledge above the fireplace. "And that's something to gloat over?"

Alar put aside his own cup and stood up. "Aye … the Marav have ruled with an iron fist for too long."

Careful, he warned himself then. *Don't say anything you'll regret.*

However, it was as if there were an imp on his shoulder, urging him on. He moved closer, inhaling her sweet scent. His breathing grew shallow at her nearness, and his pulse started to hammer in his ears. Fuck, how he wanted her. She had no idea of the thoughts that had plagued him since their handfasting. The *urges.* Right now, all he wanted to do was strip off her clothes, drag her into the furs, and tumble her until they both collapsed from exhaustion. But he wouldn't.

Leaning in, he brought his mouth close to her right ear. "It's time for you to share power with the rest of us."

Lara lay amongst the furs, staring up at the stone ceiling of the sleeping nook.

And all the while, the Slew screamed and wailed. She could almost taste their fury.

Right now, it matched her own. She glanced over at where her husband slept a few feet away. Alar had rolled over with his back to her, although she could tell by the rhythm of his breathing that he was sleeping.

Her jaw clenched. *Callous prick.*

However, the anger that churned in her belly wasn't just at him—but herself.

She'd walked right into that.

What was she doing, being so vulnerable with the Half-blood? He'd sniffed out weakness and gone straight for her throat. Even now, the glint she'd seen in his iron-hued eyes, the roughness of his voice as he leaned close made her curl her hands into fists.

He hadn't needed to be that harsh, yet he'd been making a point.

She squeezed her eyes shut then. They were gritty and sore. She was in desperate need of sleep, yet it eluded her.

Humiliation burned like a hot coal in her chest. Thank the Gods that Bree, Cailean, or Mirren hadn't overheard that exchange. They'd think she'd lost her wits.

And she had. For a few moments.

But then, Alar had emptied an icy pail of water over her head. He'd reminded her that vulnerability was a weakness and that trust was a luxury she couldn't afford. He'd told her the old order was ending, that there was no saving it, but he was wrong.

And she'd prove it to the bastard.

29: BEYOND THE WALLS

LARA EMERGED FROM the broch and halted on the top step.

Before her, the High Queen's banner snapped in the wind. A black wolf on a snow-white field. The Whistle gusted through Duncrag this morning, its shrill notes whining as it battered the high walls. The sky above was pale blue and filled with scudding clouds.

It was a fine day to set off on a journey.

The southern enclosure was a sea of leather and mail-clad bodies, bristling spears, and horses this morning. Gazes snapped her way, and a cheer went up, echoing off stone. They were waiting for her to join them.

Lara smiled, anticipation tightening her chest.

It's time.

Since her return from Doure, the smiths of Duncrag had worked hard to provide her with enough iron. She'd have liked more weapons for this campaign—for some of the warriors would go into battle armed with nothing but pikes—but since Braewall and Baldeen had turned on her, she would have to make do. Likewise, she didn't have as many warriors as she'd hoped for, although the carpet of iron helmets spilling out of the enclosure and onto The Thoroughfare beyond reassured her. Roth had done an admirable job.

The wulvers heavily outnumbered her own army—but this would still be a *Marav* victory.

"I should be coming with you, My Queen." Lara turned to find Mirren standing behind her. Clad in a sky-blue tunic that matched her eyes, her handmaid clutched a woolen shawl around her shoulders. A deep groove had etched between Mirren's eyebrows. The lass then cast a look over at where Florie, Ani, and Lilith—dressed in thick woolen tunics and fur-lined cloaks—stood behind Lara, her lips compressing.

She'd have three rather than four attendants on this trip.

"Not this time, Mirren." Lara moved closer then, taking hold of her hands and squeezing gently. "I may not return for a moon or two … in the meantime, I need you to help run the broch." She nodded to where a tall, lanky figure stood a few yards away. The wind ruffled Torran's dark-blond hair. The enforcer was watching them, his grey eyes sharp. "I have left Torran in charge of defending the fort … but *you* will be my steward."

Mirren's eyes snapped wide, her lips parting.

Lara squeezed her hands once more. "Don't look so shocked," she murmured. "You haven't been an indentured servant here for a while now. Aye, you're my handmaid … but you're so much more as well. You're as sharp as a whip and strong." Her mouth quirked into a smile. "You will do me proud."

Mirren made a strangled sound in the back of her throat, even as her eyes glistened.

Releasing her hands, Lara glanced back at Torran. "You'll give my steward the guidance she needs?"

He nodded, although Lara caught the way his jaw tensed. "Of course, My Queen."

Meanwhile, panic flared in Mirren's eyes.

Gaze flicking between them both, Lara wondered if it was wise to throw these two together like this. Had they not spoken since her handfasting? Protecting and stewarding Duncrag together would bring them in much closer contact. However, they were the people she wished to leave in charge.

She didn't know when she'd be back and needed a steward she could trust. Mirren would act in her best interests.

However, there was another reason the lass was staying behind.

Lara had no family now, and she couldn't bid Bree to remain at Duncrag—her friend would have flatly refused anyway—but she *could* protect Mirren. She'd left a strong garrison behind too—despite that those warriors would have been useful in the North. A handful of enforcers, two sacrificers, and two bards were staying as well. The fort was vulnerable these days, both from her overkings and the Slew. She couldn't leave Duncrag exposed.

Her belly contracted then. *What if I fail?* Her father had set out from Duncrag, full of optimism and determination, but he'd never returned. She had the wulvers, but they didn't make her invincible.

And what of her fire magic? At present, it was more of a liability than a gift. She wasn't sure she'd ever learn to wield it properly—and even if she did, how would she keep it secret?

And what if the Slew returned again? They would have to be vigilant at dusk on the road north.

Her breathing grew shallow then, her chest tightening. There were many obstacles ahead, but she'd take each as it came.

Turning from Mirren and Torran, Lara's gaze traveled down the steps to where Alar approached.

Like her, he was dressed for travel. Thick leathers encased his body, and a heavy black woolen cloak rippled from his shoulders. He looked like an enforcer dressed all in black, but ever since they'd met, he'd worn no other color. His leather breastplate, embossed with the Hearthkeeper's Endless Flame, gleamed in the morning light. The twin hilts of the blades he wore strapped to his back thrust up above each shoulder.

The Whistle screeched through the yard then, catching his long dark hair and whipping it around. Pushing it out of his face, Alar secured his hair at his nape with a thong as he approached.

The sight of him made her belly clench.

They'd barely spoken since their argument. Two tense days had followed. She'd thrown herself into preparing for their departure, doing her best to avoid her husband. Yet there was no escaping him this morning.

Meanwhile, she was aware of eyes upon them. Bree and Cailean's gazes were sharp. They'd noticed the frostiness between the High Queen and the prince consort over the past couple of days. Bree had questioned Lara about it the evening before, but she'd brushed her off. She didn't want anyone to know about her lapse in judgment.

Alar halted before her, his expression inscrutable. "Your army awaits your command."

The wind pushed Lara's hood back and whipped strands of hair into her eyes. Sighing, she gave up trying to fight The Whistle. It had serenaded them all morning; its icy breath made her cheeks tingle.

She was relieved to be on her way though. Bracken's step was lively. The mare was enjoying being on the road again. After leaving Duncrag, they now rode through a woodland of sycamore, ash, and oak.

The western edge of the Shiel Range rose up to her right, etched sharply against the blue sky. Once those mountains lay behind them, they'd leave The Wolds and enter the borderlands. However, this stretch of highway was relatively safe.

The Shee held no sway here, and the chieftain of Dulross had done an admirable job of protecting his territory farther north. The trouble would likely come once they entered The Goatfells.

Misgiving feathered down Lara's spine. No word had ever come from her emissaries. The Circines wouldn't be the allies she'd hoped for.

"You're quiet this morning," Bree noted then.

Rousing herself from her thoughts, Lara glanced over at her. "Just readying myself for what's to come."

Bree nodded, even as her brow furrowed. "Any concerns?"

Lara snorted. "Plenty."

"Is your husband among them?"

Lara stiffened, her gaze shifting to where Alar rode up ahead. He was out of earshot, and the whine of the wind made it difficult for even those nearby to overhear them. All the same, she responded cautiously. "Always."

Bree's gaze glinted. "He's done something to offend you, hasn't he?"

Lara huffed a sigh. She'd hoped Bree wouldn't bring this up again. "No," she lied. "I'm just aware that a woman in power has to be careful."

"Aye … I'm sure Mor would agree with you."

Lara's lips thinned. She didn't like being compared to the Raven Queen. Nonetheless, Bree had a point. Mor was ruthless. She'd even had Bree assassinate her brother when she discovered he was plotting against her.

"Mor has never co-ruled, has she?" she asked after a pause.

"No." Bree's tone turned rueful. "She would never share power … besides, no male has the spine to equal her."

Lara's breathing grew shallow, fire igniting under her ribs. One day, she wanted people to say the same thing about her.

Toward the end of the first day of travel, they reached the village of Ardroth. It was tiny, little more than a scattering of squat roundhouses gathered around a dirt square. But as Lara rode in, she marked the damage to the sod roofs.

Gaunt-faced villagers emerged from their homes to catch a glimpse of the High Queen. However, many of them shrank back, their expressions slackening in shock when they spied the wulvers marching behind her.

"All is well," she called out. "The wulvers are our friends!"

Murmurs and oaths rippled through the crowd.

As Lara passed through the market ground at the village's heart, a woman approached her. Barefoot, her dark hair matted, she was wild-eyed. A small infant wailed in her arms.

Raising her hand to signal to the others to halt, she drew up her mare. A rumble of voices rippled out behind her, as her warriors called to those following to stop. "Is your bairn ill?"

The woman swallowed. "He hasn't been right since a boggart tried to smother him two nights ago. He just cries and cries."

Lara's pulse leaped. *Boggarts?* She'd heard plenty of tales about them, none of them pleasant. They were broonies—a household spirit—who'd turned vengeful, usually because of ill-treatment. Observing the young woman's drawn face, Lara couldn't imagine what she'd done to offend one.

"Boggarts have plagued us ever since Gateway," an old man, likely a village elder, spoke up then. Frail and bent, he leaned heavily on his cane. He kept stealing nervous glances at the wulvers. "I woke up last night with one sitting on my chest, its clammy fingers pinching my nose. When I pushed it off me, the boggart screamed insults in my face."

A chill skated down Lara's spine. Things were bad enough in Duncrag. Outside the capital's walls, things were wilder than she'd thought. And The Unforgiven weren't the only restless spirits out after dark these days. She glanced back at the woman with the bairn. "I have healers with me. They can take a look at your son … and make sure nothing is ailing him."

The woman dipped her head, clutching the howling infant to her breast. "Thank you, My Queen."

Lara nodded back, even as her belly hardened. It was but a small gesture. Not enough.

"The Weeper wails outside after dusk," another woman called out from the crowd that now gathered. "Are we all doomed?"

"No," Lara replied firmly, her pulse skittering. Like the Ben Neeya, the Weeper was a harbinger of death. Usually, her appearance—although unwelcome—was rare. "These are troubling times, but they will pass." She paused then, before announcing, "I am traveling north … to take back our lands from the Shee."

Murmurs of approval rippled through the crowd of villagers. Their brows smoothed, and their gazes brightened. It warmed her to see hope spark in their eyes.

"It isn't just the Shee we fear, My Queen," the elderly man said then, his eyes, milky with cataracts, fixing upon her. "What if the Slew attack us again?"

"Or the botach starts stealing away our children?" The woman holding the bairn clasped him closer to her breast.

Lara's breathing grew shallow. She glanced then to where her husband had drawn up his horse a few yards ahead. Alar had twisted in the saddle to observe her exchange with the villagers. Her pulse quickened when she noted the tension on his face.

Few things rattled the Half-blood. But if he looked worried, then she should be as well.

She shifted her attention back to the waiting crowd. They were looking to her for answers, and she had to allay their fears. "Once we drive back the Shee, balance may be restored," she replied, wishing she knew that for sure. "But even if it isn't, I swear, I will do everything I can to ensure your safety."

30: JUSTIFY NOTHING. REGRET NOTHING.

THE WEEPER WAILED as Lara walked through the camp, flanked by Bree and Alar. The folk of Ardroth weren't the only ones being paid a visit. The wraith's mournful cry was awful—harrowing grief distilled into one drawn-out howl.

Bree muttered a curse under her breath, although Alar remained silent. Nonetheless, there was a harshness to his profile that betrayed him.

Few could listen to The Weeper and not let sorrow and foreboding overwhelm them.

The spirit was somewhere in the oakwood to the west. Corpse candles glowed amongst the trees there too, although Lara was careful to keep her gaze averted.

It was late, and their encampment was quiet, watchful. Torches burned around the perimeter, and the enforcers had laid ward stones before Ren and her bards wove a protection sain. Gregor and his sacrificers had done their bit too, beheading pigeons and chanting to the Gods as they spread their entrails.

Fortunately, the Slew hadn't appeared, although it had been a breathless wait at dusk.

The news from Ardroth had no doubt made its way through her army. Until recently, it was faerie creatures, Mor's allies, they'd been wary of. But now the restless dead and other wicked spirits were the ones stirring up trouble.

The trio wove their way through the press of tents toward a circle of supply wagons. All three of them were cloaked and hooded, shadows in the darkness. There, they slipped between two canopied wagons and ducked into a large pavilion that had been erected beyond.

Within, Lara found Cailean and Ruari waiting for her. The druid stood before a brightly burning brazier.

This was where she'd continue her fire-wielding practice.

Halting before the brazier, Lara pushed back her hood and held out her hands, warming her fingers over the flames. A clear, crisp day had given way to a cold night; a frost was settling outdoors. She glanced around then at the four individuals who now watched her, and frowned. "I didn't expect to do this with an audience."

Indeed, until Gateway, she'd only ever played with fire in private.

She wasn't sure she could 'perform' while being watched—especially with Alar present. She didn't want him here, yet he'd insisted.

"Just pretend we aren't here," her husband drawled.

Lara cut him a sharp look and retrieved her cairn stone from the pouch at her waist. Holding up the chunk of quartz to the light, she stared into its smoky depths. "I still don't understand how a lump of rock is supposed to help me calm my emotions and focus my thoughts?"

Indeed, she'd tried using it before her departure, with little success.

"I told you," Ruari answered. "Smoky quartz is grounding and protective."

Lara glanced the chief-seer's way. Exasperation flickered in his eyes.

Embarrassed that she'd seen his reaction, the young man dropped his gaze to the grey lump of gleaming stone upon her palm. "Cairn stones are more powerful than most folk realize, My Queen," he muttered. "It should help you … contain … your ability."

Marking the catch in his voice, Lara closed her fingers tightly around the lump of quartz. Ruari had agreed to help her master this, yet he feared her ability to wield fire.

Swallowing, she shifted her attention to the brazier. "Come on, then," she muttered. "Let's get started."

"First, you need to quieten your mind … as I showed you in Duncrag," the chief-seer replied.

Lara closed her eyes. Gods, this was the most difficult part. Her first couple of sessions with Ruari had felt like she'd been trudging through a bog. Her thoughts often flitted off in various directions. But she was determined to do better this evening. There wasn't any time for a wandering mind. She had to focus.

Moments passed, and as Ruari's instructions filtered through the tent, she forgot about her audience and focused on the rise and fall of his voice.

And, eventually, a stillness crept over her.

That was better. It felt as if a calm pond had settled deep inside her chest.

"Are you ready to try again?" Ruari asked softly.

"Aye," she whispered back.

Her eyes flickered open then, and she tightened the fingers of her right hand around the cairn stone, as she had in Duncrag. Her gaze then shifted to the flames dancing in the brazier. To her surprise, she forged a connection immediately. It was so much easier in a calm state, and the reassuring feel of the stone against her palm made something quicken inside her, an understanding that she'd lacked previously.

At Gateway, she'd wielded fire like a blunt instrument, but now, it felt like a lyre. She just had to learn how to play it. Tentatively, she reached out her left hand, wiggling her fingers slightly. And in response, the flames in the brazier jumped high into the air.

Ruari muttered an oath, but Lara ignored him. She needed to retain her focus, her inner calm.

Meanwhile, Cailean, Bree, and Alar looked on intently. They wanted to see what she was capable of—and she'd show them.

An instant later, the flames were dancing on her palm, like the corpse candles had on that fateful day. The day she and Alar met.

The flames on her palm went wild, flaring upward in greedy golden tongues. Of course, they were mirroring Lara's emotions—for thinking of the man who stood just a couple of feet away caused the still waters inside her to ripple, as if stirred by a breeze.

Shit. Despite that she'd done her best to distance herself from him since their argument, he still affected her. A painful knot of loneliness, longing, and frustration clenched deep in her chest then. She was stronger than this.

Sensing her turmoil, the flames on her palm scattered haphazardly.

Lara sucked in a deep breath, frustration beating against her breastbone. *This won't do.*

"Give each thought a name, remember." Ruari's voice intruded then. "And imagine putting them, one by one, into a sack."

Lara nodded, doggedly following his instructions. She'd master this.

"Now … tie the sack up and throw it aside."

She did. It worked, and moments later, the flames danced merrily on her palm once more.

"What else can you do, Lara?" Alar asked, a challenge in his voice. "Show us."

Heat washed over her. *Prick.* He was right though: summoning fire to her palm wasn't so hard. However, she was suddenly nervous to push it further. What if she lost control?

The flames guttered.

Breathing an oath, Lara closed her eyes and let stillness settle. She hadn't realized what a bubbling cauldron of emotion she was on the inside. All it took was a few words from the Half-blood, and her temper spiked.

Fire doesn't lie.

She was going to have to work hard if she wanted to wield fire successfully with Alar present.

Opening her eyes, she noted that the flames flickered eagerly in the center of her palm now, as if waiting for instruction.

"That's better," Ruari said, his tone soothing. "Mark things rather than respond to them. The flames will respond better if you stay calm."

She loosened her grip on the cairn stone with her other hand, gently rubbing it with her thumb. And when she did, the flames formed a neat ring and began to dance like revelers around a Bealtunn Fire.

Lara's lips curved. She'd never done that before. It dawned upon her then that the flames were fickle. They didn't like to be dominated or ordered around, which she'd mistakenly done at Gateway; instead, they had to be treated with respect. Elation swept over her—reminding her of how she'd felt that evening in the woods when the corpse candle had danced like a pixie on her palm—although she quickly throttled the emotion.

Calmness returned. Continuing to rub the stone, she 'asked' one of the flames to move into the center of the circle—and it did. She then concentrated on that single flame, watching as it rose like a burning pillar.

Nearby, Bree breathed something under her breath. However, Lara ignored her. She couldn't let anything distract her from the flame.

She nudged it once more with her mind, a gentle request, and the flame began to curl and twist before splitting off into four tongues. Exactly as she'd requested.

Her eyes grew wide. It was difficult to keep calm now, not when she'd been so successful. She wanted to flash Alar a victory grin, but to do so would shatter the connection she'd formed. No, she'd celebrate later.

For now, she'd enjoy this moment. Silently.

Alar swirled the dregs of wine in his cup and glanced across at where his wife was brushing her hair, readying herself to retire. The light of the nearby brazier caught the red in her auburn hair and burnished her creamy skin. "That was impressive earlier."

Lara cut her gaze his way, her lips pursing.

His praise washed off her these days. He'd hurt her more deeply than he'd realized.

Discomfort stirred within him then. Navigating this marriage was like trying to swim across a loch infested with aughisky. One wrong move and he'd be pulled under. When Lara had confided in him, he'd panicked. They were getting too close; he couldn't let her expect anything from him. But ever since he'd pushed her away, he'd regretted his harshness.

The urge to apologize to her rose then, but he smashed it down.

Justify nothing. Regret nothing. A mercenary he'd once shared an ale with, years ago now, had told him that. He'd never forgotten—indeed, he'd lived by those words ever since.

It was getting late. They'd returned from the 'practice pavilion' and shared a silent cup of wine. Lara had ignored him as they sat by the brazier, her eyes unfocused as she stared into the flames.

"I mean it," he said, even as guilt needled him once more. "You showed remarkable control … for a beginner."

She pulled another face before dragging the hog bristle brush through her hair with more force than necessary. "It better be enough." Her tone was clipped. She refused to meet his eye.

"It has to be."

Her fine features tensed. "What if the Slew return before I'm ready?"

"They probably will." She cut him a sharp look then, her brows drawing together. However, he merely shrugged. "And you'll repel them as you did at Gateway … but with a little more control."

Lara looked away once more. "And how will I wield fire without anyone recognizing me?"

Alar lifted a hand and stroked his chin. "You're right," he murmured. "That's an issue."

"Aye … and one we can't ignore." Lara rose to her feet and moved across to the pile of furs in the corner of the royal pavilion, her bare feet sinking into the sheepskins. She wore nothing but a thin linen tunic that clung to her lithe body as she walked.

Alar blinked before cutting his gaze back to the smoldering embers of the brazier. Moments passed before he cleared his throat. "I might have a solution."

31: THE FIRE WRAITH

"THE SLEW ARE back."

Glancing up from where she'd been checking Bracken's hooves, Lara met Cailean's eye. He'd just appeared in the enclosure, next to where Bree was rubbing down her sturdy cob. The chief-enforcer's expression was grim.

Chin kicking up, Lara looked west. Dusk came early now that Gateway lay behind them and the bitter season approached. Sure enough, in the distance, she spied familiar dark, swirling clouds. "Fuck," she breathed.

Her pulse went wild then. She wasn't up to this. Not in the slightest.

They were only two nights into their journey north. Dulross was still at least three days' ride away. She'd hoped to have more time to practice, to improve on what she'd learned.

But the Gods wished to throw her to the wolves.

Ducking out of the enclosure, she strode toward the heart of the camp. Wordlessly, Bree fell in step next to her. They both knew what she needed to do. She had to get to her pavilion and don the disguise Alar had created for her.

She hoped he was right—that it would be enough. Unfortunately, she hadn't been able to come up with anything better.

Her husband wasn't with her now though. He'd ridden ahead to join his wulvers in the advance guard for most of the day and hadn't returned yet. She wouldn't be getting any last-minute advice from him, not that she wanted it.

Resolve tightened her belly as she neared the royal pavilion. Ready or not, some things had to be faced alone.

Ducking into her tent, she found Florie and the twins busy unpacking items. "Leave, please," she ordered. All three lasses startled. Heads bowed, they fled from the pavilion.

As soon as she was alone, Lara went to the satchel next to her furs and withdrew a black cloak. It was one of Alar's, voluminous with a deep cowl. It smelled of him too: leather and oak, with a hint of mint.

Trying not to let the scent distract her, she threw on the cloak. She then dug into the satchel once more and pulled out a leather mask. Her husband had made it for her the night before, cutting up a pair of leather breeches. It had holes for her eyes, nose, and mouth, although when she'd tried it on, she'd wanted to rip it off straight away. It clung to her skin, smothering her like a clammy hand over her face.

She wouldn't don the mask yet though.

Tucking it under her cloak, she ducked out of the pavilion. Bree was waiting for her. The two women shared a nod before they set off, hurrying toward the perimeter of the camp.

And as they wove through the press of tents, stepping over guide ropes and iron stakes, the shrieks of the approaching Slew cut through the air.

Her palms grew damp. Anxiety now pitched in her gut, although she managed to tamp down the tendrils of panic that wreathed up like smoke. Losing her nerve wouldn't help.

She had to keep her mind focused. Clear.

Drawing near to the western edge of the encampment, where a line of bards had begun a protection sain, she and Bree ducked into the shadow of one of the tents. There, she quickly put on her mask. Moving behind Lara, Bree secured it with ties around the back of her head.

And when her warder had finished tying the last knot, Lara pulled up her hood. Her heart was beating fast now, sweat damp upon her skin. Alar had assured her the disguise was unsettling. She hoped he was right.

"Stay here," she warned Bree. "It's best you keep out of sight."

"Be careful," her friend replied, her voice tight. "Don't let any of the druids get too close ... especially enforcers."

Lara nodded, even as her stomach pitched. Surely, once they saw what she was doing, they'd all realize she was a friend rather than a foe? However, she couldn't worry about that now.

Once she emerged from her hiding place, she needed to be confident. No matter what happened, she had to hold her ground, to focus on driving out the Slew.

Jaw set and shoulders squared, she stepped out from behind the tent.

Just in time too, for the first of the wraiths were diving—dark, winged shapes that swooped down from the sky like massive buzzards.

The pungent, familiar smell of earth magic filled her nostrils—pine and campfire—as the bards' singing grew louder, shriller.

Drawing the cairn stone with her right hand, she focused on the line of pitch torches that burned bright on the perimeter, just a few yards away. Hundreds had been shoved into the ground and lit. They'd brought numerous wagons loaded with torches made with 'fatwood' for this journey—resin-soaked pine that would burn all night, and in all weathers.

No one had seen her yet.

Sweating now, she deepened her breathing and attempted to pack her churning thoughts away. Curse it. She didn't have time for this. She needed to settle her mind. Now.

A shadow dropped from above. A bard's scream cut off mid-note as claws found her shoulders, lifting her into the darkness.

Urgency slammed into Lara. *Do it now!*

She tightened her grip on the cairn stone. It warmed against her palm as she extended her left arm, her fingers snapping straight.

With a 'whoosh', the flames spurted skyward.

She staggered back, blinking as the gloaming lit up. Gods, she'd never wielded so much fire at one time. The power of it surging through her veins was heady. How easy it would be to succumb, to let it consume her.

Resisting it, she sucked in a deep breath and held it for a few moments—as Ruari had shown her—before slowly exhaling.

Around her, warriors and druids had turned, their gazes alighting upon the black-robed figure who'd just torched the sky. A wall of flames surrounded them now, and the Slew drew back, shrieking.

The *Ord-ree seal* upon her right hand started to pulse like an ember then. Her already racing heart lurched once more. Why did her father's ring, handed down from ruler to ruler, respond to fire?

Lara contracted her fingers slightly, and the flames dimmed for a heartbeat, before she released her power once more.

Fire exploded from every torch. Flames whipped through the air, turning dusk to blazing gold. A tent caught and went up in seconds.

Did I do that?

The fire had its own hunger now. It lashed in every direction while bards scrambled back from the heat. But the Slew were retreating, their screams fading into the distance.

Her skin felt raw. Sweat ran between her shoulder blades as the power burned through her, demanding more than she could give. Her legs trembled. Around her, voices shouted in confusion and fear.

Now.

She crushed her fist closed. Darkness slammed down like a curtain.

In that blind moment, she ran.

The torches flared back to life behind her, but when the warriors turned to find their savior, only empty shadows remained.

"They're calling you 'the Fire Wraith'," Bree murmured as she speared a piece of blood sausage with her eating knife. "Everyone's convinced the Gods have sent you to protect us."

Lara swallowed a mouthful of bread before reaching for her cup. She then took a large gulp of wine. "Maybe they have." She hadn't considered it before, but what if The Five were behind her in this?

Cailean raised his eyebrows. Indeed, she'd just made a bold statement.

Her skin prickled. If that was the case, their campaign was off to a strong start.

The four of them—Lara, Alar, Bree, and Cailean—ate supper alone in the royal pavilion. Skaal had joined them too, her large body curled up before the brazier behind them. Her gentle snores reverberated through the tent.

The High Queen had deliberately dismissed her attendants so they could talk.

Lara glanced her husband's way then. He'd said little since they'd sat down to a meal of blood sausage, oaten bread, and cheese. Earlier, she'd just returned to her pavilion, shivering in the aftermath of wielding fire, when he ducked inside. Turning to him, she'd marked his flustered expression.

Their gazes had locked then, and it dawned on her that he'd been worried about her.

He'd recovered swiftly, smoothing his features and favoring her with a smile, but it was too late. She'd seen it.

"The disguise worked," she said, meeting his eye.

Alar's lips quirked. "I told you it would."

"In the firelight, the mask looked like molten gold," Cailean replied. Of course, he'd been at the perimeter. He'd watched the scene unfold. "I'm not surprised everyone thinks they saw a wraith."

Lara's fingers tightened around her cup. "Next time, I'll be faster though." Her pulse quickened then. On the next occasion she faced the Slew, she wouldn't let them take anyone. That bard's screams still rang in her ears.

Alar snorted softly as he reached for a piece of bread. "You'll speed up with practice."

"Where were you earlier?" Cailean's gaze now settled upon the prince consort, suspicion darkening his eyes. "You disappeared when we made camp."

"I was meeting with my wulvers," Alar replied with a shrug. "Keeping an eye on me, mac Brochan?"

"Always," Cailean rumbled, staring him down.

Skaal rose from the furs before the brazier then, stretching. A moment later, the fae hound padded over to the table, ignoring the chief-enforcer and pushing her furry cheek up against Alar's head instead.

Smiling, he stroked her ears before glancing Cailean's way. "At least Skaal trusts me."

"She does," Bree murmured, eyeing the fae hound as she tried to lick Alar's cheek. "How strange."

Watching her companions interact, Lara frowned. Cailean and Bree's suspicion of Alar was palpable. She'd thought they might have softened toward the prince consort, especially after recent events. *Her* relationship with him had been strained of late—if she were honest, his harshness with her that night back at Duncrag still stung—but that was personal. She still valued his opinion and respected his skills. He'd saved her life at Gateway, publicly defended her honor, and come up with a disguise that would hopefully continue to hide her identity when she wielded fire. Did it matter where he'd been at dusk?

The chief-enforcer obviously thought so. His jaw bunched, his dark brows drawing together over the sharp blade of his nose. "I'm watching you, Half-blood."

32: FAR GREATER THINGS

"CAILEAN STILL DOESN'T like you much."

Alar looked up from where he'd been unlacing the leather bracers on his forearms. His lips then lifted at the corners. "I'd noticed."

"Bree doesn't either."

Her husband shrugged. "They're both just doing their jobs." He paused then. "And they're loyal to you."

Lara smiled. "They are."

His gaze met hers then. "True friendship is rare, Lara. Guard it. Treasure it. Never take it for granted."

Something in his tone made her still. She'd just gotten up from kneeling before the shrine where her four rosewood figurines sat. It was time to retire to the furs, yet she hesitated. Things had been frosty between them for days now, yet tonight, curiosity made her thaw a little.

"Lyall and Dolph are loyal to you too," she pointed out.

"Aye." He cut his gaze away as he removed both bracers and set them down on a stool next to the furs. He then started to loosen the ties on his vest. "We're as close as brothers."

"You don't have any siblings, do you?"

"No man would go near my mother once they learned she had a Half-blood son." His voice was quiet, yet there was a slight edge to it. "She didn't seem to care though."

Silence followed this admission before Lara cleared her throat. "I had an elder brother."

"I know." Warmth flushed across her chest. Of course, he did. "Were you close?"

"Aye … you remind me of him sometimes."

His eyebrows raised as he cut his attention back to her. "Aye?"

"Calm, clever … with a wry sense of humor. There was an edge to him too. Anger that often simmered just beneath the surface."

"And why was that?"

Lara's chest constricted, as it often did when she thought of her brother. "His relationship with our father was … strained. Nothing he did was good enough."

"Why doesn't that surprise me?"

"Father used to tell him he didn't have the stomach to rule … but he was wrong."

"Maybe … maybe not." Alar's voice had veiled now. "But he wasn't destined to take the throne. *You* were."

Lara's pulse quickened then. How had they ended up talking about this? It was her fault for engaging him in conversation in the first place. However, he was looking at her intently now—in that way of his that made her feel *seen*.

"Do you think it was fated then?" she whispered.

He smiled. "You were never meant to remain by the hearth while your husband went off to battle. Look at what you did today." He paused then, his grey eyes darkening. "No, you were meant for far greater things."

Her breathing grew shallow. *Be careful*, she warned herself. The Half-blood could speak in a way that made her unfurl like a flower with one breath and bleed with the next.

An ache rose under her breastbone then.

No, she'd be a fool to let her shields down again with him. All the same, there was no denying that he believed in her. They'd crossed swords about what the future held for Albia; but when he looked at her as he was doing now, she felt capable and strong, as if there was nothing she couldn't achieve if she put her mind to it.

His belief banished her lingering doubts and fears like The Sweeper clearing away sea fret on a spring morning.

Gods, she wanted to prove him right.

A misty rain began to fall as another long day of travel ended. Rubbing her back, which was stiff after a day in the saddle, Lara walked at Alar's side through the encampment.

And all the while, her gaze kept flicking west.

The Slew always came from that direction, and she had to be ready for them. At the first sign, she'd rush back to her tent and throw on her cloak.

Her palms grew damp then. She hoped she could wield fire out here as successfully a second time.

Approaching the eastern perimeter, Lara's gaze traveled over where warriors were pushing torches into the damp ground and lighting them.

They'd camped off the road, in a wooded glen. The silhouettes of tall, dark pines stood out against an indigo sky, and the rugged outline of the Shiel Range was a faint shadow to the south. They were well into the borderlands now. Albia would grow wilder from this point on.

And among the trees, golden lights flickered. Corpse candles.

Lara halted, her breath catching.

The Mother bless her, she'd never seen so many of them. With the spirit world churned up at present, the faerie lights had come out to play in force. Nonetheless, they were far more pleasant visitors than the ravenous Slew or the sorrowful wail of The Weeper.

The corpse candles lit up the wet dusk like hundreds of lanterns moving through the pines.

Memories of that evening near Doure rolled in then, returning with vivid clarity. They called to her now too, beguiling and beautiful. The *Ord-ree seal* on her right hand flickered, answering the flames.

"Careful, Lara," Alar's voice drew her away from the flickering lights. "Don't stare at them too long."

Shaking herself free of the corpse candles' call, she swiveled on her heel and came face-to-face with her husband. She wiped the rain off her face before grimacing. "Thank you."

Alar stepped in close then, glancing around to make sure they weren't overhead before murmuring. "Your love of fire betrays you … the corpse candles sense it."

Her heart kicked, and she cut a wary glance back at where the lights still burned amongst the trees. She wanted to deny his words, but her gut told her he was right. The dancing flames were likely more attractive to her because she was a fire-wielder. It was best she kept her gaze averted from the woods at dusk in future.

She looked up at the sky once more. "No sign of the Slew … yet."

"They haven't come two nights in a row so far," he replied. "Although that doesn't mean they won't. There doesn't appear to be any pattern to their arrival."

"No," she agreed, even as her pulse sped up. Taking back The Uplands from the Shee was going to be hard enough without having to fight off malevolent spirits along the way.

Heaving a sigh, she raised her face to the rain. Its gentle caress was soothing, yet it couldn't wash away her worries. Ardroth hadn't been the only village plagued by wraiths. They'd passed through another at noon with similar tales to tell. Grimlochs had been causing problems too—putting out hearths and filling homes with choking smoke. The villagers were frightened, and they'd looked to her for answers.

However, she couldn't give them any. Not yet.

"There are so many things I need to put right," she whispered. "But I swear by The Five that I will."

Alar watched his wife as her eyes fluttered shut. A faint sheen of rain covered her lovely face. Nonetheless, there were lines of strain there. She hid it well, but he could tell this campaign was already taking its toll on her.

Unfortunately, it would continue to.

His chest tightened.

He didn't want this woman to suffer.

"You aren't responsible for everything, Lara," he said finally, choosing his words with care. The last time they'd ventured into this territory, they'd argued. But he didn't want to clash with her this evening.

Opening her eyes, Lara shifted her attention to him. Her gaze was dark, reflecting the flickering flames of the nearby torches. "Someone has to be accountable," she said huskily.

He frowned. "Aye ... but we all have our limits."

Their gaze drew out before Lara raised her chin. It was a look he'd come to know well over the turns of the last few moons. His wife was digging her heels in. The tension under his ribs sharpened then. The Hearthkeeper smite him, he wished she weren't so brave. So determined and defiant.

"You say there's no going back to how things were ... and maybe you're right." Her voice was low and steady. "But I will still fight to stop the Shee taking my homeland ... or die trying."

33: LIAR

A MURKY DUSK slid into a drizzly night. They waited, but the Slew didn't appear.

Relief settled over the encampment, although it didn't last long, for as corpse candles flickered amongst the trees, a grief-filled wail split the air.

The Weeper had returned.

The sound raked its claws through Alar, each scream winding him tighter.

Fuck it. He needed some time alone. Some time to breathe.

"I'll let Bree accompany you back to the tent," he said to Lara, as her warder approached them. "I'll join you for supper later."

Lara nodded, giving him a smile that made his insides knot. "I'll see you later then."

He watched her and Bree leave, heading toward the royal pavilion in the heart of the camp. And then, when the women had disappeared, he turned on his heel and walked in the opposite direction.

The scent of burning pine from the numerous cookfires drifted through the damp air. Making his way through tightly-packed clusters of hide tents, Alar traveled toward the northern edge of the sprawling encampment, where his wulvers had pitched their tents.

And as he walked, he gave himself a talking to.

Idiot. Get a leash on yourself.

He'd told himself he'd keep Lara at a distance, but with every furlong north, he was weakening. The truth was, he liked her far too much.

Lengthening his stride, he headed to the largest of the wulver pavilions, where his captains resided. He ducked through the tent flap to find Lyall and Dolph perched on stools, sharing cups of wine. A low brazier glowed between them, where trout fillets sizzled upon an iron plate. Usually, Alar liked the aroma of grilling fish, but this evening, it made him queasy.

"Nothing to report?" he greeted them, more brusquely than usual.

The wulvers' gazes snapped his way.

"Not yet," Lyall replied.

"You look like you could do with a drink?" Dolph gestured to the jug on a low table nearby. "Help yourself."

Alar shook his head. Instead, he folded his arms across his chest.

"Ashes, you've got a face on you tonight." Lyall stretched out his long, muscular legs, clad in leather trews, and crossed them at the ankle. "What's wrong? Is your young wife harder to handle than you thought?"

Dolph snorted. "He's already proven that. He started making concessions and promises to the woman before he even married her, remember?"

Alar stilled. His brother's jibe cut a little too close to the bone.

Both wulvers observed him keenly, their golden eyes glinting in the light of the brazier.

"It's good to be free of Duncrag," Dolph admitted then, leaning forward and flipping the fish. "I've missed the wind and rain on my face … the freedom of wide skies and rolling hills."

Uneasiness rippled through Alar at these words.

"You should be in a celebratory mood, brother." Lyall raised his cup of wine to him. "Everything is going to plan, is it not?"

There was no mistaking the challenge in his voice.

"Aye," Alar replied. "I'd tell you if there was anything to worry about."

"Good." Lyall stared him down. "Because we've all worked too hard, for too long, to let *anything* ruin this for us."

The rain had stopped as Alar made his way through the ring of tents—where the druids would bed down—back toward the royal pavilion. The air was still heavy with moisture though and laced with the scent of woodsmoke and roasting meat. He recognized the gamey smell. Grouse. Someone had gone hunting before dusk.

He skirted around a glowing firepit where Cailean, Bree, and Roth all sat playing Liar while the carcasses of three birds roasted on a spit. They were taking turns shaking dice in a lidded cup and then trying to guess whether each of them was lying about its contents.

He might have passed unnoticed if Skaal hadn't spotted him.

The fae hound rose smoothly to her feet and paced across to Alar, nudging him hard with her nose.

And despite his dark mood, he stroked the thick ruff around her neck.

Cailean's chin jerked up, his gaze narrowing at the sight of him.

Alar couldn't help it; he flashed the chief-enforcer a smirk.

Cailean scowled. *Bull's eye.* Few things annoyed the warrior druid more than the adoration Skaal had for the Half-blood. It took Alar aback too, although he didn't discourage the beast.

But then, the chief-enforcer surprised him. "How about a game?"

Alar raised his eyebrows. "Now?"

"Aye."

"Lara will be waiting for me."

"I'm sure she won't mind," Bree chimed in. "Her attendants were still readying supper when I left them a short while ago."

Meanwhile, the glint in Cailean's eye made something competitive flare inside Alar.

He hadn't played Liar in a long while, not since the time he'd spent in Braewall. It was a popular game amongst the Marav, yet he found it boring.

"What's wrong?" Roth asked as Alar hesitated, his tone goading. "Worried one of us will *unmask* you?"

"Not at all," Alar drawled. Moving across to the fire, he pulled up a stool and pushed in next to the captain. Skaal padded up and sat down behind him. Alar didn't miss the way Cailean's jaw tightened at her disloyalty. "Let's go."

"We're halfway through a round," Bree replied tersely. "You'll have to wait." Picking up the cup, she shook the pair of dice within before peeking inside. "Two fives," she declared, replacing the lid. She then shifted her attention to Cailean. Her husband had the first go at deciding whether she was a 'Liar'. After a moment, he grunted, accepting her answer. The challenge now moved to Roth. The captain's gaze narrowed as he studied Bree's face. Alar had to admit, the woman was good at veiling her expression.

Perhaps it was because she was once Shee.

"Liar," Roth said finally.

Bree whipped off the lid and thrust the cup at him. "See for yourself."

Roth peered inside before growling an oath. It seemed Bree had been telling the truth.

"Not good at this game, are you, captain?" Alar couldn't help himself.

"Let's see you have a go then." Roth shoved the cup at him.

Alar took it without comment, fastened the lid, and shook the dice.

Meanwhile, the others watched him, their faces gilded by firelight. The aroma of roasting grouse made Alar's belly rumble.

Looking inside, he straightened up. "Two sixes."

Roth gave a low whistle. "Someone just slapped their balls down on the table."

Cailean snorted, while Bree's eyes narrowed. "Are you sure?"

"Two sixes," he repeated with a shrug. "What say you?"

She stared at him for a few moments, her gaze drilling into his face. She then nodded, conceding, and glanced over at Roth. "What say you?"

The captain's lips pursed as he studied Alar intently.

Alar let him. He was starting to enjoy this; maybe Liar wasn't as dull as he remembered.

Finally, his gaze sharp with irritation, Roth nodded too. "What do you think, Cailean?"

The chief-enforcer rubbed his jaw, which was shadowed by dark stubble. "So, you both believe he's telling the truth?"

"Aye," Bree replied. "Do you?"

Cailean's woad-blue eyes drilled into him. The man had a stare that could cut through flesh. Alar wasn't intimidated though. If he were honest, he enjoyed challenging the chief-enforcer. He was a worthy opponent.

"All right," Cailean muttered after another lengthy pause. "You're telling the truth."

Disappointed that he'd been as easy to dupe as the others, Alar handed him the cup.

Cailean lifted the lid. "Fuck," he growled. "Two 'ones'."

Roth snarled something under his breath, while Bree eyed Alar, her expression cold. "Why am I not surprised you're a good liar?"

34: VOICES IN THE RAIN

LARA WIPED THE rain out of her eyes and peered into the murk.

It was as if The Hag—the Goddess who presided over this time of year—had decided to turn against them. Halfway through their journey to Dulross, the weather had changed. Autumn plunged into winter. The Gales of Complaint roared in from the north, bringing sheets of icy rain. The foul weather slowed them down, and made their horses lower their necks, flatten their ears, and tuck their tails between their legs. The road had become a mire, and the supply wagons kept getting stuck, forcing the whole army to halt while warriors and wulvers strained to free them.

Dulross was less than a day away now, yet the harsh wind and driving rain made the fort seem far off. The rain had even soaked through Lara's thick fur cloak. Her fingers were now chilled, and her teeth had started to chatter.

"You should take refuge in one of the covered wagons."

Lara cast Alar a sidelong glance. Rain gleamed on his face, although unlike her, he didn't hunch in the saddle. Years living wild amongst the wulvers had toughened her husband—but she wasn't as hardy.

"There's little point now," she replied, even as she tried to still her shivering. "We're close to stopping for the day anyway."

That was true enough, although it was difficult to keep track of time when the weather was this bad, for they couldn't follow the sun across the sky. All the same, their break at noon had been a while ago. And it appeared to Lara that the afternoon was growing steadily darker. Dusk wasn't far away.

Shifting uncomfortably in the saddle, she cut a glance up at the leaden sky. Lighting the torches would be a challenge in this weather, even with fatwood.

Alar didn't insist further. She liked that he didn't push things with her. He'd never once tried to bully her into obeying him.

And despite that she was wet and cold, and her legs chafed from riding in the rain, warmth kindled deep in her breast. Her husband was arrogant, bull-headed, and frustratingly enigmatic, but he respected her wishes. He *listened* to her.

This journey had brought them closer. The rift between them was starting to heal. She looked forward to the evenings, after her attendants had withdrawn, when it was just the two of them. They'd sit by the brazier, cups of wine in hand, and talk quietly about the day.

In those moments, it felt as if they had a real marriage.

Maybe, eventually, we could—

Lara swiftly pulled herself up short. What was she doing?

She was a High Queen on campaign. Daydreaming about her husband was foolish.

Bristling with irritation at herself, she blinked the rain out of her eyes and took note of her surroundings.

She and Alar rode, side by side, near the head of the main body of the army. Cailean and Roth were a few yards in front of them, while Bree rode just behind. Skaal loped in easy strides alongside. Her long coat hung in wet, heavy clumps. She didn't seem to mind the rain though.

The advance guard—a force of four hundred wulvers—had already disappeared into the mists ahead. The rest of the wulvers traveled with the rear guard, protecting their supply wagons, healers, slaves, and servants. For most of the day, they'd wended their way through woodland interspersed by swamps. Fortunately, the road between Duncrag and Dulross was a proper one, and this section had long ago been raised up with deep ditches on either side.

Lara's brow furrowed as she gazed around her. They wouldn't be stopping just yet. Watery marshes—interspersed with rushes—stretched on either side of the highway.

She glanced Alar's way once more, marking the groove between his eyebrows as he looked right, to where rain stippled the water. His horse snorted then and bucked. Alar kept his seat and leaned forward, placing a steadying hand on the beast's slick neck. "Easy," he soothed.

Likewise, Lara's mount startled. Bracken, usually unflappable, side-stepped, threw up her head, and gave a high-pitched squeal. Stroking the mare's neck, Lara looked around her. "What's spooked them?"

Alar didn't answer. He was too busy staring out across the marshes.

"Can you hear that?" Bree's voice cut through the rain.

Lara twisted in her saddle. "Hear what?"

"Gurgling."

Alar's hands lifted to his blades. "I hear it too."

Lara held her breath, listening. There—a wet, rhythmic burbling that almost sounded like words drowning in water.

Her stomach dropped. *Beware of voices in the rain near dusk or dawn.* Her nursemaid's warnings echoed in her mind as the bog began to bubble. Mist rose from its surface like steam from a cauldron.

Cailean's curse split the air. An instant later, Skaal gave a loud growl, her hackles rising.

Emaciated figures crawled from the marsh.

Lara's pulse went wild. *The Fuath.*

The Slew weren't the only malevolent spirits in Albia that attacked in packs—bog wights did too. The Fuath were the corrupted spirits of those who'd drowned. Ragged, water-logged clothing still clung to their bodies, but their mottled blue-green skin, slick and slightly transparent, wasn't Marav. Nor were the webbed hands and feet, tipped with curving claws, they used to pull themselves free of the bog.

Long, tangled hair flowed over their shoulders, their large fishlike eyes fixed upon the column of riders and warriors before them.

"Draw iron!" Cailean roared.

Skaal lunged forward.

Metal sang in the rain. Lara's dagger was in her hand before she'd thought to draw it.

The Fuath swarmed the road.

Alar dropped to the ground, and Lara hastily followed his lead. Horses screamed, rearing back from the onslaught. Warriors formed a tight circle around the High Queen.

A warrior went down shrieking as a female Fuath buried her fangs in his leg. Her companions dragged him into the bog. His cries cut off with a wet gurgle.

Iron hissed through waterlogged flesh. The bog wights' bodies burst like punctured aleskins, flooding the road. The sharp scent of pine and ash followed as the enforcers drew upon their strength. The strident notes of singing rose above the fracas. Ren and her bards were trying to weaken their attackers. Some of the Fuath shrank from the sound, and from Cailean as he strode into their midst, iron broadsword swinging.

One slipped past the guards, lunging for Bree. Her blade opened its throat in a spray of brackish water.

Skaal's growls punctuated the shouts and grunts of battle. Lara couldn't see the fae hound, but she was nearby. Protecting them.

"Keep close!" Bree shouted. "Protect the High Queen!"

It was too late—they'd already gotten through.

Lara's world shrank to slick skin and gaping mouths. Fear pounded in her chest like a war drum. She swiped at an attacker, her dagger blade scoring a line down a bare arm. Translucent skin burst open, and the wraith retreated with a screech. Iron left a nasty cut, but it wasn't enough to keep them at bay.

"Lara!" Alar shouted. She couldn't see him now either.

"I'm here!" she screamed back.

A lean figure with stringy hair flew at her, webbed claws outstretched. She drove her dagger up, and felt it punch through slick skin. The wight's scream sprayed her with bog water.

Another Fuath lunged at her. Claws raked Lara's throat. Stinging pain followed as she reeled back. The bog wight followed.

Salt. Mirren's voice sliced through her terror. The pouch at her belt, sealed tight against the rain, was packed full of it.

She fumbled for her pouch as teeth snapped near her face. Her fingers closed around a handful of salt. An instant later, she flung it into the wight's eyes. It reeled back, clawing at its face in agony.

Another took its place.

Twin blades flashed between them. Alar was there. Somehow, he'd cut through the press to reach her.

"Salt!" Lara screamed to anyone who could hear. "Use salt!"

She flung another handful. The wight writhed away, shrieking.

But they kept coming. The narrow road trapped her people in a column—perfect for slaughter. They were outnumbered, outflanked, and drowning in a sea of raking claws and eel-like teeth.

Around her, warriors caught on. Iron and salt flew together now. The wights' screams turned desperate, raw.

Lara pressed her back to Alar's, her last grains of salt burning in her palm. Her blade was slick with bog water and something fouler.

Bree fought her way back to them, blood streaming from her face. Her dagger opened another throat. Water crashed over them in a wave.

The screaming reached a crescendo—then silence.

The Fuath drew back into the mist, leaving only bodies and the steady drum of rain.

35: UNSTOPPABLE

BREATHING HARD, Alar turned to his wife.

Lara stood there, one hand still gripping her dagger. Her face was pale, and blood trickled down her throat. But she was alive. Defiant.

Alar's skin prickled. He'd underestimated her. When he'd realized that the Fuath had broken through the circle of warriors defending the High Queen, and that Bree was seriously outnumbered, he'd thought Lara was done for. But she hadn't been.

Stepping in close, his hand lifted to her throat. "You're hurt."

"Just a graze," she said huskily. "I was lucky."

"All the same … Eldra should take a look."

She nodded. Lifting her free hand, she placed it on his chest. "You aren't injured?"

"Just a few scratches." He was surprised to have emerged relatively unscathed, for he'd been desperate to reach her earlier. He'd fought his way in a frenzy through the press of slippery, mottled turquoise bodies, but for every bog wight he cut down, three more replaced it—claws raking, hair whipping around him like snares, and teeth snapping.

He'd lost sight of her then, although her shout had cut through the din. *Use salt!* And he had.

It had made all the difference in repelling their attackers.

They stood upon the highway, ankle-deep in stagnant water. A knot of trembling horses clustered farther down the road. Fortunately, the press of the army behind them had prevented their mounts from bolting.

Around them, the rasp of exhausted breathing cut through the darkening afternoon. The Gales of Complaint still pushed against him, whipping wet hair into his eyes, but Alar hadn't noticed during the fight.

Slowly, the water drained off the road into the ditches flanking it. However, he wouldn't relax yet. His gaze narrowed as he scanned the marshes, listening for the telltale gurgling of voices.

Nothing.

How many warriors had fallen in the fight? A dozen at least, maybe more. Men and women Lara couldn't afford to lose. No wulvers though, for they were divided between the advance and rear guards.

"We need to move," Cailean announced. The chief-enforcer stood with his wife. Bree was bleeding from several cuts, although she hardly seemed to notice them. Instead, her gaze swept their surroundings, looking for more trouble.

"Aye … dusk approaches," Roth replied. A deep cut oozed upon the captain's right arm—an injury that needed seeing to. "Let's retrieve our horses and get going."

And they did. Most of the injured were able to ride, and those who weren't now traveled in the wagons. The army moved faster now, the drum of hoofbeats echoing through the rain. And all the while, Alar kept one eye on the marshes.

"Have you ever fought a bog wight before?" Lara asked eventually.

Alar cut her a glance. His wife was shivering in her sodden clothing. They needed to find refuge so she could get out of the wet and cold. He shook his head. "I had a close brush with them once … a long time ago though."

"What happened?"

"When I was a bairn, my mother and I were returning from the village market. It was raining, and we were passing a flooded field when we heard voices." He paused then, as he recalled the incident. It had taken place decades earlier, yet he still remembered it vividly. "Ma grabbed my hand, and we fled like hares."

A nerve flickered in Lara's cheek. "They ambushed us."

Uneasiness slithered in Alar's gut as he nodded. "They did."

"The Raven Queen?"

"I don't think so," he replied cautiously. "The Shee's allies have been faerie creatures … the likes of trows and powries … but I've never heard of them holding sway over spirits."

"They don't." Bree's voice made them both turn in the saddle. She rode behind them, Cailean at her side now. "None of the living, be they Shee or Marav, can control the spirit world."

Lara ducked into her tent and pushed her hood back.

She paused then, listening for the screech of the Slew outside. Nothing. Only the rise and fall of excited voices. She'd just driven the restless dead off for the second time on this journey. The Fire Wraith had returned, and the camp was alive with talk about the flames that had erupted from its fingers.

Heaving a sigh, Lara shrugged off her cloak. Gods, she was bone-weary. Her limbs ached, her feet dragged, and she was now shivering. Chills rippled across her skin, and her teeth chattered. Quickly retrieving her favorite fur-lined cloak, she pulled it tightly about her.

Her heartbeat pulsed in the hollow of her throat. After the Fuath attack, she'd been on edge, jumping at shadows. The last thing she needed was another visit from the Slew. However, at dusk, they'd appeared.

Luckily, fire had done her bidding.

Outdoors, the rain had ceased, although The Gales of Complaint still raced across the land. They'd crossed into The Uplands now and had set up camp overnight on a rugged hillside. She couldn't wait to reach Dulross. The fort would provide a couple of days' reprieve and comfort before they struck out for Strath.

Still shivering, despite that she was now wrapped in wool and fur, she crossed to the satchel she'd left next to the furs and stuffed away her cloak and mask. However, as she did so, she marked the tremble in her hands. Curse it, she needed to pull herself together.

Alar entered the tent then.

Straightening up, she turned to face him, taking in his unkempt appearance. The rain had slicked his hair back, and streaks of mud smeared his face and bare arms. "Just in time," she greeted him with a brittle smile before gesturing to where an iron pot hung over the nearby brazier. "The water should be hot enough now for bathing."

She nodded then to the curtain made of sewn-together hare skins that shielded the far corner of the tent—the space where they could bathe or use the privy.

Alar snorted. "Are you trying to tell me something, wife?"

She grimaced. "Aye … *both* of us look as if we crawled out of a bog."

He pulled a face too, agreeing with her. She shivered then as she recalled those glistening wights. They'd wanted to drag her into the marsh, to drown her and make her one of them.

"The camp's humming about the Fire Wraith," he said then, his gaze roaming over her face. "Again."

She managed a tight smile in response. She couldn't afford to congratulate herself too much. At this rate, they'd all see her 'perform' many more times before the campaign was over. "Let's hope my disguise continues to fool them."

His gaze flicked to the satchel behind her. "You're careful not to let anyone too close?"

"Aye." An awkward silence fell then, and Lara cut her gaze away. Suddenly, she felt self-conscious around him. "The lasses will bring us supper shortly. We should wash up."

"You go first … while the water is hot."

She nodded. "Do you want some wine while you wait?"

He smiled. "Aye … thank you."

Trying to ignore the fluttering in her belly, she moved to the low table, where Florie had left a jug of plum wine, and poured him a cup. Their gazes met as she handed it to him—their stare drawing out for a moment too long. The air between them grew heavy.

Heat washed over Lara, and she cleared her throat. "Right … I'll be back soon."

Moving past him, she retreated behind the curtain, where two steaming bowls of water, blocks of soap, and drying sheets waited. Another, smaller, brazier burned in here, taking the edge off the cold, damp air. The sides of the tent billowed and snapped as the wind continued.

Lara cast off her cloak, relieved that her shivers were subsiding now. She then wriggled out of her long leather tunic, slit at the sides so she could ride. She wore simple clothing for travel, nothing that required a maid's assistance. It was a relief to peel off the wet woolen undertunic. Even the third layer, a linen shift, was damp. Standing naked on the sheepskins, she used one of the bowls of hot water to bathe, sighing as she cleaned off the sweat and grime of the road. She scrubbed at her arms, eager to remove any trace of the bog wight's touch.

The graze to her throat stung slightly as water trickled down her neck. Eldra had given her some salve for it, and she would apply some more after she'd bathed. The injury could have been far worse though. The Gods had been watching over her.

And so had her husband.

As she ate, Lara kept stealing glances at Alar.

Tonight, she and the prince consort ate alone. Lara had released Florie, Ani, and Lilith for the evening too; the lasses had retired to the small tent next to theirs.

Alar also had bathed. His long dark hair was now washed and brushed back so it hung in a heavy black curtain down his back. A clean leather vest and breeches encased his lithe body, although like her, he was barefoot. The warm glow of the nearby brazier cast a ruddy glow over his pale skin.

Underneath the grime, a few grazes and bruises from the fight with the Fuath were now evident. Fortunately, the injuries on his arm, shoulder, and thigh he'd sustained at Gateway were healing well and hadn't been reopened.

"I should put some salve on those grazes," she noted once they'd finished eating and were lingering over their cups of wine.

He shrugged. "They're fine. Don't fuss."

She raised an eyebrow. "Why not? Isn't that what a wife is supposed to do?"

Their gazes held for a few moments before Alar frowned. "That's not part of the bargain we struck, Lara."

She stiffened, marking his change in mood. Tonight, his shields were up. There was a sharpness to him.

"We never talked about the details of our marriage," she said after a tense pause. "Of what exactly we expect from each other. Perhaps we should."

He eyed her warily. "And what are your expectations of me?"

Lara stared back at him, and as she did, something inside her shifted. Maybe it was the Fuath, or perhaps it was a few days on the road with this man, but she suddenly knew what she needed. "I want our marriage to be *more* than a show put on for others," she said, her voice roughening. "I want to trust you, Alar … and for you to trust me."

A nerve flickered in his cheek as he stared back at her. "You don't—"

"I don't let others in easily," she cut him off. "Especially men. I never told you, but after my wedding night with Dunchadh, I went, in tears, to my father. I foolishly believed he'd annul our union once he heard about how brutal my husband had been." Her heart started to thunder in her ears. She couldn't believe she was telling him this. "He wasn't interested, and when I pleaded with him, he got angry and told me he didn't care what Dunchadh did to me in the privacy of our alcove." She paused then, embarrassment prickling her skin. "It was then I swore that I'd never give anyone power over me like that again."

Silence followed these words.

Alar had gone very still, his fingers clenched around his cup.

Lara's breathing grew shallow. "But you offered me your army of wulvers … and before I knew it, I was handfasted again." She paused then, feeling slightly sick now. Being this honest terrified her. "However, marriage to you is nothing like it was to Dunchadh. Things haven't been easy … yet you bring out the best in me. We could be partners, Alar. Together we could be unstoppable."

Something hot flared in his eyes then before he swallowed hard. "I'm not the man you deserve," he replied, a rasp to his voice now.

"Maybe not," she shot back. "But you're the man I *want*."

36: THE DUEL

ALAR ROSE ABRUPTLY from his seat then, dragging his hands through his still-damp hair. "Fuck," he muttered.

Pulse racing, Lara also stood up. He looked like he was about to bolt. She couldn't let him.

Moving around the edge of the trestle table, she approached her husband, stopping when they were a couple of feet apart. Alar turned to face her, panic in his eyes now.

Heat rolled over Lara. "Don't you want me … is that it?" Something inside her cringed then. He hadn't touched her since their handfasting. She'd told herself he was holding back out of respect, but she might have completely misread him.

"Of course, I want you." His voice was tight. Choked.

Relief slammed into Lara, making her lightheaded, reckless. She reached out and placed the palm of her hand on his chest. His heart was racing. "What then?"

His gaze burned into hers. "I told you … I'm *not* a good man."

"I don't care."

His mouth twisted. "You should."

Lara stepped closer still, breathing in the fresh scent of his skin. Dizziness swept over her once more. "If I'm to take back The Uplands and then deal with my overkings, I need a ruthless husband at my side." She paused then, her fingertips digging into his leather vest. "The innocent, sheltered lass I was once no longer exists. And it's just as well, for she wouldn't survive the coming war."

Alar stared down at her. His chest rose and fell sharply now, and the rawness in his eyes made her lower belly clench.

"You don't know what you're asking," he whispered, a plea in his voice.

"I do."

He breathed another curse. And then, a heartbeat later, his mouth slanted over hers. It was a fierce embrace, bruising, yet she welcomed it. For too long, they'd danced around each other. They both needed to stop fighting this.

They kissed wildly. Lara clung to him with a desperation that shocked her. She *craved* him. Likewise, he didn't hold back. His arms fastened around her, and he hauled her up against the long, hard length of his body.

And then, as the kiss deepened, he bent her back over his arm. The sensual stroke and plunge of his tongue made dizziness sweep over her. She responded eagerly, drowning in the taste of him: the rasp of his shaven chin against her skin, the graze of his teeth, and the heat of his mouth.

Gods, she'd never recover from this kiss.

It drew out, hot and hungry, and then his free hand slid up from her hip, over her belly and ribs, to where her breasts strained toward him through the woolen tunic she'd donned after bathing. His palm grazed them, and then his fingertips teased her nipples into hard, aching peaks.

And all the while, his mouth continued to feast on hers.

Lara writhed against him, the sensitive flesh between her thighs throbbing. This teasing was driving her mad. "More," she gasped. Aye, she did want more. She wanted him, naked, in the furs.

He made a sound low in his throat—something halfway between a growl and a moan—and then pulled her upright. A moment later, he bent down, grabbed the hem of her woolen tunic and the long linen shift she wore under it, and yanked them up, undressing her in one smooth movement.

His scalding mouth was on her breasts then, his hands pushing the twin mounds together as he drew each engorged nipple in, rolling it between his tongue and teeth.

Lara gasped and then whimpered. Her hands tangled through his long, damp hair, encouraging his delicious torture.

He released her then, and she cried out in disappointment.

Cursing, he swept his hand over the table beside them, sending wooden cups and trenchers flying. Before she had time to recover from her surprise, he moved her sideways and pushed her onto its now clear surface.

And then, he spread her trembling thighs wide, lowered himself to his knees on the furs, and gazed at her.

Heat rolled over Lara.

He'd looked at her like this before; even so, the intimacy of it still shocked her.

And then he leaned in.

The feel of his mouth on her sex, the hot flick of his tongue, and the pressure of his lips made her buck against him, excitement churning in the pit of her stomach. She couldn't believe he was tasting her there, or that she liked it this much. But he was, and she did.

Goosebumps pebbled her skin, even as she started to sweat. Moments later, her legs began to shake and jerk. Growling something inaudible, Alar pleasured her even more hungrily now, his tongue spearing into her repeatedly, making her arch toward him.

But when he fastened upon the nub of aching flesh nestled in the petals of her sex—and he began to suck it like he had her nipples—she went wild.

Her ragged cries tore through the tent, even as wild pleasure clenched and pulsed through her loins. She was vaguely aware then of the flames in the nearby brazier and the burning cressets that hung from the roof crosspieces flaring bright. However, she was too lost to dwell on the fire's response to her climax.

She shuddered and writhed as he continued to suck her through it. And then, when she lay there upon the table, panting and boneless, he rose from between her legs.

Their gazes met.

Alar tore off his clothing. Lara stared at her husband, her mouth going dry as she raked her gaze down his nakedness. He was magnificent. The ruddy light burnished his hard-muscled body and the snarling wolf tattoo across his chest. Its eyes glowed red tonight.

His shaft reared up from a nest of dark hair, a vein pulsing along its engorged length. Moisture glistened on his crown, and her breathing caught.

After Dunchadh, she'd vowed never to touch a man's prick, but she forgot about that now. Pushing herself up, she reached for him, one hand fastening around the base of his shaft, while she trailed the fingertips of the other up his hot, hard erection.

He made a choking sound in the back of his throat.

Encouraged, she slid the hand that gripped him up the length of him, thrilling at the way he grew even bigger and harder as she did so. She glanced up then, her gaze meeting his.

Her heart kicked. Gods. The way he was looking at her right now. It made her want to utterly forget herself. Their gazes locked, even as she continued to work him. A nerve flickered in his cheek, pleasure rippling across his aquiline features.

A thrill washed over her. She loved being able to touch him like this, to have him in her thrall.

Moments later, he grabbed hold of her wrist, stilling her.

Lara gave a cry of protest. Damn him, she was only getting started. She wanted to make him lose control. However, the next thing she knew, he'd shoved her onto her back upon the table, hauled her hips closer, and parted her thighs once more. Hooking his hands under Lara's knees, he pushed her legs back.

And then, with one, deep, punishing thrust, he drove into her.

She cried out—for it was a shock to be invaded like this— before hunger twisted in her lower belly. This was what she craved, for him to make her his. To *brand* her.

Sweat glistened on his chest and upper arms as he withdrew from her, almost to the tip. He was staring between her thighs, where their bodies joined, and the look on his face made her tremble.

It was hot. Carnal.

He thrust into her again, and this time, she angled her hips up to meet him, bringing him deeper still. Growling her name, he ground into her.

She whimpered. Pleasure coiled deep in her womb, an aching pulse that made her sweat and tremble. She was so wet now, so hungry for him.

"Is this how you want to be fucked, Lara?" he ground out, rolling his hips once more.

"Aye!" she cried, without a shred of shame. "Please!"

Pinning her legs back, he rode her in savage plunges that made the table rock. And with each thrust, she bucked hard against him. It was a duel. She wouldn't be consumed by his passion but would equal it. Thrust for thrust.

And all the while, Alar's gaze seared hers.

Held fast, Lara gave herself up to him. It was breathlessly raw to stare at each other while he plowed her. The masks they'd both donned since the beginning fell away, and at that moment, she knew he cared.

Lara's breathing turned ragged, a storm gathering inside her.

The intimacy made the pleasure clutch even harder. Emotion churned in her chest, even as her loins turned molten. Arching up, she gave herself up entirely to it, grinding herself against him, while her climax shuddered through her.

Light flared around them.

Alar snarled a curse. His lean body trembled, his eyes wild now. The roaring brazier next to them now gilded his sweat-slick skin. He shouted her name then, his spine arching as he came.

37: MY QUEEN

ALAR SCOOPED HIS wife up into his arms.

A few strides took them across the sheepskins to the pile of furs waiting for them. Around them, the brazier and cressets had settled down. When she'd shattered—for the second time—earlier, he'd thought she might set the tent alight.

Fortunately, she hadn't.

Her cheeks were flushed now, her gaze limpid, as he lay her down amongst the furs.

Alar's gut twisted, hunger spiking through him. He'd thought their wild tumble might have sated his appetite for his wife, but it had merely stoked it. He'd been tired earlier, his body aching after the clash with the Fuath, but now he felt as if he could go all night.

And he would.

He'd greedily take all this woman gave him. He'd then store it away and keep it for the dark days ahead, when he'd need reminding that beauty and light did exist in this twisted world. He kissed her then, tenderly now, heat igniting in his veins when she responded eagerly.

Lara's hunger for him, her lustiness, drove him insane. It was impossible to think straight when she fixed that luminous pine-green gaze upon him.

Idiot, a voice growled at the back of his mind—one that reminded him of Lyall—*what the fuck are you doing?*

Aye, indeed. He'd set himself strict rules since wedding the High Queen of Albia, but he'd broken every one of them.

He was supposed to remain detached, to bed her only when necessary.

He wasn't supposed to care.

Pull back. Now.

But he couldn't. The feel of Lara, pliant and wanting, in his arms, the sweet taste of her mouth, and the warmth and softness of her body, was a drug. He was nearly three times her age and had weathered much in his decades alive, but he'd never met anyone who made him see his existence for what it really was. Austere. Lonely.

He'd thought he was nothing but a bitter husk, but he'd been wrong. The lad he'd once been was still there, buried under layers of armor.

Driving all thoughts from his mind, he continued to kiss Lara, taking his time now. Their first coupling had been frenzied.

He'd been rougher than intended, yet she'd welcomed it, matched every thrust as she ground herself against him.

Exploring her body again now, he committed every curve, every smooth plane and angle to memory. She sighed and undulated under his touch, and he reveled in how responsive she was, how her fingers tangled in his hair when he suckled her breasts, and when he spread her legs and feasted on her.

Lara's gasps and throaty moans made him sweat.

He rolled her over then so that she lay on her belly upon the soft furs, propping herself up on her elbows. Covering her body with his, he spread her legs once more and entered her, gently, while his hand slid between her body and the furs and found her slick heat. He stroked and circled as he moved inside her, thrilling at the way she trembled against him, how her breathing caught, how she moaned his name.

She was close now, and he could feel his own climax gathering too. Heat ignited at the base of his spine. His self-control started to fray.

His eyelids fluttered then. He'd never forget tonight.

"Alar," she groaned his name, drawing it out like a prayer.

"My Queen," he whispered back as his sweat-slick body slid against hers. He held himself up with one elbow, his lips dragging along the soft line of her neck. This position was intimate, protective almost. She turned her head to him, and he grazed the column of her throat with his teeth before nipping.

She gave a choked cry then, and wetness flooded over his fingers as he continued to stroke her. "Aye, that's it, mo rùin," he rasped. "Give yourself to me."

My secret ... my beloved. That was what she was. His one weakness.

Her sharp cry tore through the tent, her body trembling. She writhed against him, yet he held her fast. Around them, the firelight roared. Alar barely noticed. He rode her hard now, grinding deep with each thrust. And then, his self-control unraveled. Giving in to wildness, he sank his teeth into Lara's smooth shoulder. She groaned, shuddering against him as he held her fast and drove into her again and again.

She sobbed his name once more, her quim clutching at him mercilessly now.

It was too much. He wasn't made of stone.

An instant later, he let go.

"Our names are similar … did you realize that?"

Alar's eyes flickered open, a half-smile playing upon his lips. "No … how so?"

"They have the same sounds." Propping herself up onto an elbow, Lara looked down at him. The soft light inside the tent—for the cressets had died and the brazier had burned down to mere embers—caressed his proud features.

She hadn't been able to study him like this in the past, without fear of being caught staring. But now she drank him in.

"What do you mean?" he asked.

"Well …" Her own mouth curved. Then, reaching out, she began to trace letters upon his naked chest, next to where his wolf's head tattoo gently rose and fell with each breath. He couldn't read or write, but she'd show him, nonetheless. "This is my name." She drew each letter with care. "And this is yours." Slowly, she spelled his name too. "A. L. A. R." She paused then, letting him focus on what she'd just written upon his skin. "Did you notice I used the same shapes?"

Their gazes met once more. His grey eyes were hooded, sleepy, yet something glinted in their depths. "Aye … you're right."

"A coincidence, isn't it?"

His mouth twitched. "Maybe."

"Or perhaps it's fate playing its part again."

She was straying into dangerous waters again here. However, after what had just passed between them, she felt bold.

"You think fate brought us together?" His voice was low, although she didn't miss the faint teasing note in it. "Not the Gods?"

"It's the same thing … for the Gods weave our fates," she replied.

He didn't answer that, although a thoughtful look flickered across his features. "My mother named me after my uncle."

She inclined her head, keen to know more about his past. There was so much she had to learn about him. "Aye?"

"He died before I was born … strayed too close to a ruin on a hunting trip and was attacked by powries."

Lara suppressed a shudder at this, recalling her own close brush with the murderous imps. "Lara was my grandmother's name," she replied. "She too died before I was born … although, according to my father, it was a fever that took her."

He was looking at her in that way of his that made her feel as if she was being laid bare. All signs of humor had drained from his face.

Breathing shallowly, Lara dropped her attention to where her fingertip still traced patterns upon his naked chest. Letting the moment draw out, she began to follow the outline of the wolf's head tattoo, inked in blue woad upon his skin.

"I've always wanted to ask you about this," she admitted finally. "It's beautiful."

"Thank you. A tattooist in Braewall did it."

"It's a recent one, isn't it?" Indeed, the marks were still sharp, not yet blurred by time.

He nodded. "I had it done around five years ago. The woman used to be a druid … a sacrificer who'd once served the arch-druid on The Isle of Arryn."

Lara listened with interest. Most of those gifted with druidic abilities ended up serving the rulers of Albia or the arch-druid. However, she'd heard that some druids did turn their backs on their calling, although those who did often found life difficult. Their abilities set them apart from others. Many became recluses or vagrants, not fitting in anywhere.

"Well, she's talented indeed." Lara ran her fingertip along the wolf's bared teeth. "Sometimes, I swear this wolf is watching me."

Did she imagine it, or did he stiffen slightly under her touch? The moment was fleeting though, and then he relaxed once more. "Really?" His tone was casual, too much so, and she raised her gaze, meeting his once more.

"Aye … she didn't weave earth magic into it, did she?"

He gave a soft snort. "Such a thing is forbidden, Lara … except for druids."

She held his eye. "Aye … but that doesn't mean that a former sacrificer wouldn't weave magic into a tattoo … if the price was right."

Their gazes held before his mouth quirked. "All right then … she might have."

Intrigued now, Lara placed the palm of her hand over the tattoo. "And?"

"It's nothing like druidic tattoos, if that's what you're wondering," he replied, his smile tightening a little. "I can't summon earth magic to fight ... or use it in song, to access visions or speak to the Gods ... but when she marked me, the tattooist imbued the *spirit* of the wolf."

"Strong and loyal," Lara murmured. "Yet ruthless and cunning."

She remembered then, watching him fight the Slew. He'd moved with unnatural speed and agility. Was that because of the tattoo?

"Aye," he replied. "A great need for freedom too ... long ago, I swore never to have a master."

"Is that why you did it?" she asked. "To make yourself stronger ... a more dangerous enemy?"

His eyes glinted, although he didn't answer.

Silence fell then as she mulled over this discovery. The King of Braewall would be angry to learn a former sacrificer was weaving earth magic into tattoos on common folk, but she wasn't. Nonetheless, the knowledge made her uneasy. Many people believed that it was ill luck for anyone except a druid to bear such marks, and Lara had to admit she was superstitious enough to believe such tales. Druids channeled their earth magic, while Alar's coursed through his veins with no outlet. Hopefully, it wouldn't harm him.

"It makes sense now," she said finally. "Why Skaal adores you."

He huffed a laugh. "You're right ... it's the tattoo." He paused then, eyes twinkling. "How her devotion to me pisses Cailean off."

"Oh, it does," she assured him. The chief-enforcer's bond with his fae hound was a strong one indeed—one he was protective of.

"The tattoo also gives me a kinship with wolf-kind," he added then. "Ever since getting it, I trust my own instinct and intuition better." He paused a moment, his features softening a little. "And it brings me closer to my wulver brothers and sisters."

Their gazes met and held before she smiled. "Your family."

He smiled back, although his eyes shadowed just a little. "I'd do anything for them."

Lara stirred in the furs, awaking with a slow, languorous stretch.

Her body had never been so relaxed. It ached in places she hadn't known it could, but she welcomed the sensation. It reminded her of the wild night she and Alar had just shared. Not only had they tumbled, but they'd lain together talking. She'd learned more about the enigma that was her husband, although she was eager to continue her discovery.

A smile curved her lips. She then slid her hand out, across the furs, reaching for Alar.

She couldn't find him.

Eyes fluttering open, she blinked in the dim early-morning light. A few feet away, Alar was dressing. He'd just pulled on his leather breeches and was lacing them closed. His chest was bare, his wolf's head tattoo watching her.

Lara couldn't help it; her gaze dragged over his long, lithe form, hunger igniting in her lower belly.

Even after a night of sex, she wanted him still.

She'd never stop wanting him.

"What time is it?" she whispered.

His chin kicked up, his gaze meeting hers. His lips then tilted at the corners. "Early."

"Where are you going?"

"To check all is well."

Lara pushed herself up, the furs falling away as she did so. "Are you worried about something?"

He shook his head, even as his attention slid down to her bare breasts. "No." There was a husky edge to his voice now. "But I don't like to let my guard down." He reached for his leather vest then and shrugged it on. "We should reach Dulross by mid-afternoon … and after the Fuath, we need to remain alert."

She nodded, grateful for his vigilance.

"I should get up too," she said, scooting toward the edge of the furs.

"Stay … rest a while longer," he said with a shake of his head. "You didn't get much sleep last night."

Warmth flushed over her. "Neither did you."

"I'll return for breakfast," he replied, shrugging on the harness that held the twin blades he wore on his back. "Save me some oatcakes."

She smiled. "I will."

He moved across to her then, stooped, and cupped her face with his hands, staring into her eyes. There was an intensity to his expression this morning that made her pulse flutter. Lowering his lips to hers, he kissed her. It was slow and so tender that something deep in her chest twisted.

The emotions this man roused frightened her sometimes.

She was falling for him. Hard. She should exercise a little more caution, should spend more time observing him, for their relationship was still new, but after last night, it was difficult to slow down.

Drawing back, his gaze then dropped to her shoulder. His fingers slid down her jaw and neck to where he'd bitten her, his gaze shadowing slightly. "I hurt you."

Surprised, Lara lowered her chin, peering at the livid red mark upon her shoulder. She lifted her hand, catching his. "Not really … I liked it."

Something sparked in his eyes, a hungry look that made her breathing quicken and her belly turn molten.

She hadn't lied. Being taken by him, marked by him, had unleashed something primal inside her. He'd made her his, and she couldn't wait for him to do so again.

But as their stare drew out, his expression changed. Tenderness replaced hunger, and something akin to … pain … flickered across his face. "Lara," he murmured. "I—"

"My Queen!" An urgent voice intruded, slightly muffled by the thick hide of the pavilion.

Lara stiffened, her gaze snapping to the tent flap.

"What is it?" Alar asked, his tone sharpening.

"Apologies … but this can't wait." She recognized the voice, as well as the edge of belligerence, as it addressed her husband; it was Roth.

Rising from the furs, Lara reached for her shift. "What's wrong, Captain?"

"There's something you need to see."

38: FALSE HOPE

MIST WREATHED THROUGH the camp as Lara and Alar stepped out of their pavilion.

Immediately, her gaze went to where a small group of warriors and druids had gathered before her tent. Bree and Cailean were among them, their faces strained in the murky light.

"What's wrong?" Lara asked, even as dread curled up. The heady pleasure and intimacy she'd enjoyed overnight with Alar sloughed away now, and she stepped back into her role as High Queen.

"This," Roth said gruffly. He stepped aside then, revealing a large coarsely-woven sack, stained with dark patches. "Someone left it near the northern perimeter."

Lara's pulse quickened as she moved from Alar's side and approached it.

The sweet stench of decay hit her then, and she clenched her jaw. The sack was open, and when she peered inside, she halted abruptly, her hands clenching at her sides.

She then whispered an oath.

The sack was full of severed heads, and the two at the top stared out at her with blank yet accusing eyes and gaping mouths.

Ilene and Dean.

They were the two counsellors they'd sent north to treat with the Circines.

Lara swallowed hard.

Over the past turn of the moon, as time stretched out, and no word came from The Goatfells, they'd all worried about the fate of the counselors, and the enforcers and warriors who'd escorted them. But now they knew what had happened to them. Beathan mac Glen, Chieftain of the Circines, had finally given her his answer: there would be no peace between the hill-tribes and Albia's High Queen.

Lara glanced over at where Annis stood, a thick woolen cloak wrapped around her robed form. Her round face, covered in pink scabs from her recent burns, was set, yet her eyes guttered.

"At least we know where we stand with the Circines," Cailean spoke up then, breaking the weighty silence. "There's no point in having false hope."

"Aye, they're our enemies," Roth answered, his voice flat and hard.

Lara averted her gaze from Ilene and Dean's decomposing faces. "Do the hill-tribes hate me that much?"

"Not you, Lara," Alar replied softly. With a jolt, she realized he was standing next to her now. "They hate what you stand for. Decades of oppression can't be easily wiped away with a few promises."

"He has a point," Cailean growled. That was a first—the chief-enforcer openly agreeing with Alar. However, Lara was too upset by her early morning delivery to pay much attention. "You might one day win their loyalty … but it will take time."

"I should travel with the advance guard today," Alar announced. They'd just mounted their horses and were about to ride out. "We'll reach Dulross around noon … but after this morning's 'gift', there might be trouble from the hill-tribes on the road."

Lara nodded, even as her belly tightened. "That makes sense."

And it did, although his words reminded her that the valuable alliance they'd sought with the Circines had just gone up in smoke. Disappointment wreathed up too. She liked riding side by side with her husband. After the night they'd shared, she wished to remain close to him.

She'd not admit it though. Instead, she fussed with her reins so Alar wouldn't see her expression.

"I'll take more of my wulvers forward from the rear guard … just in case."

Surprised, Lara looked up. Did he really expect trouble this close to Dulross?

"Surely four hundred is enough?" Roth called out before she could answer. Having just mounted his heavy-set stallion with feathered feet a few yards away, he'd overheard their exchange.

Alar turned to him, his gaze narrowing. "Not, if Beathan mac Glen is lying in wait. They fight alongside the faerie creatures now, remember?" He paused then. "The Shee might be with them."

The two men stared at each other, tension rippling through the air until Lara cleared her throat, irritation flaring. She was tired of her captain taking issue with everything Alar said; Roth needed to relax a bit. "My husband knows The Uplands better than most of us," she replied briskly. "If he wants to strengthen the advance guard, he can."

Roth's strong jaw flexed at this, yet he held his tongue.

Lara glanced back at Alar. His expression was keen now, his gaze sharp—the tenderness he'd shown her inside their tent was nowhere to be seen.

He called out then, in the guttural tongue the wulvers used to communicate between themselves. Moments later, tall, lean figures began making their way forward toward their commander.

Lara watched the wulvers pass by. Lyall and Dolph were among them, barking instructions as they went.

Around her, the last of the tents were loaded onto wagons. Fog still snaked through the valley where they'd made camp, although the rain had stopped overnight and the bright halo of the sun was doing its best to break through. It was time to move.

Nonetheless, instead of urging his horse forward and joining his brothers and sisters who were already stalking north, the tips of the spears they gripped bristling like spindly pines in the drifting mist, Alar hesitated. "There will be more enforcers and warriors flanking you all day," he said, his gaze flicking to where Lara's warder had just swung up onto her cob. "And Bree will watch your back, as always."

Bree harrumphed. "That goes without saying." She then nudged her horse forward and drew up on Lara's left flank. Her face was still looking a bit battered. The cuts she'd sustained the day before were scabbing now. Nonetheless, her eyes were steely.

Lara nodded to her before glancing over at Alar once more. "Go on," she murmured. "I shall see you when we reach Dulross."

He inclined his head to her, their gazes holding for a few moments.

And then the fine hair on the back of her forearms prickled.

Lara tensed. Everything about this morning felt … off. It wasn't surprising though, after receiving a sack of severed heads first thing. Nonetheless, she couldn't shake the uneasy sensation that something was wrong.

Without another word, Alar reined his horse around and urged it forward, following his wulvers north.

Lara watched him go until the mist swallowed him.

"We made a mistake … sending that peace envoy."

Bree didn't reply, and Lara cast her a sharp look. Her warder's gaze wasn't on her though. Instead, she surveyed their surroundings keenly, one hand resting lightly on the pommel of her longsword. After the day before, she was even more alert than usual. Enforcers and warriors flanked them on both sides.

Her warder was determined not to let her concentration waver this morning. Mist wreathed around them, making visibility difficult.

"Alar warned me that the Circines wouldn't treat with us," Lara admitted then, warmth washing over her.

Bree did glance her way then, her gaze narrowing. "He didn't bring that up in any of our councils."

"No … I told him about it before our handfasting … when we were alone." Lara looked away. "By the Gods," she muttered. "We can't afford to lose warriors … or druids for that matter."

"It's a blow … to be sure," Bree answered after a pause. "I don't want to remind you of this … but many more will die before the end. You need to be ready."

Lara's breathing grew shallow. They were brutal words, but they were true.

She was leading an army into battle—a war that wouldn't be easily won. The death of her emissaries was only the beginning of the blood that would be spilled in her name.

Swallowing, she nodded. "You're right," she said huskily.

"Sorry … that was harsh."

Lara looked up to find Bree watching her, her gaze shadowed.

"It's all right," she murmured, managing a tight smile. "You know I appreciate your honesty."

The two women fell silent then. The dull, rhythmic squelch of their horses' hooves on the road replaced their conversation. The morning was slowly passing. It wouldn't be long before they'd reach the sheltering gates of Dulross. The fort's chieftain, Og mac Alpin, was expecting her. There would be a fine meal and comfortable accommodation awaiting the High Queen.

They wouldn't be able to linger in Dulross long, but it was the last friendly port before they set sail onto rough seas.

"You're getting along better again these days, I see."

Bree's softly spoken comment roused Lara from her thoughts. She cut her a sidelong glance. "Sorry?"

"You and Alar."

Warmth rose to her cheeks. "Aye ... a little."

Bree's expression tightened.

An awkward silence followed, and Lara frowned. "So, you haven't revised your opinion of him?"

"No. I still think he's a sly bastard."

"Really?" Anger quickened in her belly. Sometimes, Bree took her bluntness too far. "Even now?"

"Sure, he's useful in a fight ... but I still wouldn't trust him."

"And why not?" she asked, her voice suddenly brittle. She knew Alar was flawed. Dangerous. But she still wanted to believe in him.

"Because trust is earned ... and he's yet to win mine."

"Queen Lara!"

A woman's shout carried through the misty air, slicing through their conversation.

A moment later, a leather-clad figure bent low over the neck of a lathered horse galloped toward them, down the column of warriors on horseback and on foot. The woman had fiery red hair, streaming behind her, and sweat gleamed on her flushed face.

Immediately, Bree was at the ready. Drawing her longsword, she urged her horse forward to protect Lara. Likewise, the surrounding warriors closed ranks around them, hemming the High Queen in.

Cailean rode forward to meet the woman, barring her way. "State your business."

Lara stood up on her stirrups, straining to see over the heads of those protecting her.

The rider hauled her horse to a halt. The poor beast stood there, sides heaving, as the woman faced down the chief-enforcer. "I must speak to the High Queen!"

"I'm here," Lara called back. "What's wrong?"

The woman's gaze snapped her way. Even from this distance, Lara could see that her eyes were wild. "Doure has been taken, My Queen!"

Dizziness swept over Lara. *What?*

"The Shee?" Cailean demanded.

"No," the woman gasped. "The wulvers turned on us. They butchered the Marav garrison and drove the rest of us out."

An invisible fist slammed into Lara's stomach.

"When did this happen?" Cailean demanded.

"Two days ago … I've ridden hard to reach you." She paused then, still breathing hard as she pushed tangled red hair off her face. "Word arrived from Duncrag that you were marching on Strath … and then a day later, the wulvers took the fort."

Lara's mind was wheeling, but somehow, she managed to grasp the words. "I never sent word to Doure," she replied.

The woman's face twisted. "Aye, well … someone did."

39: SHIFTING ALLEGIANCE

DIZZINESS SWEPT OVER Lara. A moment later, she swayed in the saddle before she caught hold of her horse's mane to steady herself.

She wouldn't think about what this meant. She *couldn't.*

Her mouth moved then, as if to form words, yet no sound came out.

Thankfully, those around her took action. "I'm riding ahead," Roth announced. He then gestured to the warriors behind him. "We need to catch up with the advance guard and bid them to halt. Immediately." When Lara didn't answer, he turned to her. "My Queen?"

She stared back at him, mute.

"Do it," Cailean replied when Lara didn't.

Roth nodded brusquely, gathered the reins, and dug his heels into his stallion's sides. The beast took off, heavy hooves churning up the damp ground.

Lara watched them depart, her heart pounding.

Shouting reached them then, drifting up the column from the south.

"The Mother's tits!" Cailean twisted in the saddle. "What the fuck is it now?"

No one answered. Instead, the shouting grew louder, angrier.

Finally, Lara found her voice. "Go and find out what the problem is," she ordered the warriors next to her.

They did as bid, returning a short while later. The grim look on their faces made queasiness roll over her.

"The wulvers that were traveling with the rear guard have all fled," one of them announced, his face screwing up in disgust.

"Fled?" Cailean snarled the word.

"Aye … took off into the pines. Some of the warriors gave chase, but once they got into the woods, they lost them."

Beside Lara, Bree breathed a curse.

And meanwhile, something cold and hard settled into the pit of Lara's belly.

"We need to get to Dulross," Cailean said roughly. "As soon as possible."

"Aye," Lara agreed, forcing herself to focus. "Let's go."

The army moved off, traveling faster now. The main body of it drew ahead of the lumbering wagons of the baggage train and the rear guard, their sights set upon their destination. Sitting rigidly in the saddle as her horse cantered along the road, the tattoo of pounding hooves surrounding her, Lara stared ahead.

And all the while, her mind churned.

A short while later, they met Roth and his warriors coming back in the opposite direction. They were riding hard and had to haul their horses up sharply to avoid colliding with Cailean and the other enforcers who rode up front.

Cailean reined in his stallion, Skaal skidding to a smooth halt at his side. "Did you catch up with the wulvers?" he demanded without preamble.

Roth shook his head. His face was flushed, his gaze burning. "They must have run north as if The Reaper were chasing them," he panted. "We followed on their heels to Dulross … but no farther."

"No farther?" Cailean's dark brows crashed together.

Still breathing hard, Roth cut his gaze from the chief-enforcer, instead seeking out Lara a few yards behind.

The world started to spin then, and she grabbed the pommel of the saddle. The look in his eyes was an executioner's axe.

"The gates were barred to us. They've taken Dulross too."

Climbing the wooden steps to the walls, Alar sheathed the blade he'd just cleaned. He then headed toward the heavily muscled figure clad in leather and fur standing by the guard tower. The warrior's long peat-colored hair whipped around him in the wind. Intricate knots of tattoos and bronze, silver, and gold arm rings covered his brawny arms.

"Og mac Alpin is dead," Alar announced. "'The Brooch of Albia' is ours." His pulse jolted then. Finally, the jewel he and his wulvers had coveted for years—the fort that joined The Wolds and The Uplands—was theirs.

Nonetheless, the victory was bittersweet.

They'd initially planned to take more than Dulross and Doure. The wulvers had coveted Duncrag too. Alar was supposed to have laid the groundwork for a takeover. Instead, he'd kept his word to Lara. He'd signed that cursed document, as he'd promised, agreeing that he'd step aside when she died. And then shortly after he'd wed Lara, he'd informed Lyall and Dolph that taking the capital was off the table. He wouldn't be overthrowing the High Queen.

As a result, his relationship with his brothers had been strained ever since.

Lyall and Dolph had lost trust, but Alar hoped their victory now would restore it.

Beathan mac Glen turned to face him. Streaks of woad decorated his smooth-shaven face, emphasizing the sharp blue of his eyes. The chieftain of the Circines flashed him a hard smile before gesturing to below them, to where both hill-tribe warriors and wulvers were nailing up heavy wooden planks to reinforce the massive iron gates. "The gates are almost secured."

"The High Queen's army has our battering ram though," Alar reminded him. Aye, they'd brought *Fire Wyrm* north. It was being hauled by oxen in the baggage train, although there wouldn't be any wulvers with the High Queen's army left to wield it. The Marav could do so, but even if they breached Dulross's gates, they wouldn't best the combined strength of the huge wulver and hill-tribe force within.

Beathan shrugged, nodding to where warriors were hauling iron pots up onto the top of the guardhouse. "Just as well we're preparing the boiling pitch. We'll have some fun with the shit-eaters." He paused then. "I must admit, I'm tempted to throw open the gates and engage them … however, this fort is too precious to me to risk it."

Alar nodded, even as relief washed over him. He'd just betrayed Lara, but he was reluctant to engage her in battle. He didn't want her to be harmed. Instead, he needed her to turn her army around and retreat to safety.

His stomach twisted then. His wife would be reeling right now. She'd be struggling to accept that he'd double-crossed her.

But he had. He'd waited decades to take territory for the wulvers, had thought about little else as the years slid by.

And yet, the past turns of the moon had caused something to shift inside him. Lara had been a distraction. From the first moment he'd seen her, fighting for her life as powries swarmed around her, she'd fascinated him. Worse than that—she'd roused a protective instinct that was difficult to quash.

He'd told himself he could handle her, and himself. He'd been determined to let nothing get between him and his goals. But she'd blunted his hunger for anything but her.

It was over now though. He'd unmasked himself.

Earlier, as they'd emerged from the broch after killing the chieftain and taking his family prisoners, both Lyall and Dolph had been jubilant. Today changed everything for the wulvers. For centuries, they'd been persecuted, hunted. But now Doure and Dulross—two key forts—belonged to them. The borderlands were theirs. *Finally*, they had their own slice of Albia, and allies to help them hold it.

They'd taken the fort fast, dealing easily with the garrison and any residents foolish enough to fight. Those surviving had wisely barricaded themselves inside their homes. The wulvers and hill-tribe warriors who now swarmed the narrow wynds that climbed to the broch had full control.

Dulross had been expecting the High Queen, of course, for Lara had sent a rider ahead. The gates had been left wide open as they marched in. Unfortunately for the fort's residents, the Marav accompanying the wulvers weren't the High Queen's warriors but Circines. The hill-tribe warriors had shifted allegiance, turning their backs on the Raven Queen—but it wasn't the High Queen of Albia they now sided with.

"Will the bitch queen lay siege to the fort?"

Alar's heart kicked hard as Beathan spoke once more. Hate edged the man's voice. The chieftain of the Circines carried a grudge as deep as an Upland loch toward the rulers of Albia. His people hadn't been treated much better than the wulvers over the centuries.

Nonetheless, Alar didn't appreciate hearing Lara insulted. Clenching his jaw, he checked the impulse to say anything. This time.

"She'll want to," he answered, his gaze shifting from the chieftain to the rolling green meadows that stretched south. The wind had chased away the mist, making visibility clearer. Soon, the High Queen's banner would appear on the horizon. "But since our force outnumbers theirs, she'll hesitate."

He glanced back at Beathan to see that the man's lip had curled. He likely thought Lara was weak. He was wrong.

"I wouldn't underestimate her, if I were you," Alar said quietly. "The High Queen has a will of iron." He paused for a heartbeat then. "She's also a fire-wielder."

Beathan's blue eyes snapped wide, his arrogance faltering. "What?"

"Her abilities are still new to her, yet she protected the entire encampment from the Slew twice on the way here. She could cause a lot of damage."

Nausea crept up his throat then. There it was: his wife's secret handed over to her enemies. Such knowledge was valuable. Even so, his final betrayal of her twisted his guts.

Were there no depths to which he wouldn't sink?

The chieftain continued to sneer, although his gaze wasn't quite so confident. "Lucky for us, the gates are iron, not wood then," he replied. "Although we'll make sure not to have any braziers burning on the walls tonight."

Alar nodded. "That would be wise." He paused then, his stomach tightening once more. News of Lara's secret would soon spread now. How long would it take before the rumors reached Duncrag? "I'd also have plenty of buckets of water drawn from the wells … we may need them."

Beathan's mouth thinned, although he nodded. Dulross's walls were made of both stone and timber. Fire could prove their undoing. The chieftain glanced west then, the tension in his face easing a little. "It may not come to that," he murmured. "Look."

Turning, Alar's attention settled upon the bank of dark clouds sitting over the tips of the southern Goatfells. The Sharp Billed Wind was blowing from that direction too, its icy teeth cutting into their flesh. Rain was on its way.

"The Hag is with us," Beathan added, his tone smug now.

Alar didn't reply. He wouldn't credit The Five with any good fortune that came their way.

Nonetheless, it did look as if fate had turned against Lara mac Talorc.

It had the day *he'd* walked into her life. She just hadn't known it until now. Once again, remorse knifed through him. And once again, he shoved it aside. He wouldn't take that road.

"Ah … here she is."

Beathan's voice drew his attention once more, and when he looked south, he saw it—a white wolf's head against a field of black, snapping in the wind. It struck him as an irony then, that the Albian ruling family had the wolf as its sigil. A dark column marched into view, spears bristling against the pale sky.

Alar's pulse quickened. Suddenly, the image of Lara's face that morning in the tent when she'd gazed up at him from the furs—the trust in her gaze—flashed before his eyes, unbidden.

At that moment, he'd been about to spill his guts to her, to confess all.

Thank the Hearthkeeper, they'd been interrupted. He'd been on the brink of ruining everything. Afterward, as he'd watched her kneel before the sack of rotting severed heads, he'd pulled himself together.

You can't let her get to you. The woman had enchanted him, like a beautiful yet deadly bavaan—dancing in the moonlight before draining him of blood. He'd had a narrow escape.

Alar clenched his hands by his sides. *Remember what matters. The wulvers will sing of this day for generations to come. You made it happen.*

Heat ignited in his belly. The Marav deserved this. They'd made him an outcast and hunted his wulver kin ruthlessly. He'd lain awake at night many times over the years, imagining this moment. It had kept him going through harsh winters and long, bitter, lonely nights. Even when Talorc mac Brude pushed the wulvers deeper into the northern forests. Even when the Marav cut down his brothers and sisters.

It had been his fuel. His sustenance. And it would keep him on the right path now.

40: BETRAYAL

LARA DREW UP her horse and stared at the high walls of Dulross. The fort rose proudly before her, framed by the jagged edge of The Goatfells. The mountains thrust upward, streaked in green, ochre, and slate-grey against a darkening sky.

Banners flew from the walls, snapping in the chill wind. The weather was turning again, and ominous clouds drifted in from the west. Rain wasn't far away. But despite the dull light, the banners were clear. Circine and wulver. A white eagle against woad-blue. The Eternal Flame against black.

"Those shit-weasels," Cailean growled from next to her. "Beathan mac Glen is with them."

Lara didn't answer. Bitterness flooded her mouth.

Betrayed by the wulvers, whom she'd defended and believed in.

Betrayed by her husband, whom she'd foolishly fallen for.

And now betrayed by the Circines, whom she'd hoped to ally herself with. What was one more betrayal, heaped on all the others?

Her pulse thudded in her ears as she gazed upon Dulross's proud outline, the dark line of figures wielding longbows on the walls, and the locked gates.

There it was—the irrefutable proof of what Alar had done.

"How did the wulvers manage this?" Bree bit out the words.

"It doesn't matter," Roth answered. "Each of those treacherous Circines will die for it."

"As will those fucking wulvers," Cailean added.

And still Lara remained silent. The voices of her companions seemed far away. Instead, she stood on the edge of a cliff with waves foaming on sharp rocks beneath her feet. Just one step, and she'd fall.

Someone in my household guards a dangerous secret.

That Gods-damned dream. It had tried to warn her. Her chief-seer had interviewed everyone, including Alar, but he hadn't sensed anything amiss. Of course, Alar was cunning. He'd somehow managed to shield himself from Ruari's probing. He'd been hiding a secret all right, waiting for the perfect moment.

"Our numbers aren't great enough to take them on," Bree pointed out then.

She was right. They had an army of just over six hundred warriors with barely forty enforcers. There were over a thousand wulvers inside that fort, and Gods knew how many hill-tribe warriors. They were outnumbered and outmaneuvered.

Lara's fingertips started to tingle. She could wield fire, but it wasn't any good to her at present. There were no torches nearby to draw from, not at this time of day, and if she wished to inflict real damage on Dulross, she'd need a *bonfire*. It would take a while to build such a pyre, and with rain on its way, all the wood would end up soaked. They *could* dig in and wait before building a fire, but Alar would see what they were up to. He'd know what she was planning, and he'd find a way to stop her.

In truth though, she didn't want to set 'The Brooch of Albia' alight. Why should the residents of this fort burn because of the Half-blood's treachery?

Wordlessly, she swung down from the saddle.

"Lara?" Bree's voice reached her. "What are you doing?"

"I need answers."

"From whom? *Alar?*" The thud of feet hitting the ground followed before Bree's hand fastened on her shoulder. "You can't."

Lara shrugged her off, even as a strange calm settled over her.

"It's too dangerous, My Queen." Roth had twisted in the saddle, his gaze spearing her. "*He's* too dangerous."

"I'm going." Lara pushed through the gap between Roth and Cailean's stallions. "Feel free to escort me. Just don't get in my way."

She half expected the chief-enforcer to leap from the saddle and haul her back, for her behavior was ill-advised. But he didn't.

None of them did. Maybe something in her voice checked them.

They didn't need to worry about her. She hadn't lost her wits. Indeed, she'd never been surer of her own mind.

The Sharp Billed Wind pecked at her as she walked, digging into her skin. Her green, fur-lined cloak billowed, and her hair whipped around her face, stinging her eyes.

But Lara ignored it all. Her gaze remained firmly on the high stone and timber palisade before her.

The lines of leather-clad figures on the walls watched her, longbows at the ready.

"Don't go any farther, Lara," Cailean said gruffly from behind her. "Or you'll be in reach of their arrows."

Heeding him, Lara halted. She then glanced over her shoulder to where Bree, Cailean, and Roth had followed her out from the ranks. They now stood, weapons drawn, ready to defend her. Skaal had ventured forth at the chief-enforcer's heel, her golden eyes gleaming in the dull light.

Lara's jaw tightened. They all meant well, but they were crowding her. "Move back at least ten yards," she ordered. "I need some space."

A nerve flickered in Bree's cheek. "Lara," she murmured. "I don't think—"

"Just do it."

Reluctantly, their bodies tight with tension, her escort drew back to the distance she'd stipulated. They didn't look happy about it though.

Turning to face the walls once more, Lara inhaled deeply. "Alar mac Struana!" Her shout carried through the heavy air. "Show yourself!"

Her voice echoed off stone and then died away.

Only silence answered.

Her gaze traveled the ramparts. She was too distant to pick out details. She had no idea where Alar was, but she felt the weight of his stare upon her all the same. He was up there all right—determined to ignore her.

Spots of cold rain splashed upon her face then, the day growing darker still. The rain was nearly upon them. She ignored it.

"Come down and speak to your wife, Half-blood!" she shouted once more. "I'll wait you out, coward!" Her voice echoed once more, mocking her now. "I'll stand here all day and night if I must!"

And she would.

"Well, you've pissed her off."

The amusement in Beathan's voice made irritation spike through Alar. The chieftain might be enjoying this, but he wasn't. Lara needed to retreat, to move back to safety. He couldn't protect her any longer. Not from up here.

He spied three figures standing a few yards back from the High Queen, as well as a massive wolf with its moss-green coat. None of them were close enough to defend her.

Why the fuck were Bree, Cailean, and Roth letting her do this? It was irresponsible.

His heart started to thump against his ribs.

"What will you do?" Lyall growled next to him.

Alar didn't answer. For once, he didn't have one.

"My archers have longbows that will reach her," Beathan spoke up once more. "Just say the word, and they'll bring the bitch queen down."

"Call her that again, and I'll cut your throat," Alar snarled, rounding on him.

Silence fell on the wall. Beathan stilled, his dark brows shooting up to his brow line. Long moments passed, and then the chieftain's lip slowly curled, scorn flaring in his blue eyes.

Alar ignored him. Instead, his gaze remained on the woman cloaked in green standing alone on the hillside beneath the fort.

"Tell me you didn't fall for her?" Lyall murmured.

His pulse leaped into a gallop. "I didn't."

"Liar."

He was, but it didn't matter. He had to let everything go now.

The rain swept in then, heavy, cutting swathes of it, hammering the walls and those standing upon them. And although it was only early afternoon, the world turned dark.

Time stretched out. The clouds lowered, and after the initial deluge, the rain settled into a steady, drumming rhythm.

And still, Lara waited.

"Well, as pleasant as this is, I'd prefer to be helping myself to Og mac Alpin's mead and seeing if he's got any pretty daughters," Beathan said eventually. Rain was running down the chieftain's face and dripping off his nose. Likewise, Alar was soaked. However, he barely noticed.

"He does," Lyall quipped. "Two of them."

The chieftain flashed him a grin. However, his expression turned into a grimace when it shifted back to Alar. He then wiped the rain out of his eyes with the back of his hand. "How much longer are you going to drag this out?"

Alar cut Beathan a scowl. The man's whining was starting to vex him.

"The Warrior's balls," the chieftain growled. "Just ignore her."

Pain lanced through his chest, making it difficult to breathe. *I can't.*

"She'll get tired of this game soon enough," Lyall said, stepping closer to Alar then. The rain had slicked his fur down, emphasizing the power of his massive jaws. "Maybe, it's time you just—"

Alar whirled away from the walls, shoved his way in between Lyall and the wulver next to him, and made for the steps.

"Where are you going?" Beathan shouted through the roar of the rain.

"To speak to my wife."

Lara was shivering by the time the gates creaked open a crack, and a tall, lean figure slipped out.

Clenching her shaking hands by her sides, she watched him approach in long, stalking strides. "There you are," she whispered. "Couldn't resist it in the end, could you?"

In truth, she'd started to think he wasn't going to show his face, after all—that she'd wait here until dusk settled, until the cold and wet drilled deep into her bones.

But he surprised her.

Her gaze tracked him as he approached. Like her, he was drenched, water running in rivulets down his leather breastplate. Alar's expression was wary, as if he expected her to rage at him.

She wouldn't though. She was way past that.

The rain continued to thunder down, stippling the puddles that now formed around the base of the fort. It soaked through her thick cloak and all the layers of clothing beneath. It ran into her eyes, down her neck, and between her breasts. The wind bit at her exposed skin. She felt as if she'd just emerged fully clothed from an icy dip in a loch.

Twisting, she looked over her shoulder at where Cailean, Bree, and Roth waited, weapons still drawn. Likewise, rain sluiced down their faces and plastered their hair against their scalps. All three wore grim expressions. "I need some privacy … move farther back."

The chief-enforcer scowled deeply. "My Queen." His tone was harsh. "You—"

"Just do it, Cailean," she countered, cutting him off. "I take full responsibility for my actions."

"This isn't wise, Lara," Bree answered. Her voice was strained. "Talking to him won't change things."

"It will." She continued to stare the three of them down. Roth remained silent, although he watched her with a shadowed gaze. "Move back."

Moments passed, and then, reluctantly, they obeyed her. Their boots squelched as they moved.

She eyeballed them until they were around fifteen yards distant. Well out of earshot.

That was better.

Now, she and Alar could talk.

41: A VALUABLE LESSON

ALAR HALTED A few yards away and folded his arms across his chest. The rain had slicked his black hair down, and his face glistened. It gave him a savage edge. "Hello, Lara."

"Alar."

Silence followed, broken only by the steady drum of the rain beating against the ground around them, before he asked, "What do you want?"

Lara blinked water out of her eyes. "An explanation."

He studied her for a few moments, as if wondering what to make of her calmness. Maybe he'd expected rage, tears even, but he wouldn't be getting any. "You trusted the wrong man."

"Clearly."

"I played you." An edge crept into his voice. "I used your desperation, your hunger to take back what your father lost, to get what I wanted."

"And what's that?" she asked calmly, refusing to be baited.

His iron gaze drilled into her. "'The Brooch of Albia'."

"You already had Dulross," she pointed out. "You married *me*, remember?"

"I did, but being your dog was never enough. I wanted my own territory."

"So, you allied yourself with the Circines to get it?"

"Aye, we understand each other."

"You broke our blood oath, Alar."

He snorted. "I swore an oath on Gods I don't believe in. I don't give a shit about the wrath of The Five."

Lara's jaw tightened as rain streamed like icy tears down her cheeks. She hoped the Reaper would make him pay for his blasphemy—an eternity of suffering in the Underworld would suffice. However, she wouldn't bite. He thought he'd won, but he hadn't. Earlier, she'd been stunned, flattened by his betrayal. Yet, as the walls of Dulross loomed before her, something had hardened inside her. A resolve that sank deep into the marrow of her bones.

She wouldn't let him win. And as she faced him, her strength held fast. She was soaked and chilled to the marrow, but if this bastard wouldn't break her, then neither would anything else.

"Don't look down your nose at me." His voice roughened then. "You had a part to play in all this too. You marched on Doure before you were ready. You didn't have the numbers to take, or hold, the fort successfully … but you were determined to win, no matter the cost." He flashed her a hard smile. "Never strike a bargain when you're desperate."

She stared back at him, her pulse beating in her throat. "You're right," she answered. "You've taught me a valuable lesson."

And he had.

She'd made some grave mistakes since taking the throne. She'd worried her people would think their young High Queen weak, and so she'd gone on campaign before she was ready. Then, in her quest to beat the Shee, she'd married a man with questionable morals and motives—a choice that had caused her overkings to rebel.

"I *was* desperate," she admitted then. "And there you were … appearing at the perfect moment, offering me what I needed most."

His eyes glinted. "Aye … for a price."

"There's always a price." And there was. Every choice. Every path. The road she'd taken was full of sharp thorns and jagged edges, cutting her deeper at every turn. Maybe he thought this would break her, but he was wrong.

Ironically, their marriage had been the making of her. His support, his protection and guidance, had all been a mummery, yet her response to it hadn't been. Unwittingly, he'd shown her what she was capable of. He didn't realize it, but he'd help forge her.

Silence fell between them as the rain continued to drum down, and she imagined she saw a glimmer of regret in his eyes then, a flicker of pain upon his glistening face. But it was gone in an instant. No, he wasn't sorry for what he'd done. The prick was incapable of remorse.

They stood there, cocooned by the downpour, until Alar finally spoke. "Just to be clear," he said, his voice hardening once more. Water dripped off his chin. "The lands around Doure and

Dulross … and down to Deeping Barrow now belong to me. If your army marches this way again, I will take it as an act of war."

"These lands are *mine*," she countered. "Lift your leg and piss all you like … it changes nothing."

His face transformed into a sneer. There he was. The real Alar. The man who'd saved her life, who'd put his body between hers and danger, who'd taken her passionately the night before, didn't exist. This was who he really was. "Look around you, Lara. Your realm is crumbling. You can't stop it."

"You're wrong. I'll see you on the battlefield, *Half-blood*."

His eyes darkened, his jaw tightening. Raindrops glittered on his eyelashes.

She thought he'd say something else, yet to her surprise, he let her have the last word. Moving away, he turned on his heel and headed back toward the gates through the murk.

The rain still hammered down into the sodden earth. It felt as if it would never cease.

Lara watched him go, tracking every stride.

"Let me kill him." Bree was at her side then, her voice hard-edged. "There's still time."

"No." Lara's gaze never left her husband's retreating back. "When the day comes, I want to be the one to do it."

The End

AUTHOR'S NOTE & GLOSSARY

As with *The Enforcer's Bride* duology, this one is steeped in Scottish folklore. I've been writing novels set in ancient and Medieval Scotland for years—and in 2024 embarked on my first Celtic-inspired Romantasy.

Since then, there's been no looking back. I'm obsessed!

I hope you enjoyed the Pictish vibe of the story world, as well as the dangerous mythological creatures brought to life. I wanted Albia to be mysterious, with an air of brooding menace, just like ancient Scotland.

Many of the names within this duology come from Scottish Gaelic. It's a beautiful language, yet written quite differently from how it's pronounced. As such, I have changed some of the spelling in the novel to make it more phonetic and therefore more accessible to readers.

Below is a glossary of people and places from the novel and a bit of background on meaning and the original spelling:

Albia: a variation of 'Alba', the Scottish Gaelic name for Scotland
Ben Neeya: the Bean Nighe (see note below about 'the Washerwoman')

Caisteal Gealaich: the Shee queen's stronghold. It means Moon Castle. (pronounced *castel galeech*)

Sheehallion: Original spelling is 'Schiehallion'. Located in Perthshire, it's one of Scotland's most prominent mountains and rich in legend. Its name derives from the Gaelic Sith Chaillean, meaning 'The Fairy Hill of the Caledonians.'

Skaal: Cailean's Fae Hound ('sgàil' means 'shadow)

The Marav: the name for the mortal race that inhabits Albia. Comes from 'Marbh' or 'mairbh', which means a dead person/people

The Shee: the name for the fae race that inhabits Sheehallion. This name is based on the Daoine sìth (pronounced: *doonyuh-shee)*, the Scottish name for the fairy race.

In this novel, I use 'mac' with Malav names. Of course, this is from Scottish Gaelic, which meant 'son of'. In Pictish times, 'mac' was used as a separate word in a name with the father's name following. This was the origin of many Scottish surnames we see today.

The dice game 'Liar' is based on an ancient game: **https://www.lore-and-saga.co.uk/html/dice.html**

During the novel, I refer to the *Ord-ree seal* (the ring Lara wears). This comes from 'Ard-ri' (High King in Irish Gaelic) and is pronounced *Ord-ree.*

The societal structure of Albia is based on the ancient kingdoms of Ireland and the Pictish kingdoms of Scotland, where a High King ruled several lesser kingdoms governed by 'Overkings'.

The creatures that are mentioned or feature in THE UNFORGIVEN duology, and their Scottish mythological origin:

Fae Hounds are a variation of the Cù-Sìth (pronounced *ku-shee*), a ghostly hound from Scottish folklore that roamed the Highlands. The name means 'Fairy Dog'. The Cù-Sìth were said to be the size of a bull with dark-green shaggy fur and a coiled or braided tail.

People believed the Cù-Sìth was a harbinger of death—much like the Grim Reaper. Although mostly a silent hunter, this giant dog would sometimes let out three blood-curdling howls. If you didn't get away before the third howl, you'd be overcome with fear and die from sheer terror.

Ben Neeya: The Bean Nighe (pronounced *ben-nee'-yeh*), also known as 'the Washerwoman', is an old woman seen wandering near streams and pools, where she washes the bloodstained clothes of those who are about to die. The bean-nighe is sometimes said to sing a mournful dirge. She is often so absorbed in her washing and singing that she can sometimes be caught unawares. If a person sees her before she spies them, she will reveal who is about to die and will also grant three wishes. In my tale, I've altered things slightly so that she grants you one wish.

Powries: also known as a Red Cap, or a Dunter, a powrie is a type of malevolent, murderous goblin found in Border folklore. He is said to inhabit ruined castles along the Anglo-Scottish border, especially those that were the scenes of tyranny or wicked deeds, and is known for soaking his cap in the blood of his victims.

Find out more: **https://folklorescotland.com/the-fearsome-redcaps-of-the-scottish-borders/**

Trows: these creatures feature in Shetland folklore. They are similar to humans but smaller and uglier, and they live in the hills, particularly the heathery peatlands inland from the sea. They would only come out at night, to work mischief in the human world.

Find out more: **https://shetlandwithlaurie.com/the-blog/shetland-folklore-series-trows**

Aughisky: The each-uisge (Scottish Gaelic, meaning "water horse") is a water spirit found in the Scottish Highlands (anglicized as aughisky or ech-ushkya). It usually takes the form of a horse—similar to the kelpie but far more vicious. Unlike the Kelpie (which inhabits streams and rivers), the each-uisge lives in the sea, sea lochs, and freshwater lochs. The each-uisge is a shape-shifter, disguising itself as a fine horse, pony, or handsome man. If you mount this creature while it's disguised as a horse, you are only safe out of sight or smell of water. Otherwise, your skin will stick to the creature, and it will pull you down to the deepest part of the sea or loch and tear you apart.

Find out more: **https://about-mythical-creatures.weebly.com/each-uisge.html**

Corpse candles: also known as will-o'-the-wisps or fairy lights. In Scottish folklore, will-o'-the-wisps are variously depicted either as mischievous spirits (typically fairies), or even the ghosts of the dead, eager to lead travelers off their path and to their death. The lights typically appear close to a bog, marsh, or swamp, places where straying off the beaten path can become dangerous – or even deadly.

Find out more: **https://folklorescotland.com/will-o-the-wisp/**

Bavaan: The Baobhan Sith (pronounced Bavaan-shee) is a vampiric creature of Scottish origin. Beautiful, tall women with pale skin and icy breath, they dress in flowing green robes and are said to dance in the moonlight, seducing men, to kill them and drain their blood.

Find out more: **https://folklorescotland.com/the-baobhan-sith/**

Boggart: A boggart is a mischievous, often wicked, supernatural being—a broonie that has turned nasty, often due to mistreatment. They cause trouble, hide things, make noise, and lead travelers astray. It's also said that boggarts crawl into people's beds at night and put a clammy hand on their faces.

The Unforgiven/The Slew: The Sluagh Sidhe, or 'Fairy Host': spirits of the unforgiven or restless dead who soar the skies at night searching for humans to pick off. They always approach from the west and often prey on those close to death.

Find out more:

https://folklorethursday.com/folktales/the-sluagh-spirits-of-the-unforgiven-dead/

The Botach: The Gaelic word bodach (pronounced bot-ach) can mean 'old man' and also 'specter, ghost'. In ancient

Scotland, it was the name of a mythological 'bogeyman' who comes down chimneys to steal children. He was also seen as an omen of death. The bodach was said to slip down the chimney and steal or terrorize little children. He would prod, poke, pinch, pull, and in general disturb the child until he had them reeling with nightmares. According to the stories of most parents, the bodach would only bother naughty children. A good defense would be to put salt in the hearth before bedtime. The bodach will not cross salt.

Find out more:

https://www.tumblr.com/bestiarium/65069709351159398 4/the-bodach-scottish-mythology-gaelic-mythology

Wulvers: a Scottish mythological creature that is part human, part wolf. The wulver kept to itself and was not aggressive if left in peace. They would often guide lost travelers to nearby towns and villages. There are also tales of wulvers leaving fish on the windowsills of poor families. Unlike their werewolf counterparts, the wulver is not a shape-shifter.

Find out more:

https://www.scotsman.com/news/people/scottish-myths-wulver-the-kindhearted-shetland-werewolf-2463904

Fuath: (pronounced 'foo-ah') Malevolent water spirits from Irish and Scottish folklore that emerge from lochs, rivers, the sea, or during heavy rainfall.

The Weeper (Caoineag): This is a female spirit in Scottish folklore, a type of Highland banshee, with similarities to the Bean Nighe. She is believed to foretell death in her clan by lamenting in the night at a waterfall, stream, or Loch, or in a glen or on a mountainside.

Occasionally, some of the creatures and spirits mentioned in the book are entirely a figment of my imagination, although my inspiration for them comes from Celtic mythology. For example, 'grimlochs'. These are shadow spirits that infest chimneys and hearths, snuffing out fires and filling homes with choking smoke. Or the 'clag-doo', a territorial, cat-like predator. It has long claws that grow constantly; as such, it must blunt them by scratching tree trunks, leaving scars that never heal.

Gods and Goddesses of Albia
The FIVE
The Mother: Goddess of enlightenment and feminine energy—the bringer of change
The Warrior: God of battle, life, and growth, of summer
The Maiden: Young goddess of nature and fertility
The Hag: Goddess of the dark—sleep, dreams, death, winter, and the earth
The Reaper: God of death

Gods and Goddesses of Sheehallion
The Ancestors
The Great Raven

Festivities of Albia
Earth Fire: Salute to new life and the first signs of spring
Day of the Hag: Spring Equinox
Bealtunn: Passage from spring to summer
Mid-Summer Fire: Summer Solstice

Harvest Fire: Festival to salute the harvest

Gateway: Passage from summer to winter

Mid-Winter Fire: Winter Solstice

Five 'paths' of druids

Enforcers: wear black and are the warrior druids who serve the king

Sacrificers: wear red and carry out ritualistic sacrifices to keep the Gods happy

Counselors: wear white and are the sages, you go to them for wise advice

Seers: wear green and are masters at divination

Bards: wear blue and sing and entertain, and tell lore through song and music

The Arch-druid: wears gold and is the one deemed to be the wisest

Initiates: wear brown and must choose their path

The four winds of Albia

The Whistle: high and shrill

The Sharp Billed Wind: pierces the land like a sharp-beaked bird

The Sweeper: whirling gusts that strip branches from trees

The Gales of Complaint: scatters food and crops

Source: **https://weewhitehoose.co.uk/study/the-cailleach/**

DIVE INTO MY BACKLIST!

Check out my printable reading order list on my website:

https://www.jaynecastel.com/printable-reading-list

ABOUT THE AUTHOR

Multi-award-winning author Jayne Castel writes epic Historical and Fantasy Romance. Her vibrant characters, richly researched historical settings, and action-packed adventure romance transport readers to forgotten times and imaginary worlds.

Jayne is the author of a number of best-selling series. A hopeless romantic in love with all things Scottish, she writes romances set in both Dark Ages and Medieval Scotland, and Romantasy with a Celtic vibe.

When she's not writing, Jayne is reading (and re-reading) her favorite authors, cooking Italian feasts, and going on long walks with her husband. She's from New Zealand but now lives in Edinburgh, Scotland.

Connect with Jayne online:
www.jaynecastel.com
www.facebook.com/JayneCastelRomance
www.instagram.com/jaynecastelauthor/
www.tiktok.com/@jaynecastelauthor

Email: contact@jaynecastel.com